STORM'S END

Rebecca James

STORM'S END

DOUBLEDAY & COMPANY, INC.
Garden City, New York

Library of Congress Cataloging in Publication Data
James, Rebecca Salsbury.
Storm's End.
I. Title.
PZ4.J28478St [PS3560.A394] 813'.5'4
ISBN 0-385-02633-1
Library of Congress Catalog Card Number 73–20516

To R. P. O'Connor
With gratitude.

". . . late harvest of the winter tree."
—R.J.

THE FIRST DAY

One

I must always remember my name is Constance Avery Britton and they are taking me to the house where I was born, Storm's End. We left the hospital shortly after five in the afternoon although it seemed much later, more like night. It had been raining all day but it stopped shortly before Hale and Irene came with the car. But the sky stayed dark and sullen and, barely an hour later, the day turned finally into night. I couldn't help shuddering.

"Are you cold?" Hale leaned forward, his clear blue eyes anxious, his hand gentle on mine as he reached out to touch me.

"No. No, of course not, Hale. How could I be with this warm coat?" He sat back again, reassured, and looked out the car window. It was almost completely dark by then; we were traveling down the highway between two walls of black trees against a sky already nearly as black. "It won't be much longer now, Con. Sure you're not cold? I could close the window."

I shook my head again no. "The fresh air feels good."

"We don't want you to catch a chill, in addition to everything else," said Irene crisply from my other side. She narrowed her eyes and peered out at the darkness on her side of the car. "The turnoff to the house should be along here someplace." She raised her voice to catch the attention of the young man in the front seat. "Don't miss it, Ben."

"I won't, Miss Waring." He didn't look back. He hasn't once since we left the hospital. I've seen Hale and Irene almost daily these past weeks. They were no longer strange to me. But this young man Ben . . . what is he in the household at Storm's End? He wears a chauffeur's cap and a black suit. But there was an easiness about the way he put my few things into the trunk of the car, and the way he looked at Hale and Irene, the way he spoke had nothing of the servant about it.

He had sunglasses on when he came to my room at the hospital, standing politely behind Irene and Hale. Strange, I thought, on such a dark day. He has taken them off now that it is truly dark, but I can only see the back of his head, the width of his broad shoulders above the half-raised glass between the front seat and the back of the limousine.

"Wasn't that the turnoff, Ben?" Irene's fingers twisted a little, I could see them move, white in the dark car. Why isn't she wearing gloves? It's cold for October. She hasn't buttoned her coat either. It's a sensible coat, gray wool, tailored, designed for warmth only—not to draw attention. I could see it advertised as "the perfect secretary's coat." It's not very attractive with her dark red hair and sallow skin, none of her clothes are. Perhaps she doesn't care. Ben's voice came back calmly. "We've still got a ways to go before we hit that side road."

"It's just that if we miss it we'll have to go all the way around through the village. And I want to get Mrs. Britton home as quickly as possible."

Hale's voice sounded a little sharp. He moved uneasily, still peering out at the dark trees lining the empty road. Dear Hale. If only I could take that worried look away from his eyes. The voice came from the front of the car again.

"It's the fog, sir. I can't really make the time I expected."

I could feel Hale turn toward me, his face a pale blur in the darkness of the car. "You're sure you're all right, Con?"

"I'm fine." I snuggled deeper into my coat. When Hale said he would bring some clothes for the trip I hadn't expected anything like this, a long beige coat, a silky gabardine, lined with thick dark mink inside. The collar brushed against my hair but I made no move to straighten it.

"Strange that there should be fog, with the wind rising." Irene's voice sounded anxious in the dark.

"It's not really fog, Irene. When the temperature shifts, mist rises out of the hollows. The wind will blow it away before the moon comes out." How easy Hale sounded now, relaxed, sure of himself. Anything to do with the land gave him confidence.

I could hear the wind now, even inside the safety of this big car, a constant rustle of dried leaves as we passed under the trees, low branches scraping the top of the car. "What's that? Over there? Those lights?" I could see them scattered down the blackness of what must be a valley off in the distance.

"That's Avery. The town they named after your family."

"A whole town?"

"They were a very important family in their time. You won't see the town tonight. If we hit the side entrance we can cut off about two miles. Don't worry, Con. We won't be much longer."

And then it happened, so quickly it was over before I knew it: a slap of color scraping against the windshield of the car, a loud crack, the car swerving violently, the headlights picking out trees, their trunks tall and thick and solid. And close, much too close to us. I heard Irene gasp as Ben struggled with the wheel.

"For God's sake, Ben, what's the matter?" Hale had automatically pushed one hand in front of me protectively as he leaned forward. The car steadied itself and once more we could see the thin gray roadway in front of us, the headlights picking out a scatter of branches covering the pavement.

"Sorry, boss." Ben didn't look back. "The wind blew a branch right into us. I thought it was going to break the windshield."

"Well, take it easy. Mrs. Britton's had enough shocks to last her for a long, long time."

"It wasn't Ben's fault, Hale," Irene said quietly from her dark corner. "It looks like we're driving right into another storm." Hale started to answer, and then I could feel him lean back again. I didn't need light to know how he must look: lips pressed together tightly against impatient words he wanted to say, eyes with that glint of anger that came when he was helpless to protect or comfort me. I had seen that look once or twice during the weeks at the hospital when the doctor's report had not been good, when there had been no change in my condition and none of the treatments seemed to work.

I reached out in the darkness and took his hand. How firm it felt, the skin warm even through our gloves. "Don't worry, Hale. I'm all right. Really I am."

"And once we're home, it'll all come back to you, Constance. I know it will." I could hear the hope in his voice.

"Of course it will."

"You heard them tell you that at the hospital."

"Of course, Hale. We just have to keep remembering that."

I must always remember that, I thought. Just as I must always re-member my name is Constance Avery Britton. And people who love me are taking me to the house where I was born, Storm's End.

Only why am I so afraid?

*   *   *

Dr. Gallard, in one of the sessions we had at the hospital, said, "Fear is always of the unknown." I didn't like Dr. Gallard. He was attractive enough to make the young student nurses giggle when he strode past them in the halls. And even Mrs. McKenzie, my favorite of the nurses, sometimes gave me a ribald wink as she closed the door of my room when he came for his private examinations. But there was something withdrawn about him as if he knew more than he intended to tell you or anyone. His crisp black hair, silvering a little on the sides, was al-ways neatly combed, his tweed suits fit his sturdy frame well, his shoes were always polished to a high shine. But his fingers were dry as wood the few times he touched me . . . taking my pulse or checking the pupils of my eyes. And he had none of the charm of Hale with his long legs and easy grace and soft blond hair; always a little rumpled, making your fingers itch to smooth it. And sometimes I could sense something very close to anger in Dr. Gallard's dark eyes, staring at me from under his thick eyebrows. His voice, still with a faint accent after ten years in this country, would be curt. "Fear is always of the unknown, Mrs. Britton." And then he would look away. Or I would. Because there is so much that is unknown about me. So much that I cannot remember.

What I *can* remember began six weeks ago. The first was pain. I don't think I'll ever forget that pain, the whole left side of my head aching, like a hammer battering at me. I was lying down, I knew that. And even before I opened my eyes, I knew there was something at-tached to my arm, pinching the skin. I could hear voices but not words. I didn't want to open my eyes, it was safer to stay in the darkness. But then there was a light pressing against the outside of my eyelids and I moved.

"Constance? Constance, can you hear me?"

My eyes opened. And there was Hale, leaning over me. Only I didn't know it was Hale then. I didn't know anything or anybody.

It was the next day before I began to understand what had happened. After that first moment when my eyes opened I seem to have slipped back into sleep, or perhaps it was the injection they had given me. But the next morning I was awake early. I could hear the clatter of breakfast trays on the wagon out in the hall. By the time Mrs. McKenzie came into my room I had been able to move my head and see the white blanket covering me, the pale green walls of the room, the masses of flowers on the table and the dresser by the window. And the sunlight, cheerful and warm, sliding under the shades across the floor to touch the foot of my metal bed.

"Good morning. You're looking a lot better." Mrs. McKenzie moved about the room efficiently, raising the shades, popping a thermometer into my mouth, then taking my wrist for a pulse count.

"Who . . . what . . . ?" I couldn't speak with the glass tube in my mouth.

"Now, just hold on, my girl. Plenty of time for talking when I know what your blood is up to." She checked the watch on her sturdy wrist and then released my hand. The short white curls under her nurse's cap bobbed cheerfully. "Looks like you're going to recover, Mrs. Britton."

"Mrs. Britton?" It meant nothing to me.

She looked at me, wise eyes twinkling. "Doesn't sound familiar?"

"No, I . . ."

"It will. In time. Now I'd better get the doctors. Or would you like a little breakfast first? Strictly against the rules to feed you before you've been examined. But my guess is you'll need your strength to face them and their questions." She moved quickly to the door, her white uniform crackling with starch, as stiff as the icing on a wedding cake. "My name's Mrs. McKenzie. Don't fret yourself if you can't remember it." Without waiting for an answer, she opened the door and disappeared.

I managed to inch myself up in the bed. My head still hurt and I put my hand up instinctively to touch it. I could feel nothing but a hard surface of plaster, covering my head like a cap. Mrs. McKenzie came back in from the hall, carrying a tray, each dish warming under a metal lid.

"Here now, don't try and move around by yourself. We've had enough trouble getting you up to this point." She put down the tray on the bed-side table, and then leaning over me, placed her hands under my arms and helped me to sit up. I tried to find words but nothing seemed to come. Mrs. McKenzie just smiled again and placed the tray on the bed in front of me. "You eat now. Plenty of time for questions later."

And there was. It seemed like all that morning the doctors and nurses were in and out of my room. First Dr. Henderson, the head of the hos-pital, white-haired and kindly; then Dr. Sharp, tall and thin and bald-ing. He carried a pipe he never filled or lit, just something to fumble with in his long, thin fingers. And then finally Dr. Gallard, not dressed like the others in their neat white coats. But the questions were always the same. Did I know who I was? Did I know what had happened to me? And I had no answers. There was nothing I could remember . . . beyond that one moment the night before.

Finally, when it was after two on the little gold clock on the table by my bed, there was a tap on the door and without waiting for any of the doctors to answer, Mrs. McKenzie came into the room. She took a look at the three men and then moved closer to my bed.

"That's it, gentlemen. Mrs. Britton's had quite enough questions for one day. Why don't you try giving the child some answers?"

Dr. Henderson turned to her. "Nellie McKenzie, we're having a conference here." But his lips were already starting to smile and I could see he didn't really expect to overrule her.

"Conference indeed! You're wearing the poor girl out. Time she had her lunch, and a nap. I want her rested when her husband comes."

Dr. Gallard stood up then. "Is he here?"

"Not yet. But he called at noon, as usual. And somebody at the Front Desk took it on themselves to tell him she was conscious. He'll be over this afternoon."

Dr. Gallard moved to the door after the other two doctors. He low-ered his voice when he passed Mrs. McKenzie, but I could still hear him. "I'd like to talk to him before he sees the patient." Dr. Sharp turned at the door at this.

"Alex, we can't take up all of your time like this. After all, it was just as a favor you came over here."

Dr. Gallard moved toward him. "It's all right, Don. It's not often a psychiatrist gets a chance to work on amnesia. Not a genuine case." With that he was out the door, the other two doctors following him. Mrs. McKenzie flashed a quick glance at me and closed the door softly behind them.

"Is that what's wrong with me?" I said. "Amnesia?"

Mrs. McKenzie kept her back toward me as she tidied up the room. "It may be," she said calmly. "It's nothing for you to be worried about now."

"Is that why I don't remember anything? Who I am? Where I am?"

There must have been something in my voice, because she turned around and hurried over to the bed. "Now, don't get yourself upset, child. Your name is Constance Britton." She placed a gentle hand on my shoulder.

"You're married to a very handsome lad named Hale Britton. You're in Six Counties General Hospital in upstate New York. It's the fourth of September, a Monday, and that's about all you need to know for the moment. Now let me see about your lunch."

She hurried out of the room, her white rubber-soled shoes making no noise on the bare floor. I leaned back against the pillows. I could feel my eyes closing. My head was starting to ache again but I fell asleep before the pain could reach me.

The room was almost dark when I woke up. A little breeze moved among the thin white curtains at the windows. A lunch tray, untouched, was on the table by my bed. The hands of the little clock were at ten minutes after four. I moved under the sheets restlessly. Almost as if Mrs. McKenzie had been listening, the door to the hall opened a crack and I could see the tip of her pert nose and the twinkle of her glasses as she peeked in.

"Are you awake?" she whispered.

"It's all right. You can come in."

The door opened wider and she stepped in from the hall. As she came close to the bed, her white uniform cut through the half-shadow of the room. "Feel up to a visitor?"

"Not another doctor," I groaned.

"Someone much nicer than that." She smoothed the dark hair that spilled down from under the plaster cast on my head. "There's a very worried young man outside."

"Hale?"

"You see? You're beginning to remember already." She turned on the lamp by the bed. "Now, he can't stay long . . ."

She moved to the door and opened it. Someone was standing outside. The lights in the hall cast a long shadow across the bare floor.

"You can come in now, Mr. Britton," said Mrs. McKenzie to the man outside. "Your wife is waiting for you." The shadow on the floor moved —and then the doorway was filled with a tall figure.

I can never tell Hale the truth. There was something in my eyes that afternoon that he is sure now was recognition, the first chink in the wall of darkness that surrounded me. He moved closer to the bed and I could see the questioning, hopeful look in his blue eyes. And then he smiled, a smile of such relief and boyishness I couldn't help but smile back.

"You *do* know me, don't you, Con?" He leaned over me in the bed, his fingers gently touching my face. And I nodded. Then, with almost a gasp, he knelt by my bed, pressing his head close to my body. Over his shoulder I could see Mrs. McKenzie still standing in the doorway, smiling, her eyes suspiciously bright.

No, I can never tell him the truth. That the only memory I had of him was of the night before, his voice tense and desperate cutting through the pain and the darkness. But nothing from before. There is still no crack in the wall I have built up in my mind to make me forget. My arms moved around his wide thin shoulders, holding him.

But they were holding a stranger.

Two

In the weeks that followed I learned enough to push much of the fear aside. Facts are the enemy of fear and I questioned Hale and Irene eagerly. I was twenty-four, an orphan—born at the house called Storm's End over an hour's drive from here. An old house, they told me. But nothing more. Hale and Irene would glance at each other when I mentioned the house, then change the subject quickly, trying not to make it obvious. Hale and I had met in Paris—four years before, when he was an art student. We had married there as soon as I had come of age.

Apparently I do have one relative, a great-uncle named Matthew Avery. There were no flowers from him, though; I had Mrs. McKenzie check all the cards. The flowers were from Hale. Hale and Irene. Irene is my secretary, although no one has explained yet why I need one. Brisk, efficient, she must be around thirty. She answers my questions willingly but I never found the courage to ask her about herself. She's not a person you can become friendly with easily and yet I felt she cared for me.

Earlier this summer it seems Hale and I came back from Europe and opened the house at Storm's End. He has turned one of the rooms into a studio. When he talks of his painting, his face becomes totally alive. We seem to have had a good life together. One thing I *do* know—he is very much in love with me.

But neither Hale nor Irene can tell me about the day of the accident. Dr. Gallard presses me on that, over and over again, more like a lawyer in a courtroom than a doctor trying to help a patient remember. What facts I know Hale has told me. It seems I left the house that afternoon to take a walk—they didn't miss me until supper. Then Hale in his sports car and Ben in the big limousine set out to search for me. They found me about ten that night, near the side of a little-used road, my head bleeding with what later turned out to be a concussion, my face and body scratched and bruised. I did not know who I was nor could I tell them what had happened. A "hit-and-run" driver is the explanation the hospital gave me . . . but I feel Hale doesn't believe that, nor does Dr. Gallard. But neither of them will tell me what they do believe. When we reached the hospital the only sign of life was that I kept whispering over and over again, "Storm's End."

These last few weeks have been so strange. How do you know that you like sugar in your coffee and not cream? And yet your hand reaches for the sugar automatically. Dr. Gallard questioned me endlessly about what I can remember, showing me pictures in newspapers, asking me to identify public people in the photographs. Generally I can, but I don't know how. Any more than I can explain about that evening Mrs. McKenzie was sitting with me.

Hale had left after sharing my supper with me, and Mrs. McKenzie had planted the television set on the dresser and turned it on. We were watching a movie and somehow I knew I had seen it before. I knew what the next scene would be, what the girl on the screen would be wearing in the scene, even what she would say. When I told that to Mrs. McKenzie she became quite excited—but I couldn't remember where I had seen the movie or when or with whom. What I knew from the past was like something you see moving out of the corner of your eyes, only when you turn your head, there is nothing there.

*   *   *

"But you admit she's physically well?" Hale's voice was sharp, urgent. He stood by my chair, facing Dr. Gallard.

"Yes. Medically, there's no reason why she shouldn't go home today."

"And every possible reason why she should, psychologically. You've got to admit that, Doctor."

"Perhaps."

Hale put his hand on my shoulder gently. "You've already told us this amnesia thing could end in a second—one reminder of the past, something she cared about, something she's familiar with could tear through this blackout and she'd be herself again."

"It has happened that way." Dr. Gallard moved to the windows to stand, back to us, staring out at the wet lawn.

"Isn't it more likely to happen to Constance in her own home?"

For a moment the only sound in the room was the rain lashing against the glass. Dr. Gallard turned around to face us again. "You told me, Mr. Britton, that your wife hasn't been in that house for a number of years."

"She was born there, she grew up there, until her guardian sent her away to school. We've been back there most of the summer." Hale's voice was firmer now. He was determined to get his way and Dr. Gallard knew it. "If any place can bring back her memory, it'll be Storm's End." He knelt beside my chair, taking my hand. "You want to come home, don't you, Con? You know I can take care of you."

I can't bear the look of pleading in his eyes. He'd been so gentle these past weeks, so patient. I looked up at Dr. Gallard, watching us quietly.

"I do have to go home sometime, Doctor. And if I'm well—?"

He cut in sharply. "I would hardly call you that, Mrs. Britton."

I made my voice calm, it does no good to get angry with him, I'd learned that these past weeks. "I'm physically well, at least. As for my memory—you said yourself it may be months, years even before it comes back."

"It could be less. In a controlled environment. Where we could try to find what shocked you so violently that day that you feel compelled to shut off the experience completely. And with it, the whole of your previous life."

"A *controlled* environment?" Hale's voice was quiet, but colder than I had ever heard it before. "Are you talking about some kind of a sanitarium? I won't have that, Doctor. And as Constance's husband, I have the legal right to refuse to let it happen."

Dr. Gallard made a short move with his hand, almost as if he were brushing Hale away. "I know the law in matters like this, Mr. Britton. Probably much better than you." He sighed then, almost wearily. "Of course I can't prevent you from taking her home. Officially I have no control over the situation. As you know, I am not even attached to this hospital. Dr. Henderson called me in as a friend, an associate."

Then Hale stood, so young and boyish, all the coldness gone. "Then she can come home? When? Today?"

"If you insist."

Hale turned back to me, reaching down to lift me from the chair. "Did you hear, darling? We can go home today." He held me so close I could feel his heart beating under his thick sweater.

"There is one thing, however." We had both forgotten the doctor, standing quietly by the windows. "I shall want to check on your wife's progress, Mr. Britton. Luckily that will not be inconvenient for either of us. My own home is quite near yours." He walked to the door. Hale watched him carefully.

"A summer place, Doctor?" I could tell by Hale's voice something had put him on guard.

"Not exactly. I've rented a small cottage in your town. I intend to use this year to work on a book." He opened the door to the hall and then turned back, his dark eyes catching mine. "So I won't say good-by, Mrs. Britton. We'll be seeing each other."

I didn't hear the door close behind him as once more Hale had turned to me and was holding me tightly in his arms.

I spent most of the afternoon saying good-by to the doctors and nurses I had come to know these past six weeks. By four o'clock I was back in my room with Mrs. McKenzie helping me to get ready.

"There now, you look as good as new." She stepped back and let me look in the mirror over the dresser. She had parted my dark hair in the middle and combed it in two waves on each side to hide the last of the scratches on my forehead. It seemed to make my eyes look bigger than before, a darker blue. Or perhaps it was because my skin was so pale from the long weeks indoors.

"Doesn't seem to be much in your purse in the way of makeup. Not that you need it, lamb. But there's just a bit of lipstick and some powder." She walked over to a box open on the bed. I started to fasten the buttons on the long-sleeved lavender wool dress Irene had brought over the day before in preparation for when I could leave the hospital. She had put in shoes and stockings and underthings . . . all a little loose, but then I had lost weight since the night of the accident.

"What else is in that box?" I said, coming closer to the bed. "The things I was wearing that day?"

"It's nothing very much. I suppose I should have had them cleaned but your husband said not to bother. With the weather changing he knew you'd need something warmer for the trip back." There was a ringing from the nurses' station down the hall. "Drat! That's my bell. I'll be back before you leave, dear. To say good-by."

Mrs. McKenzie hurried out of the room. Behind me I could hear the rain sliding softly down the windows. The storm was almost over, leaving the room gray with shadows. I turned on the lamp by the bed.

There wasn't very much in the box. A straw bag, no wallet, no change purse or keys. Had I been robbed that day? If so, why hadn't Hale said something? Or Mrs. McKenzie? Or the doctors? Perhaps they didn't know. They had told me I was taken straight into the examining room and then wheeled in for x-rays. Maybe no one had thought to look. A lipstick, a small compact, a crumpled handkerchief, that was all. Tiny bits of tobacco sticking to the seams of the lining . . . had I smoked? Odd, I had no desire for it now.

I dropped the purse back onto the bed. It had no clues for me, it was as impersonal as any summer purse put away in a bottom drawer and forgotten until next year.

A pair of sandals was the next thing in the box, obviously well worn, the straps of both of them broken. Had I tripped? Is that how I had hurt my head, by falling on a rock or tree stump? I put them aside. Under the sandals, folded carelessly, was a pair of khaki cotton shorts, badly ripped; a scratched leather belt and a blood-stained pink blouse. I remember Mrs. McKenzie had said that they had had to cut what underclothes I was wearing off me.

I picked up the blouse. There was no label at the neckline, just dried blood, brown against the pink cloth. By the ridge where the cloth turned over to make the collar there was something stamped, faint from the washings the blouse had been through. I held the blouse under the table light. I could barely make out the figures: $C13$. A laundry mark, I thought idly, and dropped the blouse back in the box. No point in taking any of this with me back to Storm's End.

I sat down on the bed, looking again at the contents of the box. What had I gone through when I wore those clothes that was so terrible I couldn't bear to remember it? I reached out again and touched the tan shorts and then the blouse. I turned the collar of the pink blouse toward the light once more.

C13. I could feel myself frowning. Somewhere I had heard or read that laundries mark clothes with the initial of the customer's last name. And each customer with the same initial gets a number after that, so that they can trace lost articles. Perhaps I'd read it in one of the detective stories the morning nurse had left by my bed. But then the laundry mark should have been B13. For Britton. Or possibly *A*, if I'd had the blouse before I'd married Hale.

And then I laughed. Maybe Dr. Gallard was right after all, I wasn't ready to go home. The *C* stood for Constance. I stood up and took the clutter of clothes out of the box with both hands and dropped them into the wastebasket. Whatever I needed to find my way back into my past, nothing in that box would help.

*   *   *

"There it is, Ben." Irene leaned forward in the car. Ahead, the lights cut through the darkness to show a driveway turning off the main road to the right. The car slowed down, made a slight swerve into the turnoff and stopped. Caught in the headlights was a ten-foot-high metal gate, breaking a high stone wall that stretched on either side.

"Is this it, Hale? Storm's End?" I tried to keep my voice calm.

"The back entrance . . . actually, it's on the side. The front entrance is a lot grander. But that's on the other slope of the hill; the road toward town." We waited in silence as Ben struggled with the lock on the thick chain fastening the gate.

"Can we see the house from here?"

"Just about. Only it's too dark to see much. Even with the moon. Look." He pointed out the window on his side of the car. By stretching forward I could just make out the moon, nearly full, just clearing the top of the trees. The branches were motionless now, the wind had died again. And perhaps because the car had been climbing steadily the last ten minutes, there was no longer any mist upon the ground.

Even in the car we could hear the metal creak of the gate as Ben pushed hard against it. He walked back to the car, shielding his eyes from the glare of the headlights, and got back into the front seat. Ahead of us I could see about twenty feet of gravel before the driveway turned off into darkness. Bits of grass and tiny weeds stood out sharply on the surface of the road. The car moved slowly forward between the high walls.

"You'd better close and lock the gate again, Ben," said Irene, still sitting forward, her hand braced against the back of the front seat. Ben braked the car.

"I was just going to, Miss Waring." He opened his door again, got out and went back to the open gate behind us. I could hear his footsteps crunch on the gravel.

"Is everything kept locked here?" I said, more to break the silence than for any other reason.

"It's best. What with—"

Irene was interrupted before she could finish by Hale's voice, quiet and firm: "We don't use this road very much, Con. And there have been trespassers around here . . . gangs of kids, people breaking into some of the estates that they think are deserted." Then his voice warmed and he reached out for my hand. "Don't worry, darling. You're home now and we're going to keep you safe."

The front door slammed and Ben started the car forward again. As we turned again to the right, Hale's fingers tightened on mine. "There . . . can you see it?"

I peered out his window at the darkness. The car was moving uphill again, the trees were not as thick as they had been along the main road and through them I could catch glimpses of the top of the hill. I could see lights from what must be the house, or perhaps it was several houses, as the lights stretched in broken lines for quite a distance. But of the building itself, black against the night sky, I could as yet make out no shape.

And then the limousine turned one last curve and I could see the whole of Storm's End. A large lawn sloped away from it, silver in the moonlight. As we moved closer, we passed one or two statues, frozen in gray stone, eyeless, turning their classic heads toward the thin gravel walks and the house beyond. And then the house itself—a solid mass, three or four stories high at least. The solid darkness of the building was cut by lights in windows, one enormous slash of color seemed to rise from the ground almost to the roof, stained glass on a stairwell, I thought.

We swerved and then the headlights of the car illuminated the front of the house completely: gray stone walls, black-shadowed in ivy.

"But it's a castle!" Something in my voice made Hale chuckle.

"It tries hard to be. Actually, it started out as the duplication of one. And too much Victorian money did the rest."

"Simple, but we like it," said Irene dryly from her corner.

Ben brought the car into the large clear space in front of the house, driving around the great empty stone fountain in the center. Hale leaned forward and brushed his lips against my cold cheek. "Welcome home, darling," he whispered. Ben snapped off the headlights and the house in front of us fell back into darkness again.

As Ben started for my things in the trunk of the limousine, Hale helped me out of the car. Looking up I could see the moon high above the roof of the house. Gradually my eyes adjusted to the light and I could pick out the rough shape of the building. The main part of the house was directly in front of us, silver-gray in the moonlight. Rows of more or less even windows rose up two stories to a third line of windows, small and arched, cut deep into the sloping roof. The main entrance of the house, twin doors of carved wood, divided this main part of the building almost exactly at the halfway point, and halfway toward each of the two ends of the building, great stone bays swelled out from the flat walls to rise straight up to the roof.

But at each end of the square body of the main part of the house towers and turrets of different sizes and shapes erupted: some swollen and gross in the moonlight, some tiny as blisters on the great stone building, curving and jagged in silhouette against the night sky. And all of them sliced neatly along the rooftop by the tall straight lines of the chimneys. There must be twenty chimneys, I thought. But then a place as old as this, probably all the rooms have their own fireplaces.

As Hale took my arm to lead me toward the house, the huge front doors opened and light from inside the building spilled like a carpet down the wide flat stone steps across the open space to where we stood. Before we could move closer to the house we heard the sound of a dog barking.

And then somehow the great massive mansion, the huge empty lawns,

the dark sky ceased to be frightening. However strange this place might
be, it was my home and there was a dog waiting to welcome me.

"A dog!" I cried delightedly. "Hale, you didn't tell me I had a dog."
I moved away from him and started toward the open square of light.

"Constance, wait!" Hale caught up with me quickly. Ahead of us I
could see a woman in the doorway, holding by the collar a large German shepherd.

"What's his name?"

"Thor. And he's fierce, Constance."

"Nonsense, Hale, he's welcoming me. Can't you see?" I broke loose
and started again toward the animal. And at that moment the woman
at the top of the steps released him or perhaps in his excitement he
pulled himself free, struggling and barking. He raced down the steps
toward me, pink tongue hanging, eyes glittering brown in his well-
shaped head, yelping with joy.

He was about ten feet from me when I stepped out of the darkness
into the light coming from the open doorway behind him. And then
he stopped, almost as if someone had taken a stick and hit him hard on
the skull of his head between his pointed ears. I continued to move toward him but he came no further. Most dogs recognize only by scent,
but I could tell there was something about my appearance that startled
the great German shepherd. He stayed where he was, sliding his body
back onto his stiff hind legs, his front legs bent low, paws planted firmly
on the ground, his head lowered, but his eyes still fastened on me. And
the joyous barking changed into a low growl, deep from within his
chest.

"Don't move, Constance!" Hale came behind me, grabbing my arms
at the elbow. The dog growled again. I could see in the light the muscles
on his back rolling under his fur as he made ready to jump. "Ben, grab
that damn animal!" Hale managed to move me back into the shadows,
slowly, carefully.

From behind us Ben moved forward. His broad back came between
me and the dog but I could see he had gloves on now, thick leather
ones. He reached down and with one hand grabbed the German shepherd's collar. And then, with the other hand, he brought down a hard
punch onto the dog's shoulders.

"Don't!" I could hear my voice, thin and shrill in my throat. "Hale, don't let him hurt him!"

Ben had the dog firmly under control now, one strong leather-gloved hand jerking the animal back to his side. The German shepherd whimpered softly but made no attempt to break free. "He's all right now, Mrs. Britton. But you've got to be careful. He's not exactly a pet."

"But I thought . . ." I turned to Hale. His face was in the shadows but he must have seen the questions in my eyes. "He wanted to welcome me, Hale. I know he did. And then he just . . . stopped. Like I was a stranger." I felt my face turning pink with embarrassment. "They say dogs can sense when there've been changes in people. Maybe that's it."

"They say a lot of nonsense about dogs, Constance." Hale's voice was cool, matter-of-fact. "Probably he was just glad to get out. We let him loose on the grounds at night. Once we're all safely inside. Don't try and make a pet of him, Con. He was trained to be a killer."

Irene moved between us quietly. "Hadn't we better get inside, Hale? Mrs. Janeck will be wondering what's happened to us."

We moved toward the open doorway of the house. The woman who had been holding Thor hadn't moved from where she was standing, except now she seemed almost pressed against the side of the great door. I still couldn't see her face, as the light was behind her.

As we started up the wide, shallow steps she called out nervously, "Are you all right?" Without waiting for answer, she hurried on: "He just got away from me, Mr. Britton. Thor's so strong. And he's always been so close to . . ."

Irene's voice cut through her protests lazily. "Yes, we just saw that. Didn't you feed him, Mrs. Janeck? I had the feeling he was ready to take a mouthful out of all of us."

We had reached the doorway by now and, as the woman stepped back to make room for us, I could see her clearly for the first time. A plain woman, well over fifty, with gray hair pinned back neatly and a dark dress covering her angular frame to well below her knees. It was the sort of dress that looks unfinished without the neat white of a maid's apron. She had a long face and, bare of makeup, it had no more character to it than an empty plate. Her pale eyebrows made vague half-circles over her watery eyes; lashless, the lids were faintly pink as if she'd been crying for a long time.

"No harm done, Mrs. Janeck." Hale reached out as if to touch her shoulders but she stepped back submissively and I could see her eyes move toward me.

"Yes, I've brought her home, Mrs. Janeck." Hale reached out, took my hand and led me over the threshold of Storm's End. "Con, I can't very well introduce you to Mrs. Janeck, she's known you since you were in diapers."

He stood there between us. The woman looked at me questioningly. Of course she must know what had happened. She couldn't very well expect me to embrace her and yet I could hardly just shake her hand.

Once again Irene cut through the awkwardness by moving briskly past us. "Isn't anybody going to close the door? It's cold out." Quickly Mrs. Janeck moved the heavy wooden doors into place and I took that moment to turn, and for the first time, look at the house itself.

Three

I suppose all these past weeks I had been hoping, consciously or not, that once I was safely home the clouds around my memory would instantly disappear and I would be myself again. So that first moment when I turned to look at the hall at Storm's End was the most overwhelming disappointment I could possibly have known.

The hall itself was a huge, wood-paneled well that the rest of the house seemed to have been built around. Black and white marble squares gleamed on the floor. Along one of the walls, to my left, an enormous Victorian staircase led up to the second floor, some twenty feet above. It was hard to see the landing as a magnificent chandelier floated over our heads, its heavy crystals still tinkling slightly from the breath of wind that had come into the hall when Mrs. Janeck had opened the front doors. Above the dim second floor, I could just barely make out the stairway turning again to go up into the blackness of the floor above and the roof of the house.

The wall to my right as I stood in the hallway had two tall doors, with a great long oak table between them, bare except for a large Chinese vase filled with a formal arrangement of autumn flowers. Directly ahead of me, under the landing of the staircase, was a double doorway, the match of the one through which I had entered the house. One of the doors was half open and I could see into what looked like the formal drawing room of the house.

If the outside of Storm's End had seemed to me a castle, this first glimpse of the inside reminded me of the additions Hale had said were made in the Victorian era. And none of it . . . not any of it . . . could I feel I had ever seen before.

And then I became aware that the others were staring at me in silence. Mrs. Janeck, her pale face quivering as if she were close to tears; Hale I could see was unable to hide the disappointment I knew he was feeling; Irene was standing quietly to one side watching me with what I realized was pity.

"Does any of it look familiar, Con?" Hale's voice was calm, patient. I shook my head dumbly. I think if I'd been alone I might have given way to tears. But there was too much disappointment in the faces watching me to hurt them further.

"We mustn't push Constance too hard, Hale. Or too fast." Irene moved closer, almost protectively, although I knew she was not a woman given to making affectionate gestures. "It may be some tiny thing that will reach her memory. After all, this hall isn't exactly a place you'd be likely to care about. All this wood paneling, it's like living inside a tree."

Hale turned quickly toward Irene, and I think if she had not gone on talking in her quiet level voice he would have said something sharp to her. But Irene was speaking to the housekeeper. "Mrs. Janeck, why don't you take our Constance up to her room? I'll be up in a few minutes when Ben brings in her things."

Mrs. Janeck nodded and started up the great staircase. I felt myself tremble slightly. I don't know why, but somehow I didn't want to follow that silent woman up into the darkness, not without one of the others coming with me. But I felt stupid enough without disturbing them with my fancies, so I forced myself to follow her, not glancing back at Hale and Irene.

The stairs were covered with thick wine-red carpeting, brass rails stretched along each step to tuck the carpet into place. When I reached the top of the stairs, I turned back to look down at the hallway below. Irene and Hale had not moved, they stood gazing up at me silently. And the thought passed through my mind they were like chess pieces on those black and white marble squares, waiting for the next move in the game.

"This way. Your room's this way."

Mrs. Janeck stood before me in the hall, her hand on a light switch. The half-light turned her into a faceless silhouette.

"Which room is it?" I said, and I could feel myself blushing. It made me cross with embarrassment but how could I be expected to know this house or my own room?

Mrs. Janeck made no answer, she turned and started down the long hall, turning on various lights along the way. There was nothing for me to do but follow her.

It was a strange hall, even for this curious house, more like the corridor of a hotel than a home. A thin, rather worn carpet made a path along the dark wood floor. In various corners I could see soft armchairs grouped as if in a parlor, waiting for crowds of houseguests that had departed decades ago. We passed a suit of armor half hidden in a small alcove of the landing and a massive grandfather's clock almost twice as tall as I am. And then we were into the half darkness of the corridor itself, moving past small marble-topped tables placed so closely against the walls that they seemed to be growing out of them.

"Be careful where you're walking, this is the old part of the house. You'll get used to it soon enough." Mrs. Janeck stopped now in front of a deep-set doorway.

"You mean . . . used to it *again*," I said with as much control as I could manage.

"Yes. Of course. This is your room, Mrs. Britton." Her thin fingers reached for the handle of the door. And then I felt ashamed of my coldness. It wasn't her fault what had happened to my mind. I was close behind her by this time. I reached out to put my hand on her shoulder gently, but she started and looked at me with surprise.

It was hard in that gloomy hall to be sure but I felt there was something close to fear in her pale eyes. "Please, Mrs. Janeck . . . if you've known me since I was a baby we can't be that formal with each other."

She hesitated.

"What did you used to call me?"

"You were always Miss Constance, ma'am. To all the staff. Your guardian was very strict about that."

"My guardian? That would be my great-uncle?"

"He's an old-fashioned man. But then, this is an old-fashioned house." She turned away, not coldly but making it clear she had no desire to continue the conversation. She pushed down the handle on the door and opened it, stepping aside politely to let me walk into the bedroom ahead of her.

Nothing I had seen so far at Storm's End prepared me for the room that was my bedroom. If the outside had seemed half fort, half Tudor mansion and the halls resembled the lobby of a deserted Victorian hotel, my bedroom was as delicate as the bedchamber of a princess in a fairy tale.

The first thing I felt was the overwhelming color of soft rose. It surrounded me, warmed me. The high walls holding up the cream-colored ceiling were covered in a faded satin brocade of this soft pink; the same material framed the long french windows ahead of me and draped the four posts and canopy of the huge bed against the wall. Without thinking I heard myself whisper, "How lovely!"

"This has always been the bedroom of the mistress of Storm's End. In the daytime you can stand on the balcony out there and see the terrace below. And the edge of the cliff over the river." Mrs. Janeck moved past me toward the bed.

Every possible comfort for a woman of luxury had been included in the room. There was a velvet-covered chaise longue, also in the same soft pink, near the fireplace. Tucked in the corners of the chaise were little lace pillows. A Venetian glass mirror, which even from the doorway I could see must be several hundreds of years old, hung above the delicate marble mouth of the fireplace. In front of the wall of french windows was an enormous dressing table and mirror; both the table and the padded chair in front of it were covered in the same soft rose velvet as the chaise.

I walked soundlessly across pale rug toward the fireplace. A small fire had been lit and I warmed my hands as I looked covertly again at the room and at Mrs. Janeck, busy now turning down the brocade spread on the enormous bed. "It's a very . . . feminine room," I said cautiously.

But Mrs. Janeck realized what I was asking. "Mr. Britton's room is through his dressing room here." She touched a panel on the wall. I saw then that a small gold handle had been set in the brocade. She moved around to the other side of the bed. "This door is to your bath and dressing room." She touched the handle and a door opened in what had seemed a solid wall. Through the doorway I could see a brightly lit room and a glimpse of mirrored closets.

"It's all so much more beautiful than I had expected."

"How could you know what to expect, with your memory gone, Miss Constance?" But Mrs. Janeck had added the "Miss Constance" almost as an afterthought. There was something about her face, something in her voice that made me tremble again as I had done downstairs. Not as if she were angry at me or an enemy but almost impersonal, as if her eyes were asking some question that she could not put into words.

"Good! You're settling in."

Irene came in from the hall, carrying the few things I had brought from the hospital. "I thought you might need these before we change for dinner. We *do* have time to relax for a little before dinner, don't we, Mrs. Janeck?" Irene spoke lazily, with no apparent emphasis, but it turned the housekeeper back into a quiet servant again.

"Of course, Miss Waring. There's nothing that can't be delayed until you're ready."

"Wonderful! I don't know about our Constance but I could do with a good strong drink after that drive."

"I'll see to the ice, Miss Waring."

"Do that, Mrs. Janeck. And I think we might have a bottle of champagne with dinner. Or maybe even two. Yes . . . two. To celebrate."

"I don't have the keys to the wine cellar." The housekeeper's voice was sullen now.

"Then ask Mr. Britton for them." Irene still sounded casual but there was no mistaking her authority.

Mrs. Janeck nodded and started for the door. But Irene went on, her voice a lazy purr directed at the older woman. "After all, we want to welcome Miss Constance home, don't we?"

Mrs. Janeck hesitated at the door and Irene repeated her last words. "Don't we?"

"Of course, ma'am." Mrs. Janeck bobbed her head slightly but I noticed she was careful not to look at me, keeping her eyes fastened on the floor. "Welcome home, Miss Constance." And then she went out of the room and closed the door quietly behind her.

"What have you two been gossiping about? Anything exciting?" Irene dropped her packages on the bed.

"With Mrs. Janeck? She doesn't seem the type to gossip."

"Don't be upset by her, Con. It's her nature. I don't know whether she was born that way or it came from all those years of living alone here in the house."

"Alone?"

"Well, she has a husband. Otto. Not much company, I wouldn't guess. You'll probably see him working the grounds tomorrow. Still, Esther's been caretaker here most of her life. I almost had the feeling she resented us when we came back from Europe this summer and moved in. We try to keep on her good side. It's not easy to get servants for a house like this. Not these days."

Irene had been refolding the bed jackets and robes she had brought to the hospital, her back turned toward me. Now she straightened and looked at me, holding up a small bottle in one hand. "Where do you want this?"

"Oh. Those are the sleeping pills Dr. Henderson gave me. I don't really think I'll need them."

"You're not tired, Constance? If you are, I could have Mrs. Janeck bring you up something on a tray."

"No. I feel fine. You might as well put those pills in that drawer by the bed. I think the doctor only gave them to relax me, in case I felt strange here at first."

"And you don't?" Irene looked at me, her face carefully blank of expression.

"No. Oddly enough, I feel very much . . . well, if not at home in this room, at least at peace. And curious about the rest of the house. Is it all as magnificent as this?"

"Not all. But I'll give you the grand tour tomorrow. Maybe in day-light it'll seem more familiar." And then she closed her lips suddenly as if she had said something she regretted. I walked over to her as she stood by the bed.

"Irene? Don't let's be uneasy about what's happened. If my memory doesn't come back right away . . . seeing this house, the things I should remember . . . let's not try to force it. It'll come in time. But I don't want us to be embarrassed about it, or uncomfortable. Especially for Hale's sake. He tries so hard not to show how worried he is. Let's try to make it as easy as we can for him."

Irene smiled then, clearly relieved. "That's the right attitude to have, Constance. All your doctors said that."

Then she stopped, turning as I did toward the wall of long windows. The sky was too dark outside to see anything, but we both heard the soft wail of wind. Even though the windows were closed, the ivory silk curtains moved slightly.

"It sounds like that storm has finally caught up with us," I said to cover our surprise.

"It will take a while before it ends . . . even here. Hale had the radio on downstairs. Most of the thunder and lightning are supposed to pass to the south of us. But being this high over the river, any breath of air and it sounds like a chorus of banshees wailing. Less here than at the two ends of the building. If you had one of the tower rooms, you'd really need those sleeping pills."

Then she moved toward the door to my dressing room. "Let me show you your clothes. Your bathroom's beyond. I warn you. A real turn-of-the-century horror." She started into the dressing room ahead of me. And at that moment the lights in both rooms flickered out and then almost instantly, on again.

"What . . . what was that?" I stood absolutely still in the doorway, staring at Irene. She was in the middle of the mirrored room. As she turned back at the sound of my voice, the lights came on again. And suddenly I had the feeling I was seeing five or six Irenes, like a crowd surrounding me. Then she chuckled a little and the room was back to normal.

"That's the storm. Be prepared. There'll probably be another black-out in a minute."

As she finished, the lights in both the dressing room and the bedroom behind me went out again. Then, after another second, longer than the first time, the lights flickered back on once more.

"What is it? What's happening?" I tried to control my voice but Irene was paying no attention. She had dived into one of the drawers under the mirrored closets and was emerging with two short candles in plain stubby china holders.

"Better have these ready," she said.

"Why did the lights go out?"

"Constance, dear."

Her tone was patient and a little amused. "You know they call this place 'Storm's End'. I'm sure they meant it because the family planned to be at peace here. But we *are* high off the river and sometimes I think the house is a lightning rod . . . attracting every cloud and puff of wind. And the storms do seem to stop here . . . almost as if the towers rip the clouds apart."

She smiled, weighing the candlesticks in either hand. "We are living in the country . . . some of the power systems that supply these little towns . . . and especially the old mansions along the river . . . practically date back to the beginning of electricity. I don't pretend to understand any of it but I suspect the power lines in this area are a hodgepodge of every different system that's been developed through the years. All we know is that during a high wind or a storm, the lights blink out now and then. If they only go out once or twice, we seem to be all right. But if it goes out a third time . . . well, then it means it's serious. A branch off some tree on an obscure road can have fallen across a cable and it can take hours or even days before they can track it down and fix it."

"And what do we do in the meantime?" I must have sounded more nervous than I thought, for she smiled again.

"It's not so bad. We keep candles in every room. And there's a generator in one of the cellars Ben keeps promising to fix. Then in case of a real blackout, we can be completely independent. I'll get after him about it if you're worried."

"Who actually is Ben?" I asked, not so much for information but to cover how foolish I'd been about the lights. It was so strange asking about servants I might have known for years.

"Ben? The chauffeur?" Irene looked at me, a puzzled line creasing the skin between her eyebrows.

"You've told me about Mrs. Janeck. And Otto. Ben is the only person I don't know about yet." It seemed feeble even as I said it.

"I don't think there's very much to know. He's very quiet, our Ben." She stood there, the candlesticks in her hands, her face thoughtful. "Hale hired him when we came back from Europe. In the city. Apparently he had excellent references, I didn't see them. I think he has relatives living not too far from here. At any rate, he was willing to work here in the country . . . which makes him practically unique. Hale thought we were lucky to get him. Especially since you're not much of a driver. . . ."

But then she bit the words off as if once again she had embarrassed me by talking about the past. She moved back into the bedroom, placing a candle on each of the small antique chests that flanked the canopied bed.

"Now, why don't you have a hot bath, put on something lovely from one of those closets and come down and have a drink? I don't think we're going to have any more scares tonight." She waved a hand at me cheerfully and went out of the bedroom.

And for the first time, I was alone in Storm's End.

For a moment I just stood there in the center of the bedroom and looked around me. There was a feeling of such beauty and elegance, of another time, another world. Had my mother lived in this room? What was she like? And her mother? Had they looked at this same rose brocade, smoothed their hair in front of the same Venetian mirror and then, pleased with their appearance, turned to go down to dinner with their husbands, as I would?

I looked about the room carefully now, as if to find some link to remind me of the past of this room. There were things I hadn't noticed in my first inspection . . . a gilded shadow box on delicate legs holding an ivory fan and a collection of tiny, jewel-like snuffboxes. I looked at the curve of the *bombé* chests on each side of the bed, the delicate embroidery on the sheets and pillowcases.

And then a thought sent me hurrying into the dressing room. If anything could revive my memory surely it would be the clothes I'd worn, clothes I'd chosen sometime in that lost past. I flung open the doors of all the closets . . . and stood there a little stunned. Whatever my life had been before, I had liked clothes, a lot of clothes and had the money to indulge my tastes.

My fingers moved the hangers aside one by one. There were dresses for all occasions; caftans, robes, long and short gowns, sports clothes . . . a wardrobe enough for ten women. Ten women with expensive tastes.

And after the first glance it meant no more to me than if I were glancing through the racks of a shop.

Thoughtfully I moved into the bathroom beyond. If the bedroom had seemed a luxurious dream, the bathroom brought me back to the Victorian reality of the rest of the house. The bathtub and the rest of the equipment in the room were boxed in black wood like coffins. I started a warm tub, watching the water trickle out slowly, and then I went back into the dressing room.

I went through the clothes closets again, more slowly this time, examining each dress carefully. Why would I have bought this? I thought as I touched a pair of brilliantly orange pajamas. Somehow I couldn't imagine ever buying anything in that color. Or the wide skirt of purple and green silk? But then I remembered Hale. If you're married to an artist you must expect him to have some choice in the colors you wear.

Abandoning the closets I knelt on the carpet and started to open the drawers lined up underneath. Everything was in beautiful order: piles of expensive lingerie, stockings, one drawer filled with rows of purses for every possible occasion. The last drawer I touched stuck for a moment and then finally slid open, almost coming out of the wall.

It was lined with peacock-blue satin, tufted on the sides and bottom, obviously meant for jewelry. But of all the drawers in this room, this was the only one that seemed nearly empty.

There were a few pieces of costume jewelry . . . a silver link belt, a few inexpensive pins, brightly colored earrings. But nothing that really seemed to match the rest of my wardrobe. And then my eyes caught the glitter of a circle of gold.

I picked it up carefully. It was a wide, modern wedding band, clearly expensive. I twisted it to see if there was an inscription inside. I could make out the letters now . . . "HB/CA Always."

My wedding ring! I clutched it automatically in my hand and then, after a moment, I opened my fingers again. Looking down at the ring once more, I could feel myself frowning. What was my ring doing here, forgotten in this half-empty drawer? I slipped it on the third finger of my left hand; it fit easily. There was no pale mark on the finger to show where it had been before, but I couldn't really expect that. Six weeks in the hospital had bleached me of whatever tan I had acquired during the summer months.

But why was my ring here? Why hadn't Hale said anything about its being missing, all these weeks I had been in the hospital? Why had I taken it off that last day of the accident, before I left this house? Or had I taken it off before, making a deliberate decision to place it here in this drawer?

My mind was full of questions now. Where was I going that last afternoon that I had deliberately left my wedding ring behind?

And to whom was I going?

Four

By the time I was ready to go downstairs for dinner I had made up my mind to ask as little as possible. Perhaps by deliberately turning my back on the lost past it would come back to me. Whatever estrangement I had had with Hale that had led me to abandon my wedding ring that last afternoon (for I was positive it was then I had taken it off my finger), I knew it could never have been his fault. Hale had proved his love for me these past weeks when I had lain a stranger in the hospital. Now it was up to me to return that love.

The hot bath relaxed me and I took time preparing myself for dinner. Out of the crowded closets I selected a long, straight plaid skirt of pale gray and blue and a soft gray turtleneck sweater. Even though it was only halfway through October, there was a chill in the air . . . or perhaps it was this old house, the winds off the river pushing through cracks in the walls and the loose window frames to circulate endlessly through the high-ceilinged rooms. I fastened the silver link belt around my waist snugly and turned to look at myself in the Venetian mirror.

Whether it was the warm bath or the curiosity I was feeling about what I had discovered, my cheeks were slightly flushed. None of the people at the hospital would have recognized me now, I thought. Not Mrs. McKenzie or the cold Dr. Gallard. Their pale frightened ghost of a patient was gone. For good, I told myself firmly. Starting for the door I stopped and went back to the chest by the bed where I had placed my wedding ring. I picked it up again, looked at it for a brief second and then, making up my mind, slipped it back on my finger. Whatever had happened before didn't matter. I was Hale's wife and I was determined he would never regret his kindness to me.

I walked carefully down the great staircase, half hiding my left hand as I held up the folds of my long skirt. But I was ashamed of myself by the time I reached the black and white squares of the hall below. If Hale or Irene noticed I had replaced my ring, surely it would tell them better than any words how committed I was to making a new start to my life here at Storm's End. There were voices coming from the drawing room ahead of me and I moved through the open doorway to stop just inside.

Hale had been fixing a drink for Irene, standing at the solid table in front of the window seat at the end of the room. He froze as he caught sight of me, breaking off what he had been saying in mid-sentence. Irene, facing him, caught the look in his eyes and then she too turned toward me. She was the first to speak.

"Constance! Don't you look lovely!"

Hale handed Irene her glass and smiled warmly. "The doctors should see you now. I knew all you needed was to come home. And you'd be well." And then he stopped, flushing a little, as Irene had when she talked to me upstairs. I walked across the long room toward the two of them.

"Don't be uncomfortable, Hale. It's enough that I feel wonderful. We'll worry about my past later."

He smiled again and then turned back to the bottles and glasses on the heavy silver tray. "Want one of my martinis, Constance? They'll be better than the ones I brought to the hospital." We both smiled at that. Liquor had been strictly against the rules but Hale had always managed to smuggle in a small thermos of cocktails when he came over to share supper with me in my room. And Mrs. McKenzie had only said, "If you're going to break the law, I warn you, I have to be bribed." After that Hale always made a point to bring three glasses.

"A martini'd be perfect."

I glanced around the room now for the first time. It seemed more cheerful and modern than the rest of the house, the walls painted a sunny yellow, the woodwork white. A cheerful lemon chintz covered the long deep couches that flanked the fireplace; with a wide, low table planted on the fur rug between them.

Irene went to stir the roaring fire and, as Hale prepared my drink, I wandered about the room. Pale cream drapes at the windows shut out the night and the lamps placed on the smoothly polished end tables gave the room a warm, comfortable feeling. Summer slipcovers still covered most of the chairs and even the thick dark oriental rug that stretched the whole length of the long room seemed subdued. I came nearer the fireplace and sat down in a wing armchair, facing the fire.

At that moment Hale and Irene both turned back toward me. Irene had replaced the poker in the rack by the antique trunk that served as a woodbox, Hale was holding in his right hand the drink he had been making. And they both stood absolutely still, staring at me.

"What . . . what's the matter?" I stammered. I could tell something had shocked them. Good Lord, I thought. What mistake have I made now?

"Nothing. Nothing at all, Constance." Irene glanced quickly at Hale and then settled herself calmly on the sofa, straightening the jacket of the black wool pants suit she had changed into for dinner.

Hale smiled again and walked over to me. "Something must be coming back to you, Con. That was always your favorite chair. And now, your first time in the room since . . . well, *since* . . . you picked it automatically." He handed me the glass, his blue eyes loving as he looked down at me.

I could feel myself blushing. It was silly to get excited by such a little thing. And yet, wasn't this what we'd both hoped for so much? That little things would ease me gradually back into the pattern of my life?

"How's the drink?"

I took a quick sip. "Perfect."

Then, as Hale moved back to the bar table, I saw for the first time the portrait over the mantle.

It wasn't a large painting, but I could tell the artist, whoever he was, had been excellent. It was the portrait of a young woman, hair dark as mine, half facing away from the artist. She was wearing a dress of sapphire blue velvet, cut low over her white shoulders in the style of the Napoleonic era. Around her neck and extending almost down to the cleft of her breasts was a superb necklace of what seemed to be sapphires and diamonds. She had been posed with one delicate hand raised toward the necklace, a long finger almost pointing at the enormous blue stone in the center of jewels. Behind her was a dim blue-green background of storm-tossed trees.

But it wasn't her beauty or the stunning jewelry that held me. The skill of the artist had caught something in her deep, dark eyes; a look of sorrow, almost of pleading. I knew without question she had suffered pain and unhappiness.

"You don't recognize the portrait?" Hale had come back to my chair again; he leaned over the high back, swirling the ice in his glass lazily.

"No. But I feel as if I should."

"She was the first mistress of Storm's End," Irene said calmly. "The first Constance Avery." She placed her drink on the low table in front of her and fished in a silver box for another cigarette.

"Your great-great-great-grandmother. Or maybe there's even another 'great' in there. You were never very clear about it. The artist's rather good. One of Raeburn's pupils, I'd guess. She's the real reason for this house, you know."

I got up then, to move closer to the painting. "She looks unhappy."

"She was. From what you've told me of the family history."

"Only now it's your turn to tell me." I glanced back at him, but his eyes were still fastened on the painting.

"She was born in England, daughter of some minor member of the nobility. But by the time your ancestor, Jared Avery, came over on business after the Revolution, the family was more or less impoverished. You know the sort of thing . . . lots of land, all entailed, a falling-down castle . . ."

"The original Storm's End," Irene put in as Hale took a sip of his drink. "Jared supposedly had it duplicated for his bride as a gift. Although personally from what you've told us of the old scoundrel, I'll bet he did it just to show everybody how important he'd become."

"And the necklace? It's so beautiful." But I said that absently, for it was the eyes of the woman in the portrait that fascinated me.

"Glad you like it, it's yours." I must have shown my astonishment at Hale's remark, for he laughed as I looked at him.

"No, I mean it, Con. You get it on your twenty-fifth birthday."

"And when's that?" I couldn't keep the curiosity out of my voice.

"The end of the week. If all goes well, your great-uncle will hand it to you personally."

I turned away from the fireplace then. I felt confused, too many things had been thrust at me for one day and I could feel the courage and determination I had felt when I was dressing for dinner begin to seep away. I went back to the wing chair and sat down again.

"Hale, you're making it all into a muddle. Start again. Can't you see Constance hasn't the faintest idea what you're talking about?" Irene picked up her empty glass and moved over to the bar table.

"Am I, Con? Am I confusing you?"

"I don't understand all this about my birthday . . . and the necklace. What has to 'go well'?"

"We're trying to get your great-uncle to come up here for a visit. There'll be papers to sign, family matters to attend to. You see, at twenty-five you come into your inheritance. I don't know why it wasn't at twenty-one, the way it usually is, but apparently the Averys do things in their own way." He settled down in the couch opposite the one Irene had been occupying and raised his glass in a half-toast to me.

"My great-uncle's to come up here?"

"If we can persuade him. We're none of us on close terms with him at the moment."

And then my resolve cracked. I leaned forward, my fingers plucking nervously at my plaid skirt. "Hale? Do I have to see him? Can't all this legal business be handled by lawyers? Or by you and Irene?"

Hale gave Irene a quizzical look, and then turned back to me, his face serious now. "Don't you want to see him, Constance? He's the only member left living in your family."

"You're my family now, Hale. You and Irene. And this place." I stood up, moving restlessly away from the two of them, knowing their eyes were on me. "To meet a stranger now . . . and that's what he'd be, great-uncle or not . . ."

"He won't bite you, Constance." I could tell Irene meant to be re-assuring, but I felt my nerves tighten again. The glass I held was shaking, I had to use both hands to keep it from spilling.

"How do you know, Irene?" I made my voice as calm as I could as I turned to look at her. "This great-uncle of mine doesn't care very much about me, that's obvious. All those weeks in the hospital, there were never any calls or letters. Didn't he know what had happened to me?"

"He knew," Hale said. "Or most of it. He's an elderly man, Con, not very well. We felt . . . that is, his lawyers and doctor felt there was no point in disturbing him too much."

"Fine! Then let's not disturb him at all . . . the end of this week, or ever!" The words were colder than I meant but I still felt myself shaking.

Hale came toward me then, putting his arm protectively around my shoulder. "Don't be angry with him, Constance. If there's been any break in your family, it's because of me."

"You?"

Hale nodded. "Guardians of wealthy young heiresses can't really be expected to accept a struggling young artist as ideal husband material."

"That was four years ago. He's going to carry the grudge forever?" I said it petulantly, making no move to shrug off Hale's arm.

"It won't matter, not after your birthday. He has to turn everything over to you then . . . this house, your money, the necklace," said Irene.

"I don't want to talk about it. Not now, at least."

Hale moved away from me then, his face thoughtful. "I hate to think the first thing I've brought back from your past was anger and bitterness," he said.

And then I realized how guilty Hale must be feeling, probably had been feeling these past four years since our marriage. And foolishly, because I felt I couldn't face a stranger yet, I'd made him unhappy. I crossed to him, where he stood staring at the fire, his hands stuck in the pockets of his dark trousers, the gold buttons on his blazer twinkling in the firelight. I linked my arm through his and, trying to distract him, looked up at the portrait again.

"Tell me about her. The first Constance."

"Let's see what I remember." Hale's face brightened as he too looked up at the portrait. "Apparently Jared Avery . . . that was her husband . . . was one of those self-made men. There were rumors that he'd done very well out of the American Revolution, playing both sides against each other, adding to his holdings by buying up confiscated land from the various estates around here as each army occupied the area. A lot of the Revolution was fought right in this section. Then, after the war, he determined to found a dynasty. None of his respectable Dutch neighbors with their sturdy daughters were good enough for him. Or maybe they turned him down for his trickery. At any rate, he sailed for England determined to buy himself a lady for a wife."

"And he found Constance," I whispered, still looking at that lonely, unhappy face.

"Exactly. The youngest daughter of an impoverished Baronet, she didn't have much choice. He saw her portrait someplace . . . this portrait, I gather. As I said, it's either a Raeburn or one of his pupils, the style is his. Jared managed an introduction somehow and the only dowry he asked for was that necklace. Apparently it had been given to the girl by her royal godmother."

I studied the necklace now, it was truly magnificent. The artist had captured the blaze of jewels in their intricate pattern so realistically, you could practically count each stone.

Irene, a fresh drink in her hand, came up behind us. "It's called the 'Scarf of Sapphires,'" she said. "There's a rather nasty story about how it got the name."

Hale looked down at me. "It seems old Jared had plans for that necklace," he said. "He wanted to break it up and sell it to buy more land here in America. But he found under the conditions of the wedding agreement it couldn't be sold or disposed of in any way. Apparently there was some obscure British law that the necklace would have to revert to the Crown if the original Constance didn't keep it. You can imagine that it didn't start the marriage off on a very good basis."

"And the name?" I asked.

"Yes, Hale, do get on with the story." Irene had moved closer now. I could see her eyes glittering in the light from the fire as she studied the jewels in the painting.

"Well, that first winter here, when they were building the house . . . was freezing. You can imagine this place without central heating. And it seems one day your namesake complained of the cold. And Jared is supposed to have answered, 'How can you be cold, madam? You have a scarf of sapphires.' And that's what it's been called in the family ever since."

"He must have been a monster." I moved away from the fireplace. I felt I could understand now some of the unhappiness in the eyes of the portrait, it seemed to chill this cheerful room for me.

But before Hale could answer, Mrs. Janeck appeared in the doorway to announce dinner.

Dinner was surprisingly delicious; somehow I had not imagined that Mrs. Janeck would turn out to be a gourmet chef. Or perhaps after the weeks of bland hospital food her fragrant chicken curry seemed even better than it was. And the champagne that Irene had ordered gave the whole meal a festive air.

The dining room was a dark, high-ceilinged barracks of a room, paneled in the same somber wood as the hall. We left the overhead chandelier off and settled companionably at the foot of the long dining table, Hale at the end in a great carved chair, Irene and I on each side. Mrs. Janeck had placed a huge silver candelabrum at this end of the table, the half dozen candles gave us all the light we needed. And almost as if Hale and Irene had planned to lift my spirits, we laughed and joked through the meal, Ben in a neat white starched coat serving us quietly.

We were dawdling over the last of the coffee, not wanting to leave the table, when we heard the chimes of the great clock on the landing upstairs.

"Eleven o'clock? It can't be." Hale checked his wristwatch.

"And we promised them at the hospital faithfully that Constance would get her rest." Irene moved her chair back and stood.

"But I'm not tired. Not really." Only even as I said it, I realized how exhausted I was. We drifted quietly back into the hall, Irene moving toward the drawing room.

"You two go on up, I'll just turn off the lights."

Hale took my arm gently and we started up the stairs together.

And then for the first time, in all the times he had touched me these past weeks, I felt uneasy. I was not just a guest in this house, not just the descendant of that unhappy woman whose portrait I had admired in the drawing room downstairs, I was Hale's wife.

He must have sensed what I was thinking, for he turned toward me as we reached the door to my bedroom. "Don't feel nervous, Constance. Not with me. I know I must still be almost a stranger to you. I don't expect to be treated as a husband until . . . well, until you feel I really *am*."

Luckily the shadows made the hall dark by my doorway, for I could feel myself blushing.

"You're not a stranger, Hale. It's me . . . I don't know what I feel . . . or think half the time. Until I know who I am, I can't feel anything. But if you'll just give me time . . ."

"All the time you need, my dear. You're home now. And I'm going to see that you'll always be safe and happy." He leaned forward then, bending a little, and kissed me gently on the forehead. "Sleep well, darling."

I went into my bedroom then. Mrs. Janeck, or someone, had closed the drapes at the long windows and placed a thin silk nightgown and robe across my bed. I undressed quickly, anxious to get to sleep. Somehow the day seemed suddenly to have been very long . . . the hospital, that last session with Dr. Gallard, the strange fears I had had during the drive to Storm's End, the house itself . . . I needed to rest, to let this day fade quietly away.

I crossed to the windows and pushed aside one of the full rose brocade drapes. I found a latch to one of the windows behind the thin curtains and managed to open the window a little. It was too chilly to step out onto the balcony. Besides, the moon had gone over to the other side of the house now and I knew I couldn't see anything but the dark river far below. Plenty of time for that tomorrow, I thought.

I climbed into the huge bed, it was surprisingly soft. There was one last light in the room, the bedside lamp on the *bombé* chest. I turned it off and settled down to sleep.

Perhaps it was the long day, or the exhaustion of the new experiences I had been through, but I fell asleep immediately. But it was not an easy sleep . . . I could feel myself tossing in the great bed, some part of my mind still awake. Awake and listening.

For I am sure that it was something I heard . . . something strange and unhappy that was a part of this house that made me wake, all the fears I had felt earlier suddenly back in the room with me, back inside me . . . where was I? Who was I? And what was it that I felt deep inside me was so terribly wrong in this house?

I lay there in the dark, listening. I had not seen where Irene had placed the little bedside clock Hale had brought to me at the hospital . . . it wasn't glowing on the chest so I had no idea of the time.

There was no light coming through the closed drapes of the window, but my eyes adjusted to the gloom and I could make out . . . just barely . . . shapes in the room. The canopy of the bed high above me, the mirror over the now dark fireplace.

What was it that had awakened me? I tried to remember. Was it a cry? A chime from the hall clock? Someone moving outside? There were sounds in the house, I realized now, never ending sounds. The creak of old wood, changing with the temperature. Perhaps the scurry of a mouse behind a wall. But surely it was something more than that that had startled me out of my restless sleep. Only now I heard nothing but the small sounds of an old house settling down into another long night's silence. And then it sounded again . . . the soft sighing of the wind off the river . . . like a woman's cry. The first Constance must have cried like that, I thought. Here in this room, night after unhappy night.

Then I thumped my pillow angrily. This is nonsense, I thought. They gave you pills at the hospital to help you sleep, take one and stop being such a fool. With that I sat up in bed and snapped on the light.

Irene had placed the container of sleeping pills in the top drawer of the chest by the bed, I remembered that. The room was chilly and I threw my robe over my shoulders as I fumbled for a pill and swallowed it with water poured from the carafe on the chest.

Then, suddenly, a gust of wind from the open window blew the heavy silk draperies straight out into the room toward me. I started, almost dropping the glass in my hand. The draft of air continued to billow the curtains, swelling them out. It reminded me, in that moment, of the skirt of a gown a woman might have worn in another century. Once again I thought of the first Constance Avery.

It's a good thing Dr. Gallard can't see me now, I thought as I crossed to close the window. Jumping at the least noise, my mind full of old tales . . . he'd have me back in that hospital in a minute. Or worse. In that "controlled environment" he'd talked about. I shuddered a little and clutched the thin robe tighter around my shoulders.

The window was too far open for me to reach, pushed flat, the wind banging it against the outside of the house. Wishing I'd remembered to put on slippers, I took a short step out onto the cold gray stone of the balcony.

Once I'd stepped outside it was as if I had walked into a world of dreams, more hazy and confused than that from which I had just awakened. Fog swirled up from the river, pressing against the house, flattening the silk of my nightgown to my body, chilling my shoulders. I could barely see the stone railing of the balcony. There was no light, no moon, no stars, just the damp hands of the fog, closing in on me . . . touching my skin, pressing my hair to my head.

I turned and reached for the handle of the window. It was then I saw the light, the only break in the fog and night that surrounded me.

It was a lighted window, a small square of yellow cut in the dark walls to my left. I couldn't tell how far away it was, somewhere above me, I thought. Could there be someone still awake in the house? Or was it from some other building? The lighted square twisted as I watched, thinning out, moving back and forth, or so it seemed, like a curtain moving.

And, even as I watched, the fog pressed closer, whipping my hair across my eyes. When I pulled the strands back from my face, the light was gone. I was alone again on the cold stone balcony, staring at the damp, dark night.

Pulling the window closed, I stepped back into the bedroom. I could feel the sleeping pill starting to work as I fastened the latch of the window. I moved back to the bed, it looked very inviting now. Climbing in, I turned off the light. And soon the question of who at Storm's End might still be up at this hour faded away and I could feel myself doze off into sleep.

THE SECOND DAY

Five

When I awoke the next morning I could tell from the cracks of sunlight prying through the heavy drapes that the weather had changed. I still had no idea of the time, but I had a feeling that I had slept well . . . and late.

I jumped from the bed and hurried to the windows. Pulling the silken cords that hung at one side, I opened the drapes. And it was as if I had opened a wall of sunlight into the room. I glanced out at the balcony . . . I could see the flagstone terrace below and, a few feet beyond, the low wall that marked the edge of the cliff over the river. I tried to spot the window with the light that I had seen the night before but from inside the room all I could see were the curves of the turrets and towers at the far end of the house. And I didn't want to take any more time to study that now, not with the sun already high in the sky.

I hurried to dress, picking the first outfit I found in the closets, a lemon-yellow skirt and sweater. There was a ribbon of the same color pinned to the sweater. I used it to tie my hair back and, slipping on a pair of low-heeled slippers, I started down to breakfast. I'm starving, I thought. And this time I didn't hesitate on the long staircase. There was so much I wanted to see in this house, so much I wanted to learn.

Only, when I reached the hall below, I felt confused again. The closed doors ahead of me led to the drawing room, I remembered that from the night before. But which of the other doorways led to the dining room? Luckily, at this moment the door on the left opened and Irene came out. She looked neatly efficient in a tailored gray denim dress, but there were shadows under her eyes as if she had not slept well.

"There you are," she said. "I was just on my way up to see what had happened to you."

"I was standing here, trying to remember which way to the dining room," I replied, not at all self-conscious for once.

"This way," said Irene. She led me back through the doorway. The dining room was deserted, the long table bare, the twin rows of chairs down each side empty. Irene passed down the room, the heels of her shoes clicking on the polished wooden floor.

"We never eat breakfast in here. It'd be like starting the day in a mausoleum." She pushed aside the swinging door that I had noticed the night before. I had thought then it led to the butler's pantry and the kitchen beyond.

Instead it opened onto a cheerful little room, octagonal in shape, bright with apple-green cupboards, each panel decorated with a painting of a different type of bird . . . jays and cardinals and robins. Hale was seated at the round table, finishing his coffee.

"We use this as a breakfast room," Irene said as we came in. "Look who I've found, Hale . . . standing in the front hall, looking as lost as a new girl at school."

"And as young." Hale got up then and came around the table to kiss me lightly on the forehead. "I don't have to ask how you slept," he said. "I can see it in your face."

"I slept beautifully. And I'm famished." I took the place that had been set for me, Hale holding my chair. "I can't get over this house, every room seems to be of a different period of time." I picked up the coffee cup Irene had filled for me and looked out the uncurtained bow window in front of me. This room was on the river, but that was too far below us to be seen. All I could see was the clear sky and the bright morning sunlight. Even the wall of the terrace outside was out of my sight.

"That's your first task of the day, Irene." Hale's voice was cheerful this morning. "Show Constance the house. Otherwise, we'll have to put a bell around her neck so we don't lose her."

"Is the house that big?" I turned to Irene.

"Not really. Just confusing. You're right about it's being different periods. Each generation seems to have added a little something. Then, around the turn of the century, they slapped it all over with gray fieldstone to try and pull it together. I'm not sure they succeeded."

Mrs. Janeck came in from the far door now, carrying a covered silver dish, which she placed on the green and white checked table-cloth in front of me. "Good morning, Mrs. Janeck," I said, smiling at her.

"Good morning, ma'am. I've made poached eggs, but if you'd rather have something different?" She looked tired in the morning light, as Irene did. I could see now she was older than I had first thought, probably close to sixty.

"Poached eggs'll be fine," I said, serving myself eagerly.

"So you slept well last night," said Hale.

"It took me a while, but that bed couldn't have been more comfortable."

Mrs. Janeck took the empty toast rack and went over to the sideboard to refill it.

"Did something disturb you?" asked Irene. "Or was it just a case of getting used to the house? These old barns seem to have a life of their own. Especially at night."

"I know. I tossed and turned for a while and then finally gave up and took a pill. That was when I got up to close the window. You're right about that wind off the river, it never seems to stop, does it?"

Mrs. Janeck returned to the table and silently offered me some warm toast. I took a piece from the rack and she removed my empty glass of orange juice.

"You'll get used to it. You'll find we're all 'early to bed' here." Hale poured himself another cup of coffee.

"Not everybody. Someone was up late last night."

"What are you talking about?" Irene paused as she lit a fresh cigarette.

"I stepped out on the balcony as I was trying to close the window. I could see a light someplace. From one of the towers, I imagine. I thought you said nobody slept there."

There was a clatter at the sideboard. All of us turned to look at Mrs. Janeck, who was staring at a broken glass shattered on the floor in front of her. "I'm sorry," said Mrs. Janeck. And then she bent quickly, hiding her face as she started to pick up the pieces.

"Better get a brush and dust pan, Mrs. Janeck. You'll cut your hands on the pieces." Irene's voice was as calm as always. No one said anything as the housekeeper hurried out of the room.

"I'm afraid she's getting a little old for this job, Constance." Irene took another sip of her coffee.

"We can hardly replace her, Irene." Hale signaled quietly, pointing toward the kitchen door, which was still swaying back and forth. "After all, she's part of this house."

"Did I say something wrong?" Something made me feel uneasy. "Does she sleep up in that tower, is that it?"

"Nobody sleeps in the towers, Con." Hale moved his chair back to cross his long legs. He wasn't smiling now. "Nobody has for fifty, sixty years."

"Oh. It's just . . . I was sure that . . ." My voice trailed off.

"It could have been some trick of light. And you did say you'd taken one of your pills before you went out on the balcony."

"Only just taken it." I knew I sounded stubborn, but I couldn't help it. They were treating me like a child. "No pill could have started working that quickly. Anyway, it couldn't make me see something that wasn't there, could it?"

"I don't know." Irene moved forward, flicking the ash off her cigarette. "Do you know what prescription they gave you at the hospital?"

"No . . . but I'm sure it couldn't make me 'see' things."

"I want you to promise you won't go out onto any balconies after you've taken one of those things." Hale's voice was firm. "You might get dizzy, lose your balance . . . do you promise?"

"Yes, Hale," I said, meekly. I wished now I had never mentioned the subject.

"Well, I'm off to the studio. Why don't you end the tour there, Irene?" He brushed a quick kiss on the top of my head and was gone. I noticed then that Mrs. Janeck had come quietly back into the room and was sweeping up the last shards of glass from the floor.

*   *   *

"We might as well start here in the front hall," Irene said later, when we had both finished our coffee. She had moved ahead of me, standing near the great front doors. "This is the most modern part of the house."

"Modern?" I looked up at the massive staircase, marching in square angles up to the skylight that was the top of the stairwell.

"Actually, there are two Storm's Ends . . . the oldest part, the part Jared build for the first Constance, is to the left. That's the section that has your bedroom and Hale's. The other Storm's End was built in the eighteen-fifties. The first Jared had twin grandsons, they each wanted a separate house, so a duplicate was built. That's the tower section to the right, where the dining room is now, and the kitchen and the housekeeping rooms." Irene moved toward the opposite doors. "Descendants of the twins intermarried and they built this section of the house to connect the two buildings into one."

"How many rooms are there, actually? In the whole house?" I looked around, as awed as if I had bought a ticket into a museum. I'm a stranger here, I thought. I'll never feel at home, never really belong . . . but Irene was speaking again.

"Probably forty or fifty rooms, all together. I don't think anybody's ever counted. Of course, some of them are remodeled . . . two rooms thrown together, like the billiard room. And all the bathrooms, they were carved out of other rooms around the turn of the century. And then there are all those little cubicles up under the roof where the servants slept."

"It must have taken dozens of servants to run this place," I murmured. "How does Mrs. Janeck manage?"

"She doesn't, very well," said Irene crisply. "But we've only opened a few rooms since we've been back. And there's her husband Otto for the grounds. And Ben for the heavy cleaning. And once a month we get some girls in to do the big jobs . . . the silver, and the windows."

"Girls from the village?" I asked.

"No. Not from the village." Irene's voice was curt now. "We stay away from the village as much as possible." She moved across the black and white floor toward the doors that led to the oldest part of the house.

"What's the problem with the village?" I asked, tagging along behind her.

"There was some unpleasantness between your grandfather and the people in town. Your family isn't very popular around here, I'm afraid. Come, let's see if you can get the layout of the house."

As we moved from room to room it began to be somewhat clearer to me. The house was built in the rough shape of a wide U, the bottom of the letter being the main well of the front hall and the drawing room. The twin castles at either end formed the two arms of the letter. From the outside, with its uniform covering of gray stone, the whole building looked of the same age.

Irene was right, most of the house was closed. We passed through several small rooms, used as parlors once probably, into a long narrow reception room, the walls covered in a deep maroon velvet. There had been pictures on the walls; I could see from the unfaded squares of material where they must have hung.

"The gallery," Irene explained. "Your grandfather lent most of the paintings to various museums. They can be recalled. If you ever decide to reopen the entire place."

"You make it sound out of the question," I said stiffly. I stood by a tall dusty window that barely let in the morning sunlight.

"I'm afraid it is. The days when people could afford to live in palaces like this are over, Constance. Even granting that you're about to become a very wealthy woman." She opened the door to the next room, placed at an angle to the gallery. "This was the music room."

Irene's voice seemed to echo back as she walked into the room. Following her, I saw that the walls of this room had been covered with a pale blue *moiré*. The carpet was rolled up and lay, covered, against one wall. Great cotton balloons hung from the ceiling, covering the chandeliers, and a crowd of thin gilt chairs huddled in one corner. Dust-gray sheets covered various mounds; one was certainly a harp, another I guessed to be a grand piano far longer than musicians of this century ever used.

"Is the whole house like this?" I couldn't help shuddering a little, although the room was far from cold. But it was dead, airless; not even haunted by the ghosts of the people who had spent their lives here. These rooms are just empty and deserted, I thought. And sad.

"Quite a lot of the place is like this, I'm afraid. We've closed off all the bedrooms upstairs. Except, of course, for yours and mine and Hale's." She opened another door. "The ballroom's through here."

I looked over her shoulder, not even going in. The gold paper on the walls was dingy now, peeling in long strips from the dusty ceiling. "Close the door, Irene," I said, turning away. "It's so depressing." I felt now that the few rooms we lived in were surrounded by a ghost town, pressing in on us, crowding us, waiting for the chance to take over the whole of Storm's End and make it quiet and still and dead forever, safe in its memories of the past.

I walked across the bare parquet floor of the music room. "What's through here?" I said, touching the handle of the double door.

"You'll like that," said Irene, coming over to me. "It's the cheeriest part of the house. Hale's studio." She tapped on the door politely. "Hale? Can we come in?"

From inside we could hear Hale call out, "Sure." Irene opened the double doors at the same time and I walked into the sunlight of Hale's studio.

I could tell it had been designed originally to be the conservatory of Storm's End. Three walls and the ceiling sparkled with panes of glass. But instead of plants and flowers, the room was vivid with canvases, all splashed with bright, hot colors. And even in the first glance I could see Hale had gone through several phases as an artist from romantic landscapes to slashing abstracts.

He stood at the far corner of the room, his white shirt open at his throat, his long legs in faded blue jeans planted wide apart as he studied the painting on the easel in front of him.

The painting he had been working on was a portrait of me.

"Like it?" He grinned as we came nearer. "I was going to try and keep it as a surprise for your birthday. Since you can't possibly remember having posed for it before the accident. But there've been so many changes in your face, I want to capture them too. And I found I didn't quite get them in my hospital sketches."

I remembered then the long, lazy afternoons Hale had kept me company, sketchbook held idly in his lap, his fingers moving almost mechanically. So that was what he had been doing!

"You've made me too beautiful," I stammered, looking at the painting. Somehow Hale had managed to capture a resemblance between me and the first Constance, although looking at her portrait last night I would have said the only thing we had in common was the color of our hair. But Hale had posed me in much the same position, half turned away, one hand at the neckline of a low-cut dress of that same deep blue velvet.

"Not beautiful enough. I'm no Raeburn, I'm afraid. This is more my usual thing." Hale swept his hand toward the paintings stacked against the walls; brilliantly colored abstracts, splashed across large canvases.

"You're too modest, Hale," said Irene, still looking at my portrait. "Will it be finished by Constance's birthday?"

"Only if I can get her to pose for me again. There's something about the way her eyes are now that I haven't quite got."

"I'll be glad to . . . anytime."

"Come along, Constance. There are some business affairs you have to look over. And if Hale's working, we shouldn't disturb him."

"Why don't you go along, Irene? Get everything set up. I want Con to see my work."

Irene didn't much like this, I could tell. She's a woman of order, I thought, the type who doesn't like her plans changed, not even the smallest of her plans. I must find out about you. You're far more mysterious than this house.

"Please, Irene," I said. "It'll give me a chance to see if I can find my way alone back through the house."

Irene shrugged at this and went out, closing the doors behind her. But she must not have pulled them tightly, for one slid open again an inch or two so that we could hear the tap of her heels as she crossed the floor.

"What do you think?" Hale stood beside me now as I studied a large painting. It was composed of blocks of brown and gray, overlapping each other into strong patterns.

"I won't pretend to understand it, Hale. But there's something about it I like. Something clear and positive." I turned to look at him then. "Something very much like you."

He moved away from me then, standing so I could no longer see his face.

"Is that what you think of me?"

I walked around him, to search his clear blue eyes.

"My dear," he said. "You know so little about me."

"I know that I'm safe here with you. That you . . ." I couldn't say "love" somehow, I didn't dare say it. "That you *care* about me."

"More than you know." He looked at me then, more directly than I'd ever seen him do before. For a flash of a moment I thought of Mrs.

Janeck the night before, trying to tell me something and unable to find the words.

"Hale," I said, "surely by now you know you can tell me *anything?* That whatever may have been wrong . . . or secret between us . . . I want to know it . . . and to be forgiven for it."

He moved away from me then, taking a step or two toward the portrait of me, still glistening with fresh paint. "Someday I hope I *can* tell you everything."

I made no move to follow him. What have I put this man through, I thought. What unhappiness have I given him? I looked down at the wedding ring on my finger and twisted it nervously. He turned back then, and his face softened.

"I saw that you'd put it on last night," he said quietly. "I can never tell you how it made me feel." His blue eyes grew distant now, as if he were seeing another time, another room. "I've been so . . . lost. Help me to get back to where I belong."

"Hale? What is it? What did I do to hurt you so?" I held onto his arms, gripping them tightly.

"Nothing." He pulled himself back from the time he had been remembering. "Maybe someday we can talk about it. I want to . . . always believe that . . . and remember it . . ."

And then he broke off, looking over my shoulder. His face paled and I could see him guard himself almost as if a layer of glass had moved down over his eyes. I turned myself then.

Standing there, watching us from the half-open doorway, was Irene.

Six

For a moment I felt anger sweep over me. Was Irene spying on us? Whatever position she held in this household, surely Hale and I as husband and wife had the right to a few moments' privacy.

"What is it, Irene?" Hale's voice was steady but I could tell that he was as angry as I. But Irene seemed indifferent to him.

"Sorry to bother you two, but I suddenly realized I didn't show Constance where the library was this morning." Irene stood in the doorway, a calm smile on her face. "There's no telling where she might end up if we left her to go off on her own."

Was it my imagination or was there something behind what Irene was saying? Whether there was or not, Hale stepped away from me then, his anger melted. "Of course," he said. "It's just that you startled us." He turned to me then. "Better run along now, Con. Irene has a lot for you to do."

I made no protest although I still felt furious inside. Hale needed me, not Irene. Whatever the "business" she wanted me to attend to, it could have waited. But this was no time to protest, not now that Hale had separated himself from me.

I touched his arm gently. "We'll talk another time, won't we, Hale? Maybe when I'm posing for you?"

"Sure." He didn't look at me.

I turned then and walked to the door. Irene had moved back into the music room discreetly. She closed the double doors behind me and said, the first hint of an apology that I had ever heard from her, "I'm sorry. I didn't mean to interrupt you."

"That's all right." I kept my voice cool. "Now . . . which way do we go?"

I followed her back across the long reception rooms. Something puzzled me as we walked. And then I remembered we had not heard her heels clicking on the bare floor outside Hale's studio when she returned. And yet the door had been half open. *Had* she been eavesdropping? All right, my lady, I thought. Now it's your turn to answer questions.

The way to the library was not difficult to find . . . it was the other large doorway off the main hall, the twin of the door that led into the dining room and the breakfast room beyond.

The library itself was a solemn room: heavily tufted leather furniture, surrounded by layer after layer of books laid upon each other all the way up to the high dim ceiling. And in my first glance I had the feeling that none of the books had ever been opened. They stood in long, gilt-bound sets, looking down from the shelves at the room below. Thick brown plush drapes had been pushed back to let in the morning sun. It made an island of light on the heavy Victorian desk by the windows.

On top of the desk, neatly laid out, was a stack of bills, some legal papers in pale blue covers and a large checkbook.

"I think this will be comfortable." Irene pulled back the ornately carved throne behind the desk. "I'll just stand here and show you what has to be done." I took my place as she suggested.

"I think first you'd better go through the checkbook. Familiarize yourself with the past bills, before we go on to the present ones."

I flipped through the pages of canceled checks, carefully stapled back to the stubs of the checkbook. My signature looked strange to me . . . Constance Avery Britton.

How odd . . . if I'm going to have to learn to write all over again, I thought.

"Your signature doesn't seem familiar?" Irene was at my right, looking down at me. I studied the canceled checks again. The first letter of each name of my signature was large and clear: a strong C and A and B. But then the signature seemed to dwindle away into an almost unintelligible scrawl, as if the writer had tired of all the other letters.

"It's not the way I write. Not really."

"What do you mean?" said Irene. "You haven't signed your name since the accident."

I looked up at her then. "No, but I'd scribble a note or two sometimes to Mrs. McKenzie at the hospital when I wanted to sleep late. And Dr. Gallard, during our sessions, would often have me write down the answers to his questions. My handwriting isn't at all like that. See?"

I reached forward and took a pen from the slightly tarnished antique silver pen-and-ink tray in front of me. I took a pad and wrote on it: "Today is Tuesday." And then I signed it, "Constance Avery Britton." I handed the pad to Irene. "See? It's not the same as the signatures on these checks."

"That's not surprising." Irene remained as calm as ever. "Lots of people write their names in a style different from the rest of their writing. We've already alerted your bank and the lawyers about your condition. They won't be too surprised if your handwriting has changed slightly." She picked up a pile of bills. "These should be taken care of first. Mrs. Janeck, of course. And Otto and Ben. And the hospital."

She picked up a pile of neatly typed checks. "I did these earlier. All you have to do is sign them."

I glanced through the bills, the amounts did not seem excessive, mainly because none of the bills dated back further than the past two weeks.

"What about the weeks I was in the hospital?" I asked. "And before?"

"Hale paid those, out of his own funds. And I lent him money to cover the larger amounts . . . the surgeons, the private nurses . . ."

I could feel myself blushing again. All this time I had been given the best of care not only by my husband but by this strange, coolly efficient woman I had been so sure, just a few minutes ago, was spying on me. I fumbled for the pen again and started to sign the checks, trying to make my signature look as much like those already in the checkbook as possible.

*　　*　　*

It must have taken over an hour to complete all the bills. By the end my signature was practically identical with the way I had written before the accident. And I had learned a great deal more about the state of my affairs.

Apparently my parents had set up a sizable trust fund for me before they died and all these years since then (for the car accident that had killed them had taken place shortly after my fourth birthday) my money had been handled by my Great-Uncle Matthew. It was he who, out of the dividends of the trust, had paid for my clothes, my schooling and my generous allowance. Then, when I turned twenty-one, I received the dividends directly and began to have some control over my own money. And now, on my twenty-fifth birthday, the bulk of my inheritance would be mine, free and clear, with no restrictions, to do with as I wished.

I asked Irene many questions, which she answered in a businesslike manner. By going over the various bank statements, I realized that she had been right when she had said earlier that I was to become a very wealthy woman. As far as I could estimate, a fortune of over three million dollars was to be turned over to me on my birthday at the end

of the week. When I finally understood the total of the amount I felt
a little faint.

"So much money?" I glanced over at Irene. Halfway through the
session she had pulled over a straight-backed chair, to work alongside
me.

"I told you. It's a fortune. Old Jared not only owned a great deal of
land both here and in New York City that became very valuable, but
his descendants invested in *everything*. And usually very wisely. And
you're the last of the family. You and your great-uncle are the only re-
maining Averys."

I got up then, stretching my cramped legs. "Didn't he ever marry?
My great-uncle?"

"No. Apparently there was some mystery about that. From what
you told us."

I moved over then to the windows. I could see the sun on the lawns
outside, warm and golden, the trees turning into their autumnal reds
and yellows. Suddenly I wanted to be out of this dark oppressive room,
away from all this dry talk of money and families. But I had promised
myself today was for learning, not just about the house and my financial
affairs, but about Irene as well. I turned my back on the windows,
knowing I was now only a silhouette to Irene, still seated at the desk.
This time there'll be no blushes to give away my nervousness, I thought.

"Irene?"

She looked up from the papers she had been sorting. I made no move
to step closer. "There's one thing that still puzzles me."

"Only one?" Her voice was as cool as always.

"I mean, of what I *can* know. How did you and I meet?"

"In Paris. I thought we told you that. Shortly after you'd met Hale
and married him."

She reached for a cigarette and lit it. That's one of your little tricks,
I thought. You take a moment to light a cigarette or put it out while you
think. I've learned that much about you over the weeks. Only what do
you have to be on guard about now?

"You told me about Paris," I went on, still not moving. "But how
did you come to work for me?"

She glanced up at me then, her eyes narrowed a little. "Aren't you
satisfied with the way I'm handling the job?" she countered.

If she expected me to falter, to run to her for forgiveness or to re-assure her, she was mistaken. I stood where I was, determined to get the truth at last.

"You know better than that. All this . . ." I motioned toward the papers covering the desk. "I don't know anything about any of it. And I can't imagine that I understood it any better before. But I'm curious about *you*. You never mention your family or your friends . . ." I took a chance now. "Or lovers."

Irene smiled. "I'm afraid I have none of those, Constance. If I don't talk about my life it's because it's always been deadly dull. I was born poor, an orphan like yourself, in downstate Illinois. Always hated it. I worked my way through college, then I took a dreary typing job to save the money to go to Europe . . ."

"Which reminds me," I broke in. "You haven't told me how much you loaned Hale. I'd like to make a check out for that too today."

"There's no hurry." She stood now, gathering the papers into one neat pile.

You're so sure of yourself, I thought. So sure you're always going to be here, aren't you? And yet there was something about her, some-thing I'd been aware of from that first day I awoke in the hospital that told me she could not be dismissed as a servant. Searching for a way to find out more about her, I tried to get the conversation back to her life.

"Why Europe?"

"The only member of my family was there." She smiled again; it was a small, catlike smile. I had the feeling even with the light behind me she had studied my face and knew she had nothing to fear. She went on after a moment's pause. "Hale. Didn't you know? Hale and I are cousins."

I'm not quite sure how the meeting ended. I think I must have stam-mered out some stupid question like, "Are we through?" And she had nodded. And feeling like a schoolgirl dismissed by her headmistress, I had muttered some feeble excuse about wanting to get some fresh air. Walking quickly out of the room, I crossed the hall to the great front doors.

Once outside I walked down the wide shallow steps to the open gravel space in front of the house. Which way to turn? To the right meant going toward the end of the house where Hale had his studio and I had no desire to see him. Not now. Not until my thoughts were clearer. Why hadn't he told me about Irene?

But to turn left meant to pass the side of the house where the library was. And I wasn't going to let Irene see me again until I was under control. So I set off directly ahead, down one of the gravel walks that ran away from the side road we had used last night to enter Storm's End.

Irene was Hale's cousin? I knew then why she had seemed so secure in this house, so easy with Hale, so firm with the servants. Somehow in that dark past I had been too weak to prevent her from running this house, running all of our lives. And perhaps I still did not have the strength to resist her. And never would have.

By now I'd reached the first trees that edged the lawn at the front of the house. They were on the far side of the wide driveway that sloped down to what must be the main gate to the house. But the driveway curved and the gate was out of my sight. I stopped now and looked back. If someone were watching me from one of the windows they couldn't see the expression on my face, not from this distance.

I sat down on the faded grass, leaning back against the thick wide trunk of the tree behind me. So I might stain my yellow skirt, I thought. I was going to be a millionairess. I wouldn't ever have to worry about cleaning bills again.

Again?

I sat bolt upright then. Why had I thought "again"? I had seen the amount of money I had been living on all these years, surely I never could have worried about something as small as a cleaning bill?

But that word "again" had come automatically into my head. From what part of my past did it come? I found myself thinking about it, probing it, the way the tongue touches a sore tooth.

Why should I have ever worried about money . . . to the point of even thinking about something as trivial as a cleaning bill? And yet, somehow, somewhere, I knew I had.

It was warm in the sunlight and I found myself looking across the lawn at Storm's End. It's the first time I've really seen it, I thought. Last night it was a shadow in the darkness, now it lay there in the October morning as placidly on view as a monument.

It was not really the grandiose castle it had seemed the night before. Now that I knew something of its history . . . the original building, the mate that had been built in the middle of the last century, the connecting link of the hall and the drawing room; it all seemed smaller, more a real building than a fantasy castle.

I looked at it now with clear, cold eyes. The uniform cover of gray stone *did* make it into one building after all. The turrets and towers at either end of the central part of the building seemed a natural extension, almost a flowering, of the main hall. The fake battlements may have only been built to cover the drains along the roof, the peephole windows in the tiny turrets of the towers were probably there to allow light into the servants' staircases, but seen across the long, dead green lawn, Storm's End had the beauty of another world. It needs people, I thought. Cousins and aunts and children playing, servants in the background carrying tea trays, sweeping the grounds and the terrace with their long black serge uniforms.

Servants.

I remembered then the talk at breakfast. I stood up, searching all the towers at the left end of the house. What room up there had been lighted the night before? Because now that I had talked to Hale and Irene I was somehow sure that they had lied to me. Or, at least, had kept something from me. I *had* seen a light in a window the night before. And the window was in one of those towers. But which one?

Standing there, I studied the building. My room was on the other side of the house, I knew that, facing the river. And yet the towers curved around to the front of the house . . . it might have been any of the windows I now watched, glinting in the morning sun. Only which window was it? And why was it bright last night?

Suddenly I felt sure of myself again. I knew now that there were secrets in this house that neither Hale nor Irene wanted to tell me. Nor anyone else, as I thought about it. Certainly not Ben or Mrs. Janeck. And whatever it was, it was not necessarily something wrong that I had done in the past.

I took a last look at the house, so beautiful in the autumn sunlight. "You're a building," I said aloud, laughing a little to be talking to myself. "That's all you are, Storm's End. But even if my mind isn't clear and I don't know everything that's going on, I warn you, no pile of stones is going to frighten me."

Still laughing at myself, I turned away from the sun on the house, sharp against the morning sky, to take one of the smaller paths down through the trees.

It was quiet then, closed in with branches and leaves, all dark spinach color in this semi-forest; the early frosts of fall hadn't touched the trees here. I had the feeling I was going downward and yet I knew my feet were on a level, if little-used, path. I thought of turning back. This was not, could never have been a pleasant walk on the grounds and yet something led me forward.

After about a hundred feet the overgrown path widened into an open space, backed by a low building that looked like a string of garages. The trees overhead were thick here, I had a feeling of being closed in, as if I were walking underground. There was silence around me now, the silence of a root cellar or the neglected corner of some seldom visited park.

The long, low building at one side of this empty space was covered with the same gray stone as the main house. In front of it, like a miniature model of the grim structure behind, was a stone line of kennels, entrances cut at certain distances as neat and symmetrical as croquet hoops.

Who had been the dog-lover in the past? I wondered. Some cousin? Some earlier Avery who had ridden to hounds? I walked closer, studying the empty shelters. And then, from out of one of the openings, came an animal.

I saw at once it was Thor, the beautiful German shepherd that had greeted me so strangely the night before. He was fastened to a long steel chain, bolted to the side of his opening of the kennel. He came out confidently, having heard the sounds of my steps on the gravel path.

For a long moment we stood where we were, watching each other. He wasn't afraid now, I realized. Nor was I. We stood staring at each other for a long moment, his brown-black eyes searching my face.

"Thor?" I spoke quietly. "You're not just a watchdog, are you? You were *my* dog, weren't you? And you know me. You have to know who I am."

He did not move. He stood there, regarding me gravely. Trusting the look in his eyes I moved forward slowly, holding out my hand to pet him.

Then, with the snap of muscles suddenly released, he raced toward me, his jaw open, his teeth white and long in his triangular-shaped head. I was too surprised to step back, his body had stretched the end of his chain, a straight metal line leading back to his kennel.

He was on me before I could retreat . . . but the distance between us was enough that his paws could do no more than scrape at my outstretched hand. I pulled back, a scream coming out of my throat, stunned to see the drops of blood rising out of the broken skin of my hand.

Thor started to bark then, not the low growl of the night before, but a furious barking, angry and disturbed. Somehow, I knew it was not because of me, for I knew even then that his response had been instinctive, one he already regretted. He crouched down a few feet away from me. There was no desire in him to attack again and we both knew it.

From one of the stone buildings in this gloomy, green-branched cave came a stolid gray-faced man. He walked toward me, sure of his place here. Otto Janeck, I thought. Esther's husband. He was thick-figured; any other man of his size I would have said was fat but I had a feeling from the way he moved that his thick trunk and short legs were all muscle.

"You Mrs. Britton?"

I nodded, holding my bleeding hand. I was still too stunned to wonder why he didn't know who I was. I tried to stop the blood with the edge of my sweater.

"You shouldn't be here. Thor's no lapdog. I thought they told you that." He made no effort to help me, just stood there by the dog, who was whimpering softly. He bent down over Thor, his arm already raised to hit him. And then a cold black wave started to sweep up over me, toward my head, and even as it happened, I found myself thinking, "I've never fainted before . . ."

*   *   *

When I came to, Irene and Hale were holding me. I could see Mr. Janeck standing close to the kennels. Thor was no longer in sight, his chain led into one of the dark entrances and I could hear him growling softly.

"Con? Are you all right?" Hale's face was as white as when we had turned to see Irene in the studio doorway earlier. Only now his eyes were on me, his arm strong behind my shoulders. I could feel the sharp gravel of the path beneath me.

"Otto said Thor only scratched her," said Irene. But I could see she too was worried. In a perverse way I was almost pleased to see her upset. And then I felt ashamed that I had had the thought.

"I'm . . . I'm all right," I said as I struggled to sit up. It wasn't Hale or Irene that disturbed me now, I knew. It wasn't even Thor, I had seen before I fainted that he had been sorry. No, it was the stolid gray man by the kennel that made me angry.

"We've got to get her to a doctor," Hale said firmly, as if he expected an argument.

"The hospital's almost two hours away, Hale," protested Irene. "It *is* just a scratch."

"Then we'll take her to the village," said Hale. He was in no mood to be crossed, even I could tell that. "They must have doctors there."

There was a flicker of worry in Irene's eyes as she looked at him. The village was out of the question, I knew, from what she had told me. Didn't Hale know?

"I really am all right," I said, trying to stand. But Hale continued to hold me in his arms and I had to remain where I was. "But if you think I should see a doctor, there *is* Dr. Gallard. I'm supposed to check with him anyway. Remember?"

I don't know why Dr. Gallard's name came to my mind . . . except I did recall that he had said his house was near Storm's End. Surely I didn't look forward to another interview with him. I could imagine only too well how foolish he would make my accident seem. But this seemed to satisfy Hale.

"Dr. Gallard it is," he said, picking me up in his arms. I was aware of so many things as he started to carry me up the path . . . Hale's strength, the worried look on Irene's face, the cold brutal hostility of Otto Janeck.

And from deep in the darkness of his kennel, I caught a glimpse of the sad eyes of the great dog. It's all right, I thought, hoping the animal knew. I don't blame you.

Only . . . why aren't we friends?

Seven

If I had thought where Dr. Gallard would choose to live, I suppose I would have imagined a long modern building, all sharp angles and sterile metal furniture. Something that could be converted into an operating room or a sterile laboratory at any moment.

But the driveway we turned into ten minutes later led to a small white New England cottage with a low shingle roof and the last of the summer's rose vines still clinging to its neat walls. It looked more the home of an old-fashioned country doctor than that of a modern French psychiatrist.

Irene had hurried to call the doctor and find how to reach his house while Hale carried me to his low red sports car and placed me gently on the front seat. By the time he had started the car and raced it up to the front door of Storm's End, Irene was out on the stone steps with the directions. Hale made no move to have her come with us, for which I was grateful. The ride was brief . . . the doctor's rented house was barely half a mile from the main gate. Beyond his house, which stood on a hill, I could see the roofs of the small town of Avery, perhaps another mile farther down the road.

Hale braked the car and hurried around to my side. "Shall I carry you?" he said.

By now I was more embarrassed than frightened. Or perhaps I was still frightened but it was not because of the scratch on my hand. What am I going to say to Dr. Gallard? I thought. He already dislikes me. And now, this silly accident . . .

"No. Of course not, Hale." I struggled out of the low car. "Thor only scratched my hand. Not my legs. And see . . ." I held up my hand, taking off the handkerchief Hale had given me to bind it. "It's almost stopped bleeding."

"Thank God!" He put his arm around my shoulder as we started up the short path to the house. It felt good to feel him next to me. I could smell the clean freshness of his white shirt, feel the warmth of his slender body under it.

We went up onto the porch. Somehow I had expected the door to be open when we arrived, surely the doctor had heard the screech of the car tires as Hale turned into the driveway. Hale hesitated, looking for a doorbell, and then raised his hand to the polished metal knocker.

And at that moment, Dr. Gallard opened the door.

My first thought was that we'd come to the wrong house. Even though that last interview at the hospital had only been the day before, so much had happened, I had seen so many new people and places, the doctor seemed almost a stranger to me. Always before at the hospital he had been neatly dressed, quiet suits and ties, somehow always reminding me of the city rather than the country. Now, here in his own home, he looked completely different. His crisp black hair was as neatly brushed as ever, but he was wearing sand-colored corduroy trousers and a deep brown turtleneck sweater the color of his eyes.

Looking at him that first moment I couldn't help comparing him to Hale. Hale was much the taller, all long legs and arms, his silver-gilt hair tousled by the drive, a flush on the clear skin of his fine, well-bred face. Dr. Gallard was shorter, barely six inches taller than I, and I could see now he had the sturdy muscular frame of a man used to hard physical work.

Dr. Gallard looked at the two of us standing there in the sunlight, and one of his thick eyebrows lifted slightly. It gave his face a cynical expression I had grown only too familiar with during our sessions at the hospital.

"At least the patient is well enough to walk," he said dryly. "Come in." He stepped back to allow us to enter the house.

We walked directly into the main living room, a small white room, with black timbers across the low ceiling. The furniture, what could be seen (for most of it was covered with books and pads and reports), looked relaxed and comfortable. It isn't really his house, I thought, resisting the idea that the doctor would pick something so cheerful. He's only renting it. But there was a string of green plants flourishing along the edge of the bay window and fresh flowers in the bowls on the mantel and I knew someone must have been taking care of them. Does he live alone? I thought. Or is there someone else? This is a day for surprises.

"Sit down over here." The doctor swept a pile of books and papers off the sofa in front of the fireplace.

"Aren't you going to look at her hand?" said Hale. Whatever charm the house had for me had not softened his attitude toward the doctor.

"In a minute. I need some information first." He led me to the sofa and sat beside me, studying me carefully. "This dog that bit her . . ."

"Scratched her," Hale interrupted.

"He's had his rabies shots?"

"Yes."

"Good. That's one less thing to worry about."

"We're sorry to disturb you, Doctor," I said. "Hale just thought . . . well, I fainted. I suppose it must seem rather silly to bother you over a scratch."

"Silly? Dogs can kill people."

"He was on a chain. And I *did* warn Constance last night." Hale's mouth was a thin line, I could see he was growing angry.

"Oh? The animal tried to attack her last night as well?"

"Not exactly . . ." I fumbled for words. I could feel Hale's antagonism growing. Fighting Dr. Gallard never helped; over the weeks in the hospital I had learned that. "The dog was startled to see me. He *is* a watchdog, after all. Not a pet."

"Are you going to look at her hand, or aren't you, Doctor?" Hale had refused to sit; he looked down at the two of us on the couch.

"Yes. I think that might be a very good idea," replied the doctor, more mildly than I expected. "Come along, Mrs. Britton. I think I have the necessary things in the bathroom."

"Bathroom?" Hale looked a little surprised.

"I don't have an office here, Mr. Britton," said Dr. Gallard as he helped me to my feet. "I took this house to write a book."

"We're sorry to disturb you," I said quickly, before Hale could speak again. "Except that they were all so worried and I was so foolish. And the hospital is a couple of hours away."

"There are doctors in town," Gallard said, but he wasn't looking at me, he was studying Hale now as if he had never really seen him before. "I'll be glad to write down their names. If anything like this should happen again."

There was no mistaking the sarcasm in his voice now.

"Do you want us to leave, Doctor? Or are you going to take care of my wife?" Hale's face was flushed; he was no longer bothering to control the hostility he felt.

"I'll take care of her, Mr. Britton." I could see the doctor was refusing to be baited into an argument. "I just thought you might not know there were other doctors nearby. Since you are all relatively new here."

And then, before Hale could answer, Dr. Gallard steered me toward the open doorway at the end of the room. Barely bothering to glance back at Hale, he said curtly, "Wait here." And we were out of the room before Hale could protest.

We walked down a short hall to the bathroom at the end. The rest of the cottage may have dated back to the American Revolution but the bathroom was modern and spotlessly clean. Dr. Gallard switched on the light over the washbasin and, taking my hand, began to examine it under the light. The scratch was still bleeding faintly, it made an angry red line about six inches long on the back of my hand.

"Yes. This needs attention."

"It's not serious, is it?" I watched the doctor prepare a warm cloth to clean the wound.

"No. You won't need any stitches. But, if you'd been any closer . . ." He didn't finish the sentence but began to clean and treat the wound, his strong, square fingers moving efficiently. "Now . . . tell me what you think of Storm's End. Has seeing it brought back your memory?"

I winced a little then, less from the sting of the solution he was painting on the scratch than from the question.

"We never expected my memory to come back overnight," I said stiffly.

"Didn't we? I thought your husband was convinced of it. So . . . one whole day . . . and nothing has happened?"

I couldn't answer that. So much had happened. And yet what could I tell Dr. Gallard that wouldn't make me seem even more of an idiot?

I knew he was studying me again, his dark eyes probing my face as if they could see into my brain, his hands still holding mine.

Maybe it was his closeness or the embarrassment I still felt for having provoked Thor, but I knew the color was rising in my cheeks. "What could have happened?" I countered weakly, my mind thinking, Why doesn't he let go of my hand? And yet I felt powerless to pull away . . .

He looked down at my hand once more and then he released it. "I see you've found your wedding ring." He turned away then, to prepare the bandage. I bit my lip nervously. He *would* notice that.

He was winding the gauze around my hand, his voice quieter now, so quiet I could barely hear him, when he said:

"I had hoped, perhaps, you might have seen something that puzzled you. Or learned something strange of your past, of the relationships of the people around you. Or even found yourself thinking something that seemed totally apart from your life as Mrs. Britton."

How could he have known?

Luckily, he didn't seem to expect an answer. He finished the bandage and began replacing his supplies on the neat shelves by the window. One more look from his deep eyes and I had the feeling he would see all the questions I had been asking myself these past hours. And yet . . . what were my questions? That I had walked automatically to a chair that was a favorite of mine? That I may or may not have seen a lighted window in a tower that was long deserted? That Hale and Irene were cousins? That I had found my abandoned wedding ring and wondered why no one had asked me about it before? These, and the other things that troubled me, how foolish they all seemed when I added them up.

I stepped back out into the hall. "Are you through? May I go now?"

"Of course." He followed me, snapping off the light behind him. "But remember, Mrs. Britton, we're still to continue our sessions. That was the condition for allowing you to leave the hospital."

"I'll remember."

"Good. And if you don't, I'll come after you."

There was something different in the way he said that. It wasn't friendly, in fact, almost to the contrary, but I realized it was the first time he had spoken to me as a person, not a patient. Again his eyes seemed to be searching my face. And then, abruptly, he walked past me toward the living room. "And try to stay out of trouble," he said, matter-of-factly. "I have more than enough to do with my own work."

*   *   *

Hale was still angry as we got back into the car but at least we had managed to leave the doctor's house without any further argument. As Hale started the engine and began to maneuver the car around the narrow driveway, I leaned my head back against the seat. I felt tired and yet, somehow, for the first time that day, oddly free. Had the house disturbed me that much? Or was it the challenge Dr. Gallard had all but thrown at me to regain my memory?

On impulse I reached out and touched Hale's arm. "Hale? Do we have to go back to the house right away?"

"Do you want to take a drive? It's almost lunch." He put his sunglasses back on against the brightness of the noon.

"I thought . . . since we're so close . . . couldn't we just drive into town? Just drive through?"

"I thought we'd told you. The Averys aren't exactly popular in town."

I couldn't see the expression in his eyes through the dark glasses but his arm was rigid under my fingers. I sat back again, tightening the knot of yellow silk ribbon that tied back my hair. "I know, but . . . well, you're not an Avery. And neither am I, any more. I'm Constance Britton. And after all, what can they do? Throw rocks at us?"

"Probably not. But I'd just as soon nobody in town knew Storm's End was open again." The car had reached the end of the driveway by now and automatically he turned it in the direction of the house. Away from town.

"You mean . . . nobody knows we're here?"

"It seemed best. They have long memories in these parts. There were some ugly incidents in the past, or so you told us."

"What . . . what sort of incidents?" I could feel my voice grow tight. Somehow the October sun didn't seem so warm any more.

Hale made no answer. Up ahead loomed the high iron gates that led to the main driveway. Otto must have closed them after us. From here it was impossible to see the house, just the wall that surrounded the property.

"Hale? Can we stop here? Just for a minute? There's so much I don't know."

Hale swerved the car over to the side of the road and braked it impatiently. "All right," he sighed. "Ask anything you want."

"This business about the town. Begin with that."

"As far as I can piece it together it started sometime during the Depression. There was a chance a factory might be built here. Not on this side of the town, the far side. The local people needed it badly, you can imagine there weren't many jobs around here even in the best of times."

"And my family was going to build the factory?"

"No. But they held the land the company wanted to use. Your grandfather . . . and I suppose your great-uncle as well . . . absolutely refused. Said it would destroy the value of Storm's End. The 'charm' of the place. Since most of the town was out of work, and half their houses were mortgaged to the Averys . . . well, you can see why there was a lot of bad feeling."

I shuddered a little. Even years later it seemed a cruel thing to have done.

"Gradually the young people in the village left, to find work elsewhere," Hale went on. "Now it's almost a ghost town. Except for a few people with long memories. Esther tells me Storm's End has been broken into a couple of times, even when the family wasn't here. I believe there was even an attempt to set it on fire once."

There was something in the back of my head now, a question I meant to ask Hale, but I couldn't seem to remember what it was. Waiting for it to come, I turned toward him.

"But, Hale, if we're going to live here, make our home here . . . shouldn't we start by making peace with the town?"

He looked at me then and put his hand out to take mine gently. "I'd forgotten. You can't possibly remember what we decided, can you?"

"Something we decided . . . before?" The word hung between us.

"We talked about it so many times in Paris." Hale's voice was confident now, almost cheerful. "We were only going to come back here for your birthday . . . and to settle your affairs. After that's done, we'll be able to go anyplace we want in the world." There was a smile on his face, I could tell his thoughts were many miles away.

"We?" I repeated quietly. "That means you and me . . . and Irene?" I took a deep breath. "Why didn't you tell me she was your cousin?"

If I had expected some reaction to that from Hale, I was disappointed. He barely glanced at me, his smile still confident.

"Irene said you seemed surprised about that. I don't know why. I'm sure one of us must have mentioned it to you when you were in the hospital."

It was the same tone of voice that he had used at breakfast, when I had mentioned seeing the light the night before. As if I were a child. I felt my back stiffen.

"There's nothing wrong with my memory of the last six weeks, Hale!" And then I forced myself to calm down. It will do no good to irritate him, I thought. "Will Irene be coming with us?" I said carefully. "To wherever it is we're going after we leave here?"

"I suppose so," said Hale carelessly. "She can be a lot of help. And she has no other family." And then he turned to me, his face alive and excited as a small boy. "Con, it's going to be so wonderful! All that money . . . we can live anywhere we want! One of the Greek isles, maybe. Or Capri. Or some place warm in the Caribbean. I'll paint . . . Irene'll do all the household stuff . . . and all you'll have to do is to sit back and look beautiful. We'll have a wonderful life!"

You and I and Irene, I thought, bleakly.

"And Storm's End?" I said it softly; it was hard to resist his enthusiasm.

"Close it up," he said promptly. "Let it rot there until it falls into the river." He looked then at the long wall in front of us, the massive closed gates. "It's dead, Con. Can't you see that? It'd be like living in a museum. A winter here . . ." He shuddered a little. "We'd freeze to death. There are no people, no friends . . . no life. No, Con. Once we get everything settled after your birthday . . . that's the end of the week . . . then maybe another couple of weeks to make our plans . . . and we leave this behind. All of it. And make our own life."

He got out of the car to open the gates, not waiting for me to say anything. Not that I had any answer. It had grown chilly, parked here under the autumn trees. It would be grim here in winter, the first Constance Avery had known that. Hale was right. I should be happy. I knew there was no future for me at Storm's End. And yet . . . and yet what would my future be anywhere else?

*   *   *

Lunch was a quiet affair, and simple. Mrs. Janeck had prepared a salad and baked fresh, warm nutbread. We ate the meal in silence, I think all of us had too many things to think about to make conversation. Hale with his plans for the future, I with the questions that seemed to be coming more and more frequently, and with never any answers. And Irene? Who knew what was going on behind her mask of a face?

Ben had set a table up for us on the terrace facing the river, but clouds had started to fill the sky, blotting out the sun, and we were forced to move into the long formal dining room.

After the meal was over, Hale suggested I take a nap. And I realized then just how tired I was.

"You didn't get much sleep last night," he said gently. "And with all that's happened this morning . . ." I nodded and tried to smile, but it was an effort.

I walked across the black and white floor of the main hall and up the wide staircase to my room. A rest would be good for me, I thought, as I slipped out of my sweater and skirt.

And then I remembered the question I had been meaning to ask Hale ever since Thor had attacked me. Otto Janeck. When he appeared he had *asked* me who I was. "You Mrs. Britton?" I could still see the sullen expression on his gross face.

Why didn't he know who I was?

I pulled on a warm wool robe and tried to settle back comfortably on the large bed. But the question kept picking at me. Was he a stranger here as well? But *I* wasn't a stranger. He must have seen me before the accident. Why hadn't he known me?

I knew then the question would bother me the rest of the afternoon. I got up again and tightened the sash of the robe around my waist. If Hale had gone back to his studio, perhaps I could speak to him quietly, without Irene knowing. I slipped on a pair of light bedroom slippers and went out into the hall.

It was dark already in the corridor, minus the warm morning sun. I moved through the shadows toward the stairwell that led down to the main hall.

But before I could step out on the landing, I heard the voices coming from the floor below.

Eight

I could tell at once that some sort of argument was going on. Instinctively I stepped back again into the protective shadows of the corridor leading to my room. From here I could not see the hall below but neither could whoever was quarreling see me. It was, I realized after a moment, Hale and Ben.

They must be in the library, I thought. From my vantage point on the floor above I could see the very top of the tall doorway leading into the library. The double doors were slightly open.

"I don't like it, Hale." Ben's voice was low, stubborn, but I could hear him distinctly. Hale was trying to quiet him, I could tell from the low murmur that let me catch only a few of the words he was saying.

". . . had to do it." Then he said something more that I couldn't hear, ending with the words: "There's nothing to worry about."

"We've got to move fast. We agreed on that." Ben's voice was still urgent and angry but there seemed to be something else in it now, a trace of fear.

Why would he be arguing with Hale? I thought. Over what? And what was his position in this house that he called Hale by his first name, for I had heard that distinctly. Perhaps another cousin, I giggled to myself nervously. And then I put my hand over my mouth to stifle the sound. Hale's voice seemed nearer now, had he heard me?

"We can't go too fast. It would look suspicious. And if she finds out . . ."

But the rest of the sentence was lost as Hale banged the library door shut.

After that I could hear nothing.

I stood where I was, half hidden in the shadows of the corridor. The question that had led me out of my room seemed unimportant now. What had Ben and Hale been arguing about? What was it that "she" mustn't find out? Was the "she" they were talking about me? Or was it Irene? Or could it all be some simple domestic matter involving Mrs. Janeck?

I shivered a little then. The scarlet robe I had pulled on suddenly seemed too thin. And the corridor in the early afternoon shadows was a lonely, frightening place. I felt then as if someone was watching me. I whirled around . . . but the long tunnel behind me was empty. And then, more frightened than I cared to admit to myself, I hurried back to the safety of my room.

Once inside I leaned against the door to the hall. My fingers touched the key in the lock and on impulse I turned it, locking myself in. And without allowing myself to ask from what, I ran across the room and climbed up into my bed.

*   *   *

It was about an hour later that I heard the scream.

I had been dozing fitfully, trying not to let my brain ask the questions that seemed to circle my head like a rope, pressing tighter and tighter. I must have fallen asleep, for I was dreaming that I was running down the long corridor outside my room. Running through the darkness and shadows knowing that there was no end to the tunnel and, at the same time, knowing that I was running toward something terrible.

It was then the scream woke me. I sat directly up in bed, awake in an instant. This was no vague sighing of the wind or creak of the house such as had disturbed me the night before. Nor was it a fantasy I had made of the first unhappy mistress of Storm's End. This was a scream from a woman's throat, sharp and real and full of pain.

I sat there in bed for a moment, not moving. There was no sound now. No scurry of feet in the hall outside, no voices of people on their way to aid whoever had cried out. Nothing but silence.

Quietly I got up out of bed, sliding my feet into my soft slippers. I crossed to the door of my room and pressed my ear against the dark wood. I stayed there for a long moment, hoping to hear *something*, but even as I did, I knew the house was silent once more.

Who was it who screamed? I refused to let myself think that I had dreamed it. This was something real, I was sure of it.

I don't know how long I stood there without moving before I decided to go out into the hall. It seemed like ten minutes but I knew the marking of time can be deceptive. Perhaps it was no longer than a minute. By then my courage had come back and I straightened my shoulders, and knotted the sash of my robe again. This is my home, I told myself. I have the right to go anywhere in it that I wish. With this new resolve I turned the key, opened the door and stepped quietly outside.

Once out in the corridor, now even darker with shadows than before, I felt my determination weaken. The house was as silent as if I were alone in it. And yet I knew the others must be somewhere.

I took a few steps back toward the stairwell. By standing on tiptoe I could see the doors to the library were open again. There was no sound of voices now, the room must be empty.

I turned back to face the long corridor leading to my room and beyond. To my right was the alcove to Irene's room. The door was closed. I stood there, holding my breath, listening for some new sound. But there was nothing. If she was inside, perhaps she too was taking a nap. Only why hadn't she heard the scream? In my head I could hear it echo still . . . that long frightened cry for help.

But had I really heard it? Or was my damaged brain making me imagine things now?

Nonsense, I told myself. I had heard someone scream, someone inside this house. But where had it come from?

I started quietly down the corridor, my feet making no sound on the worn carpet. It's like my dream, I thought. Except I'm not running. And there *is* an end to this corridor.

I moved past the door of my room. It was still half open and I pulled it shut carefully. If someone should pass by, there was no reason for them to know I was awake and exploring the house. Beyond my doorway was the entrance to Hale's bedroom. His door was closed too. I hesitated for a moment, listening, but there was no sound from inside his room.

He's probably in the studio, I thought. And Irene could have gone shopping; somebody had to buy supplies for this place. And Esther and Ben would have enough work to occupy them downstairs . . . there's no one who'll disturb me.

I started down the hall again. There was no reason for secrecy and yet I knew I didn't want the others to know what I was doing. I turned on no lights, there were enough small, oddly shaped windows along the corridor to allow me to see where I was going, the afternoon sunlight barely making it through the streaked glass. Irene had been right, this section of Storm's End was not lived in and from the look of it, had not been for a long time.

The first doorway I reached after passing Hale's room I stopped, trying to decide whether to open it or not. Should I chance whatever it was that I might find? Or should I just go to the end of the corridor and back?

Stop being a coward, I told myself. You are going to find out where that scream came from. And you can't do that if you're frightened of a closed door. I turned the handle.

The room was almost pitch-black, the drapes at the far windows were drawn carefully and only a few chinks of light came through the rips and tears in the material. It was another bedroom, not as large as mine, the furniture covered with dust sheets, bulking in the shadows like fierce animals ready to spring.

I could see in the half-light a thin gray veil of dust spread evenly and undisturbed on the floor. No one had been in this room for a long, long time. I closed the door softly and moved on down the hall.

I suppose my search would have taken longer if the rooms I looked into had been cared for. As it was, I could stand in the doorway of each room as I opened it and see that same layer of dust covering the floor, unmarked by footprints.

I picked up the skirt of my long robe and looked at the hem. It was still clean. So the corridor at least had been dusted. Dropping the material, I started along the hall again. There were bedrooms all along this corridor, some on each side, for now I was in the oldest section of the house, the end of the building where the towers were. I forget how many rooms I opened, moving down the hall, my long robe sweeping the carpet behind me. There could have been ten or fifteen bedrooms . . . all dark, the furniture draped by some careful housekeeper many, many years ago.

And all of the rooms were deserted.

They changed shape now as the corridor curved and bent with the walls of the building. The floor became uneven, there would be an odd step up and then, further on, two or three more, so that it was almost impossible to know exactly which floor I was on.

The boards beneath the carpet were old, I could hear them creak as I walked. But after the first shock at the sound I became almost used to it. The hall had been kept fairly clean, my slippers made no prints on the faded carpeting, but each door I opened showed the same gray undisturbed floor of dust.

I could tell I was rising higher in the tower section now, the rooms began to take on strange shapes. Some were as wedge-shaped as a piece of pie, some completely circular. And some had a curving outer wall to match the turrets and then became strangely angled inside.

Obviously this part of the house had been used by the less important members of the family, governesses perhaps, and poor relations. There were no antique furnishings in the rooms now, just plain metal beds, with thin mattresses rolled up and carefully tied. No drapes or shades kept out the light, the October sun shone weakly into the barren rooms through dirty windows. The paper in several of the rooms was peeling off the walls and there was an occasional brown stain on the ceiling, giving mute testimony to leaks in the old roof.

Only one room was different from the others, the last of the large rooms. The faded paper on its walls had been a cheerful nursery print. There were still a few toys discarded in one corner . . . a forgotten teddy bear, bits of a train, a battered rocking horse with only one eye, looming above the pile, a sentinel for many years. Who was the last little boy to ride you? I thought, and moved on.

I was reaching the end of the corridor now. I could see a small gothic window at the end, a pale arch half hidden by the edge of the gray wall. To my left there was a dark alcove, barely big enough to be a closet. And then, beyond this, the last door of the hall.

I stood in front of the door and for a moment I hesitated to open it. The scream I thought I'd heard was no longer echoing in my ears, somehow the whole search seemed a little foolish now. If you leave this room unexplored, I found myself thinking, you can always convince yourself you really did hear something. Otherwise you'll have to admit that your mind is playing tricks with you again. Either that, or search the whole house . . . the other wing, the tiny servants' rooms up under the roof, the dark caves of the cellar.

But then I pushed the thoughts away again. Let's at least do this floor thoroughly, I said to myself, and opened the door.

The room inside was small, almost completely round except for a flat wall to my right that held a fireplace and chimney. The windows faced west and the afternoon sun streamed in, making a wide yellow path across the floor to where I stood on the threshold. Pale, honey-colored wood paneled the walls and ceiling, matching the wide boards of the floor. The mantel and chimneypiece were also covered with the same smooth wood.

There was no furniture in the room at all, no drapes or pictures, no rolled-up carpet. It was completely empty. And yet I felt it was the most beautiful room I'd seen at Storm's End.

It could have been a charming sitting room, I thought. For the lady of the house. The first Constance Avery might have used this room. And somehow, standing there in the doorway, I knew that she had. And that she had been happy there, down the corridor from the nursery.

I crossed to the windows. Down below I could see the setting sun warming the faded autumn green of the lawn, touching the gold and orange leaves of the trees that edged the park. I looked back at the door that I had entered.

And then I realized what made this room so different from the rest.

It was clean. Even cleaner than the hall leading to it. There was no dust on the floor to show my footprints, the bare wood shone as if it had been waxed that morning. And the glass of the windows had been washed. Someone was keeping this room in perfect condition. But why?

I thought. It was so far away from the rest of the house that we were using.

I moved over to the fireplace, as empty as the rest of the room. The mantel curved gently; underneath it, to decorate the space above the opening of the fireplace, some master carpenter had carved a delicate design that looked like vines and berries.

I crouched down on the bare floor to study it. No, it isn't vines, I thought, tracing the grooves and ridges with light fingers. It's some other pattern, something that seemed vaguely familiar, teasingly out of reach of my memory. The toys in the abandoned nursery could have belonged to any child, but there was something about this carving that I knew.

My fingers moved over the design again. What is it? I thought. What does this remind me of . . . ?

"What are you doing here?"

The voice ripped the silence. I whirled around, my robe sweeping the floor where I had been kneeling.

Irene stood in the open doorway, her hands placed on each side as if she were guarding the room. I could see her face clearly in the sunlight coming through the windows, her skin paler than usual, her green eyes glittering.

"I said . . . what are you doing here?" she repeated. She was trying to keep herself under control, her voice polite, but the tiny muscle on the side of her jaw was twitching angrily.

I stood then, taking a moment to think before answering. I knew instinctively that I did not want to tell her about the scream that had started my search.

"I . . . I decided to explore the rest of the house," I said, the half-lie coming out smoother than I would have thought possible.

"Dressed like that?" Irene said, caustically, indicating the long robe I had put on for my nap.

"There wasn't much point in getting dressed again when we'll be changing for dinner soon," I said, trying to keep my voice cool.

"And what did you find in your search?"

"Cobwebs and dust mostly. I see what you mean about the house being closed up."

"That's why we never come here," Irene said, crossing to stand with her back to the bare fireplace. "Never."

"Why?" I said. "It's such a charming room. Did it belong to the first Constance Avery?"

"So they say." Irene was studying me carefully now, her eyes curious, her anger almost under control. "There's even a rumor that it's supposed to be haunted."

"This room? I don't believe it." But then I forced myself to speak with an air of innocence. "If it is haunted, I'm sure it's by happy ghosts. I can't imagine anything bad happening here."

"Then nothing has . . . disturbed you? That made you want to search this section of the house?" She had picked her words carefully, but I knew at once what she meant. She too had heard the scream. It wasn't just my imagination! Only she didn't want to admit it . . . and I knew I couldn't either. I had to get away from her, away from her prying eyes before they guessed the truth.

"What could disturb me?" I made myself smile demurely. "Oh, there are noises, of course. As you said this morning, these old places have a life of their own. But I'm not the type to imagine things." What a skillful liar you're becoming, I thought.

"Very wise of you." Irene took a step or two toward me. She looked taller then, stronger, very sure of herself. You'd make a dangerous enemy, I thought.

"But I must insist you don't come up here again."

"Why?" The question slipped out before I knew it.

"This is the oldest part of Storm's End," Irene explained calmly. "The flooring hasn't been looked at in years, some of the doors are badly warped. You could have an accident in one of these rooms, get trapped and we might not find you for days."

So that's going to be your story, I thought. How quickly you picked it! But why? What is the real reason you don't want me in this room? There was something frightening about Irene's face, as she walked nearer. I've got to get away from you . . . and *now*. I looked down quickly, trying to hide from her what I was thinking.

"All right. If you don't think it's safe for me to come here, I won't." I stepped back from Irene, out into the corridor. "It's time we were getting ready for dinner anyway."

"I'll come with you," Irene said, following me out into the hall. She closed the door of the little room firmly. If there had been a key in the lock, I think she would have turned it.

Why are you lying to me? I thought, as we walked back the long corridors to our rooms. Why do you say that room is deserted, when it is kept so perfectly?

Who keeps it that way?

And . . . more important . . . *why?*

*   *   *

My second evening at Storm's End was quiet. Hale disappeared immediately after dinner to listen to a concert that was to be broadcast from New York. Not wanting to be alone with Irene, I made the truthful excuse that I was tired and went up to my room.

My bed had been turned down neatly once more and I noticed that fresh sheets had been placed on it. Whatever the condition of the rest of the house, I, or at least my rooms, were to be looked after carefully. The drapes had been left open and after I had made myself ready for bed, I went over to the window. I couldn't resist looking out. But there was no light in the towers tonight; they stood black and deserted against the starry sky. I pulled the drapes closed and went back to bed.

For the first time since Dr. Gallard had bandaged my hand I was aware that it was throbbing a little. You're not going to keep me awake tonight, I thought, and deliberately took a sleeping pill before turning out the lights.

THE THIRD DAY

Nine

I slept soundly, no dreams, no noises, the pain in my hand disappearing during the night. The bedside clock, which I had finally found, told me when I awoke it was just nine. Feeling better for my deep sleep I washed quickly and then went back into the dressing room. It was warmer today, one of those last summer days that sometime happen in October, to console you for the long winter months ahead. I wanted something light and simple to wear, but that was the one thing hard to find in the full closets. I finally settled on a sleeveless cream-colored blouse and a dark green cotton skirt.

There was a gold pin in the jewelry drawer and I used it to fasten back my hair. The last scratches from the accident had healed and my face was clear again. Grabbing a dark green cashmere sweater for my shoulders, in case the weather changed, I hurried down to breakfast.

"Out here, Con."

I saw Hale through the french windows of the deserted dining room as I made my way toward the breakfast room. He was standing outside on the sunny terrace, wearing a red and blue knit shirt and white jeans and looking young and happy. He waved to me again and I saw a table had been set outside.

"It seemed silly to waste this sunlight," he said as I joined him. "There won't be too many more days we can have a meal outdoors. Not here at Storm's End, at least."

He held my chair for me and I realized as I sat down that the table was set with only two places. "Where's Irene?"

"Gone to the city. Something to do with your estate." Hale took his place opposite me. His skin glowed in the morning sunlight as if he'd been scrubbed and he was grinning like a child let out of school. "There was a call last night. Ben drove her over to catch the morning train down to New York."

He handed me a covered basket. "Have some blueberry muffins. Mrs. Janeck made them fresh this morning." He grinned wickedly. "I didn't wait for you, so there aren't too many left."

"Was it anything . . . serious? About the estate?" I asked as I buttered the warm muffin.

"No. At least, I don't think so." Then, almost as if placating me, he added, "You see, Con? Irene *can* be useful. Lord knows I don't know anything about money, except how to spend it. And I can't see you turning into a financial genius. You never were before."

"Yes, Irene has her uses," I said, carefully.

"Con? Is something wrong? Didn't you sleep well?"

"Perfectly. No lighted windows, no creaking timbers . . ." And then I decided to chance it. "Not even any screams in the night." But there was no flicker in Hale's eyes. Irene may have heard the scream the day before that had started my search, but I was sure now that Hale hadn't.

"Speaks well for the thickness of the walls here," Hale said, leaning back lazily. "I would have thought that soprano could have been heard all over the house."

"Soprano?" For a moment, I couldn't think what he meant.

"My concert last night. Not one of the better ones. Glad it didn't disturb you." He took another sip of his coffee, gazing over the low stone wall at the river below. "What are you doing today?"

I was startled by his question. What *do* I do here all day? I thought suddenly. "I . . . I don't know. I still haven't seen the whole house. I suppose I could get Mrs. Janeck to take me around. Or maybe rummage through the books in the library."

"That's wasting a perfectly good day." Hale was in good spirits, I could tell, like a young colt restless to race. "Why not come and pose for me? You promised, you know. And in an hour or so, the light'll be perfect."

"All right. If you really need me."

He looked at me then, the smile that had lighted his face a moment before disappearing. He looked very serious then. "I need you, Constance," he said quietly. He reached across the table and touched my hand. "More than you realize. And I'm going to make you happy. I promise that."

I felt uneasy then, there was something so shadowed about his expression at that moment. I took his long fingers in my hand. "You do make me happy. Just in this short time that I can remember."

He held my eyes for a long moment. "You mean that, don't you? Yes, of course you do," he added. And then he got up, abruptly, to stare again at the blue river, glittering in the sun below us.

"You'll have to forgive me, Con, if I don't always seem to be as sure of what you say as I should be. There've been so many lies in the past. So many clever tricks. Sometimes I think I've lost the ability to know what is the truth."

I walked over to him and stood beside him. Something in his voice told me this was a part of Hale I'd never seen before. Certainly not in the time since my accident. It was suddenly very important to know what he meant.

"Tricks, Hale?" I looked up at him, his face was grim and unhappy. "Lies? You mean I lied to you?"

He glanced down at me then, pulled back to this sun-filled terrace, so quiet in the morning light.

"No, not you," he said. "Remember, whatever's happened, none of it was your fault."

"But . . . what *did* happen?" I stammered, touching his bare arm. "Please, Hale, you must tell me. I don't want there to be secrets between us."

"Nothing." He was on guard again, I could tell. "I'm just talking nonsense."

"Please, Hale . . . if there's something in the past I should know, please tell me." I moved away from him, not wanting him to see my face. I was closer to tears than I wanted to be. "You can't know what it's like living in this . . . *fog*. To be afraid every minute that I might say or do something innocently that will hurt you. And I'd never want to do that."

He put his hands on my shoulders and turned me around to face him. "Con? Don't worry. Everything's going to be fine." And then he smiled, cheerful again. "What are we being so somber for? There's still a little bit of summer left . . . let's enjoy today! I'll get Mrs. Janeck to make up a picnic basket for us. After we've done a couple of hours' work in the studio, we'll take the afternoon off, go for a drive. Would you like that, Con?"

I nodded. How happy he was that morning . . . with Irene away.

*   *   *

He left me then, warning me to join him in an hour. After I had finished breakfast, I left the table and walked to the far end of the terrace. I hadn't seen this side of the house before, the curving towers of the "new" wing of Storm's End. It was easier to see on this side of the house where the separate buildings had been joined together. I turned then to look over the low wall at the river far below.

The house was built right on the edge of the cliff over the Hudson. There was barely ten feet of flagstone between the windows of the house and the low retaining wall. Bending over the wall, I could see now that the ground sloped steeply down to the river, over a hundred feet below. The house had not been built in earth, but dug out of the stone. The cliff stretched down to the water, broken here and there with tenacious roots and branches that clung to the rock. And far below, angry little patches of white shattered the blue-green of the river as the current splashed against the jagged rocks. It would be a long way down to the river, I thought. If one were to fall . . .

"Be careful, miss!"

I whirled around, almost losing my balance. Mrs. Janeck stood in the long windows to the dining room. There had been no sound to warn me, I had no idea how long she'd been standing there.

"You . . . you startled me," I managed to gasp out.

"You should be careful not to lean too far over. That wall's old, like everything about this house. I don't know how safe it is. We wouldn't want to have an accident. Would we?"

Her face was expressionless as always, but there was a flicker of something in her pale eyes. What was it? A warning? A threat? I walked away from her then, not making an answer, and started on the stone walk that led around the far end of the house. I hadn't been in any danger until she startled me . . . was that what she was *trying* to do?

And then I forced myself to look at the incident clearly. I was imagining things again . . . the way perhaps I had with Irene in the tower yesterday . . . or just now thinking there was something strange in Hale's words. You're a fool, I thought. A good brisk walk is what you need before you go to the studio.

I'd reached the front of the house by now, coming out just at the side road that we had taken the night we arrived at Storm's End. After twenty feet the gravel road turned into the trees and, looking back, I could no longer see the main house behind me.

And I could not hide from myself a feeling of relief.

But *why?* Was I afraid of someone spying on me? What could be more harmless than a walk down the side road to the highway?

And yet I felt again as I had yesterday. I didn't want anyone to know where I was or what I was doing. Was this some part of my lost life? I wondered. Was I always secretive, and if so, why?

Or was it that I was always afraid?

There was a stone bench by the side of the gravel driveway and I sat down, thinking busily. Something had happened in that past, that I was sure of. It was something that made Hale unhappy to remember, some secret that Irene knew about, perhaps even shared with me. It frightened Mrs. Janeck . . . perhaps it was even the reason Thor attacked me. But what was it?

"This must be mental telepathy."

I looked up to see Dr. Gallard standing in front of me, his sturdy legs planted wide apart on the road. I must have shown my surprise, for he laughed, his teeth white in his tanned face. He was wearing the corduroy trousers he had on the day before and a tan windbreaker, open at his bare throat.

"Or didn't you come halfway down the road to meet me?"

"No. I . . . I was just taking a walk."

"Sitting down? Or do you get tired so quickly?" He moved closer then and sat beside me. It was quiet there under the trees, the sun breaking through the branches above us to make a pattern on the road. I could hear a few birds chirping domestically and across the gravel road we could see the long lawn of Storm's End stretched out golden in the sun.

"Why were you coming to see me?" I asked after a moment.

"If we are to have sessions to work on your mind, we should start them, don't you think?" His voice was low, only occasionally could I hear the hint of an accent that showed English was not the first language he'd learned. "And besides, I was curious about your hand."

He smiled again, a warmer smile than I had ever seen before on his face. "It's been a long time since I actually practiced medicine. How did I do?"

"My hand's fine."

"All the same, I think I'll take a look at it." He didn't wait for me to offer it but took my hand and carefully peeled back a corner of the bandage. "Yes, this seems to be healing well. I'll make you a fresh bandage if you like. Although probably in a day or two you won't even need a Band-Aid."

He continued to hold my hand, his fingers warm on mine. Where did I ever get the feeling in the hospital that his hands were cold? I thought. And then I took my hand back, suddenly a little embarrassed.

"So much for the physical problems of my patient. Now . . . how is the rest of you? You seemed very deep in thought when I came up."

I wasn't eager to continue this. Whatever my problems at Storm's End, I had no intention of revealing them to the skepticism of Dr. Gallard. I turned to him, looked at him directly.

"How did you get on the grounds? All the gates are locked." I said it bluntly, hoping to discourage him. But his lips twisted slightly into a shadow of a smile.

"I have my little ways. Gates aren't much good if the wall itself is falling down. And it is"—he pointed off—"a little to the right of that side entrance. It's hidden by the bushes, I suppose that is why it hasn't been repaired. I just walked through."

"You could have called the house. I would have had somebody let you in."

"Would you? Or would the housekeeper have said politely that you'd gone to the city?" I looked at him, then, surprised.

"Oh yes. I saw the limousine go past this morning. Just in time to catch the train to New York."

You don't miss much, I thought. Suddenly I felt a surge of anger. Was the doctor spying on me? Was all this interest in my hand and my lost memory covering something else? I determined to be on guard.

"The car was taking Irene to the station," I answered coolly. "She has some business of mine to attend to in the city."

"Business of yours? Then your memory is coming back?" There was no mistaking his tone now, this wasn't conversation; he was interrogating me as he had at the hospital.

"No. Not exactly." I faltered and cursed myself for walking into his trap.

"But something has happened to you, hasn't it? Some memory? Some disturbance?"

"Why do you pick that word . . . *disturbance?*" I said angrily.

He hesitated for a moment then and, looking across the driveway at the golden lawn, he went on almost apologetically. "It seemed the right word. Perhaps my English is not as good as I thought."

"Your English is perfect, Doctor. And you know it. However, I am *not* disturbed."

"You have missed my meaning. Your mind was blocked six weeks ago. With what must seem like a wall. Only that wall isn't solid." He looked up then and pointed to the bits of sky we could see between the branches. "The wall blocking your memory is like those clouds. How thick and white and permanent they seem. And yet the slightest current of air could shift them . . . and show us the clear sky beyond."

I watched his hand as he pointed. How strong it looked, I thought. Beyond the edge of his sleeve I could see his sturdy wrist, the black hairs on the back of his hand glistening in the sunlight. It wasn't a hand like Hale's, long and graceful. Then I looked away quickly, wondering why I always seemed to find myself comparing the two. When I glanced back at the doctor, he had turned and was staring at me again.

"Now," he said quietly, "tell me what has happened here."

"Nothing! You asked me that yesterday. Nothing has happened!" My voice was more angry than I meant it to be but I was afraid of his questions and he knew it. "Why do you always keep after me and after me?"

The expression in his dark eyes changed then, I could almost believe for a moment he felt sorry for me.

"Because I think you are genuinely lost," he said softly. "And I am trying to help."

"By picking on everything I say or do?"

"I said 'genuinely lost.' I haven't always been convinced of that."

Now it was my turn to stare at him. "You mean . . . the amnesia? You thought I was pretending?"

He nodded. "It has happened. In the past."

"But *why?*" I stammered. "What reason could I possibly have to pretend that I'd lost my memory?"

"That I don't know," he answered calmly. "Not yet. However, Constance Avery Britton is known to be a very wealthy woman . . ."

"But that doesn't make sense," I broke in. "What has my money got to do with my losing my memory?"

"I've found that money usually turns out to be behind most mysteries."

"Are you deliberately trying to be cryptic, Doctor?" I made no attempt now to hide my dislike of him. Dr. Gallard may have changed his stiff suits and ties for country clothes, but his mind was just as cold and implacable and *infuriating* as it had been at the hospital.

"No. I am trying to help you to think."

"I can do *that*," I said, crossly. "What I *can't* do is remember."

"Yes, I believe you."

"Now. But not before? Why should I have lied to you? To Hale? To everybody? What could I possibly gain?"

"I don't know." His voice was as reasonable as always; my anger, as usual, had not made the slightest impression on him.

"Perhaps I am . . . shall we say, suspicious? Because this whole *ménage* appears to be supported by you. It *is* your fortune your husband lives on, is it not?"

"I could almost believe you're jealous, Doctor." It was a weak retort and he brushed it aside as if I were a child. "Unknown artists don't command large fees," I persisted, and then I couldn't keep the sarcasm out of my voice. "I should think a Frenchman would know that."

"Ah . . . you see yourself as a patron of the Arts." It wasn't a question or a retort, just an impersonal statement.

How I'd like to make *you* angry someday, Doctor, I thought. But even as I did, I realized how frightening that might be. This was not some gentle man who could be teased or cajoled out of a bad mood. The discipline that controlled his emotions had taken long to learn, I knew instinctively. And it had been learned because the feelings underneath his calm surface were dangerous.

"I don't think there's any point in our going on with this . . . session, as you call it." I stood up, trying to make myself look taller and more dignified. Let's see if you can at least end this without acting like a child, I told myself.

But the doctor made no move. "I want you to remember something," he said after a moment. "If you need help . . . or a friend . . . I would like to be that as well as your doctor."

"You talk as if I were deserted here. I have a family, friends . . ."

"Remember what I said." He got up then, his eyes still on my face. "In any case, I shall look in on you again. With or without your permission."

He turned then and started down the driveway, not even waiting for my answer.

*　　*　　*

I ran then. I wanted to be away from that quiet part of the estate, away from the bench where we had sat, away from the questions he had put in my head. Just to feel myself free of all the doubts that seemed to close in on me whenever I let myself think.

I crossed the park, almost as if I were fleeing the doctor, although I knew he would not have looked back. The sun was warm on the open park, and when I reached the trees at the far side, I was happy to stop, to lean against the trunk of a large elm that stood on the edge of the lawn.

I am not going to think about you, Dr. Gallard, I told myself when I had caught my breath again. I am going to take a peaceful walk back to the house. I am going to pose for Hale and then we are going to have our picnic, someplace far away from here.

And I am not going to question myself again.

I started up the path that would lead me around the end of the house where Hale's studio was. It was quiet here, under the trees, and the midmorning sun seemed far away, almost as if I were indoors. My feet were silent on the gravel path, there was no sound now of birds, I could have been alone in the whole world.

The path took a bend to the right and I followed it . . . and stopped short.

There, only a few feet in front of me, was Thor.

He was off his leash, worrying something among the plants on the side of the path. I froze where I stood, noticing there was no one . . . not even Mr. Janeck . . . in sight. Perhaps I can move back before the dog sees me, I thought. But my feet seemed stuck to the path.

Then the huge dog sensed something, or perhaps I had made some slight movement, for he looked up, stiffening as he did. He was looking straight at me now, his body tense beneath the thick fur of his pelt. What am I to do? I thought, panicking. I can't scream . . . no one will hear me.

But I couldn't move.

And then, not looking away from me, his nostrils quivering, Thor started slowly toward me.

Ten

I stood there on the path, frozen. A scream grew inside me but I was powerless to let it out. Thor was coming slowly nearer, his paws making no sound on the path, his well-shaped head up, his eyes glinting brown-black in the gloom of the woods.

I started to tremble. There was no way to escape the huge German shepherd. He could run far faster than I even if I could move. His jaw hung loose, I could see the sharp white teeth in his mouth, half hidden by the pink of his tongue. He's going to kill me, I thought. Here. In the next minute.

And then, when he was barely a yard from me, he stopped. He was still looking at me but there was no sound coming from his throat, no low growl of anger and disappointment. I don't know how long he stood there staring at me. The world around us was shut out and silent. Waiting for him to spring, I could see nothing but the glitter of the dog's eyes as he gazed at me.

And then he started to move again, deliberately, as if he had made up his mind about something. He came to my right side and began to rub his head gently against my skirt. He was making sounds now, but they were soft, almost as if he were asking to be petted. Gingerly I let my hand touch the top of his head. His ears went up, alert, and I scratched the soft fur behind them. He stretched his neck then, almost gratefully.

And for the first moment since I had turned the corner of the path and seen him, I felt myself take a breath.

"Are we friends now, Thor?" I asked softly. "Is that it?"

The animal continued to rub his body against me, asking me not to stop the tickling of his fur. I knew then he recognized me, the moment had come that I had been waiting for since that first night, when I had heard him barking inside the great house.

I crouched down on the gravel walk beside him and held his head with both hands, making him look directly at me. "You *do* know me, don't you, Thor?" I could feel the strong muscles of his shoulders and neck under his thick fur, but they were relaxed now, there was no menace in him.

Then my fingers touched the half-hidden collar around his neck. He let me examine it, standing there patiently as I turned the collar around to the name tag. Carved into the metal strip attached to the thick leather band was an inscription: "Thor of Storm's End. I belong to Constance Avery."

So he *was* my dog! I'd known it all along, from that very first night. They had all lied when they'd said he was only a watchdog. Now he had recognized me, I was his mistress and I could tell from the busy wagging of his tail that he was glad to see me.

I felt at last I was home. Let Dr. Gallard ask his cryptic questions, or Hale and Irene have their secrets. I was Constance Avery and my dog knew me.

"Get away from that animal!"

I stood and turned as the heavy figure of Otto Janeck came out of the woods. He was carrying a rifle and for a moment I thought he was about to aim it . . . whether at me or Thor, I had no idea.

"Why?" I refused to step back, although he had startled me. "Thor's mine. Or didn't you look at his collar?"

"He's dangerous. You were told that. And you were told not to walk here."

"Put down your gun, Mr. Janeck." He did, reluctantly. "This is part of my land," I went on. There was no point in being friendly to this man, I'd known that from the first time I'd seen him. For some reason, he hates me, I thought. Well, this time I don't need you to protect me from Thor. And you're not going to frighten me either . . . not any more.

"Your land . . ." He repeated the words, but not as a challenge, almost sullenly, as if he had to accept an unpleasant truth.

"That's right. And I intend to walk anyplace I wish. Is that clear?"

"You gotta lot of snap to you for a woman with no mind." He stood there, a thick heavy bulk on the path in front of me, the tiny eyes in the folds of his face gleaming with spite.

"Enough 'snap,' as you call it," I answered coldly, staring him down, "to have made out your salary check yesterday. Unless you want it to be the last check, I suggest you get out of my way."

He stepped to one side at this and snapped his fingers for Thor. I could feel the dog stiffen at the sound, but I kept my hand firmly on his collar.

"Thor will walk me back to the house, Mr. Janeck."

"He's not allowed off his leash. Not in the daytime. That's the rule."

"He's off it now," I said. "And he'll stay off it. I'll not have him chained to that kennel, not any more."

"I don't take orders from you."

"Yes, you do. I may not know what happened here before, but from now on you take all your orders from me. Do you understand?"

His ugly eyes appraised me carefully. And then finally, with what I might almost have taken as a grudging respect for all his dislike, he said, "I understand you think you're in charge. For the moment." Then his thick lips split into a caricature of a smile. "But just for the moment."

He plunged off the path then into the thick bushes and undergrowth pressed along both sides of the walk. When he was out of my sight, I looked down at Thor, still standing obediently at my side, his head raised to look at me.

"We handled him, didn't we, Thor? Don't worry. I'll see he doesn't hit you again." And somehow I felt the great German shepherd understood me. He gave a low growl and then started ahead of me toward the house.

By the time we had reached the main entrance, Thor and I had become good friends. He'd brought me a stick, racing up with it, and we'd played a game of toss and fetch on our way back, a game we'd both enjoyed. And yet when we reached the clear area in front of the house, he dropped the stick without my commanding him and contented himself with trotting along quietly at my side.

Hale's red sports car was drawn up in front of the main door and he was standing on the top step talking to Mrs. Janeck. I could see on my first glance that something had happened to our plans for the day. Hale had changed his clothes; he was wearing a beautifully tailored navy blue suit, a subdued silk tie knotted at the neck of his crisp white shirt.

He saw me then. "Oh, there she is, Mrs. Janeck. I'll explain myself." He hurried down the wide shallow steps to meet me. "I was wondering where you'd gone to. Listen, darling, I've got to go into the city . . ."

"Hale? What's happened?"

"Nothing. There's no reason for you to look so serious. It's just that Irene called, there are a couple of things that have to be attended to . . . signatures, that sort of thing. She doesn't have the authority as your secretary. Naturally, as your husband, I can take care of it better than she can."

"What sort of problems? The signatures on the checks I made out yesterday?"

"That, among other things."

"I'm going with you." I started up the steps to the main door of the house. Mrs. Janeck had disappeared inside, but one of the double doors was still half open.

Hale grabbed my wrist and stopped me. "No, darling, really, it's not necessary."

"But why shouldn't I go?" I turned back to him impatiently. "Hale, if we're going to travel to the ends of the earth after my birthday, surely I'm up to a trip into the city!"

Hale hesitated, and then, finally, he said, "Con, it isn't just business affairs. Irene thinks we . . . that is, I should see your great-uncle. Talk to him before he comes up here."

I pulled away then. "I thought we'd settled that my first night here. I don't want to see him."

"Con, I know that. And I'll try to persuade him not to make the trip. But it's hardly a job Irene can do."

"I suppose not," I said sulkily. "Only . . . couldn't I come with you? I don't have to see my uncle."

"It wouldn't be much point in making the trip just to sit outside in the car." Then his voice softened and he leaned forward and kissed me gently on the cheek. "No, darling. You stay here. Get a good night's sleep and we'll be back tomorrow."

"You'll be gone overnight?"

"It's a long ride, Constance," Hale answered impatiently. "I'm not anxious to make it twice in one day. Besides, it'll probably be after banking hours when I get to town. There may be matters that will have to be settled in the morning."

He started down the steps then, eager to get to his car. I followed him, leaning over the near door as he turned the key and started the motor.

"I was so looking forward to our picnic," I said, aware that I was sounding very forlorn.

"So was I, darling." Hale's voice was gentler now, but I could see he was anxious to be on his way. "But we'll make up for it, I promise. Now, be a good girl, get lots of rest and don't worry about a thing." He gunned the motor then and I stepped back. With one last wave, he shoved the car into gear and drove off down the driveway to the main gate.

I stood there, watching the car disappear. I couldn't hide from myself the feeling of disappointment. I felt deserted . . . Hale and Irene both off in the city. I was like a child left behind by her parents. Only it's been so long since I had parents, I thought, how could I know what it felt like?

He didn't even notice that I'd made friends with Thor. And then I looked around for the German shepherd. But he had disappeared. He must have gone back to the woods while Hale and I were talking.

I started up the stone steps to the entrance of the house. The day didn't seem so bright and warm any longer.

My lunch was a sandwich on a tray brought by Mrs. Janeck to my bedroom. I would have tried to make conversation with her but she seemed busy and preoccupied, so I let her go and settled down to finish one of the books I had brought home from the hospital.

Now that I was alone at Storm's End, I had no further desire to explore it. Hale was right, there was no point in staying here. I knew who I was, even Thor had told me that. I didn't need this house with its air of desolation or the nearby Dr. Gallard to keep reminding me of all I had forgotten. Let it *stay* forgotten! I could make a new life with Hale . . . and Irene, if necessary. Someplace else. And bring Thor with me. That I was determined to do.

The afternoon dragged on slowly. Since I had made up my mind not to take a sleeping pill that night, I refused to let myself nap. Instead I spent the last hours of the afternoon going through the closets of the dressing room again. If we were to leave Storm's End after my birthday, I should start deciding what to take with me. I tried on various clothes and wondered again why I had chosen some of them.

By five, I had selected what I wanted to keep. I took a long hot bath and slipped on a loose caftan of sand-colored silk, light and comfortable. Down in the drawing room Mrs. Janeck had started a fire in the fireplace and put ice in the silver bucket. But the room was lonely without the others. I felt like the last guest in a summer hotel after all the other vacationers had gone.

Mixing myself a light drink, I moved around the long room restlessly. I could see from the bay window a stiff wind was blowing clouds across the twilight sky. I shivered a little and turned back to the fire.

Standing in front of it, warming my hands, I looked up at the portrait of the first Constance Avery. Perhaps because tonight there were fewer lights in the drawing room I seemed to sense a different expression on her face. There was something in her eyes beyond the sadness, something that looked at me almost in warning. The graceful hand that touched the "Scarf of Sapphires" almost seemed to me now as if it had been caught in motion, as if she had stopped before she could raise her finger to her lips to caution me to silence. What a strange fancy, I thought.

But I couldn't make it disappear.

The wind outside was stronger now. It rattled the glass in the windows, causing the chintz curtains to billow slightly, the way the drapes in my bedroom had that first night.

I continued to stare at the painting almost as if I could will the wind outside to bring her voice to me. "What is it?" I whispered softly, looking at the dark eyes of the portrait. "What are you trying to tell me?"

But there was no answer. I glanced around the shadowy room, embarrassed. Suppose someone had seen me? They would think I had lost what was left of my mind.

I deliberately walked away from the fireplace then, keeping my back to the portrait. But still I could feel those sad dark eyes following me wherever I moved.

It was then that Mrs. Janeck announced dinner. To my dismay she had set the long table in the huge dining room just for me. My place seemed so lost in that great expanse of white damask.

I had expected Ben to serve the meal but it was Mrs. Janeck who brought in the first course, a cup of clear consommé. When I asked her about the chauffeur-houseman, she muttered something about this being Ben's day off.

"Where does he go? There doesn't seem much in the way of amusement around here."

"I think he has a girl somewhere," the housekeeper answered evasively. "I'm sure he had Miss Waring's permission to be away." This was said hesitantly but with what I felt was a certain finality.

A filet of sole *amandine* followed the soup, excellent as all of Mrs. Janeck's meals were. I tried to compliment her but she refused to be drawn into a conversation. After serving a delicate strawberry mousse, she announced that she would bring my coffee into the drawing room and I was left with no more information than before.

As I made my way back to the drawing room I tried to think of some way of making her talk. I thought about the sullen behavior of her husband and I pitied Mrs. Janeck for the life she must lead married to that brute. It was there, in the drawing room, as she brought me my coffee, that I remembered the question I had meant to ask Hale the day before.

"Why didn't your husband recognize me yesterday, Mrs. Janeck?"

Her hand trembled as I took the cup from her and she stared at me, her pale eyes wide.

"I . . . I'm sure I don't know what you're talking about, ma'am," she said.

"When Thor scratched me, Mr. Janeck came out of the garage. His first question was if I was Mrs. Britton. Didn't he recognize me?"

"Perhaps . . . you were mistaken, ma'am?"

"No. Doesn't your husband know me?"

"Otto's been . . . away for a long time." She slid the tip of her tongue over her dry lips nervously.

"You mean . . . this whole summer? He never saw me before the accident?"

"I suppose maybe he didn't."

"Didn't he remember me from when I was a child?"

"Otto's been away a long time." She hesitated then, a little flush burning her cheeks. "He told me you'd made friends with the dog. I'm glad of that."

"You were all lying to me, weren't you?"

"Lying?"

"Before. When you said Thor wasn't my pet."

But her eyes refused to meet mine, she looked down at her fingers smoothing and resmoothing the crisp white of the apron she had put on to serve dinner. "I'm sorry you had words with Mr. Janeck, ma'am. He's been through some bad times. He doesn't always mean things the way they come out. I'll talk to him about staying out of your way."

I got up then and, putting my cup on the low table in front of the fireplace, I walked over to her. " 'Bad times,' you said, Mrs. Janeck? Did they happen here at Storm's End?"

"No." She looked at me, a frightened rabbit. "Oh no, ma'am. It was a long way from here." And then, anxious not to say any more, she hurried to the door. "I'd better be getting at the cleaning up. If you don't need me any more tonight."

Without waiting for my answer, she scurried out of the room.

So Otto is new here too, I thought, as I poured myself another cup of coffee. A more recent arrival even than the three of us, back from Europe this summer. One thing I didn't have to think about. I knew Mrs. Janeck was afraid of him. And I didn't blame her.

I went up to bed shortly afterwards. I was determined to fight the night through without a sleeping pill and it seemed foolish to delay any longer.

But going up to my room was difficult. Mrs. Janeck had disappeared and it was up to me to turn off the lights in the house before I went to bed.

The drawing room was easy, even with the lamps off there was still a glow of light from the dying fire. But the switch to the great chandelier that lit the main hall was at the foot of the staircase and there was only a feeble glow coming from the hallways above.

I stood by the light switch a moment before I could bring myself to turn it off. How dark the house seemed then, the great well of the hall crisscrossed with shadows all the way up to the black square of the skylight in the roof. I trembled a little, although it was not cold, the warmth of the day still held the walls of the house.

I remembered now that Irene had told me the Janecks lived in a small apartment over the old garage buildings. With Hale, Irene and Ben all gone, I was for the first time completely alone in Storm's End.

I picked up the long skirt of my caftan, determined not to let myself be frightened by shadows. It's only a house, I said to myself as I climbed the stairs to the second floor. But I had to force myself to walk slowly, I had a wild desire to run for the safety of my room and, once there, lock the door behind me.

When I reached my bedroom I saw that the bed had again been made with fresh sheets. Because of the warm weather, Mrs. Janeck had laid out a thin white nightgown and a peignoir of frothing white lace. Both of them seemed too beautiful to wear. I placed the robe on the chaise longue and slipped into the nightgown. It was cool against my skin and long enough to touch the pale carpet under my bare feet. I must always have worn high heels, I thought, picking up the full chiffon skirt of the gown as I crossed to the windows to close the drapes. But even as I thought that, I saw the cupboard in the dressing room that held my shoes. Most of them, certainly any I could have used for bedroom slippers, had the thinnest of flat heels.

Strange . . .

I stood for a moment at the windows, looking out at the night. The low wind had stopped and a thin mist was rising from the river far below. From what I could see of the outside of the house, the rooms were all dark. All except mine.

I closed the drapes and went to bed.

The next hour was spent tossing and turning in the dark, feeling the fresh sheets wrinkle beneath me as I twisted restlessly, trying to sleep. There was no reason for me not to sleep. The house was silent, no strange creaks or rattle of the wind against the panes. And yet I could not force my mind to rest. I wish there was a switch inside my head, I thought, thumping the pillows for the fourteenth time. Then I could just turn my brain off until morning.

Finally I got up. Perhaps the room was too warm. I slipped my feet into the little white satin slippers I had found placed by the bed. Turning my back on the *bombé* chest that held my sleeping pills, I crossed to the windows. I am *not* going to take a pill tonight. If I stay awake until dawn . . .

I found I could make my way in the dark without turning on a light. I pulled open the heavy rose drapes and moonlight poured into the room. Fumbling with the latch of the window nearest me, I stepped out onto the balcony.

There was a breeze from the east now, off the river. It slipped through the thin silk of my nightgown and cooled my body. The clouds had disappeared and the black sky above the house was studded with bright stars. A faint mist still clung to the low wall that edged the terrace below and swirled like a veil around the far corners of the house.

And then looking up I saw the lighted window in one of the towers, the same window I had seen that first night.

I stood staring at it for a long moment. This time no drug could be said to have twisted what I was seeing. There *was* a light, and it was coming from a window in one of the deserted towers. But the mists made it impossible to place exactly the location of the light. But it was in the section I had explored and it was coming from where I had thought I'd heard a woman scream.

I stepped back quietly into my bedroom. Suddenly I was angry.

There were too many secrets in this house, too much I didn't know, too many questions no one would answer. The moonlight filling my room was so bright I did not need to turn on a lamp. Slipping on the lace peignoir Mrs. Janeck had laid out for me, I started for the hall.

Tonight I was going to have answers from someone.

Oddly, I felt no fear. Soneone had lit that light, someone real, and I was determined to find out who it was.

I moved down the corridor, turning on every light I passed. Let the house blaze with light, I thought. The white lace ruffles of my robe trailed silently behind me as I went from room to room, throwing open door after door, turning on each light. Once satisfied a room was empty, I moved on to the next.

It was like a fury in me to light this massive house, to fling open the long-deserted rooms . . . it was my challenge, not only to the secrets that possessed Storm's End but to the shadows that veiled my mind.

Only when I reached the end of the corridor and the last door, the door to the honey-colored paneled room, did the anger begin to seep away.

I had found no one. Nothing but silent, empty rooms. And I knew before I opened this last door that I should find nothing here as well. But I opened the door and walked in.

This room was as filled with moonlight as my bedroom. I had no need to reach for a light switch and yet I did, only to find nothing. I could see well enough to search the plain walls. And then I realized what I had not noticed in my visit the previous afternoon. This was one room in Storm's End that had not been fitted for electricity.

I stood there in the center of the empty room, not wanting to move. Again I felt a sense of peace about the place, the same feeling I'd felt before in daylight. Only now there was something more . . . as if the room were alive and aware of me . . . almost as I had felt with the portrait of the first Constance Avery when I had studied it this evening before dinner.

This is nonsense, I tried to tell myself. Go back to your room. Go back to bed and stop chasing after shadows. Only it isn't a shadow, I thought stubbornly. It's a light. And ghosts of the past don't need lights. Or do they?

I felt tired then, the energy drained out of me. The comfort of this quiet room seemed to be fading away, leaving me, not afraid exactly, but somehow lost and depressed. What was I? A married woman, soon to be twenty-five . . . whose mind had been born only six weeks ago. Even in that first waking moment at the hospital I had never felt more alone.

I walked slowly out of the room then and closed the door behind me. I must have imagined the light. *I must have!* There was no one here. What I had fancied or imagined was only some trick inside my head.

It took me a long time to make my way back to my bedroom. I made myself turn off each light in each room along the corridor, and close each door carefully. When I finally got to my own room, I was tired. I dropped the robe wearily on the chaise.

What a fool I'd been! Dr. Gallard was right. I could see his sardonic face then, the way it had been today when he hinted there was something far more wrong with me than the loss of my memory. Wasn't he really trying to tell me that I was insane?

I crossed to the window again to close the drapes. But then I made up my mind. I couldn't sleep unless I looked one more time. Stepping out onto the balcony I deliberately turned toward where I had seen the light before. Those rooms are empty, I told myself as I looked up. There will be no light, because there is no one there.

But once more I saw the light. Somewhere in the towers of Storm's End that I had explored so carefully there was a room. With a lighted window.

I stood there, staring at the lighted window. The moon was behind the towers now, turning them into a solid mass of black, except for the light.

I stepped quietly back into the bedroom behind me and crossed the moonlight-covered floor to the chest by my bed. There was my little clock, I could see the numbers gleaming in the darkness. Ten after eleven. I picked up the clock and went back to the balcony, staying carefully close to the full drapes, and resumed my watch.

Seven and a half minutes later the light disappeared. I had not taken my eyes off that lighted square during all that time . . . trying to puzzle where the light was coming from. But I could learn nothing. It was too far away and higher than the floor I was on. I couldn't even tell if there were curtains on the window through which the light was shining or whether I was seeing it through bare glass. It was even too distant to tell what kind of a light it was. Sometimes it seemed to flicker as if someone were holding a candle or a lamp, then for long minutes the light never wavered. Staring at it for so long and with such concentration made my eyes weary but I was determined not to give up until the light went out.

When at last it did and the towers of Storm's End were completely dark again, I went back inside. Putting the clock on the chest I moved silently to the hall door.

I didn't really expect to hear anyone moving outside. I tested my door again, it was still safely locked, as was the door to Hale's dressing room. Once back in bed I didn't even try to sleep. There was too much to think about.

I knew then whatever was happening in this house was *not* in my imagination.

Only what *was* happening? Was it possible that somebody was hiding in the towers that no one in the house knew about?

My first reaction was to dismiss this as impossible, but I forced myself to consider it. Some drifter could have managed to get into Storm's End, the place was large enough, goodness knows, to hide a regiment. But how would a stranger live here in secret? He'd have to have food, supplies, at least the light that had given his presence away. Even if he managed to steal from the kitchen or the house, surely Esther would have noticed. No, it didn't seem possible for a stranger to hide here on his own.

But the other alternative, if there was a stranger here, was that someone in the house was helping him. I knew neither Otto nor Esther Janeck had told me everything they knew.

Suppose it wasn't a stranger? Suppose the light had been carried by someone in the house? But why? Why at night? Why in secret?

Were they searching for something? My mind instantly conjured up pictures of buried treasure, missing paintings from the gallery downstairs, perhaps. Important papers . . .

And if it wasn't a stranger, if it was someone from the house . . . who?

I had to dismiss Hale and Irene, they were in the city tonight. Ben? There was something sinister about that young man, I'd felt it that first day, when I'd seen him at the hospital. And there was that strange argument he'd had with Hale . . .

But most important of the questions I asked myself was . . . *where* was the light coming from? I'd been all through the old wing and had found nothing but empty rooms. Except, for all my searching, somewhere there was a room that wasn't empty. Or dark.

THE FOURTH DAY

Eleven

It was close to two in the morning before I felt drowsy enough to lean back against the pillows and try to sleep. My dreams were vague and frightening, that much I knew when I awoke the next morning, but luckily I remembered nothing of them. If it had not been a good night's sleep at least it had sharpened my determination. For my own sanity I knew it was necessary to learn the whole truth.

The sky was covered with white clouds, the sun was weaker than it had been and I could see from the movement of the trees outside that a wind was blowing. We were into autumn now, yesterday was the last we were to have of summer.

I managed to find a comfortable pair of dark slacks and a black sweater to wear over a loose pink shirt. Wherever my investigations of the house took me today I wanted to be able to move easier than I would in a skirt.

*   *   *

"Tramps, ma'am?"

"Tramps . . . or thieves, Mrs. Janeck."

I put down my piece of toast and reached for my coffee again. I was almost finished with my breakfast in the octagonal green room and so far Mrs. Janeck had made no more conversation than her usual "yes" and "no." Now I was going to try once more for answers.

"Hale . . . Mr. Britton . . . mentioned that Storm's End had been broken into in the past. I was wondering about it. Were they tramps?"

"That hasn't happened for a long time, ma'am."

"But who were they? He said there'd even been an attempt to burn the house down."

"Local gangs. They never caught them."

Mrs. Janeck seemed easier now. Whatever she was afraid of revealing, it had nothing to do with the people of the town. "You know about
the problems there've been in the past?" she said. "Between the family
and the town?"

"Yes, I know. Mr. Britton reminded me." I wasn't to be sidetracked.
"I was just wondering if anyone had ever broken into the house. Actually got inside? There'd be a lot to steal in this place. And since you
and your husband don't actually live in the house itself . . ."

I let the sentence trail off, hoping for her to answer it for me.

"We've never had any trouble with theft, ma'am. Not even so much
as a slice of bread," she answered severely. She wasn't being cautious
now, it was as if I had been going over her accounts. But it answered
one of last night's questions. No one was hiding here that she didn't
know about.

"Those other times," she went on, "they were just mischief. From the
town boys. And there hasn't even been any of that since Mr. Britton
ordered the gates locked and chained. I suspect nobody in town even
knows we're here."

I was tempted to mention the section of the wall that Dr. Gallard
had found crumbling and how easy it had been for him to enter the
grounds of Storm's End, but I stopped myself. There were many reasons not to let Esther know about that.

"And of course with Thor on the grounds at night . . ." Mrs. Janeck continued as she cleared the table. "No, it would be difficult for
any stranger to break into Storm's End."

"I suppose so," I said, trying to keep my voice casual. "How long have
you lived here, Esther?"

"Almost all my life. Your grandfather hired me when I was a young
girl."

"Then you knew my parents?"

"They were away most of the time." She kept her back to me, so that
I couldn't read the expression on her face.

"And when you married Otto . . . I suppose Grandfather found a
place for him?"

"Something like that, ma'am." She was definitely evading me now.
"Would you like some more coffee?"

"No, thank you." That was a mistake, for she started at once for the safety of the kitchen. "Don't go, Esther!"

She turned back then, but I could see she was on guard. How could I break through her defenses?

"This strange old house . . . spending all these years here, I should think it would be a little frightening."

I was stalling for time and she knew it. I could see her relax, the way she had when I had mentioned the people from the town.

"Oh no, ma'am. It's just a house. Bigger than most, of course. But nothing to be afraid of."

"No . . . ghosts?" I tried to say it lightly but it sounded obvious and rather foolish even as I spoke the words.

"I don't believe in such fancies, ma'am."

"Don't you even think about them?" I persisted. "This house seems made for ghosts. Noises in the night . . . unhappy memories of the past. Even from the very beginning . . . the first Constance Avery . . ."

"Has something disturbed you in the night, ma'am?" Her eyes were sharp on me now, waiting for my answer. And I knew that I would not mention seeing the lighted window again. I could learn more by finding out what Mrs. Janeck *wasn't* afraid of.

"No. Actually, since that first night, I've slept very soundly."

She smiled a tight little smile then, as if she knew I was lying. "I'm glad, ma'am. Otto and I thought we saw lights in the house last night. All along the upper corridor."

She had trapped me now, and we both knew it. Just as I knew that she would have a ready answer if I mentioned seeing the light that had started my search.

"Yes." I forced myself into a lazy drawl, the way Irene talked when she was very sure of herself. "After I'd gone to bed, I started thinking about Mr. Britton's plans for this weekend. There's a possibility my great-uncle may come up for my birthday."

"Miss Waring mentioned that to me," Mrs. Janeck said, her eyes never leaving my face.

"It isn't decided yet," I replied, with more sharpness than I had intended. This game of questions and answers was being turned on me now and I didn't like it. I forced myself to go on more calmly. "At any rate, last night I started wondering which rooms would be ready for guests. You know how something simple like that keeps you from sleeping. So I decided to look for myself."

Can you prove that isn't the truth? I thought as I smiled at her innocently.

"You should have asked me, ma'am. All guests are put in this section of Storm's End. What we call the 'new' wing. The furnishings are more modern, and it's kept in better repair. So it's safer. I always keep the bedrooms on this side of the house ready."

"How thoughtful of you." There wasn't much else I could say. "Then I didn't really need to wander through the old wing last night, did I?"

"Not unless something disturbed you." She said it quietly but there was no mistaking the question in her voice.

"No, of course not. It was just a fancy. I suppose I was trying to think like the mistress of the house."

"No need for that, ma'am. That's what I'm here for. And Miss Waring. We can manage things. And it'd be better if you stayed out of the old wing. It's none too safe there."

My second warning. I could feel a little chill on the back of my neck. I got up then. It was obvious Mrs. Janeck wasn't going to reveal anything to my clumsy questions.

"And I wouldn't worry about ghosts, ma'am. There's nothing strange about this house." She gave a little nod and, picking up the tray with the breakfast dishes, went into the kitchen.

Liar, I thought as I crossed the main hall. You're lying to me! And yet there was no way I could prove it. Anything I said, to anyone, even Hale, would just be put down to what had happened to my brain in the accident.

"You're imagining things, Mrs. Britton."

"Why don't you lie down, dear?"

"It must be the medicine you're taking, Con."

And yet I knew what I had seen!

I opened the great oak doors to the library and walked into the room. I can play this game as well as any of them, I thought. Let them wonder how much I *did* know, how much I *had* seen, until I have some proof.

I sank into one of the deep tufted leather club chairs and curled my legs under me. Who is the "them"? I considered.

Not Hale, I couldn't believe he was any part of this conspiracy, for that is what I was beginning to think of it. Mrs. Janeck and Irene were part of the secret, I was almost sure of that. Ben? I'd seen too little of him to have any opinion, but there *was* that strange argument with Hale. Otto? I hesitated over him. He was gruff and mean and, I was sure, cruel. But I couldn't see him wandering through the dark halls of Storm's End at night, exploring strange rooms.

The room!

That got me to my feet. Perhaps if I could find the room where the light had been, I would know more. I began to examine the bookshelves carefully. Surely in a house this size and age there must be building plans somewhere. I decided to start with the bookshelf nearest the door.

Two hours later I was hot, dusty and discouraged. If there remained any plans of Storm's End, they were not in the library. Or at least I couldn't find them. I'd been through all of the bookshelves, crowded with expensively bound sets of Victorian authors. There were no blueprints, no descriptions of the house, no diaries or journals of the house's long history. The cupboards near the floor contained nothing but stacks of old-fashioned novels, not grand enough for display, all of them covered with dust and cobwebs. Irene had been right. Mrs. Janeck could barely keep the surface of the main rooms of the house in order.

I left the library then, moving through the far door into the billiard room. It looked deserted and gray in the pale morning light, the huge table in the center of the room covered with a black rubber sheet. Crossing the bare wood floor, I opened the door at the end of the room and entered into what must have been the all-purpose room for the sportsmen of the family.

The furnishings were heavily Victorian. Rows of rifles were stacked in locked cabinets along two of the walls. There was a rough fieldstone fireplace, sagging wicker chairs, empty humidors on the scratched wood tables. A pile of battered snowshoes was stacked haphazardly in one corner and a clutter of long dusty skis was in another. There were various chests and old trunks placed around the room; one held nothing but discarded bathing suits and tennis shoes, all smelling of a long-ago dampness.

I was about to leave the room when I made the one discovery that justified my morning. I had been examining a wooden bureau near the streaked french windows that led out to the side of the house. The wind was rising outside, I could hear the branches of the trees as they scratched against the house. The last drawer of the bureau was stuck.

I might have left the drawer closed but it almost seemed to me that the wind was warning me not to give up. Or perhaps it was my natural stubbornness, for I kept on pulling at the knobs of the drawer, and finally, with one enormous tug, I managed to get the drawer open.

And there, inside, the only object in the drawer, was a long, double tube of cracked leather.

Binoculars, I thought as I struggled with the rusting metal catch. I took the glasses out of their case and trained them on the far side of the room. Instantly the gun cabinets were in front of me, I felt I could touch the glass doors if I put out my hand. Some avid racing fan in the past must have used these years ago and they had lain here forgotten ever since.

I went outside then, slinging the leather strap of the binoculars around my neck. The next time I saw that lighted window in the towers I would be prepared.

It was chilly outside, the wind whipped at my hair and I wished I'd thought to bring a scarf to tie it back. The yellowing grass was still wet with the night's dew, even though it was nearly noon. I started around toward the front of the house. Now that there were only the Janecks on the place, I didn't hesitate to study the upper floors. Which window was it that I had seen lighted the night before?

Because it had to be *one* of the windows. Raising the binoculars, I studied the house carefully, shifting my gaze from window to window. But there was no movement in any of the rooms, although the glasses were powerful enough to show me even the smudges on each window pane.

It was then the idea came to me.

If I went through the old wing and the towers and marked every window I found . . . and then came back out and checked the outside of the building with the binoculars, at least I would know if I had checked out every room in the house. Not that I expected to find some secret hidden room, that seemed too fanciful to consider. And yet . . . what other possibility was there?

My mind was working furiously by now. Surely in a building as old as this there must have been alterations during the years. A room *could* have been blocked off and forgotten. And if somebody knew about it . . .

I hurried into the house. I could hear Mrs. Janeck cleaning in the drawing room but the doors were closed and my sneakers made no sound on the stair carpet. It was just as well, I had no desire for anyone to know what I planned to do.

Once inside my room I dropped the binoculars on the bed and stopped to think. The plan that had seemed so simple when I was outside seemed impossible now. What could I use to mark the windows? I paced the long bedroom back and forth. Bits of cloth, maybe? I suppose I could tear something up. But suppose some of the windows wouldn't open. And there was something rather ridiculous about the idea of the whole house tagged with scraps, flapping in the breeze from each window.

I'd stopped now in front of the massive dressing table. And then I knew a way out. I sat down on the velvet-covered chair in front of the table and started pulling out the drawers. They were all full of cosmetics, enough to satisfy a movie star. One compartment held nothing but lipsticks.

I grabbed up a handful. These would do for marking. They lay in my hand, glistening golden bullets. Quietly I went to the door and out into the hall.

There was no sound in the house now. Mrs. Janeck, I knew, would be busy for some time downstairs. Otto was probably out on the grounds and the others were still away. This was the one time I could safely conduct my experiment.

I passed the door to Hale's bedroom. That was too near, I was sure, to have been the source of the light I'd seen. And then I went back. If I'm going to do this, let me do it thoroughly.

I opened the door to Hale's bedroom and went in. I must have seen the room the night before when I had raged down the corridor, turning on all the lights, but it had made no impression on me. It was a large bedroom, nearly as large as mine, but furnished simply. A wide modern bed, a plain chest of drawers, two bedside tables. The white jeans and polo shirt he had been wearing yesterday morning lay discarded on the faded carpet.

I went directly to the windows. Mark each one, I thought. Then I moved into his bathroom. His dressing room had no windows, it was simply a large closet, connecting my room to his. I marked each window in the bathroom, using a lipstick of pale beige. Just a small dot, but I knew with the powerful binoculars I would be able to see it from the terrace below. And when I let the thin curtains fall back into place the tan speck on the glass was invisible from inside the room.

I moved quickly then, hurrying down the long corridors, into the rooms on each side, not worrying about the footprints my sneakers left on the thin carpet of dust that spread through this wing of the house.

By the time I reached the tower section the lipstick in my hand was blunted and worn. Outside the wind was growing stronger, it whipped at the windows in the tower, trying to get in. I opened another tube of lipstick; this was a purplish hue, a color I felt I could never have used on my lips.

At least with the different colors I'll be able to tell where the rooms are, I thought. The tower rooms were as silent and empty as they were before; even with the wind whistling at the glass, the rooms seemed airless and closed. I moved as quickly as I could, trying to avoid the places on the old floor that I remembered had squeaked.

And then I was at the last room in the tower, the first Constance Avery's sitting room. As I opened the door, it seemed as if the wind outside stopped for a moment. There was no sound, no rattle of the glass in the windows. I crossed the bare shining floor and crouched down to mark each of the two windows, even though I knew they faced the front of the house. I wanted to stay there in this room, there was a serenity about it, the peace that I had felt before; but there was still one more window to mark, the tiny gothic arch in the hall outside.

I forced myself to stand and walked out of the room, closing the door behind me. Turning to the left, I went over to the window, half obscured by a jog in the wall. For the first time I noticed the reason for the jog: there was a small circular iron stairway, leading from the floor below up into the darkness of the servants' quarters on the floor above.

I'd better do that floor too, I decided, although the thought of that string of tiny airless cubicles under the roof was not very inviting. But before I could start up the metal stairs, I heard the sound of feet coming up from the floor below.

I looked over my shoulder quickly. Where could I hide? The steps were getting louder. I could see the top of a man's head now, coming up the stairs . . . Ben's shining black hair.

I stepped back silently, pushing my back against the wall behind me. I was in the little alcove next to the paneled room, barely closet-deep.

Luckily my clothes were dark; unless somebody passed directly by the alcove, I wouldn't be seen.

Ben had reached this floor by now, the feeble light from the little window was blocked out as he stood in front of it. I held my breath. I could hear him tunelessly humming.

Then there was the click of a door being opened and the gray light from the little window spread again across the worn hall carpet. He's gone into the paneled room, I thought. Would he see the two tiny purple dots on the bare windows?

Then I heard him step out and close the door behind him again. He was still humming the same little tune.

If he walks past me now he'll see me. And he must if he's going back to the center of the house. I could feel my body stiffen as I waited.

But instead I heard the click of his heels as he started up the metal stairs to the floor above.

I let my breath out slowly. I could hear his footsteps overhead now, moving leisurely from room to room. This was not the time for me to experiment with the windows on the top floor.

I wanted to stop trembling, to make myself move out of the safety of this dark alcove, but it took me a long moment before I could get my feet to move.

And then I ran. As fast as I could, my feet silent on the thin carpet. Now to check the *outside* of the house!

Twelve

I reached my bedroom without being seen and grabbed up the binoculars. If I could just get outside without being noticed! Opening the door to the hall carefully, I glanced at the corridor to my right. Empty. To my left I could see the great stairs also looked deserted. Holding the field glasses tightly to my side, I tiptoed toward the staircase.

I had just set foot on the top step when I heard Ben's voice, calling down from the floor above.

"There you are."

I looked up, trying to keep the glasses hidden behind me. "Were you looking for me, Ben?" I said, trying to sound casual.

"We were wondering where you were." His voice seemed to echo in the air of the hall.

"'We'?"

"Mrs. Janeck and I. It's almost time for lunch."

"I'm not hungry." I was moving down the stairs now, but he was keeping pace, step by step, from the floor above. It was like some kind of dance; a spider moving along its web after a victim.

"Now, that's not good, Mrs. Britton," he said, an insolent smile curving his full lips. "Mr. Britton won't like it if we don't look after you properly while he's away." And he moved down onto the second-floor landing.

I made a break then, hurrying down the last stairs for the front doors.

"I'm fine," I said over my shoulder. "Tell Mrs. Janeck I'll have a sandwich later."

"Wait! Where are you going?"

I looked back at him, my hand still on the front door. He seemed so strong and powerful, the cloth of his black jacket stretched tight over his muscular arms, as he leaned over the banister of the stairs.

"I'm going out." I gave a tug to the massive door. Thank heaven it opened easily. And I was outside the house, hurrying down the shallow steps.

I don't know whether Ben had noticed the binoculars I was carrying; somehow they seemed more innocent in the open air than they had inside. I moved quickly across the wide gravel square in front of the house. On the far side, sitting as if he had been waiting for me, was Thor.

I reached down to pat him, sneaking a look back at the front doors. The one I had come out was still half ajar. I couldn't tell if Ben was behind it spying on me or not.

Thor stiffened then, as if he'd guessed my thoughts, and looked toward the door. His ears went back and he let out a low, menacing growl.

"It's all right, Thor," I whispered, bending over to pat him. "Nothing's going to happen to me with you here." That seemed to reassure him. He glanced back up at me, his tail wagging happily. "Come on, boy. Let's go for a little walk."

He followed after me obediently. In case anyone was watching, I found a stick and threw it ahead of me. Thor ran after it and brought it back. Keeping the game going, I strolled leisurely toward the conservatory that was Hale's studio. This took me along the front of the house that led to the old wing.

I made elaborate use of the binoculars, scanning the trees as if I were bird-watching, then stopping to toss the stick again for Thor. I felt . . . no, I *knew* someone inside the house was following every move I made. But even having to disguise my search I was able to examine the windows carefully through the glasses.

All along the building I spotted the little dots of color, one to each window. They were invisible without the binoculars; with them I could count off each one: the front bedrooms, the sitting rooms, the thin slits that lit the upstairs hall. I could afford to take my time, for I knew it would have been impossible for me to have seen a lighted window on this side of the house. But I had to be sure.

I made a long toss of the stick. It disappeared around the corner of the building and before Thor could race it back, I hurried to join him. It was easier to use the binoculars here. The trees grew tight against the stone walls and I could innocently stare at the moving branches above me and check the tower windows at the same time. The windows were all marked. With the powerful glasses I could even

see where I had switched lipsticks . . . the tiny purple dots that marked
the tower windows were vivid through the lenses.

By now I was on the cliff side of the house. There were no trees I
could use to camouflage my search now, so I raised the glasses boldly,
like a tourist gawking at the outside of a museum.

Yes, that window had a dot, and that one. And that one.

I was almost under my own bedroom by now. Thor was nosing at a
corner of the retaining wall at the edge of the terrace, accepting that
the game we had been playing was over. And then I stopped, the field
glasses heavy in my hands.

There *was* one window without a mark!

I examined it through the glasses carefully. One window, high in
the largest tower, had no mark on it, not anywhere. I examined it
again, and then the windows on each side. None of the others seemed
near it; it was carved into the curve of the tower, below the servants'
rooms up under the eaves.

I lowered the glasses and studied the whole wing carefully once more.
If the window was at the end of the building, it must be near the
honey-colored room. But that was on the other side of the house. And
there was no door in that room, other than the one that opened into
the hall . . .

I studied the unmarked window again, twisting the binoculars to
their strongest power. The narrow glass was as dirty as all the others,
streaked and gray. I couldn't possibly see into the room beyond, not
from down here on the terrace. But there *was* a room, I had not
imagined it. Somewhere in those towers and turrets there was a hidden
chamber.

I went inside then, through the terrace windows of the drawing
room. I was prepared to face Ben now if I met him, prepared even
to tell him what I had discovered and watch his reaction. But the great
hall and the stairs were empty. I could hear a telephone ringing somewhere far away. I paid no attention. Once back in my bedroom I opened
the french windows and stepped out onto the balcony. I lifted the
binoculars once more toward the tower. Now that I knew where to
look, perhaps I could see into the secret room from here . . . only,
where was the unmarked window?

Surely I would be able to see it from here. After all, I'd seen the light both nights from here. I held the binoculars steady as I searched each of the windows in the towers to my left . . . counting each tiny dot of color.

But every window had one now!

I went over each window again and again, searching for the unmarked glass that I knew was there. But it was gone. All of them were marked.

There was no hidden room.

I think I must have become hysterical then. I couldn't stop shaking, still holding the glasses to my eyes, moving them from tower to turret and back again, searching desperately. It was hard to see, for I was crying now, the tears bending and distorting what I saw. It was as if the windows, no, the whole of Storm's End was laughing at me.

I stumbled back into my bedroom finally and fell across my bed, the glasses dropping discarded to the carpet. I had to face it now: my deepest fear, the fear I'd kept from Hale and the others, that Dr. Gallard had guessed was coming true. I was losing my mind.

I had imagined the whole thing.

The lighted window, the scream, the feeling that they were keeping secrets from me . . . it had come from some strange injured part of my brain. It wasn't just my memory that was gone. It was something much worse.

They'll put me away, I thought dully. For the rest of my life.

I am insane.

Somewhere down below I heard the slam of a car door. Hale's back. I'll have to tell him everything. I forced myself to sit up then. Not bothering to smooth my hair or wash the tears from my face, I started downstairs. I moved almost automatically, like a sleepwalker, and yet some part of me was still back on that cold balcony, searching the towers of Storm's End for an unmarked window that was not there.

The hall was empty, but someone had gone into the drawing room, for the double doors were half open. I moved across the black and white marble squares and stopped on the threshold, the way I had that first night.

Dr. Gallard stood at the fireplace, staring up at the portrait of the first Constance Avery. I must have gasped, for he turned to face me.

"It's you . . ." I said, my voice close to cracking.

"You sound surprised. I told you we'd continue our sessions." But then something in my face must have startled him, for he crossed the room with long strides, quicker than I would have thought possible for such a muscular man. "Good God, what's the matter with you? What's happened?"

He held me by my arms, searching my tear-stained face. And then I must have collapsed. Or at least the tension I had been under finally snapped and I found myself sobbing bitterly, leaning against his rough tweed jacket as he held me gently, trying to comfort me.

"What is it, child? What have they done to you?"

"It's not them! It's me. I'm going insane!"

"Hush, hush," he murmured. "Nothing's going to happen to you. I promise." He led me over to the deep sofa then, and sat beside me, holding me with his strong hands. "Now . . . tell me what's wrong. Start from the beginning."

I tried then to tell the whole jumbled story sensibly, but it poured out in a torrent of words, in any kind of order, as I tried to remember every detail. It took a long time to tell all that had happened . . . the light in the tower, the way Otto had acted and Thor . . . the scream I'd thought I'd heard, the frantic search I'd made last night through the deserted house, the quiet wood-paneled room . . .

He listened patiently, moving only once to hand me his handkerchief to dry my tears. The only reaction I could see on the calm mask of his face was a slight smile when I told him about marking the windows with lipstick.

"What else could I do?" I said, almost defensively, hurt by his treating it so lightly.

"Nothing," he said, but he was still grinning. "It was a very . . . sensible plan. And did you find the window?"

"That's why I know I must be losing my mind! I thought I saw it, out on the terrace. But when I went up to my room, all the windows were marked."

"And so you think you're losing your mind?" His voice was quiet in the long room.

"I have to be! Don't you see? It was from the balcony that I saw the lighted window." I pulled away from him then, not wanting to look into his searching brown eyes. "What's going to become of me? Will you lock me up? Will it be forever?"

"No one's going to lock you up." He stood then and paced back and forth on the thick rug, obviously considering something. What? I thought. What lie will I hear now? Is there anyone I can trust?

Almost as if he had heard my thoughts, he turned back to me. "Will you believe me if I tell you you can trust me?"

"Haven't I?" I dabbed again at my eyes with the handkerchief. "I've told you everything. You were right, Doctor. I should never have left the hospital. I should be put away someplace."

"Stop that!" He sat down beside me and grabbed my hands again, as if to control me. His grip was strong, I could feel his fingers like a vise around my wrists, and yet, somehow, I wasn't afraid of him. Maybe because it was such a relief to have finally told the truth.

"Look at me." His voice was calmer now, and when I raised my eyes to his, I felt I was seeing him for the first time. The cool sardonic mask was broken now, I could sense the strength in him, the honesty.

"There's one thing I want you to remember . . . and you must never doubt it again. You are *not* going insane. You are *not* losing your mind."

"But . . ." I protested feebly.

"Listen to me! We may not have too much time." His grip was still strong on my wrists, but there was no mistaking the warmth and kindness in his eyes. "Part of what you're going through may be because you are *regaining* your memory."

"Seeing things that aren't there?" I said it bitterly, but I made no effort to break free.

"That's possible. It's also possible that they *are* there. There may be a simple explanation. Or there may be a more complicated one." His voice was very quiet now, hardly more than a whisper. "A more evil explanation."

"I don't understand you . . ." But he wouldn't let me continue.

"Please, will you trust me? I have only suspicions now. If I told them to you . . . well, you might think me mad. Or it might put you in danger, worse danger than you're in right now."

"Danger? The only thing I'm afraid of is myself."

"And that's the only person you shouldn't be afraid of."

I pulled free then, shocked by what he had said. "Didn't you understand what I told you? It's me that's crazy. Not the rest of the world."

"That's not true!" His voice snapped like a whip. "You must promise never to think that again. Now . . . promise!"

I looked down at my hands. They seemed lost now that he had released them.

"All right. I promise. Only . . . what do I do?"

"For the moment, nothing. Keep everything you see . . . or suspect . . . to yourself. And when we see each other again . . . and I assure you, it's going to be every day from now on . . . tell me everything you've found out. Maybe together we can come up with some answers."

"Why you?" I said it stubbornly, jerking my chin up. But it wasn't in defiance . . . I desperately wanted him to reassure me once more. "Why should I feel I can trust you?"

"Perhaps you can't. But try!" He touched me gently on the shoulder, letting his hand rest there. "I think there are secrets in this house, dangerous secrets. I want to help you."

I looked at him. There was something strange in his voice when he spoke. The old suspicions came back . . . who was this man? Why should I trust him? I had a loving husband, friends . . . "Are you part of the secrets?" I asked him, directly.

"Perhaps . . ." But before he could go on, he stiffened and turned toward the doors to the main hall. Outside there were voices. I stood up quickly. Dr. Gallard made a swift gesture to his lips for silence just as the doors to the drawing room opened.

Hale and Irene had come home.

Thirteen

"Dr. Gallard! This is a pleasant surprise."

Hale was in a good mood, I could tell, his cheeks flushed, his blue eyes sparkling. Irene stood discreetly behind him, carrying some packages. She'd had her hair done in the city and for the first time I realized she could be an attractive woman.

"A surprise? Surely the gatekeeper told you I was here? I had to call first to be sure I would be let in."

"We've found it safer to keep the gates locked," said Irene, dropping her armload of packages on a chair. She came toward me then and I realized for the first time how I must look, my face still tear-stained, my hair tangled. "Constance, what on earth has the doctor been doing to you? You look terrible."

I could see Dr. Gallard's face over her shoulder, his eyes warning me to be careful. "I was napping when the doctor arrived. I suppose I should have taken a little more time to make myself presentable," I said lamely. I stepped back then to keep the light from the window behind me. "How was your trip?"

"Wonderful, Con." Hale came over to me and draped a long arm over my shoulder. "We got everything done. No more business problems. The bank couldn't have been more amiable, once we talked to them."

"And we saw your great-uncle," said Irene as she put out the match for her cigarette, her voice carefully empty of comment.

"How is he?"

Hale looked down at me, his face serious then. "Not very well, Con. His eyes are giving him real trouble."

"Eyes?" said Dr. Gallard.

"He's suffering from cataracts, Doctor. He wants to see Constance before he has the operation."

"Not that he really can see her," added Irene. "Not now. The poor man practically has no sight left. But it's been so long since they've met . . . and, well, I think he's afraid this may be the last time."

Hale stepped to one side then to look down at me. I knew what he was going to say.

"We've asked him up here, Con." I made no attempt to protest but he went on as quickly as if I had. "Please . . . it means so much to him. I think he's never quite forgiven himself for the way he acted when we were married. He wants to make up for that."

"I won't know him, Hale."

"He understands about that, Con. We told him about the accident.

But he's an old man and I think he's trying to put his affairs in order in case . . . well, in case anything should happen. I couldn't refuse him." He turned to Dr. Gallard then. "It can't hurt Constance to see him, can it, Doctor?"

"Not if she wants to." Dr. Gallard's face was a mask once more. I couldn't tell what he was thinking.

"When would he come?" I asked, moving away from the others. I wanted time to think of this new arrival but it all seemed to have been decided around me.

"Tomorrow," Irene said clearly.

"*Tomorrow?*"

"It *is* your birthday, Con." Hale was relaxed now that he had got his own way. "Twenty-five. She doesn't look it, does she, Doctor? In that outfit she could still be a child." I was suddenly aware of the loose slacks, the too-big sweater. "We're going to have a full celebration, Con. Irene's been making plans all the way back here. One last grand banquet at Storm's End for your birthday."

"I should start with Mrs. Janeck right away," Irene said, thoughtfully. "And we'll need some local people in, if we're going to have the place ready for tomorrow night."

" 'One last banquet,' you said, Mr. Britton?" Dr. Gallard was watching Hale carefully, I couldn't make him look at me.

"Didn't Con tell you? We'll be going away soon. We only came back to America to settle her inheritance. And now that's done . . . or it will be tomorrow when her great-uncle hands over the proper papers. We'll have no reason to stay on."

"And a lot of reasons to leave." Irene sounded sincerely concerned. "This hasn't been a very happy trip, Doctor. Not for any of us. Especially poor dear Constance."

"But she needs time . . . and someone to work with her if she's to regain her memory." Only Dr. Gallard made it a statement, not a protest. Whose side are you on? I thought.

"It doesn't have to be done here, does it? There must be specialists all over the world." And when Hale went on, he seemed almost embarrassed. "I'm afraid you were right, Doctor. Bringing Constance to Storm's End hasn't accomplished what I'd hoped it would. Maybe the opposite. Has she been telling you that she's not been very comfortable here?" I tried to look at the doctor then quickly, but even without catching my eye he shook his head no.

"Well, she's been uneasy, even if she won't admit it," Hale went on. "So there's no reason for staying on, is there? Is there, Con?" He swung back toward me then, startling me so that I could make no answer. "Besides, a winter here would be grim, even if we could get enough fuel to keep this museum warm."

"I'm sure Mrs. Britton can afford the fuel," answered the doctor, dryly. "With her inheritance."

"Only why waste the money, Doctor? When we can be lying on a tropical island, soaking up the sun?"

"And her memory?"

"Let's worry about the future, not the past," said Hale crisply.

This is what I'd thought before, when everything seemed normal. Now the thought of a strange new place frightened me. Only how could I say it?

"Is this what you want, Mrs. Britton? To leave?"

Dr. Gallard turned to me then, as did the others. The silence in the room seemed to stretch as they watched me, waiting for my answer. Say something, I thought. Anything. Only how could I protest when I didn't know whose side I was on or even what it was I *did* want? The doctor's face was cold now, his eyes impersonal as they had been all those times he'd examined me at the hospital.

"I . . . I want what my husband wants," I stammered finally, not knowing what else to say. Was it my imagination or was there a flicker of disappointment in Dr. Gallard's eyes? It was too quickly gone for me to be sure.

"And what will happen to this house?" said the doctor.

"We'll close it, of course. I can't imagine anyone wanting to buy it, can you?" Hale tossed off the problem as lightly as he had when we had first discussed it in his car.

"So tomorrow night will be the last of Storm's End." Dr. Gallard said it quietly, not moving, his eyes still searching Hale's face.

"And we're going to make it a real occasion. You're invited, of course. I imagine Constance's great-uncle would like to talk to her doctor about her progress."

"I'm afraid I'll have little to report."

"But you'll come anyway, won't you?" Irene leaned forward on the couch where she was sitting, her smile open and friendly. "Please? We'll need you. To balance the table."

Hale turned to me, grinning. "Your great-uncle has a lady friend, Con. Did we tell you? A very chic old party, a genuine princess. Never goes anywhere without her, he informs us."

"I suppose it must be necessary, with his eyes. He can't very well travel alone," I said stiffly. Somehow, I resented Hale's flippancy.

"I think it's a bit more than that. Imagine, Doctor . . ." Hale addressed Dr. Gallard again. "They're probably both over seventy and from what I gather, they've been involved with each other for over forty years. On several continents. Without marriage. And people talk about our generation being permissive."

" 'Involvements,' as you call it, can become sacred. Given enough time. We understand that in France."

"I don't know about its being sacred, but it's certainly accepted." Hale gave a short laugh. "Everybody, from bank managers on, seems to know about it."

"The Princess speaks excellent French, by the way. Won't that tempt you to come, Doctor?" Irene smiled again. She looked different when she smiled, very poised and attractive. The doctor hesitated only a second.

"Thank you. I'll be delighted."

"Seven o'clock then," said Hale. "And we're dressing. We've got to do the old place proud." There was no doubt Hale's words were a dismissal.

Dr. Gallard nodded politely and started for the door. But then he stopped and looked back at us. "Since it's a birthday party, I must bring a present. Do you like old jewelry, Mrs. Britton?"

He was gazing directly at me and once again I had the feeling he was trying to tell me something that he could not put into words. "Yes . . . yes, I suppose so," I stammered.

"Good. There's a quaint little store in town. You might stop in and see if there's anything there you like."

"In town?" Irene's voice was cold, an icicle stabbing at the doctor's suggestion.

"Yes. The town of Avery. Surely you've been there since you've come back?"

Hale shifted his feet restlessly. "Didn't you explain to the doctor, Con? About Avery?"

Hale and Irene were both looking at me now. I felt like a child called upon to perform. "We never go into town, Doctor. They're not too fond of us there."

"Too bad. I think you might have liked this shop. It's right off the main street, just behind the drugstore." The doctor's eyes were still on me, I could feel the force of something inside him trying to reach me.

"I really don't think Con will need any old jewelry, Doctor." Hale was leaning against the mantelpiece now. He raised one languid finger toward the portrait of Constance above him. "After all, tomorrow she gets the Scarf of Sapphires."

The doctor glanced at the portrait and then back again at Hale. "*Naturellement*. It was just a thought. Until tomorrow at seven, then." He bowed once more slightly and then, as he straightened, he looked at me again. "Get a good night's sleep, Mrs. Britton. That's what your pills are for."

And then he was out of the room.

The rest of the afternoon passed quickly. Hale insisted I pose for him, as he wanted my portrait finished by the time my great-uncle arrived. I could hear Irene on the phone, making arrangements to bring in extra help for the following day. And then, later, deep in lists of what had to be done with Mrs. Janeck. The whole house seemed to quicken with the excitement of this one last party.

I went up to bed shortly after dinner. Hale was still busy in his studio. Irene and Mrs. Janeck had disappeared down into what seemed to be a strong room under the butler's pantry and began to bring up the gray felt bags that covered the massive silverware of the house.

The night was quiet outside the house but I refused to let myself go out onto the balcony. Close the drapes and go to bed, I said to myself.

And so I did.

THE FIFTH DAY

Fourteen

I slept well that night, even without one of Dr. Gallard's pills. If there were any strange noises or disturbances in the house, I didn't hear them. But when I awoke in the morning for a moment I could not imagine why I felt so well. I looked up at the rose brocade canopy over my head and tried to puzzle out my feelings. Nothing had changed since I had panicked yesterday afternoon, except, of course, for what Dr. Gallard had said, and even that, as I went over it, was as mysterious as the rest.

What kind of a man was he? I wondered. He's obviously living alone here. But does he have a family? A wife? Either dead or divorced . . . or just absent? In all these weeks that I'd known him, he'd never said anything about his own life. One more mystery, I thought, as I jumped out of bed.

I pulled on an oatmeal tweed jumper over a thick white turtleneck sweater. The jumper had deep pockets and I crammed into them what things I might need for the day, including my wallet and a chocolate silk scarf for my head.

Downstairs the house was in the process of a thorough cleaning. Ben was shining the marble floor of the hall with a heavy machine. Somehow, dressed in a work shirt and baggy trousers he no longer seemed the sinister figure he'd been the day before.

Two pink-cheeked girls of high school age looked up at me shyly as I crossed the dining room. The long black walnut table was heavy with ornate silverware . . . carafes and *epergnes* and candelabra, which they were busy shining. They nodded when I said good morning and then ducked their heads back again to their work.

Outside on the terrace I could see Irene instructing two middle-aged workmen. One of them carried a ladder, the other had already started washing the drawing room windows. I went in to my breakfast.

Mrs. Janeck was busy through the meal in the kitchen. Another young girl, brown-haired and still plump with baby fat, brought in my coffee and toast.

"What's your name?" I asked.

"Nancy." She wasn't as shy as the girls working in the dining room, her quick gray eyes were busy taking in everything. "Mrs. Janeck says if you want something special, I'm to get it for you."

"Toast and coffee is fine," I said.

"I *can* cook," she went on eagerly. "Only not like what Mrs. Janeck is planning for the party. There's going to be cucumber sandwiches for tea. And real caviar before dinner." She looked at me, slightly puzzled. "Do people really like caviar?"

"It's supposed to be a great delicacy," I said, sipping my coffee.

"I tried a little," Nancy admitted. "But maybe it isn't supposed to be good in the morning. Gee, Mrs. Britton," she went on, "I was so excited when Mrs. Janeck called Ma last night for me to come and help. I've been dying to see what the inside of this place is like for years."

"Are you from around here?" I said, smiling a little at her enthusiasm. It had only been a few days since I'd felt the same way.

"I'm from town. You know . . . Avery. I never met anybody that had a whole town named after them. Like your folks," she added happily.

I stared at her then. She was from the town?

"I . . . I thought . . . well, that my family wasn't very popular with the town people. That they didn't like us, wouldn't work here?"

"Oh . . . that." Nancy dismissed it with a superior flick of her eyebrows, instantly a very sophisticated sixteen. "That was back in the Dark Ages, practically. Honest, we're all wild to see you. Ma says she hasn't laid eyes on you since you went to school here."

My coffee cup clattered down to the saucer.

"Oh, you've spilled that. Want me to get a napkin?"

"No . . . thank you," I said quickly. "I went to school here? With your mother?"

"She was a substitute teacher, don't you remember?" Suddenly my head began to throb. "Elsie Hoag. Well, she was Elsie Kretchner then. You had her in sixth grade. Then they sent you to one of those fancy finishing schools and Ma never saw you again."

"Excuse me, which one are you?"

We both turned then. Irene was standing in the doorway. She must have come in silently from the terrace through the dining room. She was, as always, neat and controlled, but there was a patch of scarlet high on her cheekbones as if she had brushed on rouge too hastily and I knew she was furious.

"I'm Nancy. Nancy Hoag," the girl said, shy now.

"I hate to tear you away from your conversation, Nancy, but there's a lot of work to be done here today."

"Yes, ma'am." Nancy was suddenly subdued. I knew how she felt. Irene giving commands could do that to anyone.

"I'm sure Mrs. Britton can get the rest of her breakfast herself. Meanwhile you might help me in the gallery." Irene held the swinging door to the dining room open and stood there, waiting. Nancy gave me an embarrassed smile and scurried into the other room.

"Is there anything I can do to help?" I said carefully. How much had Irene heard of our conversation?

"I don't think so, Constance." Irene went on checking off the list in her hand efficiently. "But you might stay a little . . . distant . . . from the people working here today. They'll talk your head off. And naturally they're curious about the place. But if we're going to get the house in order for the afternoon train . . ."

"I'll stay out of their way," I promised hastily.

She glanced at me then, her eyes narrowing slightly. "You weren't planning on going anyplace, were you?"

"No . . ."

"Good. I may need you to try on your dress for tonight. It's a very special gown, it might require some alteration."

"Gown?"

"You'll see." Then she smiled swiftly and went out. I could hear her voice in the dining room giving instructions to the girls working there.

I sat there alone for a long time, thinking. They had lied to me, Irene and Mrs. Janeck. Even Hale.

Or was it a lie? They'd never actually said I *hadn't* gone to school in Avery. Somehow I knew the word "school" was important to me, it made my head throb as I thought of it, as if some part of my lost past was trying to break through.

But they had all implied that the town hated my family, that we had nothing to do with them, and hadn't since the Depression years. But was it the family the town hated, or was it me? Something I'd done in that forgotten past that made them all feel they had to protect me with lies? For I remembered now that every time the town had been mentioned there had been uneasiness among them all. Why? The local girls had seemed friendly enough this morning.

I made up my mind then and started for my room. Ben was still cleaning in the great hall, a workman had joined him with a ladder and they were getting it into position to clean the crystals of the chandelier. I nodded politely and hurried up the stairs.

And all the time I kept hearing Dr. Gallard's cryptic words about the shop in town: ". . . off the main street, behind the drugstore." You want me to go there, don't you, Doctor? I thought as I scrambled through the closets of the dressing room for a coat. All right. I'll go.

I slipped on a dark brown suede jacket and knotted it at the waist. No one would miss me for a couple of hours, not if I kept my bedroom door closed. Only how was I to get out of the house? The main entrance was impossible. Ben and the workman would be busy there most of the morning. The circular iron stairway in the old wing might lead down to a side door, but it was dangerously close to Hale's studio. And I knew he wouldn't approve of what I was planning.

My mind was racing furiously. The new wing, there must be a staircase there! I dimly remembered the high line of colored light I'd seen that first night as we drove up to Storm's End. I'd thought then the stained glass must be a stairwell, only I hadn't explored the new wing yet.

Of course, it might lead straight down into the kitchen. If Mrs. Janeck saw me . . . well, I'd have to risk it. She'd never dare order me to stay inside, not with an audience of giggling, wide-eyed local girls only too eager to find something to gossip about. The new wing it was.

But once outside my room I realized I couldn't get to the new wing without crossing the open landing of the main hall. And if Ben looked up . . .

I moved quietly now toward the landing. I could hear Ben, busy again with his machine on the marble floor. Pressing myself against the far wall, I hesitated in the shadows of the corridor. Across the open landing I could see the matching corridor of the new wing. If I could just cross the twenty feet of the landing without being seen!

Through the spokes of the railing I could see the top of Ben's head, far below. He was working the machine across the black and white squares near the front door. And his back was toward me. Now was the time to move.

I slipped out from the safe shadows and, hugging the wall, took one step. Then another. One more took me into the safety of the alcove that led to Irene's bedroom. I hesitated for a moment, then moved softly out of the shadows of the alcove toward the great grandfather's clock that stood halfway across the landing. I pressed against it tightly, hardly daring to breathe, although I knew no one could have heard me over the sound of the machine in the hall below. One last scurry, to the far bedroom alcove, and I would be safely past Ben's sight.

Now . . . careful . . . don't make a sound . . .

Then over the railing popped a head. I realized at once it was the workman I'd seen before on his way up to clean the chandelier. He'd obviously balanced his ladder against the balcony railing and was climbing it to reach the top crystal pendants.

For a moment we stared in silence at each other. He must have been near sixty, with a long thin face, heavily lined from forehead to chin as if his head had been squeezed in like an accordion. He looked at me, nodded slightly, and went silently on with his work.

I took a deep breath and bolted for the far corridor. And behind me, the hum of Ben's machine continued uninterrupted.

The stairway was easy to find, right beyond the first turn of the corridor. I saw now what Mrs. Janeck had meant about the new wing. It was much brighter and cleaner. The heavy wood paneling that made the hall outside my bedroom so dark and gloomy was, on this side of the building, painted a glistening white. The carpeting was a thick, pale blue and the pictures on the walls were gentle pastels in simple modern frames. Everything seemed in perfect repair.

I stood at the top of the staircase. The stained glass of the stairwell made patches of purple and scarlet and emerald green all the way down to the ground floor. I hesitated before I started down. I could handle

Mrs. Janeck, but suppose I met Irene. How could I explain exploring this part of the house and, worse, the coat I'd put on, obviously to go outside?

I squared my shoulders. I'd had luck with me so far, and she *had* said she'd be busy in the gallery. I'd have to chance it. I started down.

At the bottom of the stairs I found no one. I had come down into a small passageway, closed doors surrounded me. If I remembered my geography of the house, one of the doors should lead into the game room, where I'd found the binoculars. Only I hadn't remembered seeing another door in that room. The other closed doors probably led to the butler's pantry, or the servants' dining room—the utility rooms of the house.

Only, which door should I pick? The wrong one, and I might come face to face with Mrs. Janeck or Irene. I listened for a second, trying to hear some sound that would guide me. But there was nothing but silence. Boldly, I opened the first door on my left.

I'd walked into the empty game room.

The door swung silently shut behind me and I realized why I had missed it before. It had been built into the wall, part of the paneling, invisible unless you knew exactly where it was. Crossing the empty room, I stopped by the french windows and tied my scarf over my hair. Once outside I'd be at the far end of the new wing of Storm's End. If I could make my way through the tall bushes without being seen I could pick up the side driveway we'd used that first night.

I opened the french window quietly and slipped outside.

The trees grew thick and close to the house and the bushes were thick. For once I was glad I wasn't any taller. I could move quickly through the underbrush, fairly safe that my dark jacket and scarf made me part of the autumn foliage. The dead branches snapped under my feet, the falling leaves, yellow and orange and brown, dropped softly around me, making a thick carpet underfoot.

About fifty feet from the house I came out on the gravel driveway, just past the last turn that swept it up to the open area in front of the great front doors. No one was in sight and I knew from here to the main road I couldn't be seen by anyone inside Storm's End.

But there was still Otto. He must be somewhere about. Odd, with all the work being done this morning, I'd not laid eyes on him. If he saw me . . .

I started to run, my shoes crunching loudly on the gravel driveway. Up ahead I could see the side gate to the highway. I stopped dead then, trying to catch my breath.

The gate was closed, padlocked.

I suppose I'd been hoping with the local people coming in to work that it would have been left open. But the chain was securely fastened to the thick iron bars. I looked at the wall. Stone, and at least ten feet high. I could have shaken the gate then with frustration, and then I heard Dr. Gallard's voice in my head again—about a break in the wall . . . a few feet to the right.

I tried to push aside the bushes near the gate. They grew close against the wall and I could feel the branches pulling my hair, snapping and scratching my suede jacket. Where was that opening? I felt trapped in this thicket, moving slowly along the wall, feeling with one hand as I tried to protect myself from the bushes with the other.

And then I felt vacant space. The wall had crumbled here, exactly as if some giant hand had ripped it from the top almost to the ground. It was a narrow opening, I could barely squeeze through. How had the sturdy doctor managed? I wondered as I scrambled up on the broken stones.

But then I was perched on the edge of the wall, the highway a few feet below me. I jumped, landing sprawled on the road. Looking up, I could see a low-hanging tree had draped a branch over the opening, anyone driving by would have missed it.

I stood up and brushed off my hands. I was free! I was outside Storm's End on my own for the first time. I set off down the road confidently.

Now for the town of Avery!

Fifteen

It was further to town than I thought. As the road passed the massive iron gates of Storm's End, without quite knowing why, I left the highway and moved carefully through the bushes on the side of the road until I was safely past the entrance. Only now the whole secrecy of the morning began to seem a little foolish to me. I had no real reason to think that Hale or Irene or anyone in the house would have done anything if I had insisted on going into town by myself. And yet I knew I wanted to keep this excursion secret.

It was a gray day, the sky low and overcast, dimming even the vivid autumn leaves as they fell around me. But instead of being depressed by the weather, I felt more alive than I had in all these weeks since the accident. I tried to puzzle out why I should have felt such freedom. After all, I'd not been a prisoner at Storm's End. But none of my reasons made much sense to me and after a while I pushed the troublesome questions aside and just enjoyed the walk.

By the time I'd reached Dr. Gallard's house along the road I was ready to stop and rest. And perhaps to ask him more about what he had meant the day before. But I could see from the entrance to his driveway that the door to his garage was open and his car was gone.

Why did he have to be out *now?* I thought, impatiently. There are a few mysteries about you, dear Doctor, that I'd like to have answered.

I was tempted to peek through the windows of the cottage. The one brief glimpse I'd had of it the day Hale brought me had piqued my curiosity. It seemed such a strange setting for the cold psychiatrist, showing a human side I'd not expected, that I wanted to see what else I could find. But the possibility of his coming back and catching me spying was enough to send me hurrying down the road again toward Avery.

About half a mile beyond the doctor's white cottage the highway dipped and I saw, when I reached it, that I was on the top of a hill overlooking the whole town. There wasn't very much to see, only a few scattered buildings, half hidden among the yellow trees.

The town seemed to be one straggling main street. Actually, the highway itself was the street, with a few buildings lining each side of the road. I could see a post office, and a grocery store, what looked like a bar and grill and a diner. All of them had the tired look of failure about them, as if they had been neglected for a long time. Or perhaps it was the grayness of the day that made me think that.

I started down the hill.

Coming closer I could see that years of poverty had settled over this small village like a fog. There wasn't a house where the paint didn't seem to be peeling. There wasn't a stairway that didn't seem to have a missing banister or broken step. The wooden porches were rotting, the planks sagged as if they had given up hope of ever being repaired.

The few shop windows I passed were so gray with dirt I could barely see inside. The cement sidewalks, the one concession the town had made to make the highway seem a street, were cracked and had settled into odd angles, so that walking was difficult.

And still I saw no one.

At first I didn't notice the absence of people. It was after noon by now and I supposed that most of the town was still at lunch. But even the diner seemed deserted as I passed it. The whole town can't be empty, I thought. Go in and have a cup of coffee and you'll see. The counterman must be busy in the back someplace. And yet I didn't want to go in. Perhaps, I thought, with a tingle on my spine, no one will be there.

The feeling of adventure I'd had earlier began to desert me. I felt as alone on this quiet street as I had been searching through the old wing of Storm's End. This is nonsense, I thought. Of course there are people here, you're just trying to frighten yourself. Still, I found I was walking faster, hurrying past the silent buildings. I realized now I'd seen no one, no farmer or passing car, no dog or cat, no sign of any human life since I'd climbed over the wall of Storm's End.

And then I stopped and stared ahead of me.

There was the drugstore. What was it Dr. Gallard had said about the shop he'd so pointedly wanted me to visit? Something about its being directly behind the drugstore?

I crossed the narrow road that straggled off the highway and stood on the curb in front of the store. It seemed as desolate as every other building I'd passed. The shades on the double doors were half drawn, the windows were full of a clutter of suntan oils and bathing caps, covered with dust. Put out for the summer trade and not changed, although it was now almost winter. I shivered a little as I stood there, my suede jacket no longer warm.

I looked past the store in the direction Dr. Gallard had indicated. This side road was black tar, dwindling in less than a block into an open field, the wild grass growing high, sad old trees huddled together as if for company. But halfway down the road there was a low yellow brick building. A wooden sign, hanging lopsided from one hook, swayed over the entrance. The paint was faded but I could still make out the words: ANTIQUES***BUY OR SELL.

And then I heard the sound of a motor. I whirled around. Suppose it was someone from Storm's End come after me? But all I saw was a great truck, lumbering down the same hill I'd traveled. The truck didn't slow down as it moved through the village, but continued on, past where I stood, the driver looking neither to the right nor left.

I don't know why seeing the truck made everything real again but it made me smile at my fancifulness. There were other people in the world after all! The truck was now gone from sight. Go and investigate the store, I told myself. That's what you're here for. And you'd better hurry if you want to get back before the others miss you.

I walked toward the yellow building. It was only one story high, but longer than I had first thought. In the back I could see sheets hanging from a clothesline, swaying slightly, although there was no breeze.

I hesitated on the concrete steps. There were store windows on each side of the shop door, crammed with odds and ends of old furniture; battered lamps and mildewed books. Junk. Why had the doctor wanted me to come here?

For a second, I thought I'd come to the wrong place. And then I noticed in the corner of one of the windows a fly-specked sign, hand-printed: "We Buy Old Gold." I went up the two steps and opened the door.

It took my eyes a moment to adjust to the gloom. The gray day outside barely penetrated the store windows and yet there was only one light in the shop, hanging bare from a long cord. There was a counter to my left, I could see it was full of old jewelry all jumbled together on dingy velveteen trays.

The bell on the door continued to tinkle faintly. As far as I could see, there was no one in the place. I started toward the back of the shop, picking my way carefully down the narrow path between the second-hand bureaus and bookcases. Even in the faint light I could see thick dust covered everything.

And then a door opened at the back of the shop.

"We're not open."

It was a girl's voice, clearly uninterested in whoever might have invaded her privacy.

"I'm sorry, I wanted to look at your jewelry."

The door stayed open and I heard the faint sounds of someone moving, like the scurrying of a mouse. From behind a yellow pine armoire a head peeked out cautiously. The girl must have been somewhere in her twenties, but she seemed much older. Her thin brown hair hung lifelessly on both sides of her long face. She wore glasses with old-fashioned metal frames, but they seemed less "mod" than something she had been fitted for years and years ago and never bothered to remove.

"What do you want to look at the jewelry for? Most of it's just junk." She didn't say it hostilely or with curiosity; it was a simple statement of fact.

"A friend of mine told me I might find something interesting."

"I doubt it." She came around the armoire now and stood there, scratching her elbow. She was so colorless she seemed almost part of the battered dusty furniture that crammed the shop. It was as if the store itself was talking to me, as if the antique sideboards and clutter of kitchen chairs had been given a voice. But her resistance only made me stubborn.

"Could I at least look around?" I asked, not moving.

"I haven't got time to watch you," she said, grudgingly. "I've got the baby to feed." But she moved a little closer now, her eyes still uninterested behind her thick glasses. "The store's my brother's. I'm only watching it for the day."

"He has some interesting things," I said politely, trying to find something that would merit that description better than the pile of old magazines that stood between us.

"Junk," she repeated.

"But the jewelry?" I touched the counter on my left.

"I wouldn't know the price of it anyway. Carl was handing out money right and left, buying it. For what? I told him. Nobody's going to come here. But he wouldn't listen. Not Carl."

She moved behind the counter now, giving it a careless slap of her hand as if she could hurt it. "Being a farmer wasn't good enough for Carl. No, he had to sell Dad's old place and buy this stuff. Spending money that should by right have been split up with the whole family."

From the back of the shop came a short angry yell. The girl glanced in that direction with distaste.

"That's Darleen. You got me right in the middle of feeding her."

"Perhaps your brother could show me the jewelry?"

"He's gone today. I told you. Poking his nose into those farms up in the hills, looking for more trash. Folks round here just laugh at him." The baby let out another howl. "You wait a minute," she said curtly, and disappeared down the path through the old furniture.

I took the time to glance at the counter in front of me. The girl was right, most of the jewelry was worthless. I could see lodge pins and rhinestone clips, bits of moonstones and garnets and colored glass, all in what looked like lead settings, half of them broken or missing a piece.

But one tray was different. Through the smudged glass of the counter, I could see the glitter of gold . . . solid bracelets, a modern watch, knotted chains.

The girl reappeared quietly, holding a fat baby on one hip, her other hand pushing a bottle in the infant's mouth. The baby eyed me crossly.

"See, I told you there wasn't anything worth looking at."

"That one tray there . . . could I see that?"

"I told you. I wouldn't know the prices."

"If I found something, I wouldn't have to take it today." This only seemed to confirm her opinion that my visit was useless but since I made no move she finally heaved a long sigh and pulled out the tray I had indicated.

"This is more expensive. I can tell you that right now," she said.

I looked down at the jewelry on the tray in front of me. My guess had been right, the pieces were all gold and they were good. But the doctor had said "old jewelry." The objects in front of me were all modern in design. Had I been mistaken? Had I come to the wrong place? Or had he just been making idle conversation?

"Is this the only antique store in town?" I said carefully.

The girl snorted. "Pawnshop's more like it. Carl'll never get his money back."

She watched me suspiciously as I touched various ornaments.

"But this *is* the only store in town with old jewelry?" I persisted.

"Folks round here don't have money to spend on nonsense." The baby snuffled a little, trying to work her mouth free to cry. "You hush, Darleen." Shifting her slightly, the girl gave the baby a grim look. The baby, subdued, went back to sucking the bottle.

I picked up a gold pin from the tray. The pin was a heavy abstract design but on a second look I could see it was three initials woven together: C and A and B.

"Why . . . that's a coincidence." The girl made no answer. I started to rummage through the other pieces now. Inside the wristwatch I found another inscription: "H.B./C.A." Those are my initials, I thought. Mine and Hale's. Hale Britton/Constance Avery. Could this be some of my jewelry? I saw again the blue satin drawer in my dressing room, almost empty. Only how could my jewelry be here?

"Do you know where your brother got these pieces?" I asked the girl. She was still watching me, but disinterest had replaced suspicion.

"No." Her thin lips tightened in memory of some past quarrel. "He bought them sometime this summer when I was away. I never would have let him put out good money for fancy stuff like that, I can tell you."

"It's just that I'm curious. Some of the pieces have initials. See? This pin, it's a C and an A and a B."

The girl was jiggling the baby now, almost automatically. Her eyes barely flickered over the pin as I held it up. "You'd better come back sometime when Carl's here," she said finally.

"You don't understand. They're *my* initials. C. A. B."

"What are you talking about?" There was a different tone in her voice now but I hurried on, picking up the watch to show it to her.

"And this . . . it's got my husband's initials as well as mine. 'H.B.' Hale Britton. I'm Constance Avery Britton."

"No you're not."

I looked at her. A faint flush began to blotch her colorless skin and her eyes were for the first time alive. And angry.

"What?"

"You're not Constance Avery." She stared at me, her eyes steady. "But . . . but . . ."

"Look, I don't know what kind of game you're up to, but I *knew*

Connie Avery. The one who lived up at the big house? Storm's End? I went to school with her. Right here in town."

"I'm sorry if I didn't recognize you." My voice was shaking and I couldn't control it. "I've had an accident."

"Don't give me that." Her eyes were hard. "You're no more Connie Avery than I am."

"But that's my name!"

She was quivering with anger now. The baby in her arms stared at her, frightened into silence. She took a step toward me and instinctively I pulled back. There was a kind of madness in her now. She's insane, I thought. She must be!

"You get out of here," she said coldly. "Before I call the police. You think I wouldn't know Connie Avery if I saw her? Even after all these years? What are you trying to take me for?" She plumped the baby down on the counter unceremoniously and went to the shop door. The bell jangled wildly as she pulled the door open. "Go on . . . get out of here! I got no time to be playing games today."

"I . . . I don't understand . . ."

"I'll just bet you don't! Coming in here, wasting time, playing tricks! Now, you get! And don't go around this town telling folks you're Connie Avery . . . some of us remember her!"

I stumbled past her, through the open door. The attack had been so violent, so senseless and unexpected, I could make no answer.

Behind me I heard the door slammed shut and then the lock turned.

I don't remember much of the walk back. I was still too stunned by what the girl had said. Was she crazy? I kept seeing her wild eyes. Or was it some twisted hatred for me and my family? It had been years, of course, since we'd been in school together, but could I have changed that much?

Admittedly I had no memory of her but I couldn't have expected that, not with the accident. But still . . . why had she said what she did?

And why had the doctor sent me there? Or was that too something that I had only imagined? But the girl, in all of her anger, had seemed so . . . *positive.*

But if I'm not Constance Avery Britton, then . . . *who am I?*

* * *

I don't remember whether I saw other people on my way back. I was still shaking, still frightened. All I wanted was to be back at Storm's End with the others, back where it was safe. I didn't even dare ask myself questions.

I climbed back through the opening in the wall and started up the side driveway to the house. The great long black limousine was parked in front of the main entrance. It must be late, I thought dully. They've probably missed me, I must make up a story. But it didn't seem worth worrying about. I had too much else to concern me.

Because . . . supposing the girl was *right?*

Then, what kind of a monstrous fantasy world was I living in?

As I started up the wide stone steps to the house, the doors opened and Irene came out. I could see she was disturbed.

"There you are! We've been looking all over for you." She grabbed my wrist and practically pulled me into the hall. "Where have you been?" She didn't wait for an answer. "They're here! They've been asking for you!"

"My great-uncle?"

"He's gone up to rest before dinner. Hurry! The Princess wants to see you."

I pulled off my scarf and tried to smooth my hair. "I'm . . . I'm not ready."

Irene stopped and looked at me sharply. "You'll do. Here, let me take your jacket. Now . . . go into the drawing room, she's waiting for you. I'll get Mrs. Janeck started on tea."

Irene was practically pushing me toward the closed drawing room doors.

"Irene, please. I can't . . . not now." I fumbled for words. I couldn't face anybody now, not after what had just happened.

"Get in there!" Irene's face was grim. She stood absolutely still behind me, tall and straight, her fingers tight on my wrist. "You heard me. You're the mistress of Storm's End. Go in there!"

I had no strength to resist her. I turned the handle on the drawing room door and opened it.

At the far end of the room, seated on one of the long sofas, was a woman. As I drew nearer I could see she was no longer young, but my first impression was of great beauty. She was tiny, shorter even than I, but she sat so erect she seemed as tall as Irene.

She was elegantly dressed in a coral suit, a soft felt hat of the same color covered most of her curly silver hair. A thick sable scarf had been dropped on the sofa beside her, and she was smoking a cigarette in a long white jade holder. Her great dark eyes watched me as I came closer, and then she stubbed out her cigarette and rose. Smiling, she held out both hands to me. I caught the glint of a huge ruby ring as she said, with a warm smile, "Constance, my dear. How good it is to see you again!"

Sixteen

"I . . . I . . ."

"But of course, you don't even know who I am. I'm Olivia. A friend of your Great-Uncle Matthew."

"Yes, I know. Your Highness," I added, belatedly.

She laughed then. It was a pleasant laugh, deeper than I would have expected from such a small woman, but with a silvery quality to it that made you want to laugh with her. And it changed her face; her skin became full of delicate wrinkles like tissue paper that has been crumpled and then smoothed out again. I realized now she must be close to seventy.

"Don't call me that, my dear. It's Olivia."

"But you *are* a princess? That's what they told me." I could feel myself blushing slightly from embarrassment. The woman dropped my hands and sat down on the sofa again, touching it lightly to indicate I was to sit beside her.

"Yes, Constance. Olivia, the Princess Respelli. To be formal about it. But all that was so long ago. I've been a widow for so many years. Now the title is just a convenience for making reservations at hotels."

I crossed to the sofa and sat beside her, trying to study her face. "And you *do* know me?" I managed to get the words out.

"Of course, child. Why shouldn't I?" There was an amused smile on her carefully painted face. "Although it has been a long time since we've met. In the years you were growing up I was not considered a proper influence for children. But we *did* meet . . ."

She leaned back and studied me. "You must have been thirteen or fourteen then."

Suddenly all that I had been feeling since the outburst of the strange girl at the shop swept over me. I could feel tears stinging my eyes. I tried to wipe them away but the Princess was not fooled. She leaned forward anxiously, touching my arm with her delicate fingers.

"My dear . . . what is it? Why are you crying?"

"So much has happened . . ." The Princess quickly pulled a square of lace from her purse and handed it to me.

"Here, child. It may seem delicate, but don't be afraid to use it. It's wiped away tears before."

I dabbed at my face, aware she was still studying me. Then something she saw seemed to satisfy her, for she leaned back and smiled once more.

"Now, what is all this about?" she said.

"I . . . I can't quite explain."

"Hale . . . your husband . . . said you were recovering. Was he wrong?"

"I don't know. Sometimes I feel it's not just my memory that's gone. That there's something else, something sinister that's happening to me." I looked at her then. Her face was in shadows, her dark eyes glowing in the half-light. "I'm not sure who I am," I added, lamely.

"Hale warned us about that. We're prepared, my dear. I've made Matthew promise there'll be no little reminiscences about the past, your childhood days and that sort of thing. Not that you saw Matthew that often. A man with a small tolerance for children, I'm afraid," she added with a sigh.

"Tell me about him. Tell me what he is like." I leaned forward anxiously. "You can't know how . . . lonely I've felt, not knowing anything except these last weeks."

"Poor child . . ." She would have gone on but there was a tap at the door. Without even glancing away from me, the Princess raised her voice and said, "Come in." It was as natural for her to take charge in her elegant way as it was for Irene. I leaned back against the cushions of the sofa gratefully.

The door opened and Mrs. Janeck, followed by Nancy, now neat in a black silk uniform, came in. Mrs. Janeck carried a heavy silver tray. Behind her Nancy was pushing a small tea cart. I could see plates of delicate sandwiches, small iced cakes, warm scones steaming in a basket. It was obvious great effort had been made to entertain our guests lavishly.

"Oh, good! Tea! Just leave it there, Mrs. . . . Janeck, is it? We'll serve ourselves."

Mrs. Janeck edged her tray onto the low table in front of the Princess, and Nancy, her eyes wide with curiosity, rolled the tea cart to my side.

"Perfect," said the Princess. She busied herself with the tea things, not even looking up as they started to leave the room. But just as Mrs. Janeck reached the drawing room doors, the Princess said quietly, "Close the doors after you, Mrs. Janeck. Constance and I have a great deal to talk about."

I glanced at Mrs. Janeck then. It seemed to me her face was even paler than usual. But she did as she was told.

And yet, once we were alone, the Princess seemed determined to keep the conversation light and inconsequential. I wanted to ask her questions about my past, my childhood, my parents, but she dodged them gracefully, either saying she didn't know or had been out of the country too long to remember. Nor would she talk about my great-uncle.

And so, gradually, I regained control of myself. I had wanted so desperately to talk to her when I'd first come into the room, to tell her all that had happened, all the contradictions and mysteries. She had seemed so genuinely warm and kind. But now I realized, as I regained my composure, she was pointedly withdrawing from any intimacy. Why? I thought. Why, when you greeted me so tenderly, are you now pulling back as if you don't want to hear my questions and don't want to give me the answers?

I drank my tea quietly and tried to turn the conversation back to my great-uncle again.

"Is he very ill?" I asked.

"Not . . . ill, exactly." I sensed Olivia was picking her words carefully. "Like most men who have never known bad health, now that he is faced with something serious, it has frightened him."

"But this operation on his eyes . . . it can be successful?"

"We hope so. If he goes into it confidently. Unworried." She glanced at me then, as if there was something she was weighing telling me. "My dear, I know you're troubled, but I want to ask a favor." Her voice was softer now, barely above a whisper. "Try to make this visit happy for Matthew. It can mean so much to him."

And to you, I thought suddenly. Because of his illness? Or is there something more?

"I'll try," I said. And then I made up my mind. "But I shall want to talk to him. There's so much that confuses me, so much I don't know."

She reached out then and took my hand in hers, her eyes almost beseeching me.

"Later. Oh, my dear, can't you wait until later?"

Now, I thought determinedly. Let me at least tell her what I suspect, what I've been accused of. The image of that strange girl in town flashed before my eyes. But before I could speak, the doors to the drawing room burst open. We looked up to see Hale in the doorway.

"How are you two doing?"

He'd showered quickly, I could see his fair hair was still damp and he had changed into his blazer and gray slacks.

The Princess smiled sweetly. "Dear Hale, we've been doing very well. Come and join us."

"I'm afraid I've got to send Constance away. Irene wants to get her dressed for dinner." He came over to the Princess and took the cup of tea she offered him. "Grand doings tonight, Princess."

"The last banquet . . . It's such a shame."

"You can't want us to stay on here?" said Hale.

"Oh, I understand your reasons. As does Matthew. But I hate to see these old houses go. To be deserted and locked up and forgotten." She smiled a little sadly. "I've seen it happen so many times in my lifetime. The end to all that's gracious and charming.

"Oh, I know, I know," she went on impatiently, although neither Hale nor I had tried to interrupt her. "This kind of life doesn't exist in this century. Everything has to be modern and plastic and hideous."

"There wouldn't be much point in Constance and me rattling around in a castle like this, would there, Princess?" I could see Hale was only amused by Olivia's outburst.

"I suppose not." The anger was gone now. She seemed suddenly frail, like a last autumn leaf clinging tenaciously to a bare branch, knowing that the wind can pull it away at any moment. "It's just that I miss the old days. I think the world will too, when we're all finally gone. Only it won't know how to bring them back again."

She fiddled absently with the huge ruby on her little finger. "It isn't just the beauty of these old houses. My dears, I've seen so many of them go!" Her eyes were far away, deep in memories. "Palazzos and Schlosses and the great mansions of the world. All gone. Leveled for rows of squalid little shoebox houses. Full of squalid little shoebox people."

"That's not very tolerant of you, Princess," Hale drawled. He was half laughing at her and she knew it.

"I'm too old to have to be tolerant!" she snapped. And then she shuddered slightly, as if she felt a chill. "All those beautiful houses! What are they now? Even if they managed to escape the wreckers? Funeral homes and guest lodges and girls' colleges. Disgraceful!" She took a sip of her tea as if to quiet her anger. When she spoke again, her voice was thoughtful. "But it isn't just the grandeur I miss. We had standards then. Honor and decency . . ."

I didn't dare look at Hale. I knew his eyes would be twinkling as he placed what she was saying against the unconventionality of her long liaison with my great-uncle. Almost as if she could read our thoughts she glanced at us, a wry smile tugging her thin lips.

"Strange words to hear from me?" She shrugged. "Not really. We had a code, and we lived by it. A code of kindness and gaiety . . ." She looked directly at me, measuring her words so that I could not escape her meaning. "And sacrifice. No matter how much pain we felt, it seemed our duty to keep it from other people . . . if it could hurt them."

You want me to keep silent in front of my great-uncle, I thought. For his sake? Or is there something else behind that carefully painted mask of yours?

"That code still exists, Princess," Hale said politely. "I'm sure none of us want to disturb Matthew. This *is* what you're talking about, isn't it?" So Hale had felt her warning too!

The Princess made no answer. She got up and moved toward the fireplace. With her back to us she could have been a young girl. She studied the painting over the mantel for a long moment.

"The Scarf of Sapphires . . ." She seemed almost to be speaking to herself now. "Matthew would never let me wear it, you know. I wasn't *family*." She made a little *moue* as she said the last word. "Of course it's much too heavy for someone as small as I." She moved away from the fireplace, straightening the white silk bow of her blouse absently. "It should have been broken up years ago. But the family would never allow that."

"Con, dear? Irene *is* waiting." Hale touched my arm gently. I glanced at him, but there was no expression in his eyes, they were blue glass. I stood up.

"All right. Perhaps we can talk later, Princess. After dinner."

"Perhaps, my dear," she said, looking at me with her wise eyes. "And do call me Olivia. We must all be friends tonight. For Matthew's sake."

*　　*　　*

When I got to my room, it was empty. But through the open doors to my dressing room I could see Irene in the bathroom beyond, drawing me a bath. She looked up and came to the door of the dressing room, leaning against it casually.

"How did it go?"

"All right." I started to unhook the tweed jumper. "She seemed to know me."

"Why shouldn't she?"

"No reason." Should I tell you about the strange girl in the village? And the questions racing through my head? But I knew I wouldn't.

"You'd better take your bath. I'll be back in a little while." Irene walked toward the door to the hall, not looking at me.

"What am I to wear?"

"Don't worry about it. I'll bring it." She disappeared out into the hall, leaving me alone.

By the time she returned, I was seated in my robe at the dressing table, brushing my hair.

"You're ready. Good." She placed the packages she was carrying on the bed carefully. Irene had changed into a clinging dinner dress of cocoa jersey, long-sleeved and high-necked. It softened the angles of her lean body, making her look almost elegant.

"What are those?" I said, pointing to the boxes she was opening.

"Your dress." She lifted out a long gown from the tissue paper. "It belonged to your great-grandmother. She had it made by Worth when she was on her honeymoon in Paris. Hale thought . . . well, since it is the last night, your great-uncle might like to see you wear it."

I came over to the bed to look at the dress. It was a deep sapphire blue velvet, the same color as the gown the first Constance Avery had worn in her portrait.

"Will it fit?"

"I think so. Slip off your robe and we'll see."

She gathered up the gown from the bed. I could see it was intricately constructed; a wide collar covering tiny puffed sleeves, a boned bodice and a great sweep of material forming a long train. I stepped into the gown as Irene held it for me, feeling the taffeta lining rustle against my skin, smelling the faint odor of roses. It must have lain all these years in sachet, I thought.

"It's almost stiff enough to stand by itself," said Irene as she started to fasten it, and it was. This was no soft clinging velvet, but rich and thick as plush. And it looked as if it had never been worn.

"But it must be sixty or seventy years old!" I exclaimed as I adjusted the neckline. It left my shoulders quite bare, the collar scooping deep in front, showing the curve of my breasts.

"It wasn't worn every day," Irene said dryly. "They called it the 'portrait' dress. What the brides of Storm's End wore when they received the Scarf of Sapphires." She finished the last hooks and stepped back. "How does it feel?"

"All right." The waist was snugger than I was used to, but not uncomfortably so. I looked down at the floor, the deep blue velvet swirling around me. "I don't know whether I can walk in it, though. It's much too long."

"I had a feeling it might be. I bought you some slippers in the city." She unfastened the shoebox on the bed and brought out a pair of high-heeled pumps of a sapphire blue satin that matched the color of the dress exactly.

"I hope they fit." I sat down on the edge of the bed and slipped them on.

"They will. I was very careful about the size. Now, stand up."

The shoes did make a difference, raising me enough so that the hem of my gown barely brushed the carpet.

"Can you walk in them?"

"Really, Irene, they're not my first pair of high heels." I smiled at her and went over to the long windows. Outside I could see the sky was darkening with the night. Soon the stars would be out. I turned back to look at Irene, being careful to move the train to one side.

"How is the gown?"

"It's heavy," I admitted. But the velvet was soft under my hands and the rustle of the silk lining was a gentle whisper as I moved. "What else do I have to put on?"

"Nothing. The necklace is always the only ornament. Take a look." I glanced at my reflection in the mirror over the fireplace.

"I look . . . beautiful!" I said, surprised out of my shyness.

"Very beautiful," said Irene, crisply. "Now, come over to the dressing table and let me fix your hair. You can't go around looking like Alice in Wonderland, not in that dress."

*   *   *

Irene was clever with her hands. Since the hospital, the only days of my life I could remember, my hair had been hanging loose to my shoulders. The only attempt to fix it had been when Mrs. McKenzie had combed the waves over the last scratches on my forehead. Now Irene swept the mass of my hair up onto the top of my head, again making me look taller.

With pins and spray she managed to fasten my dark hair into a neat pompadour. When she had finished and finally let me look in the mirror I barely recognized myself. It was as if I had been transported back into another age, out of the casualness of this century. If I didn't look exactly like the first Constance Avery, I resembled her far more closely than I would have believed possible.

"Satisfied?" Irene had stepped back, a pleased smile on her face.

"I never thought I could ever look like this," I stammered. "Thank you, Irene." I reached out for her, but she stepped back.

"Careful! Don't get yourself mussed." There was a tap on the door. "That'll be Hale, come to take you down. Stand up . . . I want him to see you in all your glory." I did as I was told.

"Just a minute, Hale," Irene called out. She led me to the center of the room, under the glittering chandelier and arranged my train as carefully as the mother of a bride. Then she stepped back, half in the shadows of the four-poster bed.

"You can come in now, Hale."

The door opened. Hale had changed into dinner clothes, the black cloth setting off his fair skin and silver-gilt hair. He took three steps into the room and then stopped. His blue eyes grew bright as he stared at me.

"My God! You look magnificent!" There was almost awe in his voice.

"Have the others gone down?" Oddly enough, there was almost a note of irritation in Irene's voice. Wasn't she proud of her creation?

"A few minutes ago. And Dr. Gallard's arrived. Looking very dashing, too." Hale moved closer, not taking his eyes off me. "You go ahead, Irene. Tell them we won't be long." I glanced at Irene. I could see she didn't like the tone of command in Hale's voice but she fastened her lips together tightly and, making no answer, swept out of the room.

Hale came toward me then. There was a new look in his eyes, one I had never seen before in all these weeks. It was a look of desire, the look of a handsome man who wants something and intends to get it. I moved away from him uneasily, suddenly aware of how low the dress was cut.

"Haven't you seen the dress before, Hale?" I managed finally. "Didn't I wear it when you were painting my portrait?"

"No. And you should never wear anything else the rest of your life." He came close beside me, I could smell the faint hint of the aftershave lotion he sometimes wore. "By God, you *do* look like the first Constance!"

He put his hands on my bare shoulders. His fingers were trembling and his eyes glistened. He's going to kiss me, I thought. Truly kiss me, for the first time. This would be no gentle touch of his lips on my cheek or my forehead, but the kiss of a man who had come to claim his wife. How long had I waited for it? And yet, now, for some strange reason, I didn't want him to. He seemed different, a stranger again.

"Hadn't we better get downstairs?" The words came out shakily, but they stopped him. He dropped his hands from my shoulders.

"I suppose so," he said. "If you don't like being touched." His voice was ice cold now.

"It isn't that, Hale. Truly." I reached out for him instinctively. "It's just Irene spent so much time getting me ready."

"I understand." There was still no warmth in his voice, his face was carefully without expression. I felt ashamed then. He'd been so patient.

"Later, Hale . . . we'll have time for ourselves. I promise." It was a lame excuse, but it at least broke the frostiness of his look.

"Sure, Con. Later. When we're by ourselves again. We'll have all the time in the world." The thought seemed to lighten his mood and he held out his arm formally, bowing gracefully. "All we should remember tonight is that we are the last master and mistress of Storm's End. And our guests are waiting."

I made a small curtsy to match his mood and took his arm. And together we walked out of the room.

Seventeen

It was a curious feeling, walking with Hale down the corridor to the main staircase. I felt as if I were many women, not just myself but all the brides of Storm's End, that long parade of wives back to the very first Constance. Perhaps it was the period gown, the long sweep of velvet trailing behind me, the formal arrangement of my hair, but I found myself walking with my back straight and my head held high. In that moment I was finally part of the tradition of this house, going down the great staircase on my husband's arm to greet our guests.

The main hall was blazing with light. Irene and Dr. Gallard were standing together; they looked up at us as Hale and I started down the staircase. Irene had already seen me, so there was an amused smile on her face as she watched the doctor's reaction.

Dr. Gallard stared.

That is the only word I can use to describe it. He was elegant in his black dinner jacket, the crisp white of his shirt setting off his strong face. He gazed up at me as we began the long descent and I realized he was looking at me as I had never seen him look before. There was a glint of desire in his eyes as there had been in Hale's, but there was also something more: admiration and even respect. I couldn't help thinking to myself, trying not to smile, that maybe Hale was right! I should always wear sapphire blue velvet!

By the time we had reached the foot of the staircase, Dr. Gallard had regained his composure and the usual sardonic smile curved his lips.

"*Très élégante,*" he said. "The perfect hostess for this great house."

"The loveliest of the Avery brides. I'll bet on that," said Hale.

"I was just about to take the doctor in to your great-uncle," Irene said. "Dinner won't be for a while yet. I warned Mrs. Janeck we'll all need time to get re-acquainted." She went on ahead, opening the doors to the drawing room.

From the main hall I could see two figures in the room beyond. Olivia had changed into a long robe of jade green satin, stiff with gold embroidery. She looked delicate, but regal, like a Manchurian princess.

And beside her, seated on the sofa, staring as if he could force his eyes to see me, was my great-uncle.

Hale brought me across the room. As we drew closer, I could see my Great-Uncle Matthew more clearly. His hair was thin on his handsomely shaped head and nearly snow-white, as was his neatly trimmed beard. He was formally dressed in white tie and tails, a thin line of miniature medals decorating his breast pocket. His skin was clear and pink as a baby's, barely wrinkled by his great age.

But it was his eyes that held me. Under his thick eyebrows they were dark but clouded, the way delicate crystal looks when someone breathes on it. His head had gone up as he heard us enter and with the aid of a slender ebony cane, he began to pull himself to his feet. Olivia reached out as if to assist him but he shrugged her aside.

"I'm not helpless, Olivia," he said, his voice deep and resonant for an old man. And he straightened himself.

He was enormously tall, well over six feet, so that even Hale seemed short beside him. He reached out his free hand to me.

"Constance . . ." His voice was a question for a moment, then as I came nearer and took his hand, he repeated my name, but more firmly. "Constance."

For a moment I didn't know what to do. I could feel the others watching me. Hale had stepped back and I stood alone in front of my tall uncle, his hand, dry but strong, holding mine. And then I felt a surge of pity and love. Whatever anger there had been between us in the past, surely the time for it was over. The accident had made me forget and I felt he wished for the same. Impulsively I took a step forward, and, raising myself on tiptoe, I kissed his cheek gently.

"Welcome home, Uncle Matthew," I said.

He reached out then with both hands to embrace me formally. There were tears glistening in the corners of his clouded eyes but he had too much control to allow himself to be sentimental.

"Dear child," he said. "I can barely see you, but surely you've grown even more beautiful?"

"It's the gown," I answered. "Your mother's gown."

He sighed. "For a moment, when you walked in, I thought it was she again. Old men have such fancies." He moved back and allowed Olivia to help him to his place on the sofa. "I'm in a strange position, Constance. Somewhat like Abraham in the Bible . . . here to give you your inheritance without even being able to see you."

"Only there's just Constance," said Hale lightly. "No brothers to be cheated of their birthright."

"What a solemn conversation!" Olivia was clearly determined to lighten the atmosphere. "Matthew, you'll frighten the girl. And this is to be a happy time. You promised. It's a birthday party and I refuse to let us all become somber."

"Olivia, you speak with the authority of one born to the divine right of kings. You only married that prince, you didn't arrive with him in his cradle." Matthew's words were caustic but I could tell from his tone that the raillery between him and the Princess was an old game, one they both enjoyed.

"Which you never let me forget, do you, Matthew?" said Olivia, not at all ruffled. "Poor Fredrico! His family strain has improved a great deal now that it has a little of my American blood in it."

"You have children, Princess?" Dr. Gallard had taken a glass of champagne from the table near the window and now joined the group near the fireplace.

I don't know whether he caught the quick anxious glance the Princess gave him. It was almost one of caution, as if he had made some horrible mistake. But then, in a second, a deliberately bright smile covered her face and she laughed her musical laugh again.

"Several children, Doctor. All far from here, I'm happy to say. And all of them impossible. But then, I'm not a very maternal person." But she was looking at me now, her eyes suddenly sad in her painted face. She nodded her head slightly toward my great-uncle as she spoke, a clear warning to change the subject.

"I want some champagne," I said quickly, moving toward the silver tray where tall lily-shaped glasses stood, already filled. "It's my birthday and I intend to celebrate. Isn't anyone going to join me?"

The awkward moment was over; we all moved about the room getting our glasses. Irene passed the tray of canapés to Matthew and Olivia.

"Olivia? Have they all got glasses?" Matthew said, looking around like a great fierce eagle. By now we all realized how little he could actually see.

"Yes, Matthew."

"Good. Then it's time for a toast. The first of the evening." He had again managed to stand. I could see his body was still strong and vigorous, it was only the uncertainty of his sight that occasionally made him hesitate.

"To Constance," he said, raising his glass. And so did the others, all of them turning to me. I could feel myself blushing as they raised their glasses in salute. Hale stood by Irene. How happy and confident he seemed. She, as always, kept her face blank of expression but there was a graceful dip of her glass as she raised it to me, almost a wave of respect. Olivia was watching Matthew carefully, her lips smiling but her eyes shrewd. And Dr. Gallard stared at me thoughtfully, standing as he had been since I entered the room, a little to one side.

It was too formal a moment. I kept thinking of the eyes studying me.

And I felt perhaps for the first time they were wondering what *I* was thinking. I moved toward the fireplace, feeling the long velvet train of my gown dragging along the carpet behind me. The fire was crackling brightly although the evening had stayed warm. Above the mantel I noticed my portrait, framed to match that of the first Constance. They hung side by side. Hale had been clever. The portraits were of two women who could have been sisters.

"Ah, Matthew! You should see her now," sighed Olivia. "Can you? At all? She looks so like the first Constance."

"I can see that, Olivia." He handed her his glass and came toward me. "I'm not completely blind, my dear child. Just that things . . . blur a little. And it isn't just these infernal cataracts. Perhaps tonight there are memories cheating my eyes as well."

I touched his arm gently. "I'm glad you're here, Uncle. I too know something about living a life that is . . . clouded."

His stern face softened. "Hale finally told me about the accident. But surely it will get better, your memory? Won't it, Doctor?" He focused on Dr. Gallard then, his voice imperious once more.

"We hope it will. In time. With luck."

"I don't believe in luck, sir." My great-uncle's voice was a stern rumble. I could see how terrifying he could be if he were angry. "There are other doctors, clinics. Surely a matter as important as this cannot be left to chance."

"Of course not, Matthew," Olivia said smoothly, moving to his side. I caught a hint of her perfume as she moved, a delicate gardenia. "But it's still only a few weeks. We must give the child time." She placed her hand on his arm. She had removed the ruby ring on her little finger and a large piece of jade, the color of her robe, had replaced it.

"All right, Olivia. I promised to be on my good behavior tonight." From habit he looked down at her, although I wondered how clearly he could see her. Perhaps the blurring of his eyes made her seem young again, as young as when they had first met . . . how many years ago? There was clearly such affection between them, such love that I thought again . . . why had they never married?

"Some more champagne, Mr. Avery?" Irene moved closer to the Princess and my great-uncle, holding a full glass.

"Not just yet. Even my dim eyes can see our Constance is missing something. Olivia?" He looked down again at the tiny elegant figure at his side. "Will you fetch the case?"

She patted his arm lightly and then moved to the table behind the sofa. I could see there was a large thin blue leather case on the table, about the size of a small platter. She brought the case back to Matthew, holding it gravely. "Will you take it, Matthew?" she said. He reached out for it, handing her his cane. I could see she had already opened the catch of the case, all he had to do was raise the lid. This must be the Scarf of Sapphires.

I glanced at the others. Dr. Gallard still stood to one side, watching us all with detached curiosity, as if we were under a microscope. But it was Hale and Irene who held my eyes. They stood together, leaning forward slightly to get the first glimpse of the inside of the case. There was a patch of scarlet on Irene's cheekbones, the way I had seen her when she was angry, but now her eyes shone with anticipation. And Hale; there was something strange in his expression. I felt as if I had never seen him before.

But my great-uncle was speaking . . .

"My dear, you know what this is?" He held the closed case slightly toward me.

"The Scarf of Sapphires?" I managed to get the words out.

"Yes. It's yours now, part of your inheritance. Not the most valuable part. That's still to be handed over to you in dull papers and signatures. But this is the symbol of your coming of age, of being the last link in the traditions of the family. When I turn this over to you it means you are no longer a child, but a woman, in full charge of your own life."

"Matthew, dear," Olivia protested, "you sound like you're opening a bridge. Or something equally pompous."

To my surprise, my great-uncle did not take offense. He let out a loud laugh, his head going back in amusement, like a lion roaring.

"I can always trust you to cut me down when I get too grandiose." He stopped laughing then, although he continued to smile wryly. "What should I do? Omit the ceremony and just slide it under her dinner napkin like a party favor?" He couldn't resist another smile as he considered the possibility.

"Just give it to her, dear. We're all waiting to see how it looks."

Matthew opened the case then and handed it to me.

I had of course seen the necklace as it appeared in the portrait of the first Constance. But that had not really prepared me for the actual sight of the jewels. The Scarf of Sapphires rested on a bed of beige satin, obviously designed generations ago for the necklace, as each jewel fitted neatly into its own nest in the fabric. The deep-blue stones twinkled up at me and I realized now why it had been named a "scarf." The necklace seemed an intricate net of diamonds and sapphires, the stones in various sizes, all surrounding the largest sapphire, placed in the center of the arrangement like a spider in the center of its web. I thought as I stared at it the pattern of the necklace seemed somehow familiar. But then I had seen the portrait of the first Constance often.

"It's . . . lovely," I said. But even as I said it, I realized I was lying. The jewels were too imposing to be an ornament, they belonged in the collection of a museum, or to be worn for the coronation of an empress. And there was something almost menacing about the necklace. It looked rigid, an expensive yoke, too heavy for a woman's shoulders.

The others were still watching me, waiting for me to lift the Scarf of Sapphires out of its case and put it on. And yet I felt I didn't want to touch it, as if the cold blue and white stars would burn my fingers if I did. And yet I knew they were waiting and I had no choice. I picked up the necklace. It was not as heavy as it looked but I did not want to feel it around my neck.

"Put it on, Constance," said Irene, her eyes mesmerized by the glittering stones.

"You'll have to have help, my dear. I'm afraid I couldn't possibly manage with my fingers," said Uncle Matthew. "And the catch is quite intricate, as I remember."

"Let me." Hale moved eagerly to my side and took the necklace from me. I could tell he was surprised at the weight of it. "It's heavy." Then he looked at me and smiled. His eyes were as blue as the sapphires in his hands. "Turn around, darling."

I did as I was told. He placed the great bib of jewels around my neck. It was cold on my bare shoulders, the last dangling stones touching the curve of my breast above my velvet gown. I could feel him struggling with the catch, his breath warm on the base of my neck.

"It's got one of those tricky safety chains," he muttered.

"It's a very valuable piece, young man. I can remember my mother used to have it sewn to a neckband, just to make sure it wouldn't fall off." I could see my great-uncle was not seeing me at this moment, his eyes were looking far back, across the years to another time, another woman in this same gown. And yet his words made me shudder. To be sewn into this heavy web of jewels, to be chained into it . . . I felt as if I wanted to claw it off with my fingers.

"There. That does it." Hale stepped back. Automatically my hand went up to my throat as if to straighten the heavy jewels, but really to ease the rim of stones clinging too closely to my throat.

And as I did, suddenly the room seemed to shatter in front of me. It was still there, the long low drawing room with its pools of lemon light, the people watching politely, but I was seeing another room at the same time, as if two camera slides had been placed over each other. The other room was smaller, a dining room, I think, simpler in its furnishings, and there was a woman looking at me, middle-aged but handsome. And I was also touching a necklace at my throat. Only this was of pearls, a single strand. And I was happy and I knew the woman staring at me was some sort of relative . . . but *who*?

It was only for a second, this double image. But it was not something I'd dreamed, some fancy. I knew it was something that had happened in the past, something in the dark years I'd forgotten. And the act of putting on the necklace, as I had in that other room, had brought it back to me.

"Constance? Are you all right?"

The other room disappeared. I could see Irene's face burning through the double image, her eyes watchful. But before I could stammer out an answer, there was a wail of wind rattling the glass at the windows of the drawing room. The evening had been so quiet that it startled the people watching me. They all turned to stare. One of the french windows had pulled open and the long drapes billowed in the breeze, the material swelling in graceful curves as it had in my bedroom before.

The first Constance, I thought. Has she come to see the new owner of her necklace?

Hale hurried to close the window, Irene gathering in the folds of the drapes as they flicked at the table where the champagne glasses stood. My great-uncle and the Princess continued to watch them and I had a moment to collect my thoughts.

"What did you see just then?"

I had forgotten Dr. Gallard. He stood beside me, his voice low but urgent.

"Nothing," I whispered. "Nothing at all."

"That's not true. I was watching you. Just as you touched the necklace something seemed to change in your eyes, as if you were someplace else. Someplace in the past."

I moved away from him then. I was afraid the expression on my face would betray me and I had no desire for the others to hear our conversation. Luckily Hale was having trouble with the catch of the window and the others were paying no attention to us.

"Perhaps I *did* see something. But it's gone. It didn't mean anything." I looked at him. It was one of the rare times when I felt he wasn't hiding behind his usual sardonic mask. His eyes showed his concern. If I could just trust you, Doctor, I thought. "Please. Let's not talk about it," I added lamely.

He stiffened as if I had slapped him. Once more he was studying me with cool amusement, his dark eyes mocking me. "I didn't bring a present for your birthday," he said, so softly I could barely hear him. "Did you find anything in that store in town? The one I mentioned?"

I stepped back then. So much had happened since this afternoon I had almost managed to bury the memory of the strange girl in the store. So it was not an accident that he had sent me there. What do you know, Doctor? I thought. Or are you trying to find out what I know?

Before I could manage an answer I heard a discreet cough from the far end of the room. Turning, I saw Ben standing just inside the drawing room doors. He had changed into a starched white linen jacket and stood there politely as a well-trained butler.

"Yes, Ben?"

"Dinner is ready, Mrs. Britton. Whenever you are."

I knew he could not have heard what the doctor had whispered to me and yet I felt uneasy, knowing he had seen us together. But there was nothing in the way he looked at me, or spoke, that betrayed anything. Still, I moved away from the doctor quickly and went over to my great-uncle.

"Uncle Matthew? Will you take me in to dinner?" I said.

He got up to his feet then and held out his arm. Hale came quickly to the side of the Princess to escort her, leaving the doctor to bow to Irene, the two of them trailing behind us as we left the drawing room.

I was determined to keep the conversation as light as possible at dinner, knowing that at least the Princess would be on my side. There was too much to think about, too many contradictions pressing in on me that I did not want to consider; not here, with all of them present, staring at me.

Hale took his place at the head of the long table, and Ben held the thronelike chair for me at the foot. Since we were six, the table divided evenly . . . my great-uncle on my right in the place of honor, the doctor on my left. Beyond him was the Princess, on Hale's right, and across from her, Irene. I made up my mind to keep my conversation with the doctor as inconsequential as I could. And as short.

The room had been beautifully arranged for the dinner. The white damask cloth looked as if it had never been used, the creases that showed where it had lain folded (for how many years?) were straight and sharp as knives. The table was heavy with silver, the pieces the girls had been cleaning that morning glittered in the candlelight, and fresh flowers, delicate roses in green baby fern nests, dotted the great length of the table, surrounding the gleaming candelabra, blazing with tall white candles. There were candles in the sconces along the dark paneled walls as well, and in the chandelier overhead, flickers of light touched the crystal prisms, turning them into emeralds and rubies and diamonds.

As we took our seats, I had one moment to study them all without being observed. How elegant they all looked! And yet as strange to me as if I were seeing them in a painting. Even Hale and Irene seemed different tonight, alien to me. I felt in that moment as if I were a ghost, but not of the past, of the future—of today. They were the past, this dinner party seemed as distant to me as if it had gathered a hundred years ago.

"Constance? Is something wrong?" My Uncle Matthew had leaned forward, his voice quiet. At the far end of the table Hale had said something to make Irene and the Princess laugh.

I lowered my head quickly, although I knew Uncle Matthew could not have seen the expression on my face.

"No, Uncle. I . . . I was just thinking how beautiful everything looked." I took a sip of the turtle soup in front of me to distract him.

"The last dinner here." He sighed heavily. "For me, at least."

"It is definite, then? You are closing Storm's End?" said Dr. Gallard. There was something under his polite words that turned my great-uncle's head toward him.

"There'd be no point in keeping it open now, Doctor. Even if servants were possible, which these days they aren't. A place like this only serves a function if it houses a family. A large family. And that means children." His strong voice hesitated for a moment, his face had become stern, the lines on both sides of his mouth were deep furrows. "And of course there will be no children," he added quietly.

"I'm afraid . . . I do not understand." As always when he was puzzled, the faint accent in Dr. Gallard's speech became stronger. At the far end of the table, Hale was watching us quizzically. The Princess had turned toward us, the blood drained from her face so that her makeup seemed harsh and unreal, like a mask.

"Constance agreed to that, when she knew the circumstances of her background." He looked at me and for the first time that evening I felt he was really able to see my face. "Don't you remember, child? Not even that?"

I shook my head dumbly. I could feel my fingers tighten on the napkin in my lap, anything to keep from trembling. Did I know? Was this what would bring back my memory?

"If I have intruded on a family matter . . ." Dr. Gallard tried tactfully to fill the silence in the long room.

"No, Doctor. If this is also part of Constance's forgotten past, it is well I remind her. And now. In front of her doctor. There will be no children. The Avery strain will die with us."

"Matthew? Surely another time?" The Princess reached out one delicate hand.

"Unpleasant things do not disappear because they are not mentioned, my dear. You, of all people in this room, should know that. Constance vowed never to have children, Doctor. There is bad blood in our family. There has been since the first Constance. In the past, the early generations, perhaps it went ignored. Rich people were allowed to be . . . eccentric. Perhaps no one noticed." He smiled a bitter smile, his clouded eyes suddenly dull and tired. "Protected by servants and money, this house became an island of safety for the occasional . . . strangeness that seemed to crop up at least once every generation."

Irene, at the far end of the table, moved restlessly as if to interrupt, but then closed her lips again in silence. My great-uncle went on as if he had not noticed.

"But with this century, Doctor," he said quietly, his voice filling the room, "we have learned more about such disorders. My brother . . . Constance's grandfather, was willing to take the risk. I was not."

I could see there were tears now in Olivia's eyes, although she made no move to wipe them away. How old a tragedy this must have been to her! Was this why she had married her prince, whom she obviously had never loved, and then, freed of the burdens of being a wife and a mother, had returned to my uncle, to spend these last years with him?

"I am afraid I still do not quite understand. Surely Constance's mother and father . . . ?" The doctor was trying to choose his words carefully.

"We never knew whether the taint was there or not. They died too quickly. An accident. Or was it? We never knew that either." There was no warmth in my great-uncle's voice now, no sadness or regret. He was as coldly impersonal as a judge pronouncing sentence. "But when there is a history of madness in a family, Doctor, it is well that that family cease to exist."

Eighteen

I don't quite know how I got through that dinner. The courses came and went, the heavy china plates placed before me silently by Ben and as silently removed, almost untouched. Mrs. Janeck had prepared a lobster salad, followed by partridges that I remember hearing Hale say to our guests had been shot on the estate. The tall glasses in front of me were filled with various wines, filled and emptied, and yet my throat remained dry under the heavy web of the Scarf of Sapphires.

Oh, God, if I can just get through this meal! Get back to my room upstairs, rip off this necklace and this heavy gown, comb my hair free. And think.

My great-uncle had said "madness." The worst fear I'd had since the afternoon when I'd first felt Hale's arms around me in the hospital and had not known him. I knew now it had been haunting me, that fear, all these weeks, these last few days here at Storm's End. It seemed to have been in back of every moment I'd spent here; when I'd looked at the lighted window that was not there, could not be there in the empty towers. The fear had been with me, laughing softly, when I'd awakened to hear the scream of that woman who also was not there. When I'd stared at the first Constance's portrait and felt her speak to me.

And wasn't it also in Dr. Gallard's carefully chosen words . . . whenever he talked to me? He had feared it too. Why else would he have . . . ? And then, in the midst of that endless dinner party, I saw again the face of that strange girl in town, her eyes blazing with anger.

Mad. I must be mad.

Luckily, whether by design or accident, nobody seemed to notice my preoccupation during dinner. Hale, flushed with wine, was being more amusing than I had ever seen him before. He kept up a running conversation at the far end of the table, including us all, joking, then laughing at his own jokes, flirting lightly with the Princess, drawing the others out, until even Uncle Matthew roared with laughter. It was as if all of them had quietly agreed that there was to be no moment of silence that evening.

Only Dr. Gallard seemed no part of the conspiracy. I caught him glancing at me from time to time, when he thought no one was looking, his eyes puzzled. And gentle.

Apparently I too had been successful in pretending there was nothing wrong. I could hear my voice, but distantly, as if it were someone else speaking, making the proper responses, my lips smiling until I thought my face would crack.

It was only when the last plates were cleared before the entrance of the birthday cake I knew was to crown the meal that I felt I had come back to the room. Hale had turned the conversation to travel and had kept it there firmly for most of the meal, drawing reminiscences from my great-uncle and Olivia and even making the taciturn Dr. Gallard join in.

"Greece, I think," he was saying when I again became aware of the conversation around me. "At least for the winter. After that, who knows?" Something in my eyes must have caught his attention; for the first time since my uncle's announcement, Hale directed the conversation toward me. "What do you think, Con? Would Greece appeal to you for a couple of months?"

"Shouldn't she be in a hospital? Having tests or therapy?" said my uncle. Was he answering for me because he too had noticed my distraction? "What do you say, Doctor?"

"I think a quiet peaceful life for a period of time might be as effective as any other treatment."

"Perhaps I don't want to remember." I said it bravely, the wine finally having some effect on my nerves. I could see all of them at the table turning toward me, their eyes shrewd and penetrating. "I'm serious," I went on. "Perhaps the ability to forget is a blessing. I can start fresh now. Wouldn't all of us like that? To forget some part of our lives?" I finished, daringly.

If I had hoped to prove I could be part of the light conversation once more, it was a dismal failure. Olivia opened her mouth to break the silence and then closed it again, abruptly. Then Hale, looking past me, stood. The others looked in the same direction and I knew the door to the butler's pantry had opened and they were bringing in the cake.

"All together now, everybody! For Constance." And he started to sing "Happy Birthday."

I made no further outbreaks. Because of the smallness of the party there was no separation of the ladies and gentlemen after dinner. Instead, we all arose from the table together and then, to my surprise, Great-Uncle Matthew led us into the library instead of the drawing room.

"Business, my dear," he whispered, bending down from his great height. "There are papers to be signed, dull matters, but it must be done. And as long as we have the good doctor here as a witness, it would be foolish not to get the affair attended to." He glanced back over his shoulder at Irene. "You too, Miss Waring. We should have witnesses that are not members of the family."

For a second I caught Irene's eye. Should I mention that she was Hale's cousin? But before I could decide, Irene stepped forward, bowing slightly to Olivia.

"I think the Princess should have that honor, Mr. Avery," she said.

"Very well." My great-uncle smiled at the tiny figure. "Olivia? Do you think you can see well enough without your glasses?"

"I'm not the blind one, Matthew," she replied calmly, and once again I was surprised at my uncle's reaction. Instead of being hurt or upset by the frankness of her speech, he laughed and walked over to the huge desk.

The desk was covered with papers, folders that were far from new, yellowing pages, black with type. Hale busied himself fetching brandy for the others as my uncle tried to explain the various details to me.

"Surely you can talk about her business affairs some other time," said Olivia after we had spent a quarter of an hour over the various documents. "This *is* a party, after all, Matthew."

"Of course, my dear." Matthew turned to me, smiling a grave smile. "I suppose I'm aware of time drawing short for me. And I wanted to get this done . . . while I can."

I touched his arm gently. "I *am* grateful, Uncle Matthew. Really."

"Now, now, you mustn't pity me. It's just a very simple operation, this business with my eyes." He turned then toward Dr. Gallard, who stood behind me, waiting to sign the last document. "Isn't that right, Doctor?"

"Of course, sir." But Dr. Gallard's face was grave and I knew that Olivia had not been deceived.

"Matthew? Wasn't there one more present you had for Constance?" Again she was deliberately changing the conversation, guiding it into safer channels. I noticed Hale and Irene, standing a little apart from us, exchange a glance. Was it to be more jewelry? Whatever it was, they were as unprepared for this as I.

Almost as if answering the unspoken question, my great-uncle glanced at me, looking up from the heavy old-fashioned leather brief case that had held the documents we were signing that gave me complete control of my fortune.

"It has no particular monetary value, Constance. This last present." He straightened then, and I could see he was holding a small morocco-bound volume, with a large tarnished metal lock holding the covers together.

He came back to me, still holding the book in his hands. "I thought you might be interested in this, especially now . . . with, well . . ." He hesitated, trying to phrase it tactfully. "With so much of the family history that you've forgotten. It's a diary. The diary of your namesake. The first Constance."

He handed the slim volume to me then. It was a curious feeling, to sit in this formal room, the shelves of books surrounding us, the fire crackling quietly, knowing that I was wearing *her* necklace and now, in my hands, held her own story.

"Thank you, Uncle," I managed to say, my fingers feeling the worn leather. "I'll treasure this." I fumbled with the catch, but it was stubborn and refused to open.

"Matthew, my dear, you've forgotten to give her the key," Olivia said with amusement.

"How foolish of me." And then he removed a large chain of keys from his pocket and, by touch, selected the smallest one and detached it. "It's an interesting volume, I scanned it years ago. Poor woman! She seems to have been very afraid of Jared. That was her husband. She only hints at certain things, of course. I never quite knew whether it was the reticence of the time or whether she was afraid he might someday ask to read the volume."

"Or force her to give it to him," said Olivia quietly. "He was not a kind man."

I longed then to ask if the madness my uncle had mentioned came from her, that first lonely mistress of this great house, or if it had come from Jared, her husband; but there was something grim and forbidding about my uncle's face now and I did not quite dare.

"Thank you, Uncle," I said again. "This is the nicest present I've received."

And I meant it.

Dr. Gallard left shortly afterward. The evening had been a long one for all of us, I realized. My uncle was visibly tired, seated quietly beside the Princess on the worn leather sofa, his clouded eyes staring at the flickering fire. Irene went to get Ben to drive the doctor's car to the door and as Hale was detained pouring a nightcap for the Princess, it was left to me to see the doctor out.

"It's been an . . . interesting evening," he said, carefully, as he put on his overcoat in the great hall.

"It's been a terrible evening," I said, shortly. "And you know it."

"Too many surprises?" He looked at me. His eyes revealed nothing of what he was thinking.

"*Madness?* You call that a 'surprise'?" I couldn't keep my voice from trembling now that we were alone.

"In the Avery family. That doesn't necessarily mean that you have it." His voice was calm, his face blank of comment.

"You of all people know better than that!" For a moment I almost hated him. How could he be so cool, so controlled, when he must know what was worrying me? "All of the contradictions . . . the strange things that have happened . . . the fancies or illusions or whatever the clinical word for them is that I've experienced? What else could they be but signs of madness?"

He put his hands on my bare shoulders then, as if to steady me. His fingers were warm on my skin, and strong. "You must not lose control. It may not be what you fear."

"Is that supposed to comfort me?" My eyes blazed as I stared at him, but I made no effort to move away. In a curious way, angry as I was, the touch of his hands on me was oddly soothing. For the first time that evening I felt as if I were safe. "The way you sent me into town? To see your mysterious store?" But the words were less angry than a question I had to know the answer to.

"So you went?" he said quietly. "And what did you learn?"

Once again he was the cold psychiatrist he had been at the hospital, all those long weary weeks. Probing, questioning. No longer a friend. I made myself break free then, stepping back out of his reach.

"Nothing! Too much, or too little. I don't know." I could not bear to face him now. "What did you expect me to learn?"

We could hear his car outside, the tires crunching on the gravel. He glanced at the massive front doors impatiently.

"Listen to me," he whispered quickly, knowing that at any moment Ben or Irene would interrupt us. "I am your friend. Believe that. If you need me, you know where I am. Trust me." He repeated the words, his voice soft and urgent. "You *must* trust me."

I heard the great doors behind me opening, and felt the cool night air on my bare shoulders. But I did not turn to see who had come in to tell the doctor his car was ready. Nor did I answer the doctor. There was nothing to say.

My head high, I walked back into the library.

Shortly afterward the party was over. Perhaps the doctor's departure had speeded it; we all felt then that we could relax, with the one outside guest gone. Olivia touched Matthew's arm discreetly, and, without a word, he rose to his feet and helped her up. Hale glanced at me. I think he wanted to ask me to stay and talk but I too was tired. Irene had her back to us as she scattered the last of the embers in the fireplace.

"I think, if you don't mind, my dear, it's time to end the evening. At least for us," said Matthew, looking down at the tiny Princess, standing quietly at his side.

"Of course, Uncle." I picked up the slim volume he had given me. The soft leather felt warm in my hands. "Thank you for all your . . . presents. And thank you for being here tonight." I stood again on tiptoe and kissed him gently.

"Dear child." His worn hand touched my shoulder gently. "You've made me very happy tonight." Looking past him I could see the Princess's face. She too was smiling, but there was something more in her eyes, a look of understanding and sympathy, and yes, perhaps even of pity.

"I'll see you upstairs," I said, not looking back at Hale and Irene as I started ahead of Matthew and Olivia toward the hall.

"Constance?" I heard Hale's voice calling out behind me.

"Tomorrow, Hale. I'm very tired," I said, not looking back.

The blaze of lights in the main hall had been turned off and the stairway was lit only by the massive chandelier overhead. But tonight the shadows seemed friendly as I preceded Olivia and my Uncle Matthew up the long stairs. When we reached the landing, I stepped to one side to let them pass me. Their rooms, which I knew were connecting, were in the new wing; my room was in the old section of the house. Matthew hesitated for a moment, as if unwilling to say good night.

"I suppose I should go through the house tomorrow, before we leave. See it for one last time." He sighed. The thought was not pleasant. In his memories the house was full of people still, though I knew all of them were long since dead.

"Why depress yourself, Matthew?" said Olivia softly. "One of the few things the years have taught me is not to look back."

He nodded silently, in agreement, and then he stepped forward one more time and kissed me gently on each cheek. "Sleep well, Constance," he said.

"And you."

I saw them go down the corridor toward their rooms, that incongruous couple. He so tall and stiff, using the thin black cane carefully to make his way; she, a tiny doll clinging to his arm, the stiff green satin of her robe sweeping the floor behind her. I wanted to hurry after them, to hold them once more, to touch them and feel their kindness and love. But I knew I could not, it would frighten them and they would not be pleased. How vulnerable they were! How vulnerable, and how gallant!

When I saw they had almost reached the door to my uncle's room, I hurried quickly away from the landing. I would not have them turn and think I was spying on them.

The door to my room was slightly ajar and I remember thinking idly that Hale must have left it open when he took me down to dinner. Or perhaps Mrs. Janeck had when she came to turn down my bed.

For the first time it crossed my mind that there had been no other people helping through the evening. Nancy, the bright young girl who claimed her mother had known me when I was a child, had disappeared after serving tea. And only Mrs. Janeck and Ben had been present to serve during dinner.

I stopped then, in the middle of the room, and found myself listening for sounds of life around me. Odd, surely after a party this size there should have been some noises from the kitchen, from the dining room:

the cleaning up and putting away that would be necessary after such a banquet. And yet I heard nothing. Nor could I remember hearing anything while we had all been in the library. The house was as silent and still as if I were again alone in it.

And then I smiled, the first smile I had felt naturally all evening. With the walls as thick as they are at Storm's End, I told myself, you couldn't hear an explosion in the hall, let alone the clatter of dishes in the kitchen.

I started toward the windows, but stopped as I passed the fireplace. Catching a glimpse of myself in the Venetian mirror above the mantel, my reflection caught and held me for a moment. The baroque frame seemed to turn the glass into a portrait. I stared at myself. My bare shoulders, rising above the deep blue velvet of the gown, the unfamiliar formal arrangement of my hair made me feel I was looking at a stranger.

But it was the necklace that held me. I had never seen it on me, not since the moment Hale had fastened the catch before dinner. I stared at the jewels reflected in the glass.

What was it about the pattern of the necklace that seemed so familiar? I raised one hand to touch the stones . . . and then, as I had when Hale had first put the necklace around my neck, I saw another room, so different from the drawing room downstairs, or this rose brocade bedroom. I saw again the loving face of a handsome middle-aged woman looking at me and smiling, and once more I was not touching the heavy antique sapphires and diamonds now around my throat, but a simple strand of pearls.

The moment disappeared as quickly as it had downstairs, and trying to repeat the motion of my hand would not bring it back again. I shivered a little, although the night was not cold. Suddenly the Scarf of Sapphires seemed tight around my throat again.

I should have asked Hale or Irene to remove it before I came up to bed, I thought idly. I clawed it loose finally, desperate to feel free of its clasp around my throat. The dress was harder to remove, the hooks and catches were complicated, but at last it dropped to the floor, a pool of velvet at my feet. I placed it on the chaise carefully. I felt so light now that I was free of the necklace and the long gown.

A fresh silk nightgown had been placed, as usual, on the bed and I slipped it on and tied the ribbons around my waist. Now for my hair! It felt stiff to my fingers, as rigid as if I were wearing a hat. I sat in the low chair in front of the dressing table and started taking out the pins.

It was then I saw it.

The piece of paper was propped up in front of the silver-backed hair-brush on the velvet-covered top of the dressing table, just to the left of the antique mirror. Someone must have known I would have had to sit down here at the mirror, to brush out my hair, and had placed it so that only I would see it, in case someone else had come into my room to say good night.

It was about the size of a postcard, a piece of stiff white notepaper with the inscription, "Storm's End," and the family crest, obviously taken from the drawer in the library desk downstairs that held the stationery of the ladies of the house. The message that was printed on the paper was short and blunt, the thick black ink standing out sharply on the cream paper.

"Your life is in danger. Get out of this house at once."

I stared at it until the letters seemed to burn into my eyes. I could not move, it was as if I were frozen and would be forever. Then my hands reached out and I picked up the note. I blinked my eyes and looked at the note again.

The words were still there. This was not something I was imagining, this was not part of the illusions that had haunted me these last days, nor even a sign of the madness that I had feared and which I had learned this evening was part of my family blood.

The message was real. I ran one finger over the letters, as a blind man might. There was no way I could tell who had written it, the printed words could have been by anybody.

Then I felt the blood come back to my head, and my hands started to tremble. And the curious thing is, not even in that first frozen glance, nor in the moments that were passing now so slowly, so quietly, did I doubt that the warning was real.

And that the danger was real.

Only, who could have put it there? My mind was racing. Could it have been one of the people who had come from the village to work that day? That was impossible. They had all left before I had come down for dinner and the note had not been here when I was dressing. Mrs. Janeck would have had the opportunity. And Ben. I went over the evening, trying to remember as much as I could. The others, had they ever been out of my sight since Hale had taken me downstairs? I could not be sure. Irene had moved in and out, arranging the party. And Hale. I couldn't remember Olivia or my great-uncle excusing themselves during the course of the evening, but so much of it was still a blur, I could not be positive.

The only person I was sure had not been upstairs was Dr. Gallard.

And yet he was the first person I thought of, not to accuse, but to turn to. I stood up then, almost surprised to find my legs strong enough to hold me, and stepped back from the dressing table, the note still in my hand. I wanted to throw it into the last embers of the fire, still glowing under the pink marble mantel, but even as I started for the fire, I knew I couldn't. This was the only proof I had that I was not mad, not imagining things.

A curious burning seemed to go through my head, I was as dizzy as if I were about to faint, but my hands were steady now and I could feel my strength coming back. And yet there was this strange whirling in my head, as if storm clouds, whipped by the wind, were breaking and parting, all inside me. I knew then whatever there had been in my past was trying to force its way through the blank wall I had built in my mind. Let me just hang on, I thought. It will come. It *must* come!

But the moment passed.

I stood there, weak and limp. Nothing had changed, after all. I was still Constance Britton, with only the memory of the past few weeks. It had been so *close!*

I became aware again of the note still clutched in my hand. And then a new feeling swept over me, more than fear, closer to anger. I had to get out of this house! Now. Tonight. It wasn't just the warning on the scrap of paper; the very walls of the room, the whole of Storm's End seemed to be closing in around me, pressing against my skin, like the heavy necklace had around my throat.

I knew in that moment there was only one place I could go. Dr. Gallard. Whatever was wrong, he would know. He had said to trust him, and I knew, somehow, standing there in the middle of that stately bedroom, the rose drapes moving slightly in the breeze that pushed its way through the cracks of the closed windows, that he was the only one I *could* trust.

It never crossed my mind what would happen when I got to him . . . the lateness of the hour, the difficulty of getting through this silent house, through the dark grounds, down the highway to him. It was enough that I had a place where I felt I could find shelter. What the others would say in the morning . . . I pushed the thought aside.

I didn't wait to change my clothes. I felt the passing of minutes, precious minutes, might mean my life. I had to leave now. This instant. Grabbing the fur-lined coat they'd brought to me at the hospital, I flung it over my shoulders and started for the door.

I had to get out of Storm's End!

Nineteen

The hall outside my room was dark. I hesitated for a moment on the threshold of my room, then closed the door behind me quietly. After a second, my eyes adjusted to the blackness around me and I started to make out some of the shapes nearby. The full moon outside managed to pierce a few of the narrow windows of the hall and I knew once I reached the main staircase there would be moonlight coming through the skylight of the roof of the house to show me my way.

I moved as quickly as I could, down the center of the hall. There was less chance of bumping into odd corners of furniture if I could keep my feet on the narrow strip of carpet as a guide. Once I reached the staircase, it would be easy enough to feel my way down through the darkness to the main doors. And then? I could only pray that they were unlocked or that I could manage to open them somehow. If I couldn't, well, I would break open a window. But I was determined to leave this house tonight.

When I reached the main staircase I stopped for a second and listened. All around me were people in their various rooms, already in bed, or preparing for it. Uncle Matthew, Hale, Irene, the Princess . . . Esther must have gone back to her rooms over the garage. And Ben?

I'd never known where he slept but I could only hope earnestly wherever his bed was, he was safely in it.

There was no sound in the house, it was so quiet I could hear myself breathe. The creaks of old wood, the scurry of mice, the rattle and whispers of the wind off the river were all still tonight. Moonlight came through the skylight above me, it made the old walls silver where it touched them, turning the newel-posts of the staircase into strange gargoyles as I picked up the skirt of my nightgown and started slowly down the stairs.

The moon made an island of light on the black and white marble floor below, turning the shadows around it into dark caves. I tried to remember which steps creaked but I could not think of anything but that I must get out of this house, now, this minute!

I could feel my long coat brush against each step as I made my way downstairs, it seemed as loud as a shout in that quiet house. If I can just make the front door without waking anybody!

The great doors were locked, as I should have known they would be, but after fumbling with them desperately for what seemed like hours, I managed to slide the bolts free. Now to open the door . . . just a crack to let me slip through!

And then I was outside. The full moon seemed to light the great empty area in front of the house to the brightness of day. If anyone were looking out the windows above me, they would see me long before I could reach the side road that led down to the highway. But I would have to chance it.

The night was cooler now. I shivered a little, pulling the coat tighter around my shoulders. Why hadn't I thought to dress? Suddenly I realized how incongruous I must seem standing here against the doors of Storm's End, only a coat over my nightgown, trying to make my feet flee in terror to a man I barely knew.

Is this what had happened the other time? The day of the accident? The day I'd left my wedding ring behind and gone . . . where? To whom? But I could not let myself think about that, not now. Now I needed all my courage to make myself race across that great open space in front of the house until I reached the safety of the dark trees lining the side road.

I picked up my skirt then and ran. Down the great stone steps, then feeling the gravel under my thin slippers as I crossed the empty park. The full moon had turned the world silver around me, the leaves and bushes, the fading grass of the long lawn, the path ahead of me, my fingers and bare arms as they clutched my long skirt.

And there was no sound to break the stillness, no birds in the trees, no wind among the branches, no cry of someone from one of those dark windows behind me. Only the scratch of my slippers on the gravel. A few more yards and I'd reach the safe shadows of the trees!

I heard the long howl of a dog in the distance. Thor. They'd let him loose tonight. Well, that wouldn't frighten me. We were friends now. If he was all that stood between me and freedom, I was as good as safe. A low branch pulled at the coat I'd placed over my shoulders like a cape and it fell to the ground. I stopped to turn back for it, safe in the shadow of the trees, and looked at the dark house from which I'd escaped. Storm's End was beautiful in the silver light. The full moon showed every detail of the stone facade, the rows of windows, black now in the walls of the building, the great front door, the turrets and towers at each of the ends of the building, all silent and still as a castle in a fairy tale, caught forever under a spell.

Except for one window.

High, high in the furthest tower, one window was lighted. Even as I stood there, trying to catch my breath, I knew it was from the same tower as the lighted window I had seen from my own room.

But this was different!

I'd seen that light from my bedroom, and that was on the other side of the house! I couldn't be seeing the same light, not from here! It would be impossible. I took another step back into the shadows of the thick elm that marked the beginning of the side road we'd used that first evening. Who could be in that empty tower tonight? Matthew? The Princess? They'd not been here before. Hale? Irene? They'd been in the city the second time I saw it.

Or was it the first Constance, coming back to visit her lovely little wood-paneled room? That would be on this side of the house, I'd seen the great lawns myself from its windows.

Then I made myself turn away from the house. I put on my coat and tied the sash securely. Storm's End could keep its secrets. I was leaving it. And I knew, in my own head, I had determined to leave it forever. I started down the side road.

I had to walk slower now, for the road was dark with the thick trees overhead, only an occasional patch of moonlight sliding through to silver the dark road. If the gate was locked, well, somehow I would climb through the break in the wall that the doctor had found. How I would manage in a thin silk nightgown, I didn't bother to consider. Somehow I would do it.

I had barely gone fifteen feet when I heard the sound.

I stopped then, my heart thudding. Something was moving in the darkness nearby. An animal? I knew the woods were wild around the house. I'd been warned. Or was it something else? Otto, on his rounds?

Oh, God, don't let him catch me! Not when I'm this close to freedom!

There was a scratching on the gravel road behind me and I turned to face it.

Trotting slowly toward me, his eyes gleaming black in the half-light, was Thor. I stood absolutely still. I knew we were friends now, but I couldn't help remembering the first two times I'd seen him. Would he go back to that now? The snarling, angry animal, ready to kill?

He stopped when he was a few feet away from me and studied me carefully. Then his tail started to wag gently and I knew that he remembered who I was. He came slowly up to my side, waiting to be petted.

"Thor? You'll protect me, won't you?" I whispered as I scratched his soft fur. "You'll let me get safely away, won't you?"

He growled, but it was low and friendly. I put my hand on his collar and started again toward the side gate that led to the highway. He seemed content to walk beside me obediently.

"Stop!"

I whirled about. I could feel Thor's body stiffen against my leg. From out of the dark shadows along the road came a figure. Ben.

I froze where I was. He'd already recognized me and, as he stepped closer, I could see him taking in every detail of my appearance: the long coat, the silk of my gown touching my slippers, the frightened look on my face.

"Well, well, well! The mistress of Storm's End. Isn't it a little late for a walk?"

"What . . . are you doing here?" I had no answer and a challenge seemed the best way to counter him.

"Guard duty. We have poachers. Didn't you know?" Even in the half-light, I could see him smiling. It was not a pleasant smile. And then he stepped forward again, out of the shadows into a patch of light. For the first time I could see what was in his hands.

A rifle.

"You carry . . . a gun?" I tried not to sound afraid but he was not fooled. He shifted it easily in his hands and smiled again.

"We wouldn't want the wrong people to get in here, now, would we? It could be dangerous. For everybody."

I mustn't let him see I'm afraid, I thought. If I do, I'll never get free. He's admitted I'm the mistress of Storm's End. If I order him to go, he'll have to obey me. I raised my head, trying to look as tall and in command as I could.

"I don't like guns. And I don't approve of them here. Besides, I thought it was Otto's job to protect the grounds."

"This is a big estate. It takes both of us." His voice was a lazy insolent drawl as if he had seen through my attempt to order him out of the way and was only amused by it.

"There's no need for that tonight. Go to bed. And tell Otto to do the same." I made no move to leave, but continued to stand there, my hand still on Thor's collar. He was growling now, not as soft as before, his head up, his ears stiff.

"Of course. Ma'am." He added that and managed to give the word a contemptuous twist. "I'll be glad to have the sleep." Then he paused and when he spoke again, the words came out deliberately, with no possibility of doubting what he meant. "After I've seen you safely back to the house."

"I'm . . . I'm not going back to the house. Not just yet." I tried to keep my voice from quavering, but I knew I was not successful. Please, don't let him see how afraid I am, I prayed silently. And knew as I did, it was no use.

"I'm afraid you have to. It's too dangerous for you out alone . . . at this hour of the night. And you, not always . . . too sure of yourself."

He took another step toward me, and as he moved, the rifle in his hands came up. There was no mistaking him now. It was pointed straight at me.

"Put . . . put that gun down!"

"Sure." But he did not lower it. "Just as soon as you're safe inside the house, Mrs. Britton. After all, that's one of the reasons Mr. Britton hired me. To look after you."

I don't know where I found the courage, but I stared him straight in the eye and said, "You can't make me go back to the house. And you wouldn't dare shoot me." I even managed to keep my voice controlled.

He laughed then, and let the rifle fall. "I wouldn't shoot you, Mrs. Britton. You're too valuable. But if I have to take you back by force, I will."

"You wouldn't dare!"

"A lady like you . . . who's been having trouble with her mind. There isn't anybody who would say I didn't do the right thing." He laughed again and then, seeing I had made no move to give in, he started toward me once more.

He can almost reach me now, I thought, but I could not move, could not force my feet to run, knowing somewhere in my mind that even if I tried, he would catch me easily, hampered as I was by my thin slippers and heavy coat.

And then Thor growled once more.

I think both Ben and I had forgotten the animal, although my hand was still on the great German shepherd's collar. He had pulled free of my grasp now and stepped forward, standing half in front of me, ready to protect me.

Thor started to bark now, and there was no mistaking his angry tone. He stood there on the road between Ben and me, his body rigid, his feet planted. His long jaws were open and a fierce growl was coming from deep in his chest.

"Call that damn dog back, Mrs. Britton," said Ben. But he was careful not to move.

"No." I knew I was safe as long as Thor stood between me and the chauffeur. "Thor doesn't like you, and with good reason. I wouldn't advise you to try and stop me."

"I'll stop you."

He moved quickly then, faster than I would have believed possible. With one swift move he swung the rifle at Thor's head. I could hear the sickening crack as the barrel hit the bone of the dog's skull. The dog sprawled on the gray road between us, knocked to one side by the force of the blow. Ben started moving toward me, paying no attention to the animal. Thor was quiet now, not even growling in pain. One more step and Ben would be able to grab me easily, and yet I could make no move.

"Now we're going back to the house."

He reached out for me, but before I could feel his hands on my arm, he was knocked sideways by a sudden blur of fur and muscle. Thor had sprung for him. I could hear the long angry snarl of the hurt animal, in that one moment he had managed to knock Ben off balance to the ground. I could see the glittering teeth of the dog trying to reach the throat of the fallen man, hear his fierce yelps as he did at last what nature had trained him to do, fight with all his strength to protect those he loved.

"No, Thor! No!" I cried out, but the words were dry in my throat. He'll kill him, I thought, but I could not move.

They were a tangle of movement on the gravel road, man and dog so twined together it would have been impossible to separate them, even if I dared. Ben struggled violently; I could hear the slow rip of his leather jacket as the animal got his teeth into the material and pulled at it.

And then Ben, with more strength than I would have thought even he possessed, managed to get up to his knees, and with both hands around the dog's throat, pulled him off and flung him across the road.

The dog was on his feet again instantly, ready to charge once more, but even that brief moment had been too long. Ben had grabbed up the gun and as Thor gathered himself to leap once more, Ben raised his rifle and shot him.

The bullet caught Thor in midair. There was a wild yelp of rage and pain, and the great German shepherd dropped at Ben's feet. Even from where I stood, I knew the animal was dead.

We stood there, Ben and I, for a long second, staring at the dog on the road between us. "Oh, my God," I managed to say, finally.

"I had to save my life and yours," Ben answered curtly.

"He never would have hurt me. He was trying to protect me. From you." I knelt down on the ground beside the animal. Thor's eyes were still open, wide and dark. I thought even in that half-silver light I could see the pain and shock still in them. But his chest under his thick fur was still. "Poor beautiful animal," I thought. "You gave your life to save me." And I could feel the tears forming in my eyes.

Almost as if Ben had read my thoughts, he stepped forward once more and, seizing me by my arms, lifted me to my feet again. "See? It didn't work," he said. "Now will you go back to the house?"

Before I could answer, we both heard a sound in the underbrush nearby. His hands still on me, Ben turned in the direction of the noise.

Otto, sweat beading his face, pushed his way out of the bushes and came up to us on the road. "What's happened here?" he said, not bothering to lower his voice. "I heard a shot."

Ben motioned toward the dog on the ground in front of us. "He tried to kill us," he said briefly.

I pulled free then. "Not 'us,'" I said coldly. "*You.* Thor was trying to protect me."

Otto looked at me then, recognizing me for the first time. "So it's the girl," he said. He glanced at Ben for instructions. "What do we do now?"

"Bury the mutt," Ben said curtly. He reached out for my arm again, and when I shrank back, he moved in closer, his fingers a steel grip. "I'll see she gets back to the house."

"But the shot . . . somebody might have heard." I realized now this was all Otto was worried about.

"They're all asleep. And if they're not, well, it won't be the first time a poacher's been shot here." He started to pull me toward the house now. I wanted to fight, to resist him somehow, if not to break free, at least to touch the poor faithful dog at my feet one more time. "Come along," Ben said, and forced me to walk along beside him. I tried to look back at Otto, bending over the dead animal, but Ben's grip was so hard on my arm I could do nothing but follow.

"Let me go!" I said, trying to catch my breath. "If you don't, I'll scream."

"No, you won't," he said grimly. "It would start too many questions I don't think you want to answer."

Why is the moon still high? I thought dully as Ben forced me up the road to the main house. Surely it must be late by now, and yet I knew I had no idea of how much time had passed. The road was a lacework of black shadows and patches of gray light where the moon managed to slit through the trees overhead. Ben's grip never loosened on my arm; he walked so swiftly that I had to hurry to keep from being dragged by him, my other hand trying vainly to keep the skirt of my gown out of the way.

When we reached the last of the trees of the side road and could see the house clearly ahead of us, as quiet and dark as it had been when I had fled from it, he stopped for a moment. The dark windows seemed to reassure him that no one had heard him kill Thor. Even the window in the far tower was dark now, I noticed almost automatically.

"We'll stop here for a minute," he said. There was nothing of the servant in his voice now. Somehow, standing there under the dark trees there was something in his voice that seemed familiar. Somewhere it belonged outside Storm's End, I'd heard it before. But I could not think . . .

He turned to me, his face dark in the shadows, only his glittering eyes showed that he was studying my face carefully.

"If you're smart, you'll keep your mouth shut about what happened tonight."

"You can't frighten me." I managed to twist free of his grip then, or perhaps he let me.

"Oh, yes I can." A wry smile twisted his lips and I could see his white teeth in the darkness of his face. "You of all people should know that."

He reached out for me again, but now his grip was different, not gentler or even less restraining, but rather as if he were holding a bird he had no intention of letting escape. "I always thought you were a beauty," he whispered, staring down at me.

And in that moment, I knew.

I had to get away from him, before he saw what must be dawning in my eyes. If he once suspects . . . I shivered a little then, although I was not cold, but the touch of his hands on my shoulders made my skin crawl.

"They may forgive you for killing Thor," I said coldly, forcing myself not to look at him. "But not if you try to rape me."

He dropped his hands then, stunned that I had guessed his thoughts. In that one free moment, I turned and ran across the empty park toward the house. I did not think he would dare to follow me; once he saw me safely inside the house there was little more he could do. And I must not let him risk seeing my face again, reading in my eyes the knowledge that had come so suddenly.

I pushed the great doors open and went inside, closing the doors firmly behind me. Not caring whether I was heard or not, I pushed the heavy bolt back into place and started up the long stairs to my room. No dark shadows in the hall could frighten me now, no fears of ghosts or ancient memories. Locked in this great old mansion, I was more free than I had been since the accident two long months ago. I was free because the sickness was over, the dark wall of amnesia had been breached the moment Ben had put his hands on me. The past was no longer a mystery. It had all come back, just as the doctors had hoped it would, all because of one small accident . . . the touch of a cruel man's hands.

I knew at last who I was.

Twenty

My name is Rosemary Carr. I was born in Bosworth, a small town in New Hampshire. I am not twenty-four, celebrating my twenty-fifth birthday, as they have claimed. I am twenty-three.

I have lived all these years in Bosworth, under the care of my aunt, my father's sister. In one instance what I have been told and what is the truth are the same: I am an orphan. I can remember now the pain of when I was eleven and my Aunt Marian took me in her arms and gently told me that my parents were dead. A plane crashing off a small Caribbean island had ended the first vacation my parents had had in years. From then on, my home was to be with Marian.

She was a kind woman, clever and gentle. She'd never had much desire to marry, I realized as I grew older, content with her independence and the life she had made for herself as a schoolteacher. Not that there hadn't always been men who wanted to marry her. But when she took me into her life I think I satisfied forever what needs she had for love and companionship.

It was a happy life, growing up in that small town. It had a quality of peace that I think has disappeared from most of the rest of the world. The changing of the seasons, the green sprouts of spring in the small garden in front of our pre-Revolutionary white cottage meant more than reports of wars and disasters in the world outside. In the winter there was the crisp crackle of snow underfoot, the clear blue twilight sky waiting for the first evening star to appear, the warmth of hot chocolate in her small kitchen after an afternoon of skiing.

And the summers . . . hot but dry, the clear water of the streams unbelievably cold, the grass on the low hills a deeper green than seemed quite real. And then the autumn, coming in close on the summer days, chilling the nights of August and September just enough to remind you of the frozen winter ahead.

The autumn was my favorite time of the year. The leaves turned early, for we were far to the north, not far below the Canadian border. The trees grew vivid with bright reds and yellows and oranges, masses of color along the roads and high up into the hills.

They had already started to turn that September morning I had left Bosworth. I did not want to leave, and yet I knew there was no point in my staying. My aunt had died peacefully last spring, as gently as she had lived and luckily in no pain. She had had time to put her affairs in order and to give me the advice that made me leave this pleasant town.

*   *   *

It had been on my last birthday, the day she had given me the simple strand of pearls that had been in our family for so many years. I could remember that moment so clearly . . . I suppose that is why it was a strong enough impression to burn through the fog of my memory when I had received the Scarf of Sapphires.

"You mustn't stay here, Rosemary," she said as I looked at the necklace in the dining room mirror. I could see her face in the glass, it was serious as she watched me and that alone was strange, for I cannot remember my aunt when she had not been smiling.

"Why?" I looked at her, bewildered. "I love it here."

"I'm glad you do, Rosemary. You know what a joy you've been to me. And now I feel a little guilty. Your whole life has been in this town. I should have sent you away to school, I suppose. But I was selfish. I so loved having you here with me."

She smoothed the place mat on the gleaming table in front of her. We had just finished my birthday dinner, the tiny pink cake she had decorated so lovingly sat, half eaten, on the cut-glass stand before her. "I've been selfish," she went on, not looking at me. "Wanting you here. Even when it was time for you to go to college you only went a few miles down the road."

"Marian? I didn't want it any other way." I came over to her and touched her shoulder gently. "You know that. You're my family. It seems to me now you always have been."

"And what will you do with your life?" She looked up at me then, her eyes bright, searching my face. I could never lie to her when she looked at me like that.

"I . . . I don't know. Continue working at the college library, I suppose."

"And Ned?"

I couldn't face her when she asked about him. Ned Garland and I had grown up together: grammar school, high school and even the nearby college. We'd gone from sharing sled rides as children to high school dances. Now he'd taken over his father's farm and it was unspoken between us that someday we would marry. But I knew, and so did Marian, that I didn't love Ned. I was fond of him as a brother but that was not enough to make a happy marriage. I could not make him as happy as Sally Wayne would, Sally who had loved him in silence all of her twenty years.

"I . . . I don't know what to do about Ned," I said finally.

"Has he said anything?"

"Not yet. He seems to feel he doesn't have to."

"Rosemary, sit down for a minute." I took the chair opposite Marian and looked at her. Her wise eyes never wavered but there was an understanding smile curving her lips.

"I want you to be happy," she said carefully. "And if I thought Ned would make you happy, I wouldn't say a word. But I think we both know that . . . affection isn't enough between two people. Not if they're going to share their lives." She hesitated for a moment, as if allowing me the chance to contradict her, but I could say nothing.

"Rosemary, there are a lot of very good things about life in a small town like this. And I'm glad you've been happy here. But one of the bad things is that you can drift into a relationship with someone not because you desire it or need it, but simply because you've met no one else."

"Perhaps I won't marry at all," I ventured. "You didn't."

"Who could measure up to my standards?" And she laughed, taking the tension out of the room. "But I think you'd be happier married. If it's to the right man."

"And you think I'll meet him someplace else?"

"You might." Her eyes were serious again. "It's one thing to choose life in a small town, if you've seen other places. It's another thing . . . not a good one . . . just to settle into it, because you lacked the courage to try anything else."

"Marian?" Her words had startled me more than I liked. "Do you think I'm afraid of the outside world?"

"I don't know. And neither do you. We've both been so protected here. I want you to promise me that if anything should happen to me . . ." She paused, and we both knew she was talking about the pains her heart had given her the past year. "Or even if it doesn't, that you will take a year and live away from this town. Rent the house, if you can't bear to part from it forever, go someplace else. A city . . . or another part of the country. Or even Europe. But see something of the world before you settle down for the rest of your life."

She reached out then, across the table, and took my hand, her eyes holding mine. "Will you promise?"

I could not argue with her, not when I knew she was right.

"I promise, Marian."

That had been in February. Marian died in May and it took most of the summer to get her small affairs in order. There was enough money in her estate to allow me a year or more of freedom if I wished it and with Ned's help I managed to rent the house, for I could not bear to leave it forever. The proposal I had been half dreading, for I had no desire to hurt Ned, came at last and as gently as I could I refused it. I think, in a way, Ned was almost relieved, which, while it may not have been good for my vanity, made leaving Bosworth that much easier.

It was a bright September morning when I finally set out. I'd packed only my clothes in Marian's car (now mine, as was everything in her estate, for I was her only relative) and left the keys of the house with Ned, as the new tenants were not to arrive until the school term began.

It was a good day to start a journey, sunny and warm enough to ride with all the car windows open. Deep as my roots had been in the town, there was an excitement in me when I made the turn at the crossroads and started down the highway away from Bosworth.

Marian was right, I thought. I should get away. I had no plans, no job waiting for me anywhere. I was completely free for the first time in my life. And while I knew there would be many days and nights ahead of me when I would be lonely and long deeply for my home and the life I'd left, this morning I could only feel the exhilaration of going out to face the unknown.

I drove steadily through the morning, stopping only to pick up bread and cheese and some apples for a picnic when I should feel hungry, and by midafternoon, I was in New York State. I suppose I had some vague idea of reaching the city by nightfall, although I had made no plans.

It must have been around three that afternoon when I stopped for my picnic by the side of the road. It was pleasant under the old trees, there were no nearby houses and I had a feeling of peace and privacy that I'd thought I'd left behind me when I had driven away from my home that morning. After I'd finished my meal, I started for the car again and faced the first problem of the day.

The car wouldn't start. It had always had its own quirks, which Marian usually managed to handle, but no matter how I tried to remember the various tricks she had used on the motor, nothing seemed to work. I grew hot and impatient, remembering how I had ignored Ned's warning to have the car overhauled before I started the trip. And then my irritation began to disappear as I realized I might be quite a long way from help. I couldn't remember seeing any gas stations on the road behind me, not for many miles, and I had no idea what lay on the road ahead of me. I was not on a highway, just a narrow country road that I had turned into because it had looked so quiet.

Quiet, it was. There had been no traffic at all during the time I had had my leisurely lunch and I now realized it might be a long time before anyone would pass that I might appeal to for help. And they might not be willing to stop. I had a brief thought of having to spend the night on the road and suddenly the day did not seem as cheerful as it had before.

And then I heard a car approaching. It was a large black limousine, the kind of car that one would expect to see in the city, carrying a financier to Wall Street or elegant ladies off for an afternoon of shopping. I stood in the middle of the road and waved my hands frantically.

The car pulled sharply to a stop and the young man driving practically leaped out of the car. He was wearing blue jeans and a tight tee shirt across his muscular chest and he looked as if he would have been more at home on the seat of a motorcycle than driving a stately limousine.

"What are you doing here?" he said, almost shouting. And then, as he came nearer, his face changed. "Sorry, I thought . . . what's the problem?"

"Please, I can't seem to get my car started."

I was so thankful to have somebody to help me, I didn't really notice his face. He was handsome, I knew that; but he hadn't the kind of looks that had ever appealed to me. There was something insolent in his face, insolent and a little cruel.

He gazed at me for a long moment and I was suddenly aware of how brief my tan cotton shorts were and that my pink sleeveless blouse, so freshly starched that morning, was now, with the heat of the afternoon, clinging tightly to my body.

"Can you help me?" I said.

He went at once to the motor of the car. "For one thing, you need water," he said after he had examined the car briefly.

I felt very stupid suddenly. "I . . . I didn't think of that."

"Is there a stream around here?"

"Back behind those trees. I . . . . I had lunch there." I pointed off to the side of the road.

"You got a bucket?" I shook my head no, feeling more incompetent than ever. "Never mind. I've got one in the car." He turned then and went back to the limousine.

I took the moment he fished in the trunk of his limousine to fasten the top button of my blouse. There was something about the young man that made me feel uneasy about the way he had looked at me. But he was my only help if I didn't want to spend the night on the road and there was no sense in offending him.

He came toward me, swinging a small bucket lazily. "Where's this stream?"

"Over here." I started ahead of him into the thick grass by the side of the road. Past the trees a little stream burbled and splashed; it had been pleasant to dip my feet in, while I ate, and I had even thought of a quick swim before I started down the road again, knowing I could not be seen by any car passing by.

The young man followed me closely, without saying a word. When I reached the stream, he bent silently and filled the pail with water. I noticed lettering on the side of the bucket: "Storm's End." It must be some sort of lodge or resort, I thought. Where he works. That might explain his driving the limousine. Probably he was on his way to pick up some guests when I had stopped him.

"Do you work around here?" I said, more to break the silence than to make conversation.

"In a manner of speaking," he said. His voice was cold and impersonal; he obviously wasn't interested in talking.

We made several trips with the bucket, filling the empty water tank of the car. And when even that did not make the engine start, he set to work with a set of tools he brought from his limousine. Trying to be friendly, I found myself chattering on. Or perhaps the few questions he asked were deliberately designed to find out where I was going and what my life was like. I didn't realize at the time how much he knew about me until after he had finished with the car and the motor was once more working.

We had gone back to the stream then, to wash the grime off our hands, for I had managed to be of some help to him. It was then he turned to me, his eyes narrow as slits.

"So you're not expected anywhere," he said. "Just off by yourself to have a good time." There was a new note in his voice now, and I stepped back instinctively. The air around us was very quiet now; there was no breeze rustling the trees and, standing by the stream, I could not see the road even if a car were to pass.

"I . . . I'm very grateful for your help," I said. "I'd like to pay you for it." I started to move away from him. "I'll get my purse from the car."

"Oh, I don't think that's necessary." He reached out quickly and grabbed my wrist. "There are other ways of paying me."

And then he pulled me close to him, his hard chest tight against my body, both of my wrists held in his strong hands so that I knew I could not break free.

"Please . . . you're hurting me!" I tried to move my mouth away from his lips as he sought mine hungrily.

"It doesn't have to be that way," he whispered. "Most of my girls say it's fun."

I tried to struggle but there was no way to break his grip. He pressed his face forward again, his lips tight on mine. And then anger swept over me and I bit down on his lips, hard. He stepped back then, letting go of my hands, his eyes blazing. And before I could move, his hand came up and slapped me.

It was a vicious slap that snapped my head to one side. Through the red glare that instantly veiled my eyes I could see him lunging forward. I took a step back, but my foot tripped over something, a branch or rock, and I felt myself falling before he could reach me.

The last thing I saw was the bucket, fallen on its side in the high grass, the lettering painted on it standing out in the afternoon sun: "Storm's End."

*   *   *

I closed my bedroom door behind me. Here, at least, I was safe, in this warm rose-colored room that I knew now had never been mine.

It was all a lie! It kept going through my head until I thought I would scream, ripping the silence of the dark house around me. None of it had been the truth! From the very beginning . . . my mind went back to that first afternoon at the hospital, Hale standing in the doorway . . .

Hale.

That was the hardest thought to face. Somehow, all along, I'd suspected Irene and Mrs. Janeck, Ben and Otto, had felt that there was some secret behind their faces, something I didn't know.

But not Hale!

Nothing he had said, none of the kindness I'd seen in his eyes, none of the gentleness in the touch of his hands, had been real. It had all been a trick, a lie. He, of all people, knew I was not his wife.

And why? I dragged myself over to the pink velvet chaise longue and slumped onto it, knowing, as I did, the reason for all of this elaborate masquerade. Without effort, I could see the library desk covered with papers and bankbooks, the fortune that belonged to Constance Avery Britton. Wars have been fought for less than the money that held this house together. And if they could use me as a pawn in their game, for I knew they were all in it now, why not?

Were they all in it? I sat up straight then, trying to think. My uncle . . . or at least the man they had told me was my great-uncle . . . could he be part of this scheme? Was he truly so blind that he could not recognize that I was an imposter? He had not seen his great-niece for four years at least, but even so . . . Could this deception be some sort of cover for the way he had handled her fortune over the years?

And the Princess . . . how much did she know? It was hard to think of her as part of this conspiracy, but all this long day, ever since I'd met her, I'd felt there was something hidden behind her eyes, something unspoken. Even if she had only met the real Constance once, there was nothing wrong with Olivia's sight or her memory.

And then I felt myself growing cold.

The one question that I had not allowed myself to think pushed its way into my tired brain and would not go away until I faced it.

Where was the real Constance Britton?

There was no escaping it now, I had to find the answer to that question. Was she dead? And if so, how had she died? And in what way? Or was she still alive? Here, in the house? I saw again the lighted window in the tower that had tormented me, heard again the scream that had split the silent afternoon air that second day of my stay here.

If she's alive and a prisoner, *why?* What have they done with her?

I shivered then, the fur-lined coat no longer warm. Who could I trust?

And then I saw the strong face of Dr. Gallard, his dark eyebrows looking at me sardonically . . . could he have suspected the trick we had all been playing? And yet he said I was to trust him, that he was my friend . . .

I had to believe him, surrounded as I was by liars and cheaters . . . and maybe worse. Killers.

I realized now the danger I was in. They had Constance Britton's fortune now, or Hale would have it, as her husband, if anything happened to her.

To *me!*

The world had accepted me, the bankers and the lawyers, all through Matthew Avery's approval. I had served my purpose, for all of them.

I turned swiftly toward the door, as if I expected someone to enter. But it was the way it had been since I had closed it. I hurried across the room to lock it.

But there was no key.

The key had always been there! I'd seen it, glittering in the light, every day. Only now it was gone. I got down on my hands and knees and felt the carpet around it. It was not there.

I looked up then, twisting to face the door to Hale's dressing room, but even as I did, I knew that key too would be gone.

There was no way to lock myself into safety. There was no way now to lock them out.

THE SIXTH DAY

Twenty-one

I did not sleep that night, I did not even try. I pulled on my warm red robe and curled up in the center of that enormous bed and tried to think. For the first time since I regained consciousness in the hospital, I wished I had a cigarette, although I had never been much of a smoker before.

The thoughts whirled through my head. What a fool I'd been! Even with the amnesia, there had been so many signs that I didn't belong here. Otto not recognizing me . . . the faded laundry mark on my blouse with its telltale initial of *C!* The moment I'd worried about staining my yellow skirt and the price of a cleaning bill. As if anyone as rich as Constance Avery had ever thought of that! The rooms I never remembered! Thor, with his first instinct to attack . . .

And the girl in the shop in town! She had known I was a lie. No wonder she had been so angry. And no wonder they had been so very careful not to let me go down into the town of Avery, where people would still remember the real Constance.

But what was I to do now?

I had not bothered to pull the drapes and I could see the sky was beginning to turn softly gray outside the windows. I got up then and stretched my body. I had to get away from Storm's End, but how?

I thought once more of Matthew and the Princess. I did not think they were part of this conspiracy but if I confided in them, pleaded for help . . . and it turned out I was wrong? Then I would have lost the one protection I had . . . that no one, as yet, in the house knew that I had regained my memory.

If I can just get to Dr. Gallard, I thought, over and over until the words seemed so loud in my brain I was sure the house around me must hear them.

Only *how?* How could I get away?

When it was seven-thirty by the little gilt clock, I ran a hot bath and tried to prepare myself for the day ahead. No one must suspect what had happened. I hung up the heavy velvet ball gown carefully and even remembered to retrieve from my long coat the note that had warned me the night before.

Holding the card in my hand gave me the first moment of peace I'd felt that long night. Someone was trying to help me. But who? And the warning reminded me, not that I needed it, that it was no imaginary danger I was facing.

After my bath I picked a simple dress of gray wool, warm enough that I would need no jacket if I found a chance to get outside. I sat down in front of the dressing table mirror and studied my face carefully. I was pale, too pale, the sleepless night showed only too clearly. For once I was grateful for the cosmetics in the drawers; they managed to give me some semblance of the happy look I had had the night before.

I don't know whether I expected my door to be locked, but it opened as easily as always and I started down the long stairs to breakfast. They must not guess, I told myself, over and over again. They must not know what has happened.

As I crossed the main hall I could hear sharp angry voices from the dining room. There was the deep rumble of the man I still thought of as "Uncle Matthew," crossing the clear tones of Hale.

"There's no reason for such legalities, young man. Whatever has happened to her memory, Constance is perfectly capable of handling her own money."

I could tell, from the hall outside, Matthew was indignant.

"I just thought . . ."

Hale broke off as I came into the room. They had all turned toward me . . . Irene, serving herself at the sideboard, apparently not part of the argument; Matthew at the head of the table; Hale, standing to one side, a legal paper in his hand. Only the Princess did not look up. She sat at Matthew's right, elegant in a bone-white suit, calmly finishing her breakfast.

"Con . . ." Hale was angry, I could see, but there was something more. There was a flush to his cheeks, as if he had been caught doing something wrong. Matthew looked up then, trying to focus his clouded eyes on where I was standing.

"Constance? Is that you?"

Don't let them guess, I thought as I crossed the room. Don't let them know I am in any way different from the way I was last night. I bent over the old man and kissed him lightly on the cheek.

"Good morning, Uncle," I said, and was surprised that my voice did not shake. "Hale, dear . . ." I managed to slide a kiss on his cheek without letting his eyes catch mine. "You both seem in loud voice this morning."

"Just . . . business, Con." Hale sat down again sulkily.

"Does Constance know about this?" Matthew's voice had lost none of its anger. I walked over to the sideboard and began to serve myself from the covered silver dishes. I could feel Irene's eyes on me, but I did no more than nod good morning before I busied myself fixing my breakfast.

"Know what, Uncle?" I managed to get my plate back to the table without spilling it. Opening one of the great square napkins, I tried to concentrate on my breakfast.

"Your husband wants you to sign a power of attorney, so that he's in charge of your fortune." There was no doubt in the way that Uncle Matthew phrased this, what he thought of the idea.

Let me be clever, I prayed. They mustn't suspect. But I knew what it meant. To give Hale that power, Hale and Irene and the others, then truly I would be a prisoner, completely at their mercy.

And so would the *real* Constance Avery, if she was still alive.

"I think it's a very good idea, Uncle." I managed to say it coolly. Let them think I'm on their side. At least at first. "With my memory gone, who knows what might happen in the future?"

"That's what I was trying to tell him," Hale said, and I could hear his gratitude. "I had the paper drawn up, and I thought as long as he and the Princess were here to witness it . . ."

So that was the plan! How could I delay it without making it seem suspicious? But if I didn't, once the paper was signed they would have no further use for me. And there was no one anywhere in the world who knew where I was, or would be concerned. They must have learned that already through Ben . . .

"Oh, there's no reason to do it today, Hale," I said, trying to keep my voice calm. I didn't dare look at him, or at Irene, who had turned suddenly and was staring at me intently. I made myself smile at the Princess. It seemed safer to look at her. But she did not smile back. Her eyes narrowed a little as she watched me. I glanced down at my plate again quickly.

"Why not?" Without even looking, I knew that Hale was frowning.

"We'll have to go into the city soon anyway, to make our travel arrangements. Surely it would be better if we did all this at the bank . . . when we decide what to do about money and letters of credit?"

"This is a legal matter, Constance. It's got nothing to do with banks." Hale's voice was gruff; I knew he was trying to find a flaw in my answer to twist me into what he wanted me to do.

"All the better. I should get to know the family lawyers in any case, shouldn't I, Uncle Matthew?" I reached out then and touched his gnarled hand. "It's been so long since they've seen me, they won't even know me. And if they can actually see this . . . well, amnesia thing, won't it make it easier? In case something should happen . . . in the future?"

There, I thought! Let's see them try to wriggle out of that! It gives everybody what they want . . . and it gives me at least a few more days.

"That makes sense. Surely you agree to that, Hale?" My uncle turned his head toward Hale. Under cover of raising my coffee cup, I caught Hale shoot a doubtful glance at Irene and saw her head nod slightly. So you *are* in it together, I thought, although I'd known it long before.

"I suppose that's best," Hale said sulkily, flinging the document on the table beside his place. For the first time since I had entered the room, I took a deep breath. Instantly my brain warned me: be careful, you're not safe yet!

"Did you sleep well, Uncle?" That seemed as harmless a question as any I could ask.

"Lightly, child. I found myself lying in the dark . . . listening for voices long since gone." There was sadness in his eyes now, and his thin hand shook a little.

"Nonsense, Matthew. I could hear you snoring clear through the door of my room." The Princess's voice was deliberately brisk. Whatever sentiments she might feel, she was not going to let Matthew indulge in them.

And, again, as he had the night before, he surprised me by laughing. "Dear Olivia! Will you never let me have the fun of being an old man?"

"Never," she replied sedately, ignoring her own silver hair and ravaged face. "I don't like old people."

And that made him laugh again. It was only later that I considered she might have made her acrid remark deliberately, to lighten the tone of the meal. And to move it safely away from conversation about the Avery fortune.

The rest of breakfast passed without incident. It was decided that Matthew and the Princess would return to the city that day, Ben driving them back in the great limousine. I suggested that they might want to see more of the house before they left, but Irene managed to drop a sufficient number of hints as to the condition of the empty rooms to discourage them.

"No unpleasant memories of this house, Constance," Matthew said as he left the dining room, his arm in mine. "I have too many happy memories of Storm's End to want them destroyed."

Hale and Irene tactfully took him for a short walk on the grounds while the Princess went upstairs to finish her packing. On impulse I watched the others go out the main doors and then followed Olivia upstairs.

"Princess?" I stopped her when we reached the landing. "I wonder if I might ask a favor?" A plan was beginning to form in my head . . . if I could get just one person on my side!

"Yes?"

I could see her child's body stiffen, her face once more an imperious mask. Why are you on guard? I wondered again how much a part of this conspiracy she was.

I made my face as innocently demure as I could. "You'll be going to the city by way of the main highway. Could you drop me off at Dr. Gallard's on the way?"

"Why?" Her dark eyes stared at me intently. I felt that they could pierce through my skull into my brain and read every secret. But she was my only chance.

"We're supposed to work on my memory every day. I've been rather lax about it, I'm afraid. And also Hale doesn't seem to think he's doing any good." I didn't dare look at her. I stood there, smoothing the pleats of my skirt, aware I probably appeared simpleminded in addition to everything else. "But if we are going to be traveling soon, I think I should make every effort I can. While I'm here."

I looked up at her then. She hadn't moved, she was still standing in the square of weak sunlight that came down through the skylight at the top of the house. Her face was as frozen as a professional gambler's, but there was something warmer in her eyes.

"Doesn't Hale want you to see the doctor?" she said, her voice carefully without comment.

"It isn't that. He wants me to be well, I'm sure of it. But if he has to drive me there, then wait for the session, and then drive me back, well, it takes so much time away from his painting. I don't like to do that." And then I added hastily: "I don't mind walking back, but it's a little far to walk both ways."

And then she surprised me again. She stepped forward and put her hand gently on my sleeve. "Of course, child. We'll be happy to help you." And she smiled, her delicately painted face breaking into tiny wrinkles. She stood there for a moment and I could see her choosing her words carefully. "You've made Matthew very happy, my dear. I can never be grateful enough to you for that. The reason we must hurry back to the city is . . ." She dropped her hand from my arm, and it was almost as if she were alone, talking to herself. "He's due to go into the hospital this evening. This is his last venture out."

"He will be well?" Whatever part Matthew Avery had played in this conspiracy, I could not feel indifferent to him now.

"Of course he will." Olivia's voice was firm. She would allow no doubt to enter. And then she added softly: "I could not bear to lose him now."

My plan succeeded, and even the departure was easier than I had expected. Hale looked startled when I appeared on the front steps with the Princess, a gray cashmere sweater over my dress, the warning note hidden in my purse, obviously prepared to leave with them. But the Princess was in complete charge, arranging herself and me and Matthew in the back seat with a regal disregard of everybody else's opinions. The mention of Dr. Gallard caused another quick glance between Hale and Irene but they made no serious protests and no one seemed anxious to argue with Matthew, who was once again showing the belligerence he had displayed at breakfast. The walk around the grounds had obviously made him unhappy and he flared out at all of us in sullen impotent anger.

"Shall I pick you up in an hour, Constance?" said Hale, leaning into the limousine to make one last protest.

"Nonsense," said the Princess, her back stiff. "The child's peaked, a good walk home will do wonders for her." And then she added a last remark that had different meanings for all of us and effectively silenced Hale: "After all, what can happen to her now?"

The drive toward Dr. Gallard's house was short in distance, but for me, trying hard to chatter innocently, to please my two elderly companions and not to look at Ben sitting so silently in the front seat, it seemed to last for hours. At last we pulled up in front of the doctor's cottage. It was so like the house I'd left in Bosworth, I thought suddenly. No wonder I had warmed to it at first sight.

I bent over to kiss the man I still called uncle and got out of the car, trying to ignore Ben as he held the door for me formally. The Princess held my hand for a long moment and then, pulling me close, she whispered gently, "Remember, child, you are not alone. Once this crisis with Matthew is over . . ."

He interrupted then, testily. "Olivia, stop whispering. You know I can't stand secrets."

She gave one last squeeze of my hand and then I pulled away and started up the driveway to the doctor's house. Behind me I could hear the motor start again and the car pull away.

I'm free, I thought. I've made it!

Now to convince Dr. Gallard.

*   *   *

He stood there, holding the cream-colored card of warning that I had found last night, staring at it as if to memorize it. Why doesn't he say something? I thought.

I'd been here at least twenty minutes, I thought, quiet for the first time since I'd entered his house. Whatever plan I had to approach him sensibly, to state what had happened coolly and quietly, had disappeared as soon as he opened the door. The words had come pouring out, the whole story, jumbled together until I was not sure that it made sense and would repeat like a chorus, over and over again, "I'm not Constance Britton! I'm Rosemary Carr!"

I'd told him everything . . . about my Aunt Marian and the town in New Hampshire, I think I even mentioned Ned. And that quiet afternoon by the road, and Ben, and what he'd tried to do.

I'd told him everything, and still he stood there silently. Oh, God, if *he* doesn't believe me, what shall I do?

His face was as professionally impersonal as it had been during those long weeks when he came to see me in the hospital. But when, finally, he raised his head and looked at me, I saw in his eyes an expression I had never seen before.

"You poor child," he said.

And it was as if my last reserve of strength had collapsed. I found myself sobbing, the tears pouring down my face as if they would never stop. He was beside me instantly. I could feel his strong arms holding me, feel the muscles of his shoulders under his thin sweater against my cheeks and for one moment, I felt I had at last reached safety.

"You *do* believe me." I choked it out, my words muffled as he held me. "Say that you do."

"Child, child, of course I do." I could feel his hand smoothing my hair, comforting me. "I've wanted to from the beginning."

I pulled free from him then, searching his face with my eyes. It was a handsome face, I knew now I'd always thought that. Not beautiful the way Hale's was, with fine, well-bred features, but strong; a stubborn chin, the thick dark eyebrows over his deep-set eyes, the crisp black hair, the clean line of his firm jaw.

"What do you mean . . . you 'wanted to'? 'From the beginning'?"

He looked at me and I could see he was weighing his words. Then, finally, he sat back, his eyes still on mine.

"Constance . . ."

"*Rosemary*. Remember?" I couldn't help giggling a little. We were going to have to start to know each other all over again. Somehow it was something that even then I was looking forward to. He smiled back, realizing the incongruousness of the situation.

"All right. *Rosemary*. A very pretty name. It fits you much better than Constance. I always felt that was too cold, too formal for you." He reached out and held my hands, staring at me intently. "Now, Rosemary, we might as well start with some of the things that I know that *you* don't."

I could have sat there forever, safe, with his hands holding mine, but I forced myself to concentrate on what he was saying. How could I have ever thought this man cold and impersonal? When even now all I wanted . . . I could feel myself starting to blush.

He looked at me with some amusement. "You're thinking of the way I treated you at the hospital, aren't you? Well, there was a reason for that." He dropped my hands and reached for his pipe on the low table beside the sofa.

"Let me tell you a story," he began as he filled his pipe. "Once upon a time a stubborn, opinionated, rather difficult Frenchman who is also a doctor and a psychiatrist, came to America to study. After several years, he decided to write a book about what he had learned and, having friends who worked at a hospital in upstate New York, he rented a house not too far away and prepared to start on his work."

"Do you really think of yourself as stubborn and opinionated and difficult?" I broke in. "It's so like my own description of you."

"Don't interrupt, Con . . . Rosemary." But he was smiling too. "At any rate, he found a comfortable house in a quiet town. It was summer. He didn't know anybody, and that was the way he wanted it. Then one night his peaceful life was disturbed."

"The hospital." I thought of that silent room, Mrs. McKenzie, waking and not knowing where I was.

"No, child, that was later. No, this interruption was last July. A woman came to my door late one night. A woman who identified herself as Esther Janeck, from a house nearby called Storm's End."

I sat up straight then. He was right. This was something I did not know.

"She insisted I come back to the house with her." He was lighting his pipe now, taking his time, letting his words sink in. Finally he went on: "She said she needed a doctor and the one in town was out. She was worried, distracted, close to hysteria. There'd been some kind of accident, would I come?"

"And you did."

"I didn't have much choice. I think she would have pulled me out of the house by force, delicate as she is. She kept wringing her hands on the ride back, but she wouldn't tell me what was wrong, or even who was in trouble. Over and over again she kept muttering, 'They mustn't know. Promise me you won't tell anybody.' I tried to reassure her but it did no good. She just kept saying the same things again and again.

"When we finally reached the house, she let me in the main door. No one else seemed to be in the house. When I asked her if she was alone, she said, 'They're all gone, in the city. That's why I couldn't take the chance . . .' All the time she was leading me up the stairs . . . to the master bedroom of the house."

He was watching me carefully as he spoke, wondering about my reaction.

"My room? All rose brocade . . . with a balcony overlooking the river?"

"Yes. And in the bed was a young woman. Dark hair, blue eyes, somewhat of the same appearance as you. With one exception. Her face was twisted and tormented, her eyes savage, her arms punctured with the marks of drug addiction."

I felt myself wince and he reached out and touched my hand again gently.

"She was unconscious. The other woman, Mrs. Janeck, assured me she was not on drugs, had not been for a long time. But she was in a coma. Whether it had come about because someone had tried to cure her habit by making her stop at once and completely or whether it was something in her own mental state, I couldn't tell. Not at first. But she was as close to death as anyone I've ever seen."

He stood then and walked over to the bay window, not seeing the autumn garden outside, his eyes still in that terrible room. "I managed to save her," he said, finally. "I still did not know her name. The other woman, Mrs. Janeck, would not tell me. But at last the girl regained consciousness. She didn't want to know who I was, or what I was doing there. All she said was, 'Where's Hale? Where's my husband?'

"Mrs. Janeck tried to silence her, but she was too weak. The young woman kept twisting in the bed, she was getting angry, even with the sedative I had given her. 'I'm Constance Britton,' she said. 'Where's my husband?' I couldn't tell her and Mrs. Janeck wouldn't.

"When she finally fell asleep, Mrs. Janeck saw me downstairs. She made me promise not to say anything about this. When I told her I must see the patient again, that she needed help, Mrs. Janeck told me the young woman was to be taken to a private hospital the next day. She showed me to the door and told me there was no further need for me at Storm's End.

"I tried to call once or twice after that, but every time I identified myself, whoever answered would quietly hang up the phone. Then, in the village, I heard that Storm's End was closed, and, after a while, the whole incident seemed like a bad dream.

"Until one afternoon, Dr. Henderson from Six Counties Hospital called and told me he had a patient who seemed to be suffering from amnesia. Would I care to come and help the staff, since it was more in my field than theirs? I was told the patient was Constance Britton, Mrs. Hale Britton, brought there by her husband after an accident."

I began to realize what he must have been thinking all these weeks. "Only when you walked into the room, it wasn't the girl you'd seen at the house, it was me."

"Exactly. Who were you? Were you the real Mrs. Britton? That's what your husband said. Was the other woman an imposter? Or was it the other way around? Was yours a real case of amnesia? Or was it some sort of conspiracy?"

I got up and walked to his side. "So you couldn't believe me." But it wasn't an accusation, I was understanding now what had been going on behind that cold mask all this time.

"I wanted to, Rosemary." He looked down at me, his eyes troubled. "Then when you came back to the house, I began to be afraid for you. Afraid that somehow they were using you as a victim."

"So you suggested I walk into town. To find out who I was?" Suddenly everything was beginning to make sense now.

"I found the shop by accident. The man who runs it is friendly, interested in talking. He told me how he had bought the jewelry from Mr. Britton of Storm's End. He claimed that Hale had said something about his wife not liking it, but it was clear that the owner of the shop thought 'The Averys have fallen on hard times.' That was his phrase. He talked of having known Constance as a child . . . well, none of that seemed to fit in with what Hale had said, about there being some kind of animosity between the town and the family at Storm's End."

I was frightened now. The whole conspiracy seemed deeper some-how, the people involved more desperate. I wanted to feel the doctor's comforting arms about me once more, but I didn't dare move closer, not then.

Dr. Gallard seemed to sense what I was thinking. Without a word he opened his arms to me, and then, as simply as if we'd both been waiting for it for a long time, I raised my face.

And he kissed me.

Twenty-two

I will never know how long it was before we started to talk again about Storm's End, it may have been nearly half an hour. For we had something more important to discuss now . . . what we meant to each other, our future, our hopes. All these long weeks I had been fighting so hard against Alex . . . Dr. Gallard . . . and they now seemed to have been just a road I had to take to walk into his arms. With that first kiss I knew I had found what I had been hoping for all my life.

"But now we must be serious," Alex said finally, his arm around me as we sat together on the couch. I pushed back my hair and tried to look as sensible as I could. It was not a great success. Sitting close to him, feeling his arm on my shoulders, I wanted to think of nothing but him.

"I suppose so," I sighed, reluctantly.

"There'll be time for us, in the future." He had an engaging little-boy grin now, and I realized suddenly that marriage to a psychiatrist might have its difficulties. Could they always read your mind?

"We must go to the police, Rosemary."

That *did* bring me back to earth.

"Alex, we can't." He stared at me, puzzled. "Don't you see? They've been too clever."

"But, Rosemary . . ."

"No. Please listen to me. What happens if we got to the police? We tell them the whole story. They go back with us to Storm's End. Hale and Irene, all of them are very solicitous. Poor Constance, they say, looking at me so gently. She's had another bad turn. First she loses her memory, now she claims she's somebody else."

"They wouldn't dare." Alex's face was indignant. "I'd be with you . . . I'd testify to what happened this summer . . ."

"And Mrs. Janeck would deny it," I said, cutting in. "I don't know what hold they have over her, or how deeply involved she is, but she won't dare say a thing. And if we keep on protesting, they'll call my great-uncle. And the Princess. They believe I'm Constance Britton. They believe it enough to hand over her entire fortune to me."

That stopped whatever protest Alex might have made. He looked at me soberly for a moment. "Do you think they're part of this?" he asked.

"I don't know. But we don't dare count on their *not* being part of it."

"We could go back to your town . . . what was it? Bosworth? Bring the estimable Ned down here to identify you. Bring the whole town if we have to."

"Alex, all that would take time. Time for them to make their preparations. To get away even." And then I thought of something worse. "Time for them to kill the *real* Constance."

He stared at me. "You think she's still alive?"

"I'm practically positive of it. Alex, they never would have tried to kill her . . . once dead, where would her inheritance be? Matthew didn't like Hale, remember? So they would have had to keep her alive somehow until she received her fortune."

"Which you managed to do for her last night." His arm tightened around me again, protectively.

"But they couldn't be sure I'd get away with it. No, the real Constance must still be alive, somehow, somewhere." In my mind, I could see the lighted window in the dark towers. You're there somewhere, I thought. Only how do I find you?

"Mysteries within mysteries." He sighed.

"Surely you should be used to that. As a psychiatrist?"

"The *why* of things, yes, I can understand that. A failed artist, a chance at a great fortune, a headstrong young woman who'd never known her parents, retreating into drugs . . ."

"Not to mention what Uncle Matthew told us . . . If there is insanity in the family, that plus the drugs could very well have destroyed Constance."

"And if they'd presented her to Matthew in this condition . . ."

"They didn't dare, Alex. Can't you see? Matthew would have found some legal way to get her away from Hale, would have kept control of her fortune, probably would have even found some way to blame it all on Hale."

"Their great gamble lost." He moved uneasily. "But where did they get the idea of substituting you?"

"They couldn't have planned it in advance." My mind was working busily, I kept seeing that quiet place by the small stream, so far from the road. The tall grass, the sunlight on the fallen bucket, Ben coming toward me . . . "They must have had some idea that they could cure Constance by themselves. Without letting anybody know."

"Only it didn't work."

"Exactly. And after Ben tried to attack me by the stream and I fell . . . he must have panicked. Suppose, just suppose that he drove back to Hale and Irene and confessed everything. I don't quite know what his relationship to them is, but he's definitely part of it."

"Then what?"

"Hale's not a monster, Alex. No matter what's happened, I can't believe that of him."

Alex looked at me carefully, his eyes narrowing a little. Why, you're jealous, I thought. And, if I'm to be honest, I must admit I felt a great surge of joy.

"You're still fond of him?" he said, confirming my suspicions. I reached out and touched his arm.

"Alex, he means nothing to me. I know now he never has. But I don't think it's in his character to leave a girl unconscious by the side of a road.

"No," I went on, trying to reconstruct the scene. "I have a feeling they all went back to the stream. Probably I was just regaining consciousness. Remember the hospital said I kept repeating the words

'Storm's End' over and over again? I'd seen them on the side of the bucket as I fell, the last impression I carried with me."

"So there they were . . . with an injured girl suffering from amnesia, a girl who looked like Constance . . ."

"Or just enough," I interrupted. "No one had seen her in years, she'd been in Europe since she was twenty. And if they knew that Matthew's eyes were clouded with cataracts . . . well, they must have decided then to risk it."

We stood there silently for a moment. And then he took my arm and started us toward the front door.

"The police," he said. "Right now."

I pulled free and faced him. "Alex, we can't!"

He looked at me, puzzled. "I'm sure there's a way we can prove the whole story." There was a gleam in his eyes now. "Your car . . . if we can find the place where you stopped . . ."

"Alex, they would have hidden my car the first thing. Abandoned it miles from here, stripped of identification. Or else put it some place in Storm's End where they knew no one would find it."

That stopped him. He ran one impatient hand through his crisp hair. "What can we do?" he asked finally.

But I think we both knew the answer.

"It's very simple," I said quietly. "I have to go back to Storm's End."

"No!"

"Alex, it's the only way!"

"No! I absolutely forbid it, Rosemary. And I have the right to forbid you now."

I reached up and kissed him. How good it was to feel his arms around me! But I pulled myself free.

"Alex, listen to me . . ." Before he could argue again, I put my hand to his mouth. "Please listen."

He was quiet then.

"The only way to save that girl is if I go back and try to find her. I'm the only one who can."

"And if she's not alive?"

"At least I'll have tried. But I think she *is* alive. Alex, I don't think they ever meant to kill her. I think once they got the money they planned to take her back to Europe or someplace out of sight . . . that's what all this talk about traveling has meant."

"But to go back, to deliberately walk back into danger. My God, Rosemary, you can't think I'd let you do that!"

"But I won't be in danger, darling. No. Really!" I added as I saw him start to protest again. "As long as they don't suspect I've regained my memory, I'm still their pawn. Think how much easier everything will be for them if they can take me into the city, show me to the lawyers and the bankers, carefully backed by the fact that my Uncle Matthew has accepted me. That means whatever happens in the future, I've been accepted as the real Constance Avery."

I moved away from him then. It was too distracting to see his face, his dark eyes worried. "They can get her money then. All the money they want."

"And when do you think they will make that move? Take you to town?"

"Today's Saturday, Alex. They can't do anything before Monday at the earliest."

Monday! To think it had only been last Monday that I had left the hospital. It seemed years away now, standing in this low-ceilinged room.

"But what can you do if you go back to Storm's End? If you haven't found the girl by now?" He was beginning to see my reasoning, but he didn't like it.

"Alex, I couldn't find her before because I was afraid I was imagining things. Now I know the truth. She's there all right." I reminded him then of the scheme I'd devised to mark the windows in the old wing of the house.

"I thought I was going crazy that day . . . first I saw the unmarked window, then I didn't. I should have realized somebody must have spotted me and in the time it took me to get up to my bedroom, marked the hidden room." I remembered then Ben going up the stairs to the attic, searching for me. "It must have been Ben."

"But how? You were carrying the lipsticks."

"He could have taken some off the spots I'd marked on the other windows." It was beginning to be clear to me now. "Once he realized what I was doing. Then smeared it on the window in the room where they're keeping her. The hidden room."

"And you think it will be easier now to get her? When they've been guarding her night and day? That is, if there *is* a secret room. And if she still exists." His words were sarcastic but I knew it was only because he was worried.

"Alex, how I'm going to get into this secret room, I don't know. But I think I have a fairly good idea where it is . . ." I could see clearly the small wood-paneled room of the first Constance. And Irene, in the doorway, angry, ready to guard it. And then I thought of something else . . .

"The diary!"

Alex looked at me strangely.

"Alex, the diary I got last night! Written by the first Constance. If it covers the period when the old part of Storm's End was being built, if there is a secret room, surely there'd be something in there about it." I could feel myself growing excited. I could see the diary now where I'd left it last night, on the chest by my bed. All at once I couldn't wait to start back for the house.

"But suppose you fail." I looked at him then. There was no mistaking the concern in his eyes. So this is what love looks like, I thought. And knew that I would never forget it.

"I won't fail, Alex." I made my voice as confident as I could. "Besides, we've forgotten one thing. Someone in that house is trying to help me. Why else would they have left that note warning me?"

"It could have been the Princess. And now she's gone."

"No. The Princess and I talked alone, she would have said something. I think it was Esther." And then I couldn't resist teasing him. "Or perhaps it was Hale. Maybe he *does* care for me."

Alex grabbed me in a rib-crushing grip and I realized then it is not a good idea to tease a Frenchman in matters of the heart.

*   *   *

Soon after I made him drive me to the main gate of Storm's End. The gates were still open. Alex wanted to drive me all the way up to the house, but the look on his face would have given away our plans to anyone.

"You will call me tonight?" He held me close as we sat for one last good-by before I left the car.

"If I can."

"If you don't, I will come and get you tomorrow. And no one will stop me." His jaw was set stubbornly and I knew better than to argue.

"I'll call you tomorrow. Definitely. But we must not behave any differently than we have been. Too much depends on it."

I got out then and closed the door of the car. He gave me one last look, then, racing the motor, turned and drove back down the road toward his own house. When he was out of sight, I started up the gravel road.

But I was in no condition to face anybody. Not yet. Too much had happened since I'd driven down the long driveway with Matthew and the Princess and I was afraid of the sharp eyes of Irene and the others. I turned off the road then, down a path I'd not taken before.

I found myself missing the company of Thor. I would have felt so much safer if he had been with me. And I saw again his dead body on the road last night.

For a moment, I panicked. Alex was right. What was I doing coming to this house, deliberately walking into a trap that could lead to my death? For now that they had the Avery fortune and were free to leave Storm's End forever, they could not leave with *two* Constance Avery Brittons.

I started to walk faster, as if I could leave my thoughts behind. The path was growing narrower; it was barely a clearing through the brush now, but still I kept on, ignoring the branches that scratched at my face, the mossy ground damp beneath my feet.

It must have been about thirty yards off the main driveway that I saw the little building. It was fieldstone, like the rest of the buildings on the estate, a low structure like an icehouse, or someplace where the pumps that supplied the water for the main house might be kept. It seemed totally forgotten in the midst of this part of the park, surrounded by thick bushes, the trees nearby abandoned, dropping their dead branches as if no one had ventured into this part of the woods for years.

Except now I noticed this path under my feet had a twin running faintly alongside of it. The sort of marks a small car might make.

I stopped and stood there, absolutely still. The trees were thick over me. I could no longer tell if the weak sun was still out, the branches of the tall bushes were too thick around me.

There was no sound. I might have been the only person on earth. I knew I should go back, back to the main driveway. Compose my face and go up to the house and pretend that nothing had happened. Whatever had made the tracks to the small shed ahead of me could not change what I already knew. And yet I knew I had to see what was in the building, knew even if the whole plan Alex and I had agreed on exploded in my face, I still had to see if this was where they had hidden my car.

I started toward the building. Only now I was moving more cautiously, picking my steps with care, trying not to make any noise. There was no reason to suspect that anybody was nearby and yet I did not dare take a chance of being discovered. A branch snapped in my face and I let out a surprised gasp, but even as I did I put a hand over my mouth to stifle the sound.

The walls of the building had that cool, almost damp feeling of stone that has not been warmed by the sun for a long time. There were wide wooden doors on the near end of the building, solid, locked, with no windows. The doorway was wide enough that a car *could* have been driven through it.

I started to circle the building. There was no path now, just piles of damp leaves molding on the damp ground near the walls. I could walk on them without making any noise. The long side of the building had two little windows, but they were high up, a couple of feet above my head, and even by jumping, I could not see in.

I turned the corner. This wall was solid stone. If there was no way to see in on the fourth side of the building, whatever secrets the building held would stay secret.

But I was in luck. There were two windows on this side of the building as well, and almost directly under one of them, the stump of a dead tree. Someone had chopped the tree down, probably because it had leaned too heavily over the building. I thanked them silently as I climbed up on the stump.

The window was so dirty I could barely see inside. There was something in the far corner, half covered by a tarpaulin. I squinted my eyes and rubbed at the glass. I could see there were wheels under the canvas covering, but I couldn't quite be sure it was my car. But without a key to the stout doors, there was no way to be positive.

Only I knew . . . *knew* . . . this was where they had hidden my car.

I jumped down from the stump quickly and started back toward the main driveway. I didn't care now how much noise I made, I just wanted to be away from the building as quickly as possible. Somehow, feeling that my car was there, my few possessions still safe, gave me a feeling of confidence. With each step I was becoming more and more the girl who had been lost these two months. The girl Alex said he loved.

"What are you doing here?"

I'd stepped out of the underbrush onto the driveway and was starting toward the main house when I heard the voice behind me. I knew before I turned it was Otto. Had he seen which side of the road I'd come from?

"I'm taking a walk, Mr. Janeck," I said, as coolly as possible. I wasn't afraid of him now.

He looked at me, his small eyes taking in every detail of my appearance. "They were wondering where you were up at the house. They even called that doctor. He said you'd started back."

"It took longer than I thought."

"It don't pay to go roaming off the road. We got traps set in there." There was no mistaking the threat. "You could get hurt wandering around where you don't belong."

"I . . . I thought I saw some wild flowers." Don't let him question me about that. Let me think of something to say that will distract him. "Have you buried Thor?" I said, trying to keep my eyes firm on his eyes.

He nodded briefly. And then he smiled, a curiously little lopsided grin that showed his yellow teeth. "Now I'm to lock up the main gates. Since we ain't got no visitors any more."

"Ben isn't back from the city yet," I said, trying to sound like the mistress of the house. I started to walk away from him then, toward the house.

"He's got his own ways of getting in," he called after me, insolently. I kept my shoulders straight and pretended not to hear. Had he suspected what I'd seen? I'd been a fool to give in to my impulse to search the little building. It could have ruined everything if I'd been caught.

You mustn't make that mistake again, I told myself. Too much depends on your staying in complete control. If Otto mentions to Hale or Irene where he had seen me . . . I realized then I didn't have two days to discover Storm's End's secrets. Time was running short.

I might only have hours left.

No one was in the great hall when I entered the house. I ran swiftly up the stairs, trying to be as quiet as possible. Perhaps I might have time before lunch to study the first Constance's diary. Then maybe this afternoon, if Hale went to his studio and I could find some excuse to send Irene shopping, I might be able to find the secret room.

My bedroom had been put in order during the time I'd been away. The rose brocade spread had been placed neatly as always over the huge bed. The blue velvet portrait gown was packed in its oblong box, carefully nestled in tissue paper. The Scarf of Sapphires was still on my dressing table, each stone fitted into its proper place in the platter-sized case.

But the diary was gone.

Twenty-three

Curiously, I wasn't angry. I wasn't even very surprised. If I had guessed there might be some clue to the secret room in the old diary, it would have been foolish to think that they wouldn't have come to the same conclusion.

I stood there thinking, my fingers drumming the top of the chest by my bed where the diary had been. I could ask questions about it at lunch, but I dismissed that as soon as I'd thought of it. I could hear Irene being vague about the book, bantering back and forth with Hale about who had seen it last and where it was, both of them finally turning to me as they made a point of remembering that I'd taken it up to my room myself.

And then their pitying look, that look I knew so well when I made a mistake, when I said or did something that was wrong for Constance Britton.

No, I thought. I won't mention the diary is missing. Let them think it doesn't interest me, that I hadn't even noticed that it was gone. It might quiet them if they were getting suspicious. And their suspicions were my biggest fear.

If only Otto hadn't seen me!

I went down to lunch then. The Venetian mirror over the mantel told me I looked the same as always and I knew if I delayed seeing them it would only make me more nervous.

I could hear Hale and Irene talking quietly in the library as I came downstairs. How much you must have to talk about among yourselves, I thought, and then, putting on a bright smile, I opened the doors and walked in.

"Isn't it time for lunch?" I said. "I'm absolutely starving."

They looked up at me, a little startled. They'd been going over the legal papers I'd signed the night before and their expressions were almost guilty. Irene recovered first.

"We weren't sure you were back yet," she said.

"Oh, Dr. Gallard is really impossible," I pouted. "He keeps acting as if I'd made up my mind not to remember the past. As if I had any choice about it!" I came up to the two of them and linked arms with them both companionably. "Aren't you two hungry?"

"We . . . we were just going over your business papers," Hale said carefully.

"Oh, don't let's talk about that, not today. I had enough of that from Great-Uncle Matthew last night. Today I just want to relax and enjoy myself. Maybe Matthew and the Princess weren't a strain for you, but they were for me."

With my arms in theirs, I could feel them both relaxing. Good, let them think I'm being silly. Just don't let them suspect the truth.

Luncheon was a casual affair. I'd made up my mind to distract them as much as I could and while I still felt them eyeing me curiously from time to time, I kept the conversation light and inconsequential.

And all the time I was trying to find out what their plans were for the afternoon. For if the diary was gone, my only chance lay in questioning Mrs. Janeck. Somehow I had to get the truth out of her. And if she *had* left the warning note for me, she must have some desire to help.

Oddly enough, Hale solved the problem for me. We had finished lunch and Irene had led us to the library. Once again there were checks to sign, for various amounts, including one made out to Irene for her salary.

It was then I knew I had not much time left. They were putting their affairs in order.

Hale was talking, as he had through lunch, of when we would leave.

"Monday, I think, for the city," he said.

"Hale? So soon?" My mouth felt dry.

"I want to get out of here before the bad weather starts."

"Feels like we might get a storm today," Irene said as she gathered the checks together.

"It would be a little early for a blizzard," I answered, my voice tarter than I intended.

"There isn't any reason to stay, is there?" Hale was looking at me now, his eyes narrowing slightly.

"Noooo. I suppose not. But the house . . . it'll have to be closed up?"

"Let Mrs. Janeck do it. After all, you're paying her for just that." Hale's voice dismissed the problem lazily.

"But . . . clothes and things. There'll be mountains of packing to do, I don't even know what to take." I knew it was a weak excuse, but it was the only one that occurred to me. "And your paintings."

"We can come back later. If we have to. Let's get everything taken care of in the city first." I could see a look pass between Hale and Irene. The date had been agreed on.

We would leave Monday. And this was Saturday noon. Could I find Constance Avery in the time left? Not with the two of them here, watching me every moment.

And then, for the first time, my luck turned.

"Which reminds me, Irene," said Hale, crossing his long legs carelessly. "We'd better get a few of the local accounts straightened out before we leave. I don't want the natives forwarding the bills for the dinner after we're gone."

"Yes," she said, absently, busy with the thick checkbook and the other papers on the desk. She wasn't looking at him but I felt in a curious way as if something were being said between them, something I could not guess. "We could go around this afternoon, I suppose."

I felt my heart begin to pound. Anything that would take them out of this house for a while would get my wholehearted blessing. But I mustn't let them know, it could be another trap.

"Can't that wait? We don't have to drive down Monday, do we?"

"It's just a few little things, Con. The bill for the man who framed your portrait, I want to thank him personally." He came over and stood next to me, looking down with his face grave. "And I thought you'd want to be in town Monday. That's when your uncle's operation is scheduled."

Now I realized why they were rushing. They didn't dare be available to my great-uncle when he had recovered his sight. I made no further protest.

Irene went upstairs then to get a jacket and I was alone with Hale. It was harder now to make light conversation. I felt his eyes were studying me too carefully.

I walked away, over to the long windows of the library, and looked out at the park. The sun had given up its feeble struggle to come out, the sky was low and pewter gray, and far to the west I could see storm clouds building. And then I felt his hand on my shoulder.

"Oh! You . . . startled me."

"Constance?" He had the same look still on his face, suspicious, searching. "You seem . . . different today."

Oh, God, had he guessed? I made myself look up into his light blue eyes. It seemed impossible now that I could have ever found them attractive. His hands were like cold marble on my shoulders. Let me think of something . . . anything.

"But I *am* different." The words came out almost automatically. But it was a denial he was expecting and so my agreement surprised him. I made myself smile up at him even though it took all my strength not to break free of his grip and run . . . out of this room, out of the house, down the long road to Alex.

"I mean it, Hale. I feel like yesterday was examination day at school, and I've passed." He dropped his hands now, a little puzzled. "You knew how I dreaded seeing my great-uncle. All those memories and questions about the past I knew I couldn't answer. And now it's over. I just feel . . . free."

"Poor darling! I didn't realize it had been such a strain for you." And then he thought of something else . . . I could see it in his eyes as he remembered what had made him suspicious. "Is that why you went for a walk last night? In your nightgown?"

I felt my heart stop beating. So Ben *had* told him!

"Of course. Did Ben also tell you that he killed Thor?" My voice shook a little but maybe it would seem I was just concerned over the dog.

"The dog was a killer. He should have been taken care of long ago." Hale moved away then. I could see there were questions he didn't want to answer now, questions that if I were the real Constance I should ask.

"Hale, there was no excuse for what he did. That poor dog was only trying to protect me."

"You shouldn't have been outside." His voice was crisp.

"I just went for a walk. To relax enough to sleep. And I wasn't just in my nightgown. I had my coat over it." I made myself walk up to Hale, touching his arm gently. "After all, it wasn't as if I was going any place, dressed like that. How could I? And I knew I'd be safe, just taking a stroll on the grounds." Thank heaven I hadn't stopped to dress last night!

He glanced at me quickly but I was prepared for it and I knew my face revealed nothing more than my innocent concern.

"We couldn't have taken Thor with us anyway, Constance." He reached out for me again. I felt his long arms going around me, pulling me close. "Let's not think about it anymore. We've other things to talk about."

I knew my heart was beating too quickly. Surely he must feel it, even through his jacket. But I didn't dare pull away.

"You mean . . . the trip?" I said, trying to distract him.

"No. The two of us." He moved his hand to lift my chin up so that he could look into my eyes. The suspicion was still there but I could see something else now, that look he had had last night before we went down to dinner.

"You said there'd be time for us. When we were alone. We're alone now."

There was no mistaking what he meant. But behind the desire in his eyes there still lurked suspicion. Was this another test?

And then, before I could answer, we both heard another voice behind us.

"Not quite alone."

Irene was standing just inside the door to the main hall. She leaned against the doorway as if she had been there for some time and there was a wry smile on her face. But there was no mockery in her pale green eyes. "Sorry to interrupt you two lovebirds, but if we're going to make that trip, Hale, we ought to get started. It looks like there might be a storm brewing."

Hale dropped his hands from me and walked toward Irene purposefully. For a moment I thought he might hit her. I think she felt the same, for she stepped back, one hand suddenly clutching the leather jacket around her shoulders.

"Or have you changed your mind?" she said quietly.

He stopped short and looked back at me, almost embarrassed.

"You two go on, I've had enough trips outside for one day."

It was the only thing I could think of to say to break the silence, although neither of them had mentioned taking me with them.

"You'll be all right, Con?" There was obviously more Hale wanted to say, but with Irene in the room, it was impossible.

"Its nap time for me, Hale. You two run along."

He turned back to Irene. "You all set?" he said, and I realized he meant more than if she herself were ready. Is the real Constance locked up safely is what you mean, I thought bitterly. And Irene answered him just as enigmatically.

"Of course. Aren't I always?"

I stood on the steps outside the great main doors and waved good-by to them as they drove off in Hale's red sports car. Even after they were out of sight I made myself wait, just in case it was a trap and they decided to come back. A wind was starting to rise, ruffling the last leaves on the trees, bending the long grass of the park. Irene had been right, a storm was headed our way. I pulled my gray sweater tighter around my shoulders and went back inside.

If only Mrs. Janeck hasn't gone back to her quarters! I knew there was no possibility of forcing her to talk if her husband were around; he was too strong for both of us. But if I could find her alone . . . !

I went through the long dark dining room, through the small breakfast room and into the butler's pantry beyond. There was no sign of her. I walked through the immense kitchen beyond the pantry. I'd never really seen it before. It made me understand better than anything else in the house the scale of living the Averys had enjoyed in their golden years. The stoves and refrigerators, the long marble-topped tables for baking, the huge butcher's block; the kitchen was equipped to feed a hotel full of guests.

And it was empty.

"Mrs. Janeck?" I could hear my voice echoing in the big empty room. There was a door at the far end. I walked toward it and opened it. A narrow iron staircase led down into the cellar of the house. That's where the silver vault must be, I thought. Of course, she'd be putting everything away that had been used at the banquet last night.

A bare light bulb hung from a cord halfway down the stairs. I could see another light from somewhere beyond. No wonder Mrs. Janeck had not heard me, walking down those iron steps was like descending into a crypt. I made no further attempt to call her. Surprise might be on my side.

At the foot of the stairs I saw a door opened to my left. It was solid as the door of a bank vault. Mrs. Janeck stood with her back toward me, bending over a table in the middle of the small room. She was covering a massive soup tureen of silver with its gray felt bag.

"Mrs. Janeck?" I said quietly.

She whirled around, her eyes wide. If I had hoped to surprise her, I had succeeded, she almost dropped the heavy tureen.

"You . . . you frightened me," she said, her tongue moving nervously over her pale lips. I thought of when I had stood on the terrace looking down at the river below and she had come up behind me, and I felt no regret.

"I want to talk to you, Mrs. Janeck," I said, moving into the room. It was smaller than I had imagined, that room, all the walls filled with shelves, all the shelves filled with their heavy burden carefully covered with felt bags against tarnishing. There was a closed airless feeling about the place; it was as if the two of us were in a small tomb, the one light bulb swaying on its cord above us.

"I . . . I was just putting the silver away, ma'am." She turned back to her work as if afraid to look at me.

"That can wait." She glanced up again, and I could see she had noticed something different in my voice, something that frightened her. But she tried to pretend there was nothing unusual about my invading this part of the house.

"Miss Waring won't like you being down here, ma'am," she said, but she made no attempt to go back to work. Her eyes were fastened on me and I could see her hands were trembling.

"I don't think we have to worry about Miss Waring. Or Mr. Britton. They've gone out." I moved closer, making sure to keep the doorway behind me. I wasn't going to have her escape, not now. "And besides, why should I care what Miss Waring likes? This is my house, isn't it?"

She looked down as if afraid of what her eyes might reveal and so I repeated it: "Isn't it?"

"As you say, ma'am."

"Mrs. Janeck? Look at me." Reluctantly she raised her head, her mouth pursed tightly as if she were afraid by accident she might say something wrong.

"Mrs. Janeck, don't you think it's time we told each other the truth?"

"I . . . I'm sure I don't know what you mean, ma'am."

I wanted to shake her then, frightened as she was. Time was going by so quickly. I didn't know how soon Irene and Hale would return and minutes were already passing.

"Let's not lie to each other," I said boldly. If I couldn't get the truth out of her, it would be best to find that out now, while the others were away. Then at least I might still have a chance to escape. I thought for a second of Alex's arms around me, of the safety I had felt. Well, if I had to risk everything, now was the time.

"Mrs. Janeck," I began, not moving away from the door, "you left a note for me last night."

I did not think it was possible for her to grow paler, but my words stunned her.

"A note?" She licked her thin lips again nervously. She was getting ready to deny it, I knew.

"You know you did. No one else could have left it."

"You didn't show it to anyone?" The words were out before she could pull them back. Instinctively her hand went to her mouth, but it was too late.

"No. No one here."

"Why didn't you take my warning?" The color was coming back into her pale cheeks now, and she had stopped trembling. "I thought this morning . . . when I heard you'd gone to the doctor . . . why did you come back?"

It was time now for me to be honest. "You know why I came back," I said. "To find the real Constance Avery."

I thought when I finally faced her with that she might faint or grow angry or deny it. I'd been thinking about how to handle her reaction ever since I decided to tell her what I knew was the truth. But I never expected what happened now.

She just looked at me, a bitter little smile twisting her lips. "You found out," she said finally. "I thought you had this morning at break-fast. The others weren't watching you, but I was." She smoothed the work apron over her black dress, the touch of it seemed to give her strength.

"No," she went on. "They were all too busy talking about money. Not you." She glanced at me sharply. "You know who you are?"

"Yes," I said simply. "My name is Rosemary Carr. I come from a town called Bosworth, New Hampshire. By the way, Dr. Gallard knows too."

"You told him?" She was frightened again, and then she gave a small mirthless chuckle. "Well, that might be some protection. If you were outside the gates of Storm's End. It won't do you much good here."

But I wasn't going to be frightened. "He also told me about the visit you made to him this summer," I said.

"I'll deny it!" Her pale eyes were wild now. I thought for a second she might spring at me. "If you ever mention it to anyone, I'll deny it," she repeated.

"It was the real Constance Avery he saw that night, wasn't it?" I persisted. I must get her to crack somehow, otherwise she would never help me.

"Yes." She slumped onto a stool by the table then, her eyes quiet, remembering.

"Is she still alive, Mrs. Janeck?"

"Please . . . don't ask me any more . . ."

"I have to! I want to help her, if she is alive. And she is, isn't she?"

She looked up at me and then, almost pleading, said, "Get away from here. Now. While you can. Don't worry about the girl. They promised they won't hurt her . . ."

"Then she *is* still alive!" I'd finally got it out of her. But there was still so much more to learn. "Where is she?"

"You can't help her, miss. No one can. She needs doctors. But they've promised now that the money is theirs they'll get doctors for her."

"And you believe them?"

She did not answer. It was very quiet in that small room now. And then she dropped her head into her hands and I knew she was crying.

"I . . . I have to believe them," she managed to get out between sobs.

"Why? What hold have they got over you?"

But she wouldn't answer. I knelt down beside her and gently took her hands away from her face.

"Please, miss, if they ever find out . . ."

"They won't," I said firmly. "Not if you help me. Now . . . you must know where she is. They couldn't have done this without you." But still she wouldn't answer.

"It's the tower, isn't it? In the old wing? She's in some room there, isn't she?"

She looked at me then, her eyes seeing me for the first time since she started crying. When she started to speak unconsciously she dropped her voice. It was practically a whisper and I had to strain to hear her.

"It's somewhere in the tower, miss. But I don't know any more than that."

"She's been there all this time?"

"Just since they brought you back from the hospital. It's . . . some kind of a secret room. They wouldn't say anything more than that. I don't know how they found the entrance. Connie must have told them when they were in Europe. When she was well . . ." Her voice broke off then and her eyes filled with tears. "She was such a pretty little girl, miss. Wild, like all the Averys. But never bad. I couldn't believe what had happened to her when they brought her home."

She looked at me then and grabbed my wrists. She had a strong grip for such a frail woman.

"I wanted to go to the police right then. To the doctors. But they said I mustn't . . . Mr. Britton being her husband, he had the right to do it his way. And by the time I saw it wasn't doing any good, I couldn't go to the police."

Her eyes were bleak now. She looked down at her hands gripping mine and then, suddenly embarrassed, let me free. "I couldn't go to anyone then," she said.

"Why? What power have they got over you?" But even as I questioned her I had an idea of what the answer was. "It's Otto, isn't it? Something to do with Otto? Is that why you can't talk?"

Her hands went out at me, like claws. But then she stopped, her hands still in the air almost as if she knew there was no point in attacking me. Then she let them drop back into her lap again.

"Yes, it's Otto," she said finally. "I should have known all along we couldn't get away with it." She looked very old suddenly, the anger drained out of her.

"I won't tell anyone . . . if you'll help me."

"It doesn't make any difference now. I'd hoped he'd change . . . once he was safe back here, once the world couldn't get at him." She sighed. "It wasn't any good."

"Tell me."

Her bent fingers were twisting her apron again. She couldn't look at me.

"Otto . . . Otto was in jail," she said at last. "Up in Canada. It was for murder, but he said it wasn't his fault. I believed him. I'd believed so many of his other stories over the years, why should I stop now? He managed to escape . . . he never quite told me how, but I suspect there was another killing mixed in that too. And he just showed up, early this summer, at Storm's End."

She pulled herself up to her feet then, smoothing the thin strands of hair that had pulled loose over her ears.

"We hadn't seen each other for a long time," she went on. "He'd gone off on his own before, and always he'd turn up again. Broke and sick and no place else to go. That's all I ever was to him, someone to help him out, to give him a place to hide until he was well enough to walk out on me again."

She stood there quietly, remembering the long, bitter years of her unhappy marriage.

"He figured he'd be safe here," she went on, not looking at me. "Storm's End hadn't been opened in years. I was paid a steady salary to be caretaker, no one up in Canada knew he'd been married. There was no reason to think anybody would track him down."

"But they did?"

"It was that Ben." She spat out his name almost viciously. "Somehow, he recognized Otto, I don't know from where. He told the others. It was just about the time I knew something had to be done about Miss Constance.

"They called me into the library. They had all the facts about Otto. There wasn't anything I could deny. They said if I'd help, they wouldn't say anything. He could stay here. They were only going to be here until it was time for Miss Constance to get her inheritance. Then they'd be off again, and Otto would be safe. Forever.

"So I said I'd go along with them. I hadn't any choice."

"But when you saw she wasn't getting better . . . ?" I tried to make my words as gentle as possible. I'd brought back too many memories for this unhappy woman and I was afraid she would collapse before I found out what I needed to know.

"The night I went for the doctor . . . that was the worst she'd ever been," Mrs. Janeck answered, trying to control herself. "Most of the time, she just sleeps. It's like she was in a coma."

"Is she still on drugs?" I asked.

"I don't know. I don't think so. But with that Miss Waring . . . I wouldn't put anything past her." She gave me a long look. "It was she who decided to use you to fool the old man. I never thought it would work, not the way it did.

"Anyway, the day they brought you back from the hospital they took

Miss Constance into the old wing. They wouldn't tell me where. I'd prepare meals on a tray and one of them . . . Mr. Britton or Ben or Miss Waring, they'd take them up."

I thought of something then. "There was a night this week though, when no one was here . . . and I still saw a light in the tower I couldn't trace."

"Don't fool yourself." The elderly woman's lips twisted in a mirthless smile. "There was always someone here. Ben it was that night. It was a lie I was to tell, so you'd think you were alone. They wanted to find out how much you knew. You'd given them a real scare, coming down that first morning with your talk about seeing a light in the old towers."

Suddenly I felt very cold. I remembered going through the house that night, not afraid because I was so sure there was no one else there. To think that Ben might have been behind any door . . .

"Scares you a little now, doesn't it?" The old woman hadn't missed my reaction. "All the more reason for you to get out of here. While you can."

"I can't do that," I said. "If I do, they'll kill her. They can't let me go. And they won't bother to save her."

She stood there watching me, and I knew from the expression on her face that what I'd said was true.

"That's why you've got to help me, Mrs. Janeck. Before they come back. There must be some way to find that secret room." I thought of something then, the reason I'd come down here, the one thing she could do to help me.

"The diary . . . the diary of the first Constance Avery . . . where is it?"

"Miss Irene has it," she said. "She went to your room last night to help you undress and found you gone. Thank God you took my note with you. That's when she got the idea that there might be something in the diary."

"Where is it now?" I grabbed her by her shoulders, as if I could shake the truth out of her. "Quick! We haven't much time!"

"It'd be in her room, I guess. She had it in her hands when she called me last night when you'd gone out, after the house had gone to bed. She was afraid that you were poking around the tower again. Then we saw you run across the park away from Ben and she went back to her own bedroom."

"And took the diary with her?"

"She must have."

"Then we've got to find it." I started for the door, but Mrs. Janeck grabbed me by the hand.

"Oh no, miss, you can't! If she catches you . . ."

"You'll have to stand guard. There must be a hall window where you can see them if they drive up to the house."

Still she hesitated.

"For God's sake, Mrs. Janeck! It's our last chance! Now . . . come on!"

Twenty-four

As I opened the door, I realized I'd never been in Irene's room before. She was such a private person and I'd been so much in awe of her it had never occurred to me to visit her there.

It was a large bedroom, facing the cliffs and the river as mine did, but not as grandly furnished. Blue and white striped satin material covered the walls and draped the long windows. There was no dressing table in front of the windows. Heavy Victorian furniture, chests and an armoire, and a great black walnut bed filled the room.

I left Mrs. Janeck on guard and walked into the room. If the diary was hidden, it might take me hours to find it, but for once Irene had been careless. She'd left it in plain sight on her bedside table, the key still in the lock of the leather volume.

"Miss? Have you found it?" Mrs. Janeck called from the hall outside.

"Yes. Keep watching," I called back. I twisted the key in the lock and the catch loosened. With a little effort I managed to free the metal lock and open the diary.

I suppose I expected the book to be set out like a modern diary, a page for each date, all the entries neat and orderly. But instead the book in my hand was more like an account book . . . there were no headings at the top of the pages, no dates listed, the handwriting was continuous, page after page of faded brown ink on yellow pages. The paper was dry and the edges were beginning to crumble.

This could take me days, I thought, even if there is a clue here. I read the first entry . . . the writing was hard to decipher and the phrasing strange to my eyes. But gradually I began to make it out.

To London by the morning coach. Father is determined that I am to have a season, although I know he cannot afford it . . .

I flipped through the pages after that. I began to get a picture of this girl who was to become the first Constance Avery. I could see a governess handing her the little book, to start a diary of Constance's adult life. That's what a first season in London would have been for a young lady of that time.

About ten pages later I discovered the first reference to Jared Avery.

. . . and while touring the gardens, Father pointed out the rich colonist that everyone in London is talking about. His name is Jared Avery. He was on a beautiful chestnut mare, but the horse balked and he began to beat her unmercifully. I had to turn away . . . I cannot bear to see an animal mistreated. Dear Father would never allow such a thing, no matter what cause the creature might give . . .

I glanced up at the clock on Irene's bureau. Nearly four. I'd have to hurry. I flipped the pages quickly. Constance's handwriting was becoming easier to read now . . . there were mentions of balls, new dresses, going to the theater, and again and again, to sittings for her portrait.

Occasionally she would list the gentlemen present, always starting with a Phillippe de Something (I could not make out the name) and then, more and more frequently, at the very end of the list, as if showing his place in her affections, the name of Jared Avery.

Then I came across one page that was more of what I had expected. There were only two sentences:

Phillippe returned to France this night. God grant he come back safe.

And the rest of the page was empty. I was doing some rapid figuring then. It was hard to be sure with no dates, but it might have been about the time of the French Revolution. And I had a curious feeling, as I turned those pages written so many years ago, that Phillippe did not return.

There were more pages of outings, and the name Jared Avery gradually began to be condensed to the initials J.A.:

J.A. presses his suit . . .
J.A. had a long talk with Father . . .
J.A. requested I ride with him . . .

But this was no help for the information I needed. I knew how the story ended. Whether Phillippe was guillotined or not, Constance agreed finally to marry Jared and come to America.

I decided to start from the back of the volume then, turning the pages carefully. The last entry of the last page was brief:

Goodwife Asher says first babies are very often late and I must not fret myself. There is no gentleness in the way J.A. looks at me now, he eyes me as if I were part of the stock. Pray God when it comes, it be a boy. For all our sakes.

There were loose threads on the binding after this page, as if other entries had been ripped out. It needed no great imagination to realize that a young mother, running a huge household, would not have had the time for a personal diary any longer. Or perhaps she was afraid of what she might put down, and J.A. reading it.

I started through the volume again, this time working forward from the back. Several names appeared again and again, especially that of someone called Tobias:

Even J.A. is pleased with the work Tobias does . . . Tobias has carved the molding for the upper hall from my sketch of what it looked like at home. He has made it wonderous like . . . I wish Tobias had not been witness to the scene. J.A. in temper is not a pretty sight . . .

Now, this was getting more like it! I started reading again more carefully.

"Aren't you done yet, miss?" I looked up to see Mrs. Janeck standing in the doorway. I had become so absorbed in the old volume I'd almost forgotten her.

"Not quite. Any sign of them?"

"No. But it's getting late," she said, twisting her hands nervously.

"Well, keep watching. I'll try to hurry."

Esther went back out into the hall and I started going through the pages as rapidly as I could. Tobias was obviously some kind of carpenter, probably one of those traveling journeymen who went from town to town. At any rate, there was no mention of his having a wife or family. And if he felt sympathetic to young Constance . . . This might be what I was looking for!

And then, at last, I found the passage. It started simply enough:

Today my twenty-third birthday. J.A. is still away, which made it easier to feel I am the same girl I had been at home. The real Storm's End. It was this afternoon I received the best present of my new life. Tobias took me to my sitting room, as like as the tower room at home, all honey wood. He knows I fear the cold and he has made it easy to warm, as he has kept it small, not like the great chambers J.A. desires. I had told him of the priest's hole that Father had discovered at home, and without J.A. knowing, he has made the same here. He said many foolish things but implored me to keep the secret to myself. I think he fears someday I may need a place to hide, which is mere fancifulness especially now that I am certain with child. J.A. would never hurt me now. Tobias has been most ingenious, duplicating the secret of the necklace . . .

"Quick! They're here!"

I looked up to see Esther standing in the doorway.

"They're back?" I said. She nodded, too excited to speak. I stood up quickly. It would happen just now when I am so close! I heard the car screeching to a halt outside. My fingers trembled now, I thought I would never be able to get the lock fastened. I sent Mrs. Janeck downstairs then. It would give me another minute. Finally I managed to get the key turned in the little volume just as I heard the voices of Hale and Irene in the hall below. I put the diary down on her bedside table. As

far as I could remember, it was the way it had been. I started for the
door and then, just at the last moment, remembered to go back and
smooth the bedspread where I had been sitting. Now to get to my room!

I hesitated for a second in the deep embrasure that led to the hall
from Irene's room, the door closed quietly behind me. They were still
downstairs. If I could just slide past the top of the staircase, I'd be out
of their sight. I took a deep breath and moved as softly as I could out of
my hiding place.

But they had not started upstairs yet. I could see Mrs. Janeck standing on the curve of the landing, almost as if she were on guard duty.

"But it wouldn't take a moment to make tea, Mr. Britton," she was
saying as I crept past the open staircase.

"We don't want tea, we'd like to get to our rooms and clean up." I
could tell Hale was impatient, but she had given me the few seconds I
needed to scurry to safety. I did not hear any more, as I was in my own
room by then, the door closed softly behind me.

Once again I felt for the key to lock myself in . . . and realized it
was gone. Had Irene taken that too? I'd meant to ask Mrs. Janeck, but
so much had happened I'd forgot. I could think about that later. But
now, in case Irene stopped in to check on me . . .

I ripped off my gray dress and flung it on the chaise. With one quick
tug, I pulled back the heavy brocade spread on the bed. It was full
enough to cover the fact I was still wearing my slip and stockings. The
rose brocade had barely rippled into place over me when I heard a soft
tap on my door. I took a second to catch my breath and ruffle my hair
and then I leaned back again, my eyes closed.

There was a second tap. I made no move. Let her think I was still
asleep. I could hear the bedroom door open quietly. I lay there without
moving, trying to breathe as evenly as someone asleep would.

And, after a moment, I heard the door close again.

I lay where I was. This was the first chance I'd had to puzzle over
what I'd read in the diary. There was some connection between the
hidden room and the necklace, that was obvious. "The secret of the
necklace" that the first Constance had written. But what was it?

I got out of bed then and went to the dressing table to look at the necklace. But my eyes were caught by the world beyond my windows. The sky had turned dark, although it was still early. The storm clouds that I had noticed before, so far to the west, were overhead now, the wind driving them across the sky furiously. The french windows were starting to rattle, the silk of the curtains billowing.

I thought then of the first Constance, and for the first time, realized the parallels between us . . . we both loved Frenchmen.

And we both of us were prisoners of Storm's End.

The clock on the mantel chimed. It was getting late if I was to dress for dinner. The necklace would have to wait. By the time I finished bathing, the storm had started. First, the long low rumble of thunder, still some miles away. And then I could see over the far banks of the river the yellow crackle of lightning. There was still enough daylight to see the trees along the shore bending in the wind. The rain had not started yet.

I knew I should be hurrying, they would be coming for me soon to go down to dinner, but it was hard to tear myself away from the windows. I'd never been afraid of storms, nor was I unduly fascinated by them. When you grow up in a small town in the country, nature does not surprise you. A storm is something you accept. But I had never stood at a vantage point like this, high above the terrace and the cliffs, the river far below, all of it waiting for the heavens to break, the torrent of rain, the thunder and lightning to swirl around us.

My room was growing dark now, and I forced myself to turn on the lights of the dressing table. The Scarf of Sapphires was still there, in its case, in front of my mirror. I opened the lid and looked at the cold blue and white stones. What was it Constance had written? The "secret of the necklace"?

I reached then to take it out of its case to examine it and at that moment all the lights of the house flickered off. And then on again. I remembered suddenly what Irene had said that first day when they had brought me here from the hospital . . . and what would happen if the lights went out a third time. I do not think I am any more afraid of the dark than anyone else, but with what I now knew of the people of Storm's End and the tragedies of this house, I sent up a silent prayer that tonight at least the lights would not fail. The lights flickered a second time, and then, once more came on again.

And perhaps it was something about the changing lights that made the necklace look different. For that one moment, with the lights out, the crackle of lightning that snapped around the outside walls of the house lit the sapphires and diamonds at a strange angle, like the blinding glare of a photographer's flash. The jewels no longer looked like a necklace, I could see the arrangement of the stones as a pattern now.

And then the lights came on again.

But that second had been enough. I knew now the secret of the necklace that the first Constance had written about. Or at least I knew part of it. Because, as I stood there, staring down at the dressing table, that fortune of gems spread out in front of me, I knew now why it had looked familiar. I had seen it before, that pattern. Here, in Storm's End. Carved under the mantel of the fireplace of the little honey-colored room in the towers, the room Tobias had made for the first Constance.

I remembered now what she had written in that entry of her diary . . . about the "priest's hole" at the original Storm's End, across the ocean, somewhere deep in England. Such hiding places were not uncommon, I knew, built into some of the old English halls as a safe refuge, not just for priests in the times of religious troubles, but for use whenever civil wars swept the countryside. A refuge for cavaliers in the time of Cromwell, for smugglers, if the people of the great houses were involved in that trade, as many of them had been. A hiding place, safe and quiet, with only a few trusted people of the house knowing the secret of how to enter it.

I picked up the necklace and looked at it. There was no mistaking it now. The journeyman carpenter Tobias had used the pattern, dug it into the honey-colored wood of that tower room. It couldn't be an accident; whatever the secret of the necklace was, I was sure it also was duplicated in the wood of the fireplace. And it must lead to the secret room where Irene and Hale kept the real Constance Avery Britton hidden.

My fingers were trembling now as I fingered the stones. What was the secret? I turned the necklace over and studied the back of it, the flat setting for the stones. I could see the workmanship now, but it gave me no clues. Was it the placement of the stones that meant something? Or the way they were connected?

I tested the strength of some of the links; they held firm although it had been centuries since the necklace had been strung together. Turning it over again, I studied the cold stones, fingering each of the larger ones as if I could learn what I wanted by touch. The jewels were cold in my hands.

And they kept their secret.

What is it, I thought? The key is here in my hands, if I can just discover it. I sat down in front of the dressing table and held the necklace up to the light of the lamp by the mirror. I was looking for something irregular now, something that was different in the pattern. Surely a secret from so long ago would be something comparatively simple. The light came through the larger sapphires, the main stones of the necklace, twisting among the carved facets of the gems, glittering and twinkling the diamonds that edged each jewel.

Except one.

The center sapphire, the deepest clouded blue, reflected no light. It sat there in the middle of the arrangement solid and dark, no light passing through it. I turned the necklace over again. I could see now why light had passed through the other stones. They were in raised settings without a backing. But the center gem was backed with dull metal, gold probably, but it had been so many years since the Scarf of Sapphires had been cleaned it was almost impossible to tell.

Why should this one stone have a backing? True, it was obviously expensive; larger and heavier than the others. I remembered that when I had seen it the night before, it had reminded me of a spider in the center of a web. But why had it been treated in a fashion different from the other jewels?

I studied it carefully, running a light finger around the edge of the stone. Something caught on my nail. Peering at it closely I could see a little diamond had been placed at the bottom of the stone. I flicked at it and for a moment I thought it had come loose from its setting.

But it was the jewel itself that had come loose, the great sapphire had pulled free from the rest of the necklace and I could see now it had been hinged at the top of the stone, the tiny hinge covered by a cluster of diamond chips. And behind the sapphire, hidden by the dull metal backing, was an empty space.

I sat there for a moment, the necklace in my lap. Was this the secret? If I touched the bottom of what would be the main stone in the carved pattern of the fireplace, would it too open? It seemed implausible, but what else could the first Constance have meant by the "secret" of the necklace?

I looked at the little hiding place. The large sapphire, almost an inch square, covered a space big enough for . . . what? A note some lovely lady might want to hand to a gallant lover, without her husband discovering it? Or perhaps something grimmer . . . poison? I thought of the Borgias and then smiled at my romanticism. Probably nothing more important had been hidden there but a bit of cotton, soaked in the favorite perfume of the women who owned the necklace.

There was a knock on my bedroom door.

Irene, I thought, and pressed the stone back into its original position. I dare not take a chance that she might guess what I had discovered. Dropping the necklace on the dressing table, I stood up and pulled the cord of my robe tight.

"Yes?" I called out.

The door opened and Mrs. Janeck came in.

"They're wondering what's happened to you, miss," she said. She'd put on a crisp white apron over her black dress and was obviously ready for dinner.

"I'll be down in a minute," I answered. There was a roll of thunder outside, louder than before. The storm was moving closer. I could see Mrs. Janeck was trembling and she made no move to leave.

I crossed the room quickly and took her hands. She must not give away what I knew, not now.

"Are you all right?" I whispered. The door to the hall behind her was still open and I didn't want anyone hearing us.

"I . . . I think so," she murmured. Then she looked up at me, her pale eyes wide. "But . . . they seem so . . . strange, since they've come back. Almost . . . almost like they suspect something." The tip of her tongue slid across her thin lips. "Miss, I'm frightened."

I held her hands firmly. I felt no braver than she, but I dared not let her guess this. I would need her on my side tonight.

"Don't be," I said. "They can't possibly have guessed anything. Remember that."

"I'll try . . . I'll try. Did you learn anything from that diary?"

I was tempted then to tell her what I suspected, but I hesitated. She was too close to breaking to be trusted with the secret of the necklace. If they bullied her, and I knew they were capable of it, everything would come out. I patted her hand reassuringly.

"I think I have an idea. But I can't act on it . . . not with them here." I moved away from her then, walking restlessly to the fireplace. "If only I could explore the towers alone. Tonight." I looked at her. Could she help me? Or was she too afraid?

"Mrs. Janeck, I must get them out of the house. Can you think of any way?"

"No, miss." Her hands were trembling again, but this time she laced her fingers together herself to stop the shaking. And then she looked at me with almost pity in her eyes. "And Ben's back, miss. That makes three of them now."

I sat down on the chaise, my legs suddenly too weak to hold me. I knew how cruel he could be and in the back of my mind I suppose I'd been hoping the long trip to the city to deliver Matthew Avery and the Princess would keep him away from Storm's End until after I'd discovered what I needed to make my escape. Now, with him back . . . !

"Dear God," I whispered, not caring whether Esther heard me or not.

"Miss, you'd better hurry. They want dinner early. They said it's in case the storm blows out the lights. But I'm not sure it's that. Please . . . let's not get them angry."

I forced myself to stand up again. "All right, Mrs. Janeck, I'll be down soon," I said. And then, as she started for the door, I thought of something.

"The keys to my room . . . did you take them?"

She looked back at me, her gray eyes growing wide again.

"What are you talking about, miss?" she asked.

"The key to my door . . . and to Mr. Britton's dressing room. They're gone. They have been since last night."

She came closer to me then and I saw a new look in her eyes. Before she had been frightened, or worried, locked in her own troubles. But for the first time since I had met this strange woman I saw an expression on her face of concern for someone other than herself.

"You mean . . . they can get in here anytime they want? That you're not even safe in this room?"

I nodded. We stared at each other for a long moment and now it was my turn to gather strength from her. She took my hands firmly, still staring straight into my eyes. Her shoulders had stiffened and her mouth was set in a stronger line than I had ever seen it before.

"I'll help you, miss. I don't know how just yet, but I'll do my best. Whatever happens, just be prepared to take advantage of it." She gave my hands one last pat and started again for the door.

"You've had enough to face," she said, her back to me. "It's time I did my share."

"Thank you for helping me."

She stopped at that and glanced over her shoulder. Her glance was impersonal once more but the strength of purpose was still there.

"Make no mistake, miss. I'm not doing this for you. It's time I did something for Miss Constance. The real one."

And she went out and closed the door behind her.

Twenty-five

I hurried then. A half-formed plan was in the back of my mind, one too idiotic to consider seriously, but it was all I could think of. The important thing was to keep them from growing suspicious. I could not believe that their trip this afternoon had given them any real reason to suspect the truth about me, but they had had time together to talk, to exchange impressions, and I knew I would have to be doubly careful.

I needed a certain kind of dress for the evening, one with deep and, preferably, invisible pockets if what I was planning to do was to have any hope of success. I discovered a long black skirt of fine corduroy in the back of one of the dressing room closets. It was a little shorter than the other evening outfits, so that I could wear it with flat heels. And two pockets had been hidden in the side seams of the skirt.

As I put it on I thought grimly to myself of how stupid I had been

. . . never noticing how long Constance's clothes had hung on me, all of them sweeping the floor. Whatever else the real Constance Britton was, she was several inches taller than I. I found a high-necked white blouse, stiffly starched, and a pink moiré ribbon to tie back my hair. The clothes made me look young and innocent, but, more important, I could move in them quickly.

The storm clouds were thick outside now, the sky was turbulent, a purple-gray. The thunder was nearer and the crackle of lightning was not on the far side of the river any longer. It was as if the clouds were being caught on the sharp spires of Storm's End. But I could not worry about that now.

As I left my room to go down for dinner, the hall was quiet. In my bedroom I could hear the storm gathering around the house; in the dark corridor it still seemed shut out and distant.

I hesitated for a moment at the top of the grand staircase. The lights had not been turned on in the hall below, nor in the upper corridor, and the great open well that made the center of this house was in the gray half-light of twilight. As I stood there, my hand on the railing, there was one moment of complete silence. And then an enormous clap of thunder sounded directly overhead, loud enough that if sound alone could have shaken the house, I think the walls would have trembled. And almost at the same second a yellow flash of lightning hit the skylight high on the roof above me. It seemed to go through the glass, down through the open space of the stairwell. I could almost have sworn it struck the black and white marble squares of the floor below.

I stood there frozen, watching the weird yellow light twist the railings and wooden gargoyles into grotesque shadows. And then, before the light was truly gone, there was another crash of thunder, louder than the one before, and another crackle of lightning, blue-white now, burning my eyes, ripping down through the hollow well of the house.

And then, at last, the rain began.

It didn't start slowly, increasing its tempo; it seemed the world outside went from waiting for the storm to being in the center of it all at once. The rain slashed at the skylight high above. I could hear it beating on the glass of the windows in the rooms around me, wave after wave of water, as if it would not stop until the house itself was leveled and only that would end the storm.

I started down the stairs then, knowing no excuse on earth would get anyone in this house out tonight.

Before I'd even had a chance to try it, my little plan had failed.

*   *   *

But the storm did one thing for me. Mrs. Janeck's warning was still in my head as I opened the doors to the drawing room and I knew it would be harder to get through this evening pretending nothing was wrong as Hale and Irene studied me than it had been earlier. But when I walked into the room, the two of them were at the windows at the far end, struggling to fasten the catches tightly and for the first moments hardly seemed to notice me.

"Con . . . give me a hand with this." Hale was half engulfed with the long curtains that swirled around him. Irene was having the same problem with the tall window on the other side of the bay. She had changed into a loose rust-colored paisley robe and the full sleeves seemed to be getting in her way.

"What happened?" I asked as I held the curtains back.

"The catches on these windows, they won't stay shut," said Hale. The rain lashed against the glass, the high wind slapping the windows over and over again as if the storm was trying to invade the house itself.

"We knew there was going to be bad weather," said Irene, tucking back the long silk curtains. "It's been on the radio all day. But this . . . !" She managed to secure the windows at last. "I've never seen anything like it."

And then the curtains hung straight again, barely moving from the wind that pushed through the cracks of the window. Irene pulled down her sleeves and went straight to the low table in front of the fireplace, where her glass was. "God, Hale, I could do with a drink now." She held up the empty glass to him.

He barely glanced at her as he took it from her and went straight to the silver tray where the bottles and glasses were. "Martini for you?" he called over his shoulder to me.

"Fine," I said, grateful that the first moment had passed without their attention fixed upon me.

"Aren't you afraid of storms?" asked Irene. She had curled up on the yellow sofa near the fireplace and her green eyes seemed almost shy as she stared up at me.

"Not particularly," I answered. I was about to explain about growing up in the country when I caught myself. Stay on guard, I thought. Every *second!*

But it was Hale who made the first slip. He turned on my remark and stared at me. "What are you talking about? You've always been afraid of storms. I remember one time in the South of France . . ." And then his voice trailed off as he recalled who had been with him there. Irene shifted her legs on the sofa. The two of them were going to have to be careful tonight too. The game was nearing its end, but I must not let it happen too soon.

"Then that's something else I've forgotten," I said as I took my glass from Hale.

We didn't linger over cocktails that evening. The storm outside was too violent; it made conversation almost impossible. The lightning glittered and crackled around us, the thunder a long low roar, like an angry animal, howling for revenge.

And it frightened Irene. Somehow I had never expected this cold, controlled woman to be frightened of anything. But each slash of light outside the windows, each crack of thunder made her wince. She'd burrowed herself into the deep pillows of the sofa, grasping her knees with her hands, her green eyes flickering at each crash of sound, her sallow skin drained white. Finally she could take it no longer.

"For heaven's sake, Hale, let's go into the dining room. We can pull the drapes there, maybe it won't sound so loud," she said when a particularly long crack of lightning had lit up the rain-swept terrace outside, electric white for a moment before it slid back into the darkness of night. The rain was relentless; it had come down so violently I had been sure it could not last, but still it continued, drumming, hard and angry, against the outside walls, changing the atmosphere inside, making the air muggy.

"Right," agreed Hale. He made himself another drink, a strong one, and led the way into the dining room, his glass in his hand.

Mrs. Janeck had lit the candles in the dining room, as well as turning on all the lights. Whatever happened, we would be prepared. We took our places as we had the other nights, Hale at the foot of the long table, Irene and I on each side. The heavy velvet drapes had been pulled tight over the windows and the storm did sound fainter here.

There was a carafe of wine on the table and Irene poured herself a glass even before she sat down. If they both could drink enough to fall asleep, I thought, and knew even as I thought it, it wasn't likely. But something of the thought must have shown in my eyes, for Irene raised her glass to me almost mockingly.

"Thinking I'm going to get drunk?" she asked. "I wouldn't mind, not on a night like this."

"The storm can't last too long," I said quietly. "Isn't this where they end?" But almost at once there was another long rumble of thunder outside. The wind had risen, I could hear it wailing around the house, caught in the towers and strangely angled walls.

"I wouldn't count on that," said Hale. "I think we're in for a night of it." He turned toward the pantry door to call for Mrs. Janeck, and at that moment the lights flickered out again.

There were enough candles lit to keep the room from total darkness and, as always, the lights came on again within a second. But Irene's hand shook enough to spill a little of the wine on the damask table-cloth.

"That's once," she muttered. "If it happens three times, we're in for it."

Almost as if the house were teasing her, the lights went out again. We sat there, none of us moving, for what seemed like a very long time but was probably no more than a few seconds, and then the power came on again. But the lights seemed dimmer now, as if they were struggling to stay on.

"Twice," said Irene. Her mouth was set in a grim line. She barely turned her head as Ben came in. He offered her the soup tureen but she waved it away without looking at him and poured herself another glass of wine. I caught his eyes on me as he served Hale and looked away quickly. There was something different about his face tonight, his eyes were insolent, probing.

He knows, I thought, panicking. And looked down at my plate quickly.

And then the lights went out a third time.

It was not like the other times, when they had flickered first. This time it was as if they just faded away. For a moment I wasn't even sure that it had happened, until I saw Irene grab Hale's hand, her knuckles tight over his fingers.

"Three," she whispered. "The lights are out, Hale. They're out for good."

"Now, calm down," he said, freeing his hand. He looked at me a little apologetically. "It may only be for a few minutes. While they trace where the power is broken." He got up and went to the hall door and opened it. We'd turned on the lights as we came in to dinner, but now it was absolutely black beyond the open doorway.

"Is the whole house out?" I asked, getting up from my chair.

"Probably the whole valley." Hale turned back then and picked up one of the candelabra from the table. He disappeared into the dark hallway beyond.

Irene glared at Ben. She was even more frightened than I thought, and she was covering it with anger.

"You didn't fix the spare generator," she said. It was not a question.

"When have I had time?" He gave her a long look, not insolent, but as if it could take the place of the conversation they could not have in front of me. When *would* he have the time, I thought bitterly, guarding the real Constance? For the first time since I had come down to dinner I thought of her. Of what it must be like in that tower room, alone, a prisoner, surrounded by darkness. I prayed silently that she was unconscious; it was terrifying enough down here, with other people and lighted candles.

The storm was growing louder now. It penetrated even this room with its closed windows and heavy drapes. Or maybe the darkness around us made it seem all that much closer. Hale came back from the hall and placed the heavy candelabrum on the table again.

"The power's out all right. I even tried the telephone. It's dead."

My last chance of reaching Alex tonight was gone. I was alone in this house with only a frightened old woman to help me and the three of them against me.

"Luckily we have plenty of candles. Don't we, Irene?" said Hale. She was about to nod when we heard the scream.

For a moment I thought perhaps Constance had managed to escape without my help, but then I realized the sound had come from the butler's pantry. The door swung open and Mrs. Janeck stood there, her white apron twisted around her hand. Even in the faint candlelight I could see the blood seeping through the thin material, dyeing it red.

"My . . . my hand . . . I cut it in the dark," she said, almost apologetically. The others surrounded her then, Hale trying to examine the cut, but it was still bleeding too heavily to be left without even the simple bandage of her apron for longer than a second or two.

"How on earth . . . ?" Irene's voice was irritable as she tried, like Hale, to see the cut.

"I was slicing the roast," said Mrs. Janeck. "When the candle went out. I had one lit. And in the darkness, my hand slipped . . ." She looked past them as she spoke, straight at me. Her words were nervous, apologetic; she sounded frightened by the accident. And the others were too busy with her wound to notice the look on her face. There was nothing frightened in her eyes, though; they stared at me levelly and I knew she had done this to help me.

"We've got to get her to a doctor," I said. "Dr. Gallard, he's the nearest."

They stared at me then: Hale, Irene and Ben. For once I'd surprised them, or perhaps the whole evening, with the storm and the lights failing, had shaken them more than they realized, for it was as if they had been waiting for me to give instructions. "Ben, you'd better drive Mrs. Janeck there at once. Irene, you go with them. Maybe the doctor's phone is working. You can report what's happened to the power here."

That would get rid of two of them, I thought. And Hale I could handle. I kept my hand in the pocket of my skirt, my fingers curled around the small object I'd brought down with me. Please, let them do what I asked!

Irene was the first to recover. "Otto could take her, he's her husband," she said, almost automatically. She might be startled by the accident and frightened by the storm outside, but she was not about to give in to someone else's commands easily.

"No! Otto can't take me." They turned back to look at Mrs. Janeck as she said that and I could see her look at each one for a long moment. I realized, as did they, what she meant. An escaped convict couldn't very well drive his wife anywhere.

"All right, Ben," said Hale, briefly. "You take her. But don't go to Gallard, take her to the hospital. That cut'll probably need stitches."

Mrs. Janeck caught my eye again and now there was panic in her look. We'd both been counting on her being able to talk to Dr. Gallard about what had happened.

"That's too far, Hale." I tried to make my voice sound calm and reasonable. "She could bleed to death on the way." And then I decided to take a chance. Perhaps I'd found out all I needed here. I had, or was fairly sure I had, the secret of where they had hidden Constance and how to get to her. Perhaps now was the time to go to Alex and then to the police. I made up my mind to risk it. "I'll go with Ben, if Irene doesn't want to."

"No." Irene said the word a little too loudly, but there was no mistaking that she had recovered from her fear. "There's no need for all of us to get wet," she went on, more calmly. "Ben can do everything that's necessary. And there's no reason not to go to Dr. Gallard, if he's available. Ben can stick with her all the time."

It was a strange thing to have said, and if I had had time, I would have puzzled over it, wondering how much Irene and the others knew or suspected about Alex. But Mrs. Janeck started moaning then, and it moved them all into action; Ben to go out into the storm and get the car and Hale for a towel to wrap around the bleeding cut. Only Irene made no move to leave us, as if she suspected the housekeeper and I had things to discuss. And with Irene watching, there was no way of passing a message. The only thing I could say to Mrs. Janeck was at the front door when, a few minutes later, Ben had brought up the car and had dashed up the steps through the rain to get the old lady. Hale stood behind us in the doorway, the candelabrum from the dining room in one hand as he tried to shield it from the storm outside.

"Just tell Dr. Gallard exactly how it happened," I said to Mrs. Janeck, holding her eyes with mine. "He'll know what to do." She nodded briefly and I hoped she understood what I meant. Ben threw an old raincoat over her shoulders and started her down the wet stone steps.

We scrabbled together a meal of sandwiches then, Irene and I. The few candles we managed to find in the old kitchen turned it into a strange dark cave, our shadows enormous on the walls around us. The peak of the storm seemed to have passed. At least the thunder was coming less frequently now and, it seemed, from more of a distance. The rain continued, though, whipped by the wind, slashing at the stone walls of the house, rattling the loose windows and forming little puddles on the floor wherever it could find a crack to let it in.

And not for one moment was I allowed to be alone. In the kitchen I had felt Irene's sharp eyes on me all the time we prepared the food and later, when we had gone back into the drawing room for our coffee, Hale had seemed to be at my side every minute.

My fingers curled around the small bottle in my pocket as I watched Irene pour the coffee. My plan had been foolish, perhaps, but it might have worked if I could have been by myself for one minute. I'd opened the capsules of the sleeping pills they had given me at the hospital and transferred the powder into the bottle directly. It was not the same substance as the sugar; it felt more like finely sifted flour to the touch, but it *was* white, and in the half-light of the drawing room, they might not have noticed. Only I'd had no chance even to try to add it to the sugar bowl; one or the other of them seemed always to be watching me. Soon it would be time to end the evening, or for them to suggest that I go up to bed, and I dared not risk their sleeping soundly enough without the drug to let me explore the tower room undiscovered.

I looked up at the paintings over the mantelpiece: my portrait and, hanging next to it, that of the first Constance. I remembered the afternoon she had seemed to warn me. In a way she had, for I realized now what her pose in the portrait meant. She had been painted with her hand almost touching the Scarf of Sapphires . . . one finger extended, almost as a hint, toward the center stone that held the secret of the necklace. And her diary had told me of the room where the real Constance was. If you could only help me now, I thought. One more time. And then, almost as if she had heard me and once again was coming to my rescue, I heard the wind rise outside. The thunder was fainter now when we heard it and we had not seen the yellow slash of lightning for almost ten minutes. The storm was moving on. Even the rain that worked its way down the chimney to make the roaring fire spit seemed fainter. But the wind had not died. It was stronger than before, almost gale force, making a strange howling sound as it circled around the house.

"Damn that wind!" said Irene, her eyes bitter. "That's one sound I never want to hear again." She took another sip of her brandy as if that could shut it out.

And then there was one great surge of wind, straight across the river, battering at the cliff side of the house with a great whoosh. The tall french windows on either side of the bay were slapped open, the silk curtains streaming straight into the room. They gave me no picture of the soft billowing of a lady's skirt now; the thin material writhed and twisted like long ghostly fingers, snapping at Hale's shoulders, swirling around Irene as she sat on the sofa.

She screamed then, as if she had felt the same thing, clawing at the material, trying to pull it away from her face. Hale had dropped his glass as he struggled with the drapes, and then both of them were at the windows, the way they'd been when I'd come down for dinner, fighting to get the glass closed against the rain and the wind, their backs toward me.

I only had a few seconds. Luckily my fingers were on the bottle in my pocket at the moment. I twisted the cover off with the bottle still in my pocket. Bringing it out, I covered it with my fingers. I was standing over the tray that held the coffeepot and cups, the cream pitcher and sugar bowl. I put my hand over the bowl, not daring to look down, my eyes still on Hale and Irene as they struggled with the windows. I could feel the powder sliding through my hand. Don't let them turn, I thought. One more second, that's all I need, just one more second!

And then it was over. No powder was touching my fingers now. The bottle must be empty. I pulled my hand back and shoved it deep into the pocket of my full skirt as they turned back from the windows.

"This should convince you we can't stay the winter here, Con," said Hale as he rubbed his hands together. "If you needed convincing."

"More coffee?" I said. I allowed myself to look down at the tray now.

The sugar looked the same. The bowl was deep enough and Mrs. Janeck had only filled it halfway so that it was impossible, even standing
directly above it, to study the contents.

"I could use some," he said. I refilled his cup and Irene's and scooped
up a full teaspoon from the sugar bowl for each of them, stirring it in
before I handed the cups to them. Irene was busy lighting a cigarette
and Hale was still staring at the storm outside the closed windows. The
wind was quiet now and, although I do not know whether I believe
in ghosts or not, I silently thanked the first Constance, if indeed it was
she who had provided the distraction I had needed.

"I'll see if there's more coffee," I said, holding up the silver pot as if it
were empty. I knew I could not sit in that room and watch them drink
from their cups without giving away what was happening.

By the time I came back from the kitchen, their cups were empty.

We went up to bed shortly after that. The lights were still out and
we each took a candelabrum from the hall table and lit it before starting up the stairs. Hale made no attempt at a romantic good night, for
which I was grateful; I was too excited now to be able to fool him with
any tricks. Irene closed her bedroom door without looking back at us
and Hale, after he had opened the door to my room for me, went without a word down the hall to his own room.

*   *   *

I made myself wait an hour. It was the longest hour I have ever
passed in my life. After I changed quietly into a pair of dark slacks, I
extinguished the candles in the great silver stand and sat there in the
dark in case any light might shine under the door to Hale's room and
give away the fact that I was still awake. The little figures on my gilt
clock gleamed in the blackness and outside the wind and rain hit
against the walls of the house relentlessly.

Finally it was time. I moved slowly, my feet quiet on the carpet. I
had found the short candle in the stubby china holder that Irene had
dug out that first night and pushed a box of matches into one of the
pockets of my trousers. I would not dare light the candle until I was
in the tower room.

In the long hour I had waited I had realized one thing. I could not
count on Alex tonight. Either Ben had decided on his own not to take
Mrs. Janeck to him or else the wound was more serious and Alex had
insisted that they go to the Six Counties Hospital. Otherwise they would
have been back by now. There were only Hale and Irene in the house,
and presumably they should be asleep by now.

What would I do if I found my way to the real Constance? I'd made
no plans for that. It had seemed enough just to discover her, but as I
left my room for the towers, I began to think of what should happen
next. If she was well enough to be moved, I could try to get her out of
the house. But I dismissed that almost at once. She would be in no
condition to be moved. I had no car and with the storm outside I
couldn't have gotten her fifty feet from the house, let alone all the way
to Alex's cottage.

No. I would have to find her first, make sure I knew how to enter
the secret room and then go to Alex myself and get the police before
Hale and Irene discovered I was missing. With any luck, it could all
be over by dawn.

Once past Hale's room, I breathed easier. I had put my ear to his
door, but I heard nothing. But still I did not dare light the candle in
my hand. I would have to make my way in the darkness.

Oddly, it was not difficult, or not as difficult as I feared it would be.
I knew the way to the tower rooms and for once I was not afraid of what
I might find. As long as I stayed on the narrow path of carpet down
the center of the hall I was fairly sure not to bump into anything. And
it was not completely dark. Even with the rain and wind still swirling
around the stone walls of the house there was still some light coming
through the hall windows, or perhaps it was less that the outside was
light than that the hall was so black. And now and then there was a
flash of distant lightning to give me a second to see where I was.

And then I was at the door of the tower room. It was closed and for
a moment I panicked, thinking perhaps Irene had locked it. But the
door gave under my push. I stepped inside. The room was as bare of
furnishings as before. Rain dribbled quietly down the windows now.
I put the candle on the floor near the fireplace and lit it. At once I saw
the pattern carved into the wood of the fireplace below the mantel,

the same pattern as the necklace as it looked stretched out in its case, practically the same size.

The candle was an orange flame, making shadows flicker in the corners of the room. I reached out for the large knob of wood that was the equivalent of the center stone of the necklace. There was no hinge on the top of it, as there had been with the sapphire. Could I have been wrong? I felt all around it, but there seemed to be no catch. Finally, getting desperate, I tugged at the knob of wood itself, feeling my fingernails scratch at the sides of the carving.

And then I felt it give a little, like pulling the handle of a drawer that has been long stuck. I sank back on my knees and pulled again, harder.

And slowly the whole wall in which the fireplace had been set began to move . . .

Twenty-six

The wall continued to slide toward me, smoothly, quietly. Whatever hinges were involved had been well oiled. I understood now why the room had been kept so spotlessly clean.

I had to move back as the wall came toward me, but it stopped, only halfway open from the rest of the room. What was behind the fireplace section was in darkness. I stood then, picking up my candle, and moved toward the open space.

Holding the candle high, I peered in. There was a space about five feet deep. I could see a thin window high in the wall, too narrow to open. The window I'd seen from my bedroom. And below it was a cot.

And on the cot lay a silent figure.

"Constance?" I whispered. "Is that you, Constance Avery?"

I sensed the figure move. I didn't want to go into that narrow little hole. It was hardly bigger than a closet and I was terrified the fireplace might swing back again. I knew there would be no way to open the wall from inside. But I dared not call any louder and I must find out who the figure was.

"Constance? Can you hear me?" I held the candle higher. I could see the figure on the cot move once more. Struggling to sit up, it turned toward me and I saw a face, the eyes gleaming out at me from the darkness like a wild animal.

It was the face of a woman, but a woman who had been through a hell such as I could not imagine. The dark hair hung lank and tangled over her shoulders. A thick gown that had once been white clung to her scrawny body. She put one hand out as if to shield her eyes from the candlelight. I saw in that moment there was no real resemblance between us; the color of her hair perhaps, or her eyes, but what she had been through had twisted her into something that was barely human.

Dear God, I thought . . . what have they done to you?

Her dry lips tried to move and she reached out a long thin hand toward me.

"Help," she whispered. "Please help me . . ."

And then I was afraid of the secret room no longer. I had to get her out of there . . . down from this tower, out of this house, if I had to drag her every step of the way.

I put the candle on the floor and stepped inside the dark hidden room. It was not as airless as I had imagined it. Perhaps the stones of the outer wall were loose in this tiny turret, for I could feel the dampness of the rain outside and a steady current of air forcing its way into this long-closed place.

"Let me help you," I said, putting my arms around the girl's thin shoulders. But she sank back then, as if she had no more strength left. For a moment I thought she was dead, but then I realized she was unconscious again. What was in her poor tortured brain at this moment? I wondered. That I was a dream?

I laid her carefully back on the cot and stepped out into the wood-paneled room again. What was I to do? I dare not close the panel on her again and yet how could I take her with me as she was? I crossed the bare floor to the window. The rain was falling quietly now, sliding softly down the glass, the fury of the storm past. The clouds above were thinning, moving swiftly across the sky, pushed by the driving wind. There was a full moon behind those clouds; in a few minutes it might break through if the rain stopped. But for the moment all was blackness.

Suddenly faint patches of light appeared on the ground. For a moment I thought it was the moon, but the sky was still dark above the house. What I was seeing was the lights of the downstairs windows spilling out onto the grounds. The power had come back on.

I caught my breath. We'd all forgotten to turn the switches off when we'd come upstairs. If the lights had come on in Hale and Irene's rooms, no drug would keep them asleep. I turned back toward the hall and, as I did, I knew I was no longer alone.

They stood there in the doorway, Hale and Irene. They were dressed as before; they had not even prepared for bed. I could see they had already noticed the open wall.

"So you know," Irene said. There was no anger in her voice, no emotion. But her sharp green eyes were glittering as she walked into the room. Hale stood in the doorway, leaning against it, not with his usual lazy grace, but as if he needed it for support.

"All right, Irene," he said quietly. "We've lost. We always knew it might happen."

"We haven't lost yet," she said grimly, not taking her eyes off me. She'd shoved her hands deep into the pockets of her paisley robe. It made her shoulders square and strong.

"Yes, you have." I couldn't move away from the window; now that we were all crowded into this small room I felt weak but my voice came out surprisingly strong. "That's the real Constance Avery in there, isn't it?" I pointed toward the dark opening behind the fireplace wall. It looked so strange, that wall, angled out from the room, my candlestick on the floor giving the only light.

Neither of them seemed to want to answer.

"She is, isn't she? Tell me the truth for once."

Hale stepped into the room now. The candlelight made him look suddenly old. "Yes, that's Constance," he said finally. "Or what's left of her."

"And this insane game . . . all these lies . . . the way you've treated her, you did all this for her money?" My voice sounded shrill but, frightened as I was, I could not control my anger.

"Be quiet," said Irene. She moved then, going to the entrance of the secret room. She stood there looking in, her back stiff, her hands still in her pockets.

"How did you find out?" Hale asked. I could almost smile at his curiosity.

"From the very beginning I felt there was something strange. Not at the hospital, maybe. You were all so kind." I could feel my lips twist in bitterness as I remembered that kindness. "But here in this house . . . from the first moment nothing seemed quite . . . right. And then last night . . ."

"You got your memory back." It was a statement from Irene, not a question. "Ben thought you had."

"Why couldn't you have left everything alone?" Hale ran his fingers through his golden hair. "We never meant to hurt you. We never wanted to hurt anybody. If only you'd kept out of all of this!"

"How could I? You made me part of it." I pointed toward the hidden room. "As you did her."

"We were going to take care of her!" His voice was rising now, as he tried to defend himself. "She's only been up here since we brought you back. By next week we would have been in Europe. We would have had her in a sanitarium, the best money could buy . . ."

"*Her* money," I pointed out quietly.

"Yes, her money!" Irene's face was livid now; it was as if all of the control she kept these long weeks was finally snapping, like string too weak to hold a package. The red patches were high in her cheeks now and her green eyes blazed. "Her money! Well, it got her into this and we would have used it to get her out." She stepped closer then. "We didn't start her on drugs, we didn't create the insanity in her family that destroyed her . . ."

"You just took advantage of it." I finished her sentence before she could.

"No!" Hale moved past Irene. I could see the sadness in his eyes now, the sadness I noticed before when he'd talked of other places, other times. Those secrets that had made him so unhappy, that once I had thought were my fault.

"Listen . . . please, you must believe us. We never meant to hurt Constance. She was rich, wild. And we were so desperately poor." He clenched his hands and then let them drop again. "But I tried to care for her."

"You . . . and your cousin." No appeal or excuse he could make would soften what I felt for them now.

"'Cousin'?" Irene gave a mirthless laugh. "You believed that?"

I stared at her now. Her chin went up defiantly.

"Hale and I aren't cousins," she said. "We're lovers. We were, years before he even met Constance. We always will be." She smiled then, the wicked smile of a sly child. "Hale's only cousin is Ben. He was the one who found Constance originally. Don't ask where . . . or how. It wasn't one of Europe's better hotels, I can tell you that. There she was . . . with the family money pouring in from America . . . no relatives, except a great-uncle she'd quarreled with, who couldn't stop her funds. And nothing to do with her life but destroy it with every drug, every crazy whim, every man she wanted. And why not? Matthew Avery had told her she had the curse of madness on her."

She gave a contemptuous glance at the dark opening in the wall. "Why shouldn't we have taken advantage of her? Somebody else would have. At least we tried to help her. And when she was a little better, she decided Hale was the man she wanted. It didn't make any difference how anybody felt. What she wanted she was used to getting." Irene's voice was quiet, but there was no mistaking the hatred in it, the hatred of a poor, plain woman who had spent her life stepping aside for the rich and the beautiful.

"You didn't have to marry her, Hale. She couldn't have forced you." He wouldn't look at me now. Whatever cruelty he'd committed, I knew some part of him was still decent enough to know shame.

"I . . . I thought it would solve so many things." He raised his head then, his eyes angry suddenly, angry and defensive. "What do you know about art? What do you know about what it is to struggle? To go without meals? Clothes? A place to sleep even? And to know, all the time in the back of your head, that the sacrifice isn't going to be worth it? That you'll never be more than a passable second-rater? And yet, even knowing that, knowing you can't give it up?"

"We're wasting time, Hale." Irene took one hand out of the pocket of her robe and put it on his shoulder. There was no love in her eyes, just cold determination. "We can go into recriminations a week from now, when we're safe on some warm Greek island."

"You don't think you can get away with this? Not now?" I took a step toward them, no longer weak or afraid.

"We haven't done anything." Hale ran a nervous hand over his mouth.

"Not yet," said Irene. "But we can't let Miss Nosey run around loose, now, can we?" She smiled at me again. It was not a pleasant sight, her lips were stretched tight, like a hungry animal. "You know what we agreed to do, if we had to . . ."

"Irene, I . . ." But he couldn't finish the sentence. It was as if he knew before he said the words it would be of no use.

"It'll be such a shame . . . poor dear Constance having another bad attack during this storm. Surely her great-uncle will remember how she hated storms. And with the lights out, for her to have wandered outside . . . and to fall in the darkness over the cliffs." Irene's voice was calm, hypnotic; it was something that had been long planned and she recited it as coolly as if she were describing a pleasant outing. "By the time we discover her, it will be too late. And the fall will be so severe that her face will be unrecognizable. To her great-uncle . . . to the lawyers and the police . . . even to the so persistent Dr. Gallard." Irene smiled at me again, that same amused confident smile. "Naturally the grief-stricken widower will want to get away from here as quickly as possible. And with the widower's share of her estate, we'll all be able to travel with all the comfort we could possibly want."

"And me?" But even as I said it, I knew she was prepared to be rid of me as well.

"We never meant you any harm." Hale made a move as if to reach out for me, but I stepped back before he could touch me. He dropped his hand again. "I swear that."

"What were you going to do? You couldn't very well have left here with two wives."

"Irene promised . . . when the time came . . . well, there are sedatives, sleeping pills . . ."

"You were going to kill me," I said coldly.

"No! Just . . . knock you out. Then Ben was going to drive you and your car back to the town where you came from. We found out about you from the things in your car. We thought . . . if we left you outside your town, people would find you. They could help you back from the amnesia. In time this whole thing would seem like some sort of a dream."

"And if questions were asked, you'd be in Europe. With the real Constance in a sanitarium, ready to be produced." I had to give them credit for being clever. Only one thing they didn't know. That Alex knew the truth. I could still fight them, if I could just stall for time. But Irene had moved back to the opening in the wall.

"You'd better get her downstairs, Hale," she said.

"No. No, Irene, I . . . I can't . . ." His hands were trembling now. He stood there like a small boy, waiting to be punished.

"They both have to die, Hale. You know that. I think you've known it from the very beginning, even though you wouldn't face it." Then she finally took her hand out of the pocket of her loose robe. The gun she held was black in the light of the one candle, still on the floor. She held the gun as if she knew how to use it.

"Would you rather we change places? You can take care of *this* Constance. Look her straight in the eyes . . . those eyes you found so appealing . . ." She glanced at me then but there was no smile on her face now. "Oh yes . . . I saw that he was falling in love with you," she said to me. And then she looked back at Hale, the gun still firm in her hand. "It's too late for other love affairs, Hale. Much, much too late. But if you want to end this one yourself, I'll gladly give you the pleasure."

He broke then, his hands coming up to cover his face, his shoulders shaking. But there was no sound of sobs in that small room, it was as if there were no more tears left in him. Then, after a moment, his shoulders straightened and he dropped his hands. His face was bleak, the light of the candle carved deep hollows in his cheeks and around his eyes. It was like looking at the head of a skeleton.

"Storm's End," he said, and it almost sounded as if he had laughed. "All my life I've felt like I was being pushed back further and further . . . until one day I knew I'd reach the end."

His lips twisted in a bitter smile. "The world isn't really round, you know. Oh no. If they push you enough, and you keep retreating and retreating, you finally get to the edge of the world." He started to raise his hand and then dropped it again, as if he were just too weary to make the effort. "And then you fall off."

"Storm's End," he said. "World's end . . ."

Irene moved past him toward the windows, keeping the gun on me. "Take her downstairs. If you're too cowardly to arrange the accident, Ben will be back soon." She glanced out the window and then back at Hale. "Hurry! The moon's starting to come out!"

I'd thought he would make one last protest but there was no more resistance left in him. He disappeared into the dark space behind the open wall and after a moment reappeared, holding Constance in his arms. She was still unconscious, her body limp in her long white robe. One arm dangled loose; I could see the scars of puncture marks along the skin, deep blue bruises in the wavering candlelight. Even though I knew Irene still had the gun pointed at me, I crossed the room and grabbed his arm.

"Hale, you can't do it!" But he shook himself free, his arms strong around the body of his wife.

"I don't have any choice. Do I?" he said. And then he was gone.

I looked back at Irene then. "Will you really kill me?" I said, and thought as I said it that for some strange reason, I wasn't frightened.

"Perhaps not with a gun," she answered. "You've been so anxious to learn the secret of this room maybe I should let you stay there. Forever." Her eyes were steady on me and I realized what she meant. She was going to trap me in the hidden room!

"Someone . . . will find me," I said. But now I was frightened. Even if Alex did search for me, even if Mrs. Janeck managed to lead him to the diary, would he be able to piece together the secret way to open the wall from the necklace as I had? And would he be able to do it before I suffocated? Or went mad?

"I think there'll be no one to find you. The room's soundproof, you can only hear someone calling for help if the wall is open." She took a step toward me now. "The way you did that afternoon. I was careless that day. But usually Constance was quiet in the daytime."

"Quiet?" I asked, not bothering to conceal my disgust. "Or drugged?"

"You're clever," said Irene, the gun in her hand never wavering.

"You understood the secret of the necklace. But no one else will have that chance. Because I have it now."

She reached in the pocket of her robe with her free hand and pulled out the Scarf of Sapphires. The necklace was like a sparkling snake twined in her fingers. She played with it for a second and then, abruptly, shoved the jewels back into her pocket.

"Yes, you were clever," she went on. "But not quite clever enough. What was it you put in the sugar bowl? Just out of curiosity, I'd like to know."

"Some of the powder from the sleeping pills they gave me at the hospital," I answered. "How did you find out? You had your backs turned toward me."

"We were at the windows, remember? With the night outside it turned the glass into a mirror." Her voice was almost amused. "If you hadn't done it, you'd be safe now. Hale was convinced you knew nothing. Even after this afternoon."

She came closer then, the gun in her hand still pointed at me. "You didn't think to ask where we went this afternoon. That was foolish of you. We went to get the jewelry we pawned, in that little store in town. You should have known we couldn't leave that here, where people might ask questions. As it was, we heard about your visit. The girl claiming to be Constance Avery."

I was trying to think now, but I couldn't make my mind concentrate, not with that gun pointed toward me, and above it, the cold, bony face of Irene. Alex and I had made so many mistakes . . . no, not Alex, I had. It was my fault that I was here, facing death. As was the real Constance . . . For a moment I thought I was going to be sick.

"But Hale would have let you go," Irene went on. "He likes you." Her lips twisted wryly. "Well, I won't have to worry about that any more. There's nothing like murder to bring a couple together."

And then we both heard it, at the same time . . . the sound of a car coming up the driveway. The headlights cut through the darkness below as the car pulled around the empty space in front of the great doors of the house.

"Ben . . . he's back!" She pulled open the window to lean out. For a moment the gun was not on me. I knew I should run, or try to run, but my feet seemed to be no part of my body and I could not move. I looked down at the long limousine as it stopped, the headlights still on. But the doors did not open and no one got out. I could not see if Mrs. Janeck was still with him.

From the angle of this tower room we could see the front doors and the wide shallow stone steps that led down to the open space where the car had stopped. The headlights of the car were trained on the entrance of the house. It looked artificial somehow, like a stage set the moment after the curtain has gone up, before the first actors appear.

And then the front doors opened and Hale walked out, still carrying that limp body in his arms. He seemed dazzled by the bright headlights for a moment and stopped, frozen, as if he were posing for a picture.

"Ben! Help him!" Irene called, leaning out the window, the gun forgotten in her hand. But still I could not move. There was something strange about the scene below, like a dream half remembered. Hale started toward the car, moving slowly down the stone steps as if he were sleepwalking, holding the body of his wife. It was as if the headlights of the car were pulling him forward in a straight line, hypnotizing him.

Irene stepped back, her body tense. She had felt what I had, that something was wrong. And at that moment the clouds pulled back from the moon and the whole scene below was covered with silver light. We could see now that the great limousine was full of people, both the front and the back seat. And at the same time, spaced at regular intervals, figures began to emerge from the trees that edged the park. Figures that even from here I knew were wearing uniforms, and what they held in their hands were guns.

State troopers, I thought, and blessed Alex.

Irene muttered something. And as if a signal had been given, suddenly the doors of the limousine burst open and I could see men scrambling out of the car. One of them was being held; that must be Ben, I thought. But we were too far away for me to see if Alex was among them.

I turned automatically to look at Irene. The skin was stretched tight on her face now, her eyes were wide, colorless in the moonlight that came through the window and empty as glass. Then she straightened her shoulders and swung the gun around, pointing it again at me.

She's going to kill me, I thought. Here. Now. And I could not move,

I could not scream; I could only stand there, helpless before her. From somewhere outside I could hear shouts, voices, but it had nothing to do with the stillness between us in that small room.

"So there's only me left." She said it half to herself, even though her eyes were on me. But I knew she was not really seeing me. And then her whole body jerked, as if in a convulsive spasm, and I saw her finger tighten on the trigger of the gun.

I must have made some movement then, although I was not aware of it, but it was enough for her to focus on me again. The candle was still sputtering on the floor beside us. It showed the twitch of the muscle on the side of her strong jaw.

"There's still time," she said, and waved me toward the door with the gun in her hand. "You'll come with me."

And then I could speak. I tried to keep my voice quiet and controlled, as someone would speaking to a madman; for I truly thought by then she *was* mad. I knew one movement, one sharp word and the gun in her hand would explode.

"Irene," I said. "It's over. Can't you see that? Give me the gun and we'll go down to the others."

"Never!" The moment of insanity was over and I could almost see her brain working. "If I can get past the police I know where your car is hidden. And with you as hostage . . ." She reached out suddenly with her free hand and grabbed my wrist. I'd always known she was strong, but her grip was like a handcuff. I could not twist free even if I had dared to try.

"Irene, they'll have the house surrounded. You must know that."

"There are a lot of ways out of this house. Hale was always too bored to listen to Constance's stories, but I wasn't. There isn't an inch of Storm's End I don't know." She twisted my arm now, prodding me with the gun toward the door to the hall. "I haven't come all this way to lose now."

I had no choice but to give in to her. Not only was she taller and stronger than I, but I could feel the barrel of the pistol against my back and I knew she would not hesitate to pull the trigger if I made any protest.

"How . . . ?" I barely managed to get the word out, my lips felt dry and cracked as she pushed me forward. We were in the hall now. We could see the long expanse of the corridor before us.

"If we can get over to the new wing, there's a staircase I don't think they could find in a week. And it goes straight down to the grounds." Her voice was curt, but I knew at least she was back in control of herself. I had a feeling this was something she had thought out weeks before, even as she had placed the Scarf of Sapphires in the pocket of her robe tonight when they'd come in search of me. The necklace might not be the Avery fortune, but it would make her wealthier than she had ever been in her life.

She started me down the hall toward the center of the house and the new wing, my arm twisted behind my back, the gun still in her other hand.

Only now we could hear voices and footsteps pounding up the stairs. I knew what it meant, as did she. The police were inside the house.

She pulled me to a stop and for a moment I thought perhaps she had accepted her defeat. And then she gave my arm a fierce yank and started to drag me back toward the paneled room.

"Irene, there isn't any way to get past them." But with her gun still in my back, I kept my voice a whisper and I wasn't sure she heard me.

She pulled me back beyond the opened door to the tower room. For a second I saw the candle still guttering on the bare floor and then we were at the foot of the circular iron staircase that Ben had climbed that day when I had nearly been caught.

"Up the stairs," Irene commanded. "We can get across on the servants' floor." She prodded me once more with the gun, forcing me to climb up the winding staircase.

It was like climbing up through a narrow open tube, up, up into the darkness of the floor above. I could not hear any voices now, although I knew the troopers . . . and Alex . . . must be searching through the rooms of the house for us. God, what will happen if they find us?

And then I thought, my stomach cold inside me, what will happen if they *don't?*

Once we were on the floor above, Irene swung ahead of me, her grip still tight on my wrist. She pulled me down the dark narrow passage, moving as swiftly and surefooted as a cat. We were practically running now through the long hall. There were doors open on each side of us.

I had a vague impression of tiny cubicles of rooms, their doors open on this passage, the curtainless windows letting the full moon paint their bare floors white. We must be near the center of the house, I thought. And still Irene pulled me forward, not slowing her pace for a moment. It was like one of my nightmares, but this was real. We had been moving forward toward blackness, only the moonlight coming through the open doors to guide us; but I never doubted Irene knew exactly where she was and where she was going.

And then the far end of this corridor was suddenly shattered with splashes of moving lights, angling and swooping against the wall, searching out like fingers. Someone with flashlights had climbed up to this same floor.

Irene stopped then and pulled me into an open doorway of one of the little rooms, her hand, still holding the gun, over my mouth.

"Who's there?" It was a man's voice that called out and I thought it sounded like Alex. A flashlight splashed light down the bare floor of the passage. It did not quite reach the doorway we were hiding in. I dared not struggle; even if Irene's hand had not been over my mouth, I think I still could not have called out. I could feel her breath move from the back of my head and I knew she had twisted her face away and was looking into the room behind us. I turned to look too, but I could see nothing in the darkness except the small round window that I knew would look down over the terrace and the cliffs to the river below.

But Irene had spied something, or perhaps she had always known it was there. She pulled me into the room and closed the door to the hall behind us. My eyes were becoming accustomed to the dark now and I could see in the far corner what looked like a metal ladder leading upwards. I could see now the ceiling of this little room was steeply sloped. There was no attic at Storm's End, we were right under the roof. And I knew what she intended to do. "No . . . I . . . I can't, Irene!"

"Get up there!" Her voice was harder than any bullet in my back and she gave my wrist a wrench that made my arm feel as if it were breaking. She went ahead of me now, climbing the thin ladder quickly, the skirt of her long robe looped over the hand that still held the gun. She reached up into the darkness to the roof and pushed it. It must have been a trap door of some kind, for it fell back with a creak of its hinges and I could see in the open square above us a few stars twinkling in the night sky.

She practically pulled me up the ladder. My foot slipped on one rung but by this time she was out on the roof and she leaned over the edge toward me, the gun pressed to my head.

"Don't try to break free now," she said. And pulled me up onto the roof.

The rain had stopped by now, the clouds swept away, and the full moon laid out the roof of Storm's End around us like the strange distorted world of a nightmare. Rows of chimneys, grown like barren dwarf trees, stood solid on the two sides of the steep slopes of the roof.

I took one terrified glance around me. I could see for miles: the twinkling lights of Avery off to the west on my right, the black river far below on my left. There was nothing above us but the stars and the great white moon. It was as if we were on the top of a mountain. Except the house almost seemed to be moving under us, as if we were insects on the spine of some primeval monster waking slowly out of a deep sleep. The rest of the world seemed miles below.

And behind, and ahead, stretched the long peak of the roof. Lining the top of the peak, straight as a tightrope, was a narrow metal ridgeway. It couldn't have been wider than the width of a narrow foot but someone had designed it for repairmen to walk on. I saw now what Irene's plan was and I knew, as I huddled on the edge of the trap door, that I would rather be shot than walk it.

"I can't, Irene! I can't do it!"

"Get on your feet!" She pulled at me, forcing me to stand beside her on the edge of the trap door. The wind had not died, it snapped at her long robe, pulling the tendrils of her coarse hair, loosening strands of it to writhe about her face.

"You'll go ahead of me," she said and the gun in her hand glinted in the moonlight. She pulled me forward, away from the safe opening of the room below us. We were close together, close as two people dancing, until she prodded me once again with the gun.

I could see the thin metal ridge in front of me, a black line separating the two slopes of the roof, the slates still shiny from the rain. I put one foot forward, then brought my other foot behind it. I was standing alone now, the wind pushing at me. I felt myself waver and instinctively I tried to crouch. Perhaps if I could crawl . . .

"Move!" She kept shouting at me, but the words were muffled by the wind. I turned to look back at her over my shoulder. She was as rigid as a statue, a tall silhouette against the night sky. But turning had made my body shift and I could feel my balance going. In panic I reached for her, grabbing the loose material of her robe. She tried to pull free but I hung on desperately, until I felt the material rip in my hands and something hard and glittering fell onto the narrow strip of the metal path between us.

It was the Scarf of Sapphires. It balanced on the peak of the roof for a moment and then slowly, slowly, it started to slide down the slates toward the gutter, twinkling and gleaming in the moonlight.

Irene let out a gasp and lunged forward, her outstretched hand a long claw as she grasped for the jewels. For a moment I thought she had them, but there was another gust of wind and they slid away from her. I was clinging now with both hands to the metal ridge, but Irene was still off balance and she sprawled forward, her hand still reaching for the necklace as it slipped further away from her.

I realized at the same moment she did that she was falling. Her face twisted back up at me and, for the first time, I saw fear in her eyes. The slates were slick from the storm and even if I could have reached out for her she was too far away from me by now. Her mouth was open as if she were screaming, but the wind pulled the sound away. All I could hear was the long scratch of her fingernails as they scraped down the slate. She slipped faster and faster toward the end of the roof. Then she reached the gutter and I saw her hands desperately grab for a hold, but the angle of the roof was too steep and she had slid down it too quickly, like a child on an enormous slide. Her body hung for a moment, and then she disappeared over the edge.

I could hear her scream now. It came like a long wail, as if the house itself was crying out all its years of pain and sorrow. Then there was silence.

I shook the hair back from my face. Somewhere I had lost the ribbon that tied it but I dared not take my grip off the metal ridge on the peak of the roof to brush it back. I looked down the shiny slates, down to the open gravel area at the front of the house, so far below. I could hear shouts now, rising faint in the night. Other cars had pulled up, their headlights making a circle of yellow light in the center of this moonlit world. In the center of the circle lay a twisted figure in a rust-colored robe. The robe looked the color of blood from here. I thought I saw the figure move once, but I could not be sure.

And then it was still.

"Reach out your hand!"

It was Alex's voice. He had pulled himself up onto the edge of the open trap door to the roof, one hand stretched out for me. But I could not move; I was frozen there, locked in panic, a great wave of darkness starting to sweep over me. I'm going to fall too, I thought, the way she did.

But then I felt his hands strong on my wrist and after that I remember nothing more.

AND AFTERWARDS . . .

Twenty-seven

The winter was milder than we expected, damp with rain, but not cold. And spring arrived early. Tulips grew in great beds at Storm's End, wide splashes of fuchsia and ivory and waxy pink. There were jonquils too, and daffodils, all growing wild and free, circles of color under the trees as they put out their first yellow-green leaves. The ivy clinging to the house softened the harshness of the old walls; the leaves darken in color in summer, but in April there is still a soft hue to the vines that climb the gray stones of the house. As I walked up the driveway each morning, I could almost fancy the house itself was being reborn with the new season.

Only it will never be reborn again.

I had never expected to spend the winter at Storm's End. That last horrifying night of the storm, the night of Irene's death, had freed me of any reason to return to the place, and the pain and suffering I'd felt that long week I'd spent there gave me nightmares that may take years to erase. But it was Alex's idea, after a suggestion of Matthew Avery's, that I should spend the winter helping close the house. And now, today, my work is finished.

The night that Alex had come to my rescue ended late the following morning. I still shudder when I think of how it might have ended. But when the power went out that night and Alex could not reach me by phone, he took matters into his own hands and went to the state police. They might not have believed him if Ben had not arrived with Mrs. Janeck. She had the courage at last to tell the truth, whether it implicated her and Otto or not.

It was dawn by the time we finished answering all the questions of the police. Hale and Ben were taken into custody and Irene's body moved to the coroner's office. There was still one more task for us that morning: riding with the unconscious Constance Avery to Six Counties Hospital. Then, at last, when I saw her safely put to bed, under the care of my kind Mrs. McKenzie, I could allow myself to feel the terror was finally over. I stayed at the hospital. Dr. Henderson gave me a sedative and it was nearly twenty-four hours before I awoke.

By that time Alex had taken charge. He had consulted with the Princess in the city and they agreed Matthew Avery was not to be told what had happened until after his operation. In the meantime, the staff of the hospital worked night and day to save Constance's life. For several weeks she hung in the balance and then, finally, almost imperceptibly, she began to gain strength. Her mind was still clouded, but her body at least was struggling back to health.

On Alex's advice, I spent those first weeks myself at the hospital. But the day came when I had recovered. Matthew and the Princess had driven out from the city and after they had spent some time with Constance in her room they came to the solarium where I was waiting, Alex with them.

I stood as they entered. The winter sunlight was bright and Matthew had protected his eyes with dark glasses. But one look and I could tell he had regained his sight. He came directly toward me and took my hand.

"How can I thank you?" he said. And he leaned forward and kissed me gently on the cheek.

We talked then, the four of us. Plans were made for Constance to be moved to a quiet private sanitarium where people could help her regain her mind. She is there now, she may be there a long, long time. The progress has been slow so far; the combination of the wild blood in her family and the violent abuse of the drugs she used may leave her permanently lost to this world, but Alex feels it is too soon to give up hope.

As we sat in the solarium that winter afternoon, there were other plans to be made. Hale and Ben were still being held for trial. It would be difficult for Ben. He had committed other crimes in the past and served other sentences and there was little chance that he would ever be allowed to go free again. I shuddered a little as Matthew and Alex talked of it, but then I remembered Ben's cold and cruel eyes and I could feel no pity.

With Hale there might be a possibility of clemency someday. I found myself defending him as Alex watched with some amusement. But I truly felt that he would never have killed Constance; even the fact that he had taken her body out the great doors, the opposite side of the house from where the "accident" was supposed to take place, argued in his favor.

"And you?" said Alex wryly. "He left you to Irene, knowing what she planned." His arm tightened around me as we sat on the sofa facing Matthew and the Princess, and I knew, despite his surface humor, Alex would neither forgive nor forget what they had done.

"She wouldn't have killed me, Alex." But even then a swift memory of that night made me shudder. The Princess put out a gentle hand, her delicate face creased with concern.

"I should have helped you," she said. "I guessed something was different about you, but I would not let myself become suspicious. I was so worried for Matthew."

"She might have died, Olivia." Matthew's voice was stern now. "I am an old man, whether I have months or years to live is not important . . ."

"It is to me," the Princess said simply.

"That is not a sufficient excuse. Rosemary could have been killed . . . and Constance as well." Olivia winced at the hardness of his words and when he went on, his voice was gentler.

"I don't blame you," he said. "If anyone is at fault, it's I. I should have protected Constance more, kept her from the mistakes she made . . ." His voice trailed off. Then he squared his shoulders and leaned forward. "Well, I shall look after her in the future. But you, young lady." He turned to face me, his white hair silver-fine in the sunlight. "What becomes of you now?"

Alex tightened his grip on my hand. "She's going to be married," he said. And then he added, with a slight smile, "That's a prescription from her doctor."

Olivia and Matthew exchanged glances. "Indeed?" said Matthew. "And when is that to be?"

"We . . . haven't decided," I said.

"Right away is what *I've* decided," Alex added, promptly. "But the lady seems to be holding back."

I turned to him then, forgetting the two elderly people watching us with such interest. "It isn't that I don't love you, Alex," I said. "Or that I'm not sure of us. It's just so much has happened. So quickly. Just in these last few months. Can it hurt if we delay a little? Just till the spring?"

"Yankees," said Alex, and made a face. "You are as stubborn as we French. And what do we do while we wait?"

"Might I make a suggestion?" said Matthew, breaking in. We looked at him then. There was a gentle smile on his face and I noticed he had reached out for Olivia's hand. They looked very peaceful together. "The house at Storm's End is to be razed, I am determined on that. It has been an unhappy place from the beginning.

"And no, I do not think it is any great loss to the world," he said, turning to Olivia, who had made no attempt to contradict him.

"I didn't say anything, Matthew," she replied serenely.

"But the contents will need to be catalogued. The books, the paintings . . ." He'd turned back to me now. "If you'd like the job, my dear, it would only be for a couple of months."

"Go back to Storm's End?" My voice sounded strained even to my ears. They were all looking at me now and even though my hands were clasped together, I knew they were trembling.

Alex was the first to speak. "Why not?" he said, to my surprise. Before I could speak, he went on: "It might be very good for you to see it is just a house. No ghosts, no phantoms, with nothing to frighten you in the night."

Mrs. McKenzie has reported my nightmares to him, I thought, but I wasn't angry.

"You can stay in one of the apartments over the garage if the house seems too enormous," said Matthew. "Mrs. Janeck has her rooms there, she can take care of you." He looked at me and even with the dark glasses I could see the shrewdness of his expression and knew what he was thinking. "She's alone, you know. Otto disappeared that night. For good, I should imagine."

*   *   *

And so it was agreed. Even Alex admitted, once he was used to the idea, that a few months of courtship before our marriage would not be too difficult, but I suspected as we knew each other better that he also welcomed the chance to finish his book before our marriage and the honeymoon he'd planned, revisiting his home in France.

The rooms I had were bright and sunny. Esther had taken some of the best of the furniture from the main house and arranged it carefully for my comfort. We became friends during the winter months, working side by side as we catalogued the possessions of Storm's End. I would have thought since so much of her life had been spent here that she would be sorry to see the house destroyed, but I soon realized she was looking forward to the last day as a prisoner might to freedom. She was resigned to Otto having gone forever and her plans included retiring to a warm climate on the pension Matthew Avery had arranged for her.

It was on Christmas that Alex gave me my last assignment. I had been admiring the beautiful diamond ring he had slipped on my finger and I did not see, in my first excitement, that he held another package in his hand. It was a large notebook, such as I had often seen on his desk these last weeks since I had returned to Storm's End.

"This is for you too," he said, and when I looked at him questioningly, he opened it to show me the blank pages. "A little therapy. For those nightmares. I want you to write down the whole story of what happened here. Maybe that will take it out of your mind forever."

*   *   *

And perhaps it will. It is April now. Storm's End is empty at last, stripped of all its possessions, waiting in silence for the wreckers that will come next week. Hale and Ben were both convicted, but Matthew tells me he has heard from Hale and he seems almost at peace in prison, with time at last to work on his painting. Constance is no better, but her great-uncle will not give in. He has plans to take her this summer to Switzerland for a new treatment. If she ever recovers, and still feels as she did for Hale, perhaps he too will someday have a new life.

As I sit here at the window, looking out at this beautiful April morning, I realize the story is over. Or, at least, the story of Storm's End. In a few minutes Alex will come to pick me up. My bags are packed. It will be a simple wedding and tomorrow we sail for France.

I can hear, in the distance, his car as it turns into the long driveway. And now, the real story of my life begins . . .